Shadows in Paradise

Books by Erich Maria Remarque

All Quiet on the Western Front
1929

The Road Back
1931

Three Comrades
1937

Flotsam
1941

Arch of Triumph
1946

Spark of Life
1952

A Time to Love and a Time to Die
1954

The Black Obelisk
1957

Heaven Has No Favorites
1961

The Night in Lisbon
1964

Shadows in Paradise
1972

SHADOWS
IN PARADISE

Translated by Ralph Manheim

Erich Maria
REMARQUE

Harcourt Brace Jovanovich, Inc., New York

F
Rem

Originally published in Germany under the title *Schatten im Paradies*
by Droemer Knaur

Shadows in Paradise

Prologue

I lived in New York during the last phase of the Second World War. Despite my deficient English the midtown section of New York became for me the closest thing to a home I had experienced in many years.

Behind me lay a long and perilous road, the Via Dolorosa of all those who had fled from the Hitler regime. It led from Germany to Holland, Belgium, northern France, and Paris. From Paris some proceeded to Lyons and the Mediterranean, others to Bordeaux, the Pyrenees, and across Spain and Portugal to Lisbon.

Even after leaving Germany we were not safe. Only a very few of us had valid passports or visas. When the police caught us, we were thrown into jail and deported. Without papers we could not work legally or stay in one place for long. We were perpetually on the move.

In every town we stopped at the post office, hoping to find letters from friends and relatives. On the roads we scrutinized every wall for messages from those who had passed through before us: addresses, warnings, words of advice. The walls were our newspapers and bulletin boards. This was our life in a period of universal indifference, soon to be followed by the inhuman war years, when the Milice, often seconded by the police, joined forces with the Gestapo against us.

I

I had arrived a few months before on a freighter from Lisbon and knew little English—it was as though I had been dropped deaf and dumb from another planet. And indeed America was another planet, for Europe was at war.

Besides, my papers were not in order. Thanks to a series of miracles I had entered the country with a valid American visa; but the name on the passport was not mine. The immigration authorities had had their suspicions and held me on Ellis Island. After six weeks they had given me a residence permit good for three months, during which time I was supposed to obtain a visa for some other country. I was familiar with this kind of thing from Europe. I had been living this way for years, not from month to month, but from day to day. And, as a German refugee, I had been officially dead since 1933. Not to be a fugitive for three whole months was in itself a dream come true. And living with a dead man's passport had long ceased to strike me as strange—on the contrary, it seemed fitting and proper. I had inherited the passport in Frankfurt. Since the name of the man who had given it to me just before he died had been Ross, my name was now Ross. I had almost forgotten my real one. You can forget a lot of things when your life is at stake.

On Ellis Island I had met a Turk who had spent some time in America ten years before. I didn't know why they were not re-admitting him, and I didn't ask. I had seen too many people deported from any number of countries merely because some official questionnaire did not cover their case. The Turk gave me the address of a Russian living in New York who, on his flight from

Russia twenty years before, had been helped by the Turk's father. The Turk had been to see him some years before, but didn't know if he was still alive. The day they released me from the island I took a chance and looked him up. Why not? I had been living like that for years. Lucky breaks were a fugitive's only hope.

The Russian, who called himself Melikov, worked in a small run-down hotel not far from Broadway. He took me right in. As an old refugee, he saw at a glance what I needed: lodging and a job. Lodging was no problem; he had an extra bed, which he set up in his room. A job was a little more complicated. My tourist visa didn't entitle me to work. Anything I found would have to be clandestine. That, too, was known to me from Europe and didn't bother me particularly. I still had a little money.

"Have you any idea what you could do for a living?" Melikov asked me.

"I last worked in France as a salesman for a dealer in dubious paintings and phony antiques."

"Do you know anything about the business?"

"Not much; some of the usual dodges."

"Where did you learn that?"

"I spent two years in the Brussels Museum."

"Working?" Melikov asked in surprise.

"No, hiding."

"From the Germans?"

"From the Germans who had occupied Belgium."

"Two years? And they didn't find you?"

"No," I said. "Not me. But after two years they caught the man who was hiding me."

Melikov looked at me in amazement. "And you got away?"

"Yes."

"Any news of the other fellow?"

"The usual. They sent him to a camp."

"A German?"

"A Belgian. The curator of the museum."

Melikov nodded. "How could you stay there so long without being discovered? Didn't anybody ever visit the museum?"

"Oh yes. In the daytime he locked me up in a storeroom in the cellar. After closing time he brought me food and let me out for

5

the night. I had to stay in the museum, but at least I was out of the cellar. Of course I couldn't use any light."

"Did any of the employees know about you?"

"No. The storeroom had no windows. I had to be very quiet when anyone came down into the cellar. My main worry was sneezing."

"Is that how they discovered you?"

"No. Somebody noticed that the curator often stayed in the museum at closing time—or went back later."

"I see," said Melikov. "Could you read?"

"Only at night. During the summer or when the moon was shining."

"But at night you could wander around the museum and see the pictures?"

"As long as there was light enough."

Suddenly Melikov smiled. "When I was escaping from Russia, I spent six days lying under a woodpile on the Finnish border. When I came out, I thought it had been much longer. At least two weeks. But I was young then; the time passes more slowly when you're young." And then abruptly: "Are you hungry?"

"Yes," I said. "Starving, in fact."

"I thought so. They've just let you out. That always makes a man hungry. We'll get something to eat at the pharmacy."

"Pharmacy?"

"Sure, the drugstore. One of this country's oddities. They sell you aspirin and they feed you."

I looked down the row of people hastily eating at the long counter. "What do you eat in a place like this?" I asked.

"A hamburger. The poor man's stand-by. Steak costs too much for the common man.

"What did you do in the daytime in the museum?" Melikov asked. "To keep from going crazy?"

"I waited for evening. Of course I did everything in my power to keep from thinking of the danger I was in. I'd been running from place to place for several years, first in Germany for a year, then in other countries. I shut out every thought of the mistakes I had made. Regret corrodes the soul; it's a luxury you can afford only in peaceful times. I said all the French I knew over to myself; I gave myself lessons. Then I began exploring the museum at night, looking at the pictures, imprinting them on my memory. Soon I knew them all by heart. Then in the daytime, in the darkness of my storeroom, I'd call them to mind. Not at random, but systematically, picture by picture. Sometimes I'd spend whole days on a single painting. Now and then I broke off in despair, but I always started in again. This memory exercise made me feel that I was improving myself. I'd stopped knocking my head against the wall; now I was climbing a flight of stairs. Do you see what I mean?"

"You kept moving," said Melikov. "And you had an aim. That saved you."

"I lived one whole summer with Cézannes and a few Degas— imaginary pictures of course and imaginary comparisons. But comparisons, nevertheless, and that made them a challenge. I memorized the colors and the compositions, though I'd never seen the colors by daylight. The pictures I memorized and compared were moonlight Cézannes and twilight Degas. Later on, I found art books in the library; I huddled under the windows and studied them. The world they gave me was a world of specters, but still a world."

"Wasn't the museum guarded?"

"Only in the daytime. At night they locked it up. Which was lucky for me."

"And unlucky for the man who brought you your meals."

I looked at Melikov. "And unlucky for the man who'd hidden me," I answered calmly. I could see that he meant no harm; he wasn't chiding me, but merely stating the facts.

"Don't get any ideas about clandestine dishwashing," he said. "That's romantic nonsense. Besides, the unions won't stand for it these days. How long can you hold out without working?"

"Not very long. How much is this meal going to cost?"

"A dollar and a half. Prices have gone up since the war started."

"There's no war here."

"Oh yes, there is," said Melikov. "Which is luck for you again. They need men. That'll make it easier for you to find something."

"I've got to leave the country in three months."

7

Melikov laughed and screwed up his little eyes. "The U.S. is a big place. And there's a war on. Another stroke of luck for you. Where were you born?"

"According to my passport, in Hamburg. Actually in Hanover."

"They can't deport you to either of those places. But they could put you in an internment camp."

I shrugged my shoulders. "I was in one of those in France."

"Escaped?"

"Not exactly. I just walked out. In the general confusion of the defeat."

Melikov nodded. "I was in France myself. In the general confusion of a supposed victory. In 1918. I'd come from Russia by way of Finland and Germany. The first wave of latter-day migrations."

We went back to the hotel, but I was restless. I didn't want to drink, the worn plush of the lounge didn't appeal to me, and Melikov's room was too small. I had been shut up long enough. "How late can I stay out?" I asked.

"As long as you please."

"When do you go to bed?"

"Don't let that worry you. Not before morning. I'm on duty now. You want a woman? They're not as easy to find in New York as in Paris. And a little more dangerous."

"No. I just feel like roaming around."

"You'll find a woman more easily right here in the hotel."

"I don't need one."

"Go on!"

"Not tonight."

"You're a romantic," said Melikov. "Remember the street number and the name of the hotel: Hotel Reuben. It's easy to find your way in New York. Most of the streets are numbered; only a few have names."

Like me, I thought—a number with a meaningless name. The anonymity suited me: names had brought me too much trouble.

I drifted through the anonymous city. Luminous smoke rose heavenward. A pillar of fire by night and a pillar of a cloud by day—wasn't that how God had shown the first nation of refugees the way through the desert? I passed through a rain of words, noise, laughter, and shouts that beat meaninglessly on my ears. After the dark years in Europe, everyone I saw here seemed to be a Prometheus—the perspiring man standing in his shop door in a blaze of electric light, who thrust out an armful of socks and towels in my direction and implored me to buy, or the cook I saw through an open door standing like a Neapolitan Vulcan in the blaze of his oven. Since I didn't understand what they said, the people I saw, the waiters, cooks, touts, and street vendors, looked to me like figures on a stage, marionettes playing an incomprehensible game from which I was excluded. I was there in their midst but not one of them; between us there was an invisible barrier, no hostility on their part but something inside me that concerned no one but myself. I was dimly aware that this was a unique moment, which would never come again.

The next day this feeling would be gone. Not that I'd have come any closer to these people. Far from it. Tomorrow or the day after I'd throw myself into the struggle for a livelihood, the daily round of parry and thrust, of deceptions and half-lies, but tonight the city held out its impartial face to me like a monstrance, every feature etched in the finest filigree. It had not yet caught me up in its net, but confronted me as equal to equal. Time seemed to stand still, as though for this one moment in the darkness the great scales were evenly balanced between active and passive.

Here I was in this haven of safety—out of danger. And now suddenly it came to me that the real danger was not outside me but within myself. For years my only thought had been sheer survival, and this had given me a kind of inner security. But tomorrow, or, rather, from this strange moment on, life would spread out before me in all its richness. Again there would be a future, but there would also be a past that might easily crush me unless I could forget it or come to terms with it.

Suddenly I realized that this was the beginning of a new life. But was it possible to start over again from scratch? To make myself at home in this new, unknown language? And, most frightening of all after all these years of fighting for survival, to learn once more how to live? And if I succeeded in coming back to life, would I not be betraying all my dead friends and loved ones?

I turned around. Confused and deeply troubled, I hurried back to the hotel, no longer looking at my surroundings. I was out of breath when I finally caught sight of the dismal little neon sign over the entrance.

The door was inlaid with dingy strips of false marble, one of which was missing. I went in and saw Melikov dozing in a rocking chair behind the desk. He opened his eyes. For a moment they seemed fixed and lidless, like those of an aged parrot; then they moved and I saw that they were blue. He stood up and asked: "Do you play chess?"

"All refugees play chess."

"Good. I'll get the vodka."

He went up the stairs. I looked around me as though I had come home after a long absence. That is an easy feeling to get when you have no home.

II

I devoted the next few weeks to learning English. In the morning I sat in the red plush lobby with a grammar and in the afternoon I practiced conversation. After the first ten days, it dawned on me that I was catching Melikov's Russian accent. So I brazenly latched on to anyone who would talk to me. From the hotel guests I acquired, successively, a German, a Jewish, and a French accent; then, confident that the waitresses and chambermaids at least would be real Americans, a thick Brooklyn *patois*.

"An American girl friend is what you need," said Melikov.

"From Brooklyn?" I asked.

"Better find one from Boston. That's where they speak the best English."

"Vladimir," I said, "my world is changing quickly enough as it is. Every few days my American ego grows a year older and the world loses a little of its enchantment. The more I understand, the more the mystery seeps away. In another few weeks my American ego will be as disabused as my European one. So don't rush me.

And don't worry about my accent. I'm in no hurry to lose my second childhood."

"No danger. Right now you have the intellectual horizon of a melancholy greengrocer. The one on the corner, Annibale Balbo."

"Is there such a thing as a real American?"

"Of course there is. But New York is the great port of entry for immigrants—Irish, Italian, German, Jewish, Armenian, Russian, and then some. What is it they used to say in your country? 'Here you're a man and allowed to be one.' Well, here you're a refugee and allowed to be one. This country was built by refugees. So get rid of your European inferiority complex. Here you're a man again. You've stopped being a bruised chunk of flesh with a passport attached to it."

I looked up from the chessboard. "That's true, Vladimir. But how long will it last?"

Someone limped into the lounge. We were sitting in the half-light, and I couldn't see the man clearly; but I was struck by his odd three-quarter-time limp. "Lachmann!" I gasped.

The man approached us.

"My name is Merton," he said.

I turned on the light, which trickled lugubriously from a blue-and-yellow ceiling fixture in the worst art-nouveau style. "Good God, Robert!" he cried. "You're alive? I thought you'd been dead for years."

"Same to you," I said. "I knew you by your walk."

"My trochaic limp?"

"Your waltz step, Kurt. Do you know Melikov?"

"Of course I know him."

"Do you live here?"

"No. But I drop in now and then."

"And now your name is Merton?"

"That's right. And you?"

"Ross. But I've still got my own first name."

"So we meet again," said Lachmann with a faint smile.

We both fell silent. The usual embarrassment between refugees. Neither of us knew what questions it was safe to ask, who was dead and who was alive.

"Any news of Cohn?" I finally asked.

That was the standard technique. You inquired first about casual acquaintances.

"He's here in New York," said Lachmann.

"How did he get here?"

"How did he get here? By chance, by luck."

None of us figured on the list of prominent intellectuals whom the American authorities made a point of saving.

Melikov turned out the light and produced a bottle from under the desk. "American vodka," he said. "We've got everything over here. California Bordeaux and Burgundy, Chilean Rhine wine, et cetera. Cheers. One of the advantages of being a refugee is that you're always losing sight of people, so when you meet again you can celebrate. Gives you the illusion of long life."

Neither Lachmann nor I answered.

A hotel guest came in, and Melikov went out to the reception desk for his key.

"A shady character," said Lachmann with a glance in Melikov's direction. "Do you work for him?"

"How could I work for a hotel clerk?"

"Oh, he's got other irons in the fire."

"For instance?"

"Girls. A bit of heroin. A little bookmaking, I think."

"Is that what you've come for?"

"No. There's a woman here that I'm crazy about. She's fifty, from Puerto Rico. A Catholic, and she's only got one foot. The other was run over. She's tied up with a Mexican pimp. For five dollars he'd even make the bed for us. But she refuses. She's adamant. She thinks God's looking down from a cloud. Even at night. I told her God was nearsighted. Nothing doing. But she takes money. And makes promises. When the time comes, she laughs. And promises again. What do you think of that? Is that what I came to America for?"

Lachmann was neurotic about his limp. He had been a great lady's man in his time, or so he said. Some S.S. men in Berlin had got wind of his exploits and dragged him to their headquarters. They were going to castrate him, but the police turned up in the nick of time. Lachmann had got off with a few scars and a broken leg that hadn't set right. He had limped ever since, and acquired a taste for women with slight physical defects. Nothing else mattered, as long as they had big hard buttocks. After escaping to France he had kept up his activities under the most difficult circumstances. He claimed to have known a woman with three breasts in Rouen—and, better still, they were in back. A marvel! He could see everything at once without having to turn her around. "And hard as a rock!" he cried in ecstasy. "Hot marble!"

"You haven't changed a bit," I said to him.

"We never change. We swear to turn over a new leaf. We even try to, when things are going badly. But as soon as the trouble passes over, we slip right back." Lachmann heaved a deep sigh. "Would you call that heroic or idiotic?"

"Heroic," I said. "In our situation we may as well treat ourselves to the best adjectives. It's no good looking too deeply into our souls. We never know what we'll find."

"You haven't changed either," said Lachmann-Merton. "Still the same taste for popular philosophy."

"I need it. It comforts me."

Lachmann grinned. "It gives you a feeling of cheap superiority. That's why."

"Superiority can't be too cheap."

"Oh well," said Lachmann. "I should talk!" He sighed, reached into his side pocket, and took out a package wrapped in tissue paper. "A rosary," he said. "Guaranteed blessed by the Pope. Genuine ivory and silver. Do you think that might soften her up?"

"Which Pope?"

"Pius. Who else?"

"Benedict XV would have been better."

"What do you mean?" He gave me an angry look. "He's dead."

"A dead Pope would give it more class."

"Oh! Still the same old wit. I'd forgotten. The last time we . . ."

"Stop!" I said.

"Why?"

"Stop, Kurt. Not another word!"

"Well, if that's the way you feel about it." Lachmann hesitated a moment. He wanted to go off in a huff. But his heart was too full. He took another little package from his pocket and unwrapped the light-blue tissue paper. "A little something from Gethsemane; olive wood from the Mount of Olives. Stamped and certified. If that doesn't melt her! What do you think?" He gave me an imploring look.

"It's bound to. Have you got a bottle of water from the Jordan?"

"No, I'm afraid not."

"Fill one."

"What?"

"Fill one. There's a faucet out in back. Put in some dust to make it look more authentic. Nobody can prove anything different. You've got a certified rosary and olive wood—all you need to make it complete is some water from the Jordan."

"But not in a vodka bottle!"

"Why not? Wash off the label. The bottle looks oriental. I'm sure your Puerto Rican woman doesn't drink vodka. Maybe rum."

"No. Whisky. Would you believe it?"

"Yes."

Lachmann pondered. "There ought to be a seal on the cork. That would convince her. Have you got some sealing wax?"

"Where would I get sealing wax?"

"People have all sorts of things in their pockets. For years I had a rabbit's paw . . ."

"Maybe Melikov has some."

"That's it. He's always sealing packages. Why didn't *I* think of that?"

Lachmann limped out to the reception desk to confer with Melikov. A few minutes later I joined them.

"It's all settled," Lachmann said triumphantly. "Look at this. Vladimir has this Russian coin that will make a beautiful seal. Cyrillic letters. Anyone would think the bottle had been filled by the Greek fathers in a monastery by the Jordan!"

Melikov produced a candle, and they set to work. I was hypnotized by the sealing wax, bright red in the light of the candle. What's the matter with you? I said to myself. That's all over. You're saved. Life is out there waiting for you. Saved! But was I saved? Had I really escaped?

"I'm going out for a while," I said. "My head's too full of words. I've got to shake them out. See you later!"

When I got back, Melikov was still on duty.

"Where's Lachmann?" I asked.

"Gone up to see his ladylove."

"Do you think he'll have any luck this time?"

"No. She'll ask him out to dinner with the Mexican. And let him pay. Was he always like this?"

"Yes. Except that he used to have better luck. He claims that he used to be normal, and that his taste for crippled and deformed women came with his limp. Maybe it's true. Maybe he's so sensitive that a good-looking woman would make him feel ashamed. We'll never know."

Melikov set up the men. "Who cares!" he said. "You can't imagine how unimportant these things seem when you get older."

"How long have you been here?"

"Twenty years."

I saw a shadow coming through the door. It was a slender, tallish girl with a small face. She was pale, with ash-blond hair that seemed to be dyed and gray eyes. Melikov rose to his feet. "Natasha Petrovna!" he cried. "When did you get back?"

"Two weeks ago."

I had stood up. The girl was almost my height. She had on a tight-fitting suit and seemed very thin. She had a hurried way of talking; her voice was a little too loud, almost jangling.

"Vodka?" Melikov asked. "Or whisky?"

"Vodka. But just one finger. I can't stay. I'm working."

"At this time of night?"

"All evening. The photographer only has time for us in the evening. Dresses and hats. Tiny little hats."

It was only then that I noticed that Natasha Petrovna was herself wearing a hat, or, rather, a cap, a little black nothing perched slantwise on her hair.

Melikov went out for the bottle. "You're not an American, are you?" the girl asked.

"No. German."

"I hate the Germans."

"So do I," I said.

She looked at me with surprise. "I didn't mean it personally."

"Neither did I."

"I'm French. You understand. The war."

"I understand," I said calmly. This wasn't the first time I had been held responsible for the sins of the German regime. You get used to it after a while. I had been sent to an internment camp in France, but I didn't hate the French. There was no use trying to explain that. I could only envy the primitive simplicity of her black-and-white approach.

Melikov came back with the bottle and three tiny glasses, which he filled. "None for me," I said.

"Have I offended you?" the girl asked.

"No. I just don't feel like drinking right now."

Melikov grinned. *"Na zdorovye!"* he said, raising his glass.

"A gift of the gods," said the girl, and, tossing her head like a colt, drained her glass.

I felt like an idiot for having declined, but it was too late now. Melikov picked up the bottle. "Another, Natasha Petrovna?"

"No, thank you, Vladimir Ivanovich. I've got to be going. *Au revoir."*

She held out her hand to me. *"Au revoir, Monsieur."*

She had an unexpectedly powerful grip. *"Au revoir, Madame."*

Melikov saw her to the door and came back. "Did she insult you?"

"No."

"Think nothing of it. She insults everybody. But she doesn't mean it."

"Is she Russian or French?"

"Both. Born in France of Russian parents. Why?"

"I once lived with some Russians for a while. Russian women seem to specialize in cutting men into little pieces. It's their favorite sport."

Melikov grinned. "You don't say so. But is it so bad to shake a man up a bit? Isn't it better than shining the buttons of his uniform every morning and polishing the boots he's going to trample innocent people with?"

I flung up my hands. "Have mercy! It seems to be a bad day for refugees. Let's have some of that vodka I turned down before."

"Okay."

Melikov pricked up his ears. "Here they come."

There were steps on the stairs. Then I heard a melodious femi-nine voice. It was the Puerto Rican belle, with Lachmann in tow. She didn't limp, and no one would have suspected that she had an artificial foot.

"Now they'll call for the Mexican," Melikov whispered.

"Poor Lachmann," I said.

"Poor? He's still able to desire something he hasn't got."

I laughed. "I guess that kind of desire is the one thing we never lose."

"A man isn't poor until he stops wanting anything."

"Really?" I said. "I thought that made him wise."

"Not at all. Checkmate, incidentally. What's the matter with you today? You're playing like a bow-legged baboon. Do you need a woman?"

"No."

"Then what's wrong?"

"General letdown now that the danger's over," I said. "You must remember that from your younger days."

"We always huddled together. But you don't seem to care much about your fellow refugees."

"Because I don't want to remember."

"Is that it?"

"Refugees build invisible prison walls around themselves. I've had enough of that."

"You mean you want to become an American?"

"It's not a question of nationality. I'd just like to be somebody after all these years. If they let me."

"That's a tall order."

"A man's got to encourage himself," I said. "No one else will."

We played a second game. I lost again. Then the hotel guests began coming in, and Melikov was busy handing out keys and tak-ing cigarettes and liquor up to people's rooms. I kept my seat. What was actually the matter with me? I decided to tell Melikov that I wanted a room of my own. I didn't know exactly why; we didn't get in each other's way, and it was all the same to him whether I shared his room or not. But it suddenly struck me as important to have a room to myself. On Ellis Island I had slept in a large room with other people, and it had been the same in the French internment camp. I knew that if I had my own room it would remind me of times I preferred to forget. But there was no help for it. I couldn't evade them forever.

III

I met the Lowy brothers late one afternoon, at the hour when the setting sun suffuses the antique shops on the east side of Second Avenue with a honey-colored glow, while the cobwebs of night are already forming on the windows across the way. As I opened the shop door, the redheaded Lowy brother stepped out of his aquarium, blinked, sneezed, peered out into the soft light, and sneezed again. Then he noticed me. "Pleasant evening," he said in no particular direction.

I nodded. "Nice bronze you've got there."

"A fake," Lowy replied, rather surprisingly for a dealer.

"I suppose it doesn't belong to you?"

"What makes you think that?"

"Because you say it's a fake."

"I say it's a fake because it is a fake."

"But aren't you a dealer?"

Lowy sneezed again and blinked again. "It was sold to me as a fake. This is an honest shop."

The whole shop began to glow as the sun struck the mirrors on the back wall. "But mightn't it be authentic?" I asked.

Lowy stepped back from the doorway and looked at the bronze that was standing on an Early American rocking chair. "You can have it for thirty dollars," he said. "With a teakwood stand thrown in. Carved!"

I still had about eighty dollars to my name. "Could I have it for a few days?" I asked.

"You can have it for the rest of your life if you pay for it."

"Couldn't I have it on approval? Just for two days?"

Lowy turned around. "But I don't know you. A few months ago I gave a lady two pieces of Meissen china on approval. She had an honest look."

"And she disappeared?"

"Oh no. She brought them back in shards. They'd been knocked out of her hands in a crowded bus. She cried as if she'd lost a child. Two children. Twins. They were identical pieces. She had no money to pay for them. All she'd wanted was the pleasure of looking at them for a few days. And showing them off at a bridge party to spite her friends. All very human. What could we do? Chalk it up to bitter experience. So you see . . ."

"A bronze isn't so fragile. Especially if it's a fake."

Lowy gave me a sharp look. "You don't believe me?"

I didn't answer.

"Leave us twenty dollars," he said. "You can keep it a week. If you sell it, we split the profit. How's that?"

"Outrageous. But it's a deal."

I accepted because I wasn't sure of my guess. I took the bronze to my hotel room. Lowy had told me before I left that he had bought it from a museum that had wanted to get rid of it when it was found to be a forgery. I stayed home that night. When it grew dark, I didn't turn on the light. I had put the bronze by the window, and I lay on the bed looking at it. During my stay in the Brussels Museum I had learned one thing: that objects begin to speak only after you have looked at them for a long time, and that the ones that speak soonest are never the best. The museum had a fine collection of early Chinese bronzes, and now and then, with my protector's permission, I took one of them with me into the solitude of my storeroom. If anyone had noticed its absence, he would say that he himself had taken it home to study it. In this way I gradually learned the feel of patinas. On summer evenings I would peer into the cases for hours, and so became a good judge of texture, though I had never seen the colors by proper daylight. But, above all, my studies in the dark had in course of time given me a blind man's heightened sense of touch. I didn't trust it entirely, but sometimes I felt pretty sure.

The bronze had had the right feel in the shop; the contours and reliefs were sharp, which may have been the reason for the museum expert's opinion, but to me they did not seem new. When I closed my eyes and felt them slowly and carefully, I became more and more convinced that the piece was very old. I had seen a similar bronze in Brussels. At first the curator had taken it for a Tang or Ming copy. The Chinese had begun long ago—as early as the Han dynasty at the beginning of our era—to bury copies of Shang and Chou bronzes; the patina on these pieces was just about perfect, and it was very hard to identify them unless there were slight mistakes in the ornaments or defects in the casting.

I put the bronze back on the window sill. From the court down below I could hear the metallic voices of the kitchen helpers, the clanking of garbage cans and the soft throaty bass voice of the Negro who was carrying them out. The door opened, and the silhouette of the chambermaid appeared in the lighted rectangle. She stood there for a moment and then cried out in horror: "A dead man!"

"Nonsense," I said. "I'm asleep. Close the door. My bed has already been turned down."

"Don't tell me you're asleep. You're wide awake. And what's that?" She pointed at the bronze.

"A green chamber pot," I said. "What did you think it was?"

"What you won't think of next! But I won't empty it. You can do it yourself. Or you can just learn to use the toilet like everyone else."

"I'll try."

I lay down again and fell asleep in spite of myself. When I woke up, it was deep night. For a moment I didn't know where I was. Then I saw the bronze and almost thought I was back in the museum. I sat up and took a deep breath. I'm not in the museum, I said to myself inaudibly; I've escaped, I'm free, free, free. I said the word "free" over and over like an incantation, audibly now, in a fervent undertone, until I was calm again. I had often done this when I woke up in the course of my wanderings. As my eyes grew accustomed to the darkness, the bronze showed a faint trace of color and seemed suddenly to come alive. Not so much the form, as the patina. This patina was not dead; it was not laid on or produced artificially with acids; it had developed ever so slowly down through the centuries. It came from the water in which the bronze had lain, from the minerals of the earth that had fused with it, and probably, along with the clear-blue stripe on the foot, from the phosphorus compounds produced hundreds of years before by the proximity of a corpse. This patina had the faint shimmer that the unpolished Chou bronzes in the museum derived from their porousness; it did not absorb the light, like an artificial patina, but reflected it, taking on the texture of coarse raw silk.

I kept the bronze for two more days, then I went back to Second Avenue. This time I was received by the second Lowy brother, who resembled the first except that he was dressed more fashionably and seemed more sentimental—within the limits possible for an antique dealer.

"So you've brought it back," he said, reaching for his billfold to return my twenty dollars.

"It's authentic," I said.

He gave me a look of kindly amusement. "It's been rejected by a museum."

"I say it's authentic. I'm returning it to you so you can sell it."

"But what about your money?"

"You'll give it back to me with half the profit. That was our agreement."

The Lowy brother reached into his right-hand pocket, took out a ten-dollar bill, kissed it, and put it into his left-hand pocket. "What can I treat you to?" he asked.

"You mean you believe me?" I felt very pleased. Nobody had believed me in a long time.

Lowy laughed. "Let me explain. I made a bet with my brother: two to one; five dollars for him if you brought the bronze back and said it was a fake, ten for me if you said it was authentic."

"You seem to be the optimist in the family."

"The professional optimist. He's the professional pessimist. That's our way of sharing the risks in these hard times. Nobody can afford to be both these days. How about a Kapuziner?"

"Are you Viennese?"

"Yes. Viennese-American. And you?"

"Adoptive Viennese and citizen of the world."

"Fine. Let's have a Kapuziner over at Emma's. The Americans are funny about coffee. They boil it to death or they make a whole day's supply in the morning. But Emma's different. She's a Czech."

We crossed the roaring avenue. A Department of Sanitation truck passed, spraying water in all directions. A lavender vehicle rushing diapers to pampered mothers almost ran us over. Lowy saved himself with a graceful leap. I saw that he was wearing patent-leather shoes.

"Aren't you and your brother twins?" I asked.

"Yes, but we call ourselves Senior and Junior to make it easier for the customers. My brother is three hours older. That makes him an astrological twin, too—Gemini, don't you know. I'm Cancer."

A week later the owner of the firm of Loo and Co., an expert on Chinese art, returned from a trip. He couldn't imagine why the museum had thought the piece was a forgery. "It's no masterpiece," he said, "but it's definitely a Chou bronze. Late Chou, transition to Han."

"How much is it worth?" asked Lowy Senior.

"It ought to bring four or five hundred at auction. Not much more. Chinese bronzes are cheap right now."

"Why?"

"Because everything's cheap. The war. And there aren't many collectors of Chinese bronzes. I can give you three hundred for it."

Lowy shook his head. "I'll have to offer it back to the museum first."

"Why should you?" I said. "It's half mine. You have no right."

"Have you an agreement in writing?"

I looked at him open-mouthed. He raised his hand. "Just a minute before you start yelling. Let this be a lesson to you. Always make your agreements in writing. I learned that the hard way myself. And now listen to me. I've got to offer it back to the museum because it's a small world—the New York art world, I mean. In a few weeks the story would get out. And we need the museum. Understand? I'll see that you get your share."

"How much?"

"A hundred."

"And how much for you?"

"Half of anything over that. Okay?"

"It may be peanuts to you," I said. "But I risked half my fortune."

Lowy Senior laughed, showing a mouth full of gold. "A crazy business," he said, "but I think I know how it happened. They've appointed a new curator. A young guy. He wanted to show that the old fogy he replaced didn't know his business, that he'd wasted the museum's money on forgeries."

We finished our coffee in silence. I was still mulling over my wrongs. "I'll make you a proposition," he said finally. "We've got a cellar full of things that we don't know too much about. We can't know everything. Suppose you look them over. We'll pay you ten dollars a day. Plus a bonus on everything we sell."

"Is that compensation for the bronze deal?"

"Partly. Of course it's only a temporary job. My brother and I can manage the usual business by ourselves. Okay?"

"Okay," I said.

"Fifty thousand to kill a man?" asked the elder Lowy, chewing furiously on his cigar. "In the First World War they did it for ten thousand."

"People are cheaper in Germany," I said. "In the concentration camps they figured out that a young Jew in good condition is worth sixteen hundred twenty marks. They hire him out to German industry as a slave laborer for six marks a day. It costs the camp sixty pfennigs a day to feed him. Amortization of clothing comes to ten more. Average longevity: nine months. That brings the profit to something over fourteen hundred marks. Then there's what they call the rational processing of the remains: gold teeth and fillings, hair, personal apparel, money and valuables, minus two marks for the cost of cremation. The net profit comes to about sixteen hundred twenty marks. Allowing for children, the sick, and the aged, whom it costs approximately six marks to gas and cremate, it still averages out to twelve hundred marks."

Lowy had gone deathly pale. "Is that true?"

"Those are the figures drawn up by the competent German authorities. But they may have underestimated a little. Unforeseen complications. There's no difficulty about the killing. At that the

Germans are world champions. Way ahead of the Russians, who are no slouches."

"I know," said Lowy in an undertone. "Our allies, whom we supply with arms."

"The trouble is getting rid of the bodies. It takes time for a body to burn. Burying isn't so simple either, so many thousands of them —if you want to do a neat job. There's an acute shortage of crematoriums. And half the time they have to shut down at night on account of the bombers. Yes, the poor Germans are having a hard time. And all they wanted was peace."

"What!"

"That's right. If everybody had done what Hitler wanted, there wouldn't have been any war."

"All right," Lowy growled. "That's enough of your jokes." His red head drooped. "How can people do such things? Do you understand?"

"No. But the men who give the orders usually think in abstractions. They don't see any blood. It all begins with a man sitting at a desk. He doesn't shoot, he's never seen a gas chamber, he just writes out orders." Lowy was very unhappy. I felt sorry for him, but I couldn't stop. "And there are always plenty of people willing to carry out orders—especially in Germany."

"Even when it's cold-blooded murder?"

"Especially when it's murder. Because an order from above frees a man from responsibility. He's free to act like the savage he is."

Lowy ran his hands over his hair. "Have you seen those things?"

"Yes," I said. "I wish I hadn't."

"And here we are," he said, "having a peaceful afternoon in a shop on Second Avenue. What do you think of that?"

"I think it feels like peacetime," I said.

"That's not what I meant. I meant: how does it strike you that people just sit around with their hands folded when such things are going on?"

"Who's sitting with folded hands? What about the war against Hitler? I admit the war doesn't seem very real to me. Real war is only in your own country. Anything else is unreal."

"But people are being killed."

"We haven't imagination enough to count very high. Most of us can only count to one. Or maybe two."

The shop door opened. A woman in a red dress wanted to buy a Persian silver cup. Could it be used as an ash tray? I took the opportunity to disappear into the cellar. I hated such conversations, which struck me as naïve and useless. Such conversations were for outsiders who thought they were doing something if they worked themselves up, for people who were not in danger. How deliciously cool the cellar was by comparison. Like a comfortable air-raid shelter. A collector's air-raid shelter. The roar of the traffic overhead was like the muffled sound of planes.

It was late afternoon when I returned to the hotel. In a surge of simplehearted generosity, Lowy Senior had given me a fifty-dollar advance. He had instantly regretted it—that was obvious—but after that harrowing conversation he hadn't dared to ask for it back. So some good came of the conversation.

Melikov wasn't there. But Lachmann was in the lobby, as usual agitated and perspiring. "Did it work?" I asked him.

"Did what work?"

"The water from Lourdes."

"Lourdes? Who said anything about Lourdes? That water was from the Jordan. No, there hasn't been a miracle. But I'm getting ahead, yes, getting ahead. All the same, that woman is driving me crazy!"

There was madness in his eyes. "If I don't get that woman soon, I'll go impotent. You know about my obsession. Those dreams have come back; I wake up screaming and bathed in sweat. Those thugs wanted to castrate me. Not with a knife. With scissors. And the way they laughed! If I don't get that woman soon, I'll dream that they succeeded. Terrible dreams. And so real. I jump out of bed and I can still hear the laughter."

"Get yourself a whore."

"I can't do it with a whore. With whores I'm impotent already. Or with normal women. You see what they've done to me!"

Suddenly Lachmann heard a sound. "There she comes! We're going to the Blue Ribbon. She likes sauerbraten. Come along. Maybe you can put in a word for me. You talk so well."

I heard the melodious voice on the stairs. "No time," I said. "But maybe she's as neurotic about her foot as you are about your limp."

"Think so?" Lachmann had stood up. "Do you really think that might be it?"

I had said that without thinking, just to comfort him. When I saw his excitement, I cursed my loose tongue, because I knew from Melikov that the woman slept with the Mexican. But it was too late to explain, and Lachmann had heard all he wanted. Already he was limping away.

I went to my room but didn't turn on the light. Some of the windows across the court were lighted; in one of the rooms a naked, hairy man was standing at the mirror, putting on make-up. When he had finished, he put on a pair of light-blue panties and a bra, which he filled out with toilet paper, so intent on what he was doing that he forgot to pull down the shade. I had seen him a few times in the lobby: a retiring sort when dressed as a man, rather noisy and bumptious in female attire. He had a weakness for evening gowns and big floppy hats. The police knew him and had him listed as incurable. I watched him for a while. Then, overcome with sadness, I went downstairs to wait for Melikov.

IV

Lachmann had given me Harry Kahn's address. His legendary feats were well known to me. He had turned up in southern France shortly after the Germans moved into the unoccupied zone. He called himself José Tegnèr, carried a Spanish diplomatic passport, and drove a car with a diplomatic license. He dressed like a dandy and was so shamelessly self-assured that even the refugees were taken in.

He drove about the country making use of his usurped position to help his fellow refugees. He looked very Jewish, but that, as he airily explained, was common among the Spanish nobility. When stopped on the road, he flew into such a rage and became so haughtily abusive that the German patrols preferred to wash their hands of him: maybe he really was a Spanish vice-consul, and what a dressing-down they would get from their superiors then! Franco was known to be Hitler's friend, and this Señor Tegnèr was Hitler's friend's representative.

He had connections with the underground Resistance. That was probably where he got his money, his car, and the gas to run it with. He transported leaflets and the first underground newspapers, little two-page pamphlets. Once, when his car was full of subversive literature, a German patrol wanted to search it. Kahn shouted such dire threats that the patrol decamped on the double. But Kahn wasn't satisfied. After unloading his incriminating cargo, he called at the local German headquarters and fumed until the commanding officer apologized for the idiocy of his men. Kahn departed with the Falangist salute, to which the officer replied with a brisk *"Heil* Hitler!"* Later in the day Kahn discovered that there were still two pamphlets in the car.

Somehow Kahn came into possession of a few Spanish passports, which he used to save the lives of refugees who were personally wanted by the Gestapo. He managed to hide them in French monasteries until he could arrange for a guide to take them across the Pyrenees. He had saved two refugees, who were already under arrest, from being shipped back to Germany. In one case he had explained to a sergeant that Spain had a special interest in the prisoner, because his knowledge of languages fitted him for counterespionage work in England; in the other he had plied the man's guards with rum and cognac and then threatened to report them for drinking on duty.

Then one day Kahn disappeared from view, and all sorts of rumors cropped up. We all knew that his one-man campaign could end only in death. He had been getting more and more foolhardy, as though deliberately tempting fate. I myself felt sure that he had fallen into the hands of the S.S. And then I heard from Lachmann that he was alive in New York.

I found him in a shop where President Roosevelt was making a speech over six radios at once. The noise was unbelievable. The shop door was open, and a large crowd had gathered on the sidewalk.

Conversation was impossible; we would have had to shout. We

ended up talking in sign language. He shrugged his shoulders apologetically, pointed at the radios, then at the people outside, and smiled. I understood; he thought it was important for the people to listen to Roosevelt's speech. I sat down by the window, lit a cigarette, and listened. I listened to the man who had made it possible for us to come to America.

Kahn was short and slender, with black hair and large sparkling eyes. He was young, not over thirty. His thoughtful, sensitive face suggested a poet rather than the daredevil he was. But Rimbaud and Villon had also been poets; and it took a poet to conceive of exploits such as Kahn's.

Suddenly the loud-speakers fell silent. "I'm sorry," he said. "I couldn't interrupt the speech. Did you see those people outside? Some of them would be quite capable of killing the President. He has a lot of enemies. They say he got America into the war and hold him responsible for the American losses."

Kahn looked at me more closely. "Haven't we met somewhere? Maybe in France?"

I told him about my problem. "When do you have to leave?" he asked.

"In two weeks."

"Where will you go?"

"No idea."

"Mexico," he said. "Or Canada. Mexico is simpler; the government is friendlier. They took the Spanish refugees in. We could inquire at the Mexican Embassy. What kind of papers have you got?"

I explained. "The same old story," he muttered with a smile. "And you want to stick to your passport?"

"It's all I've got. If I admit it's not mine, they'll throw me into jail."

"Not necessarily. But it won't do you any good. Are you free tonight?"

"Of course."

"Pick me up at nine. We need help, and I know where we can get it. Someone's having a birthday party."

"Betty!" I cried.

Under the tousled hair her round red-cheeked face glowed like a friendly moon. "Robert!" said Betty Stein. "Good Lord, where have you been? When did you get here? Why didn't you get in touch with me? But of course you have better things to do than . . ."

Betty Stein was a mother to all refugees, just as she had been a mother to every unsuccessful writer, painter, and actor in Berlin. Her affection for her protégés was unquestioning, wholehearted, and mildly tyrannical.

"Old friends, I see," said Kahn. "The reproaches begin on the doorstep. Splendid." And, turning to Betty, "You see, our friend Ross needs help and advice."

"Ross?"

"Yes, Betty, Ross."

"Is he dead?"

"Yes, Betty. And I'm his heir."

"I understand."

I explained my situation. Without a moment's hesitation she started discussing the possibilities with Kahn, who was still held in high esteem as a hero. I looked around me. The room was not large, but it had already taken on Betty's character. A number of photographs, all with affectionate dedications, were thumbtacked to the walls. I read the names. Seven of them were bordered with crepe: six who had not succeeded in escaping from Germany, and one who had gone back. "Why have you got crepe on Forster's picture?" I asked. "He's not dead."

"Because he's gone back," said Betty. "And do you know why?"

"Because he was homesick and wasn't Jewish," said Kahn. "And because he couldn't learn English."

"Because he couldn't get his favorite field salad in America," said Betty. "That made him sad."

A few days later I saw Kahn again. I found him in a mellow mood, and for the first time he told me something about his exploits. On one occasion he had persuaded the commandant of a French internment camp to release five refugees. There were also some Nazis in the camp. First Kahn had persuaded the commandant to release the Nazis, because the Germans would be arriving in a few days, and the Gestapo would be sure to arrest him if they found Nazis in his camp. Once the Nazis were released, he blackmailed the commandant, threatening to report him to the French authorities unless he freed the refugees.

"How did you get out of France?" I asked him.

"Well, the Gestapo finally got suspicious. One day I was arrested. I shouted and threatened as usual, but it didn't work. They told me to undress—to see if I was circumcised. I told them that thousands of Gentiles were circumcised. The more I stalled, the more they laughed. The funniest thing in the world, to those people, is the sight of a man struggling for his life. Finally I gritted my teeth in desperation and clammed up. At that point their leader—he wore glasses and must have been a school principal—said amiably: 'All right, you stinking Jewish pig, off with your pants; show us your circumcised pecker. We'll cut it off and give it to you for supper.' His subordinates, all very handsome and blond, went into gales of laughter. I took my pants off, and they practically fainted: I wasn't circumcised. My father was a so-called enlightened Jew; he believed that circumcision was unnecessary in a temperate climate."

Kahn smiled. "You see the tactic. If I'd taken them off right away, it wouldn't have made any impression. As it was, they were flabbergasted and embarrassed. 'Why didn't you say so right away?' asked the commandant.

" 'Say what?'

" 'That you're not one.'

"Luckily, two of the Nazis whose discharge from the French camp I had obtained were there at Gestapo headquarters, waiting to be sent back to Germany. And now they stood up for me. I was their friend. I'd done something for them. That revived my courage. I thought up some new threats and dropped a few names. In the end I had them so worried they were almost grateful when I promised to forget the whole incident. They told me to run along, and I didn't stop running till I got to Lisbon."

We were sitting in the dark in Kahn's radio shop.

"Does this place belong to you?" I asked him.

"No, I'm employed. I'm a very good salesman."

"I'm ready to believe that."

We could see shadowy figures passing on the sidewalk and, beyond them, a steady stream of car lights, but the invisible plate-glass window cut out the noise and more than the noise. It was like sitting in a cave looking out at the world.

"Have you noticed," Kahn said, "that you can't taste a cigarette in the dark? Wouldn't it be wonderful if the darkness made us insensible to suffering?"

"We suffer more in the dark because we're afraid. But what are we afraid of?"

"Of ourselves. Imagination. We ought to be afraid of other people."

"That's imagination, too."

"No," said Kahn calmly. "That's what people used to think. Since 1933 we've known it's not true. Civilization is a thin veneer; the rain can wash it off. The nation of poets and thinkers has taught us that. Supposedly the most civilized people on earth. And now they've outdone Attila and Genghis Khan."

"The darkness doesn't seem to agree with us," I said. "May I turn on the light?"

"Of course."

For a moment we sat blinking in the merciless glare. Kahn took a comb from his pocket and straightened the part in his hair.

"What funny places we land in," he said. "But the main thing is to land somewhere and start doing something. It's no good waiting around. What are you doing? Have you got a profession?"

"I'm a temporary sorter in an antique shop."

"There's no future in that. Start something of your own. Selling hairpins. Anything. I'm doing something else on the side."

"Do you want to become an American?"

"I wanted to become an Austrian; then a Czechoslovakian. Both times the Germans marched in. I tried again in France, and the same thing happened. Now I'm wondering if the Germans will occupy America."

"And I'm wondering what border they'll shove me across in ten days."

Kahn shook his head. "That's not so sure. Betty is collecting affidavits for you. She's already got Thomas Mann and Heinrich Mann lined up. Men like that have influence. But of course we need some Americans to vouch for you, too. There's a publisher who wants me to write a book about my experiences. I'll never write it, but I don't have to tell him that right now. He takes an interest in refugees. Good business, he thinks, but he's a bit of an idealist, too—which is an excellent combination. I'll call him up tomorrow. I'll tell him you're one of the people I rescued from Gurs."

"I actually was in Gurs," I said.

"No kidding? You escaped?"

I nodded. "Bribed one of the guards."

"Perfect," said Kahn with enthusiasm. "Don't worry. By hook or by crook we'll get your visa extended. A few weeks or months, time to turn around in. The first thing we need is a lawyer. Have you got any money?"

"Enough for ten days."

"You need that for yourself. We'll have to raise the lawyer's fee. It shouldn't be too much." Kahn smiled. "One good thing is that we refugees stick together. For the present at least. Misery is better glue than good fortune."

I looked at Kahn's pale, emaciated face. A subhuman, I thought, according to the code of the master race—my people—a subhuman who had to be exterminated. "You've got one advantage over me," I said. "You're a Jew. The Nazis honor you by rejecting you and your whole people. That's an honor I can't claim. I'm a member of the master race."

Kahn looked at me in silence. I felt stupid and ill at ease. "I'm talking nonsense," I said finally, to be saying something.

"Maybe you'll feel better," Kahn said, "if we do something un-Jewish. Let's get drunk."

I had no desire to drink but I couldn't refuse. Kahn seemed perfectly calm and collected; but Josef Bär had seemed just as calm that night in Paris when I was too tired to sit up and drink with him, and in the morning I had found him hanging in his wretched hotel room. Uprooted people are very unstable; a trifle can throw them off balance. If Stefan Zweig and his wife had had someone to talk to, someone to call on the phone that night in Brazil when they killed themselves, it might not have happened. And aside from being alone in a strange country, he had made a big mistake:

writing a journal, dwelling on his memories instead of avoiding them like the plague. They crushed him. That was why I kept away from mine as long as I could. In the back of my mind I knew there was something I had to do and wanted to do—but I forced myself not to think of such things, because I also knew that nothing could be done until the war was over and I could return to Europe.

The hotel, when I finally got back, seemed more dismal than ever. I sat down in the plush lobby to wait for Melikov. I thought I was alone, but then I heard a sound. A muffled sob. A woman was sitting in the far corner, half hidden by a tropical plant. It was a moment before I recognized Natasha Petrovna in the dingy light.

She was probably waiting for Melikov, too. Her weeping grated on my nerves. I dreaded the thought of a conversation. But then my gentlemanly instincts got the better of me, and I went over to her. "Is there anything I can do?"

No answer. "Has anything happened?" I asked.

She shook her head. "What makes you think that?"

"Because you're crying."

"Nothing has happened," she said.

I stared at her. "But you must have some reason."

"That's what you think!" she said, suddenly hostile.

I'd have left her to her misery if I hadn't been befuddled with drink. "Usually there's a reason," I said.

"Why can't I cry without a reason? Does there have to be a reason for everything?"

I fully expected her to say that only stupid Germans demanded reasons. Instead, she asked: "Haven't you ever felt that way?"

"I can imagine feeling that way."

"But you never have?"

I could have explained that if I had been the weeping sort, I'd have been at no loss for reasons. The idea of crying without a reason, out of *Weltschmerz* or vague melancholy, was a relic of a gentler century. "No," I said.

"Of course not. You're not the type."

There we go, I thought. Slav against German. I stood up. No use trying to comfort her if she only wanted to insult me. "I'll be running along now," I said.

"I know," she said bitterly. "There's a war on and it's ridiculous to cry over nothing. But I happen to feel like crying. And all the battles in the world won't make me stop."

"I understand," I said. "What's the war got to do with it? Suppose I stub my toe. It won't hurt any less because hundreds of thousands of people are getting killed somewhere."

I made no move to leave. Why was I talking such nonsense, I wondered. Why not let this hysterical woman have her cry? Why don't I go? And then I knew why. I didn't want to be alone.

"It's no use," she said. "Nothing we do is any use. We're all going to die. There's no escape."

Good God! I thought. That's all I needed. "Yes," I said, "but we can put it off for a while. That makes a difference."

No answer. Suddenly I had an inspiration. "Would you care for a drink?"

"I hate Coca-Cola," she said. "How can people drink such stuff?"

"How about vodka?"

She looked up. "Vodka? Where are you going to find vodka when Melikov's not here? Where is he anyway? Why isn't he here?"

"I don't know. But I've got some vodka in my room. I'll go get it."

"That makes sense," said Natasha Petrovna. What she said next reminded me of all the Russians I had ever known. "Why didn't you think of that long ago?"

I took the half-empty bottle and went down reluctantly. Maybe Melikov will come in soon, I thought, maybe he'll play chess with me until I calm down. I took a dim view of the impending session with Natasha Petrovna.

She was a different woman when I got back. The tears were gone, her face was freshly powdered, she even smiled. "Where did you learn to drink vodka?" she asked. "They don't drink it in your country, do they?"

"I know," I said. "In Germany people drink beer and schnapps. But I've forgotten my country and I don't drink either beer or schnapps. I'm not much of a vodka drinker either."

"What do you drink?"

What a fool conversation, I thought. "Anything that's handy. In France I drank wine when I could get it."

"France!" said Natasha Petrovna. "What the Germans have done to it!"

"Don't blame me," I said. "I was in a French internment camp at the time."

"Naturally! As an enemy."

"Before that I'd been in a German concentration camp. Also as an enemy."

"I don't understand."

"Neither do I," I said angrily. What a day! I thought. All day I'd been harping on the same thing. When all I wanted was to get away from it.

"Would you like some more vodka?" I asked. We really had nothing to say to each other.

"No, thanks. I'd better not. I was drinking before I came."

I fell silent. I felt utterly wretched. Betwixt and between and belonging nowhere.

"Do you live here?" she asked.

"Yes, temporarily."

"Everybody lives here temporarily. But some stay forever."

"So they say. Have you lived here?"

"Yes. I wish I'd never left. And I wish I'd never come to New York."

I was too tired to ask any more questions. I had heard too many life stories to be curious. And I really couldn't take an interest in this woman's lamentations at having come to New York. Such people belonged to a faraway shadowy world.

Natasha Petrovna stood up. "I've got to go now."

For a moment I was panic-stricken. "Won't you wait for Melikov? He'll be here soon."

"I doubt it. Felix has just arrived. He takes Melikov's place when he's not able to be here."

I looked around. Sure enough, there was Felix's bald head. He was standing in the doorway smoking. "Thanks for the vodka," said Natasha, looking at me out of her gray, transparent eyes. "Isn't it funny how little it takes sometimes to cheer us up?" she said.

She nodded and left. She was slender, and taller than I had thought. Her receding form seemed frail and vulnerable. But her heels clattered forcefully on the wooden floor, as though she wanted to trample something.

I corked the bottle and went out to the doorway. "How's it going, Felix?" I asked.

"Pretty fair," he said, gazing absently out into the street. "Nothing to complain about."

His serenity filled me with bitter envy. In that moment his glowing cigarette became a symbol of all the peace in the world. "Good night, Felix," I said.

"Good night, Mr. Ross. Do you need anything? Beer, cigarettes?"

"No, thank you, Felix."

I opened the door to my room. The past came surging out at me as though it had been lying in wait. I threw myself on the bed and stared at the gray rectangle of the window. I felt helpless, I wanted to choke somebody. I saw faces, I looked for other faces and couldn't find them, I screamed soundlessly for revenge, but even as I did so I knew it was useless. I wanted to choke somebody and I didn't know whom. All I could do was wait. And then I felt that my hands were wet and I knew I was crying.

V

The lawyer made me wait an hour. I assumed that this was the old strategy, his way of softening up a new client. There was nothing left of me to soften. I passed the time watching two clients who were also waiting. One was chewing gum, the other was trying to date the secretary, who just laughed at him. Across from the secretary, between two color prints of New York street scenes, hung a framed sign with one word on it: THINK! I had often come across this succinct command. You couldn't even go to the toilet at the Hotel Reuben without being admonished to think. Nothing I had seen in America reminded me so much of Prussia.

The lawyer had broad shoulders, a broad, flat face, and colorless eyes behind gold-rimmed glasses. He was perusing a letter that must have been from Betty. His voice, when he spoke, was so soft that I could barely hear him.

"You're a refugee?" he whispered.

"Yes."

"Jewish, I presume?"

I made no reply.

"Jewish?" he repeated impatiently.

"No."

"What? You're not Jewish?"

"No," I said in surprise. "Why?"

"I don't work for non-Jewish Germans."

"Why not?"

"I don't believe that requires an explanation. Mrs. Stein should have told me you weren't Jewish."

"The German Jews seem to be more tolerant than their American cousins," I said angrily. "What about you? Are you Jewish?"

"I am an American!" He raised his voice for emphasis, and it went up a whole octave. Aha, I thought, that's why he whispers. "And as an American I have no desire to help Nazis."

I laughed. "You regard all Germans as Nazis?"

"Potential Nazis at least."

I laughed again and pointed to the inevitable THINK! sign, the same as in the waiting room, except that his had gold lettering. "That," I said, "doesn't make any more sense than saying that the Jews are to blame for everything. The Jews and the bicycle riders."

"Bicycle riders?" he whispered.

"That's an old joke. A Gentile says to a Jew: 'The Jews were to blame for everything.' 'Yes,' says the Jew. 'The Jews and the bicycle riders.' 'Why the bicycle riders?' the Gentile asks. And the Jew answers: 'Why the Jews?' "

I expected the lawyer to throw me out. Not at all. A broad smile made his face even broader.

"Not bad," he said. "I hadn't heard that one."

For a minute or two he just sat there chuckling. But then he grew serious. "We have a fatal weakness for jokes," he said. "But I stand by my opinion."

"Think it over," I said. "The Jews left Germany because they had to; they were persecuted and in danger. If they hadn't been persecuted, some of them wouldn't have budged. The non-Jews who left Germany left because they hated the regime."

"Except for the spies."

"A spy wouldn't be coming to you for help. Spies always have beautiful passports and visas."

The lawyer waved that one away. "You say that some Jews wouldn't have opposed the Nazi regime. Doesn't that suggest a touch of anti-Semitism?"

"Maybe it does. But among Jews. It's not my idea. I got it from my Jewish friends."

I stood up. I was sick of this argument. Nothing is so tedious as a man trying to show you how clever he is, especially when he isn't.

"Have you got a thousand dollars?" the broad face asked.

"No," I said bluntly. "Not even a hundred."

He let me get almost to the door. "How were you expecting to pay?" he asked then.

"My friends will help me. But I'd rather face another internment camp than ask them for such an amount."

"Have you already been in one?"

"Yes," I said angrily. "First in Germany. And there they have a different name."

I expected this know-it-all to tell me that there were also criminals in the concentration camps, which was true. If he had, I'd have lost control. But it didn't come to that. Suddenly a melancholy voice cried out: "Cuckoo. Cuckoo. Cuckoo." A Black Forest cuckoo clock—something I hadn't heard since my childhood.

"Isn't that pretty!" I said, with all the sarcasm I could muster.

"It's a present from my wife," said the lawyer, with a note of embarrassment.

I was going to ask him if the cuckoo was an anti-Semite, but thought better of it, realizing that I had found an unexpected ally in this mechanical bird. In a tone that was almost friendly the lawyer said: "I'll do what I can for you. Call me the day after tomorrow."

"But your fee?"

"I'll discuss it with Mrs. Stein."

"I'd rather you told me," I said.

"Five hundred. In installments if you like."

"Do you think you can do anything?"

"I'm pretty sure I can get you an extension. Then we'll see."

"Thank you," I said.

Lowy Senior came down to the cellar where I was working. He was carrying a bronze. "What do you think of this?"

"What is it supposed to be?"

"Chou. Or even Shang. The patina looks good to me."

"Have you bought it?"

Lowy smiled. "Would I do that without consulting my expert? A man's just brought it in. He's waiting in the shop. He wants a hundred for it. Which means that he'll take eighty. Seems cheap to me."

"Too cheap," I said, looking at the bronze. "Is he a dealer?"

"He doesn't look like one. A young fellow. Says he inherited the piece and needs money. Is it genuine?"

"It's a Chinese bronze. But it's not Chou. Or even Han. More likely Tang, or even more recent. Sung or Ming. Yes, I'd say it was a Ming copy of an older piece. And the copyist wasn't too careful. The tao-tieh masks are inaccurate, and the spirals shouldn't be there; such spirals weren't used until after the Han period. The décor, on the other hand, is copied from a Shang piece; it's compact, simple, and strong. But the ogre's mask and the accessory ornament would be much clearer and sharper in an authentic Chou piece. And you'd never find these little curlicues in a really old bronze."

"But look at the patina! It's beautiful."

"Mr. Lowy," I said, "it is a fairly old patina, but there are no malachite incrustations. Remember that as early as the Han period, at the time of Christ's birth, the Chinese started making copies of Shang bronzes and burying them. That gives them a very nice patina, even if they're not authentic Chou."

Lowy Senior shook his head. "Did you learn all that in your nights at the Brussels Museum?" he asked with mild sarcasm.

"No," I said calmly. "I've learned that in my nights in New York with the help of your excellent public libraries."

"What is this piece worth?"

"Twenty or thirty dollars; but you know that better than I do."

"Want to come up?" Lowy asked, with a malicious glint in his blue eyes.

"Must I?"

"Only if it amuses you."

"To confound a petty crook? What for? And maybe he's not a crook. Who knows anything about archaic Chinese bronzes?"

Lowy gave me a sharp glance. "None of your wisecracks, Mr. Ross."

The tubby little man climbed the cellar stairs with puffy determination. The steps trembled and sent down a shower of dust. For a moment I could only see his shoes and trouser cuffs; the upper part of him was already in the shop.

A few minutes later the legs reappeared. Lowy still had the bronze. "I've bought it," he said. "For twenty bucks. Why not? Ming isn't so bad."

"Not at all," I said. Maybe Lowy didn't know much about Chinese bronzes, but he had a keen eye for business.

"Tell me," he said, "how much longer will you be busy here?"

"That depends on you. Do you want to get rid of me?"

"Certainly not. But we can't keep you here forever. Your work will be done soon. What did you do before?"

"Newspaper work."

"Can't you go back to that?"

"With my English?"

"Seems to me you've been learning fast."

"But I can't even write a letter without making mistakes."

Lowy scratched his bald head with the bronze. After all, it was only a Ming copy. "Do you know anything about paintings?"

"Not much. Just what I learned in Brussels."

He grinned. "That's better than nothing. I'll look around. Maybe some dealer needs an assistant. Business is slack; you can see how it is in antiques. But with paintings it's different. Especially the Impressionists. Nobody's interested in the old stuff right now. Anyway, we'll see."

Lowy stomped back up the stairs. Farewell, cellar, I thought. You've been a dark home to me. Farewell, ye nineteenth-century

gilded lamps, ye ornate *fin-de-siècle* fixtures, ye Louis-Philippe furniture, ye Persian vases, ye light-footed dancing girls from the
tombs of the Tang period, ye terra-cotta horses, and all ye silent
witnesses to dead civilizations! Born through no fault of my own
into one of the lousiest of all centuries, unarmed latter-day gladia-
tor in an arena full of hyenas, jackals, and a few lions, enjoying life
while waiting to be devoured, I salute you. I bowed in all directions, distributed blessings to right and left, and looked at my
watch. My working day was over. The evening sky stretched red
over the rooftops, and from the restaurants poured the friendly
smell of fried onions.

VI

I wandered aimlessly through the streets, afraid to go back to the
hotel. I'd had a nightmare the night before and awakened
screaming. Bad dreams were nothing new to me: I had dreamed
the police were chasing me; or that I'd lost my way, crossed the
German border by mistake, and fallen into the hands of the S.S.
Then, too, I had jumped up screaming. But I had looked out the
window at the sky, recognized that this was New York, and gone
confidently back to bed. I was saved.

This dream had been different, confused flashes rising endlessly
out of a black magma. A pale anguished woman was crying out
soundlessly for help, but I couldn't move; she was sinking into a
dense mass of pitch, muck, and blood. Only her head emerged. She
stared at me out of eyes paralyzed with terror; wordless screams
poured from the black cavern of her wide-open mouth. Then
blackness, intermingled with flares, shouts of command, a grating
voice with a Saxon accent, uniforms, a hideous smell of murder,
raging furnaces. A human form was moving, then only the hand
moved, then only one finger, slowly, very slowly, and someone was
stamping on it. And then a sudden scream. It came from all directions and echoed.

I stopped outside a shop window but saw nothing. It was some time before I realized that I was on Fifth Avenue and that this was one of New York's most luxurious jewelry shops. For the first time Lowy's cellar had seemed to me like a prison cell. I had left it precipitately, feeling a sudden need for light and life and movement.

A tiara that had belonged to the Empress Eugénie lay on its bed of black velvet, glittering in the artificial light.

Two girls stopped beside me.

"How'd you like to own that?" one of them asked.

"Too flashy," said the other.

I drifted down the avenue, stopping now and then to gaze absently at displays of shoes, cigarettes, china, fashions, anything. The tumultuous life of a late afternoon in New York passed me by. I wanted to be part of it, to swim with the stream like everyone else, but I could not be part of it; I was a lone fugitive, an Orestes pursued by the distant cries of the Furies.

Usually dreams are dispersed by daylight; only a few tatters linger on, and little by little these, too, are forgotten. But this dream kept its hold on me; I couldn't shake it off. In Europe I hadn't dreamed much. I had been too busy keeping myself alive. Here in America I thought I had escaped. But now I knew that the shadows had followed me across the ocean. And what was that acrid, yet cloying smell? Could it be the smoke of the crematoriums?

I looked around. No one was watching me. I turned to the shop windows for help. As though so much treasure could not be contained in one row of shop windows, there were more on the second and sometimes even the third floor. Never in all my life had I seen so many paintings and vases, so much furniture, so many lamp shades. Temples of luxury and comfort. A voice seemed to whisper: "Take what you need, take more than you need. There's plenty of everything!"

I yearned to embrace this country, which paints the faces of its dead, which worships youth, and sends its soldiers to die, with no idea of what they were dying for, in countries they never heard of.

Why couldn't I be part of this? Why must I belong to the army of homeless souls who climb endless flights of stairs, ride eternally up and down elevators, and wander from room to room, tolerated but unloved, and only too ready to love in return for being tolerated?

I looked into the windows of Dunhill's at the rows of deep-brown dull-polished pipes, symbols of peace and security, giving promise of long quiet evenings by the fireside—a far cry from the bitter Gauloise with which the homeless fugitive tries to quiet his nerves.

I'm getting sentimental, I thought. Seeing that Fifth Avenue was undermining my morale, I turned westward on Forty-second Street. The Public Library, the penny arcades and theaters. Then I passed through streets of brownstone houses. The grown-ups were taking the air on the stoops, while the children flitted about on the sidewalk, looking for all the world like dirty white butterflies. I looked at the people on the stoops, and, as far as I could see in the failing light, they seemed at peace with the world, not seriously worried about anything.

A woman, I thought, that's what I need. A stupid, unthinking animal with blond hair and a promising wiggle to her ass, who knows nothing and whose curiosity is confined to the state of one's pocketbook. We could drink a bottle of California Burgundy, and I'd spend the night with her somewhere, and I wouldn't have to go back to the hotel. But where was she, this woman, this girl, this whore? This wasn't Paris, and I had already learned that the New York police were very strict about the morals of the poor—the whores you could recognize by their umbrellas and outsized handbags were unknown in this town. Of course there were phone numbers you could call, but that took time and you had to know the numbers.

"Good evening, Felix," I said. "Where's Melikov?"

"It's Saturday," said Felix. "My day."

Good God, Saturday. I'd forgotten. A long empty Sunday ahead of me. Today I dreaded the prospect more than ever. I still had a little vodka left—maybe a few sleeping pills.

"Miss Natasha is here," said Felix indifferently. "She's been asking for Melikov, too."

43

I saw her in the dim light of the lobby. If only she doesn't start crying, I thought. She rose to meet me, and again I was surprised to see how tall she was. "On your way to the photographer's?" I asked.

She nodded. "I felt like a drop of vodka, but Vladimir Ivanovich isn't here today. I'd forgotten."

"I've got some vodka," I said eagerly. "I'll go and get it."

I ran up the stairs and opened the door. Looking neither to right nor to left, I picked up the bottle and two glasses. But on the way out I risked a look around. Nothing. Not a ghost in sight. The bed shimmered pale in the darkness. I shook my head at my foolishness and went out.

She seemed different from my memory of her—less hysterical and more American. A bit of an accent, but, as far as I could judge, it was more French than Russian. She was wearing a loose-fitting turban of lavender silk. "To keep my hair neat," she said. "I'm modeling evening clothes."

"What makes you come here?" I asked.

"I like hotel lobbies. They're never boring. People come and go. They meet, they part. Those are the best moments in life."

"Do you really think so?"

"Anyway the least boring. What is there in between?" She made a gesture of impatience. "The big hotels are colorless. The people hide their emotions. You feel that there's adventure in the air, but you never really see it."

"And here you see it?"

"More. The people let themselves go. So do I." She laughed. "I don't have to tell you that. Besides, I like Vladimir Ivanovich."

She stood up. "I've got to go." She hesitated a moment. "Why don't you come along? Are you busy?"

"No. But won't the photographer throw me out?"

"Nicky? Don't be silly. The place is swarming with people. One more or less . . ."

I could guess why she had asked me to come: to make up for her behavior at our first meeting. I had no great desire to go; what would I do in such a place? But that evening anything seemed preferable to sitting in the hotel. I couldn't agree with her; to me there was nothing adventurous about the place. And certainly not that evening.

"Should we take a cab?" I asked.

She laughed. "People who live at the Reuben don't take cabs. It's not far. And it's a beautiful evening. Oh, these New York nights! I wasn't made for country life. What about you?"

"I don't really know."

"Haven't you ever thought about it?"

"No," I said. When would I have had time for such luxurious thoughts?

"Then you still have something to look forward to," she said. She walked quickly, taking such long steps that her skirt seemed too tight. It occurred to me that this was the first time I had walked with a woman in America.

She was welcomed like a long-lost child. There were half a dozen people in an enormous bare room lit by spotlights. First the photographer, then two other men, hugged and kissed her. I was introduced, vodka, whisky, and cigarettes were passed around, and a moment later I found myself in an armchair off to one side, forgotten.

I didn't mind, because the scene that unfolded was quite new to me. Cartons were unpacked, and their contents—coats and dresses—carried behind a curtain. There were two other models besides Natasha Petrovna: a blonde and a beautiful brunette in high-heeled silver shoes. An argument arose. What should be photographed first?

"First the coats," said a woman who seemed to be the boss.

"No. First the evening dresses," said the photographer, a slight, sandy-haired man with a gold chain on his wrist. "Otherwise they'll get rumpled."

"They don't have to wear them under the coats. The coats have to go back first. Especially the furs. The shop is waiting for them."

"Okay. First the fur cape."

More argument about angles and lighting. I listened without trying to understand. There was something theatrical about the general gaiety and animation. Each speaker was so intense about making a point that seemed to have no bearing on reality. I was reminded by turns of *Midsummer Night's Dream, Rosenkavalier,* and one of Nestroy's farces. At any moment I expected a flourish of

45

trumpets announcing the entrance of Oberon, or at least of Casanova or Count Saint-Germain.

Suddenly the spotlights converged on a white screen, beside which a vase of artificial delphiniums had been placed. The model with the silver shoes appeared in a beige fur cape. The supervisor smoothed out the cape and gave it a little tug here and there; two other spotlights flared into life, and the model froze into immobility.

"Fine!" said Nicky. "Once more, darling."

I leaned back. I was glad I'd come. Nothing better could have happened to me. "And now Natasha," somebody said. "The broadtail coat."

And there she stood, slender and supple in a glossy, tight-fitting coat with a kind of beret to match.

"Perfect!" Nicky cried. "Hold it!"

The supervisor wanted to change something, but he shooed her away. "Later. We'll take some more. But first like this, casual, unposed."

The spotlights groped for the little face. Her eyes glittered like bright-blue stars in the glare. "Hold it," said Nicky.

Natasha didn't freeze like the other model. She had no need to; it was as though she had been immobile all along. "Good," said Nicky. "And now with the coat open."

She spread her arms, allowing the coat to open like the wings of a butterfly. The garment, which had looked so narrow before, was in reality very wide, lined with white-and-gray-checked silk. "That's it!" cried Nicky. "Like an emperor moth. Hold it!"

"How do you like it here?" asked someone beside me.

It was a pale young man with black hair and round, strangely brilliant black eyes. "It's marvelous," I answered in all sincerity.

"Of course we're not getting things from Balenciaga and the great French houses. The war, you know," he said with a deep sigh. "But Mainbocher and Valentina aren't so bad, are they?"

"Certainly not," I said, without the faintest idea what he was talking about.

"Oh well, let's hope it'll be over soon, so we can get the best again. . . ."

Someone called him away. His reason for being against the war didn't strike me as absurd; for the moment at least, I could think of no better reason.

Then it was time for the evening dresses. Natasha stood before me in a long white gown, dazzling in its simplicity. "Are you terribly bored?" she asked.

"Not at all." And then I stared at her in amazement. "Happiness must be giving me hallucinations," I said. "That tiara you're wearing—I could swear I saw it this afternoon in Van Cleef and Arpels' window."

Natasha laughed. "You have good eyes."

"Is it really the same one?"

"Yes. The magazine we're working for borrowed it. Did you think I'd bought it?"

"How would I know? Anything seems possible tonight. After all those beautiful things."

"What did you like best?"

"It's hard to say. Maybe the black velvet cape. That might have been Balenciaga."

She looked me straight in the eye. "It *is* Balenciaga. Are you a spy?"

"A spy? Nobody's ever taken me for a spy. For what country?"

"For one of our competitors. Are you in the trade? How else would you know it was Balenciaga?"

"Natasha Petrovna," I said solemnly, "I swear to you that I never heard the name of Balenciaga until ten minutes ago. Before that I'd have thought it was a make of car. I heard it from that gentleman over there. Actually, he said Balenciaga models were unobtainable these days. I was joking."

"Well, you hit it on the nose. That cape really is Balenciaga. Smuggled over in a bomber. A Flying Fortress."

"I can think of no better use for a bomber."

"Well, then you're not a spy. I'm almost sorry to hear it. But it seems we've got to be very careful. They stop at nothing."

Someone was calling her. "We're all going to El Morocco afterward. It's the custom. Would you like to come?"

She was gone without waiting for an answer. Of course I couldn't go. I couldn't afford it. I'd have to tell her that. An unpleasant task, but there was no hurry. For the moment I refused to think of the next day or even the next hour. The brunette, who had been photographed in a long bottle-green coat, threw it off to put on another. She had no dress underneath, only the strictest minimum of underthings. No one seemed interested. All in the day's work, I supposed. Besides, half the men were queer. She was very beautiful; she had the slow-moving negligent assurance of a woman who knows the cards are stacked in her favor and doesn't make much of it. Natasha, when I saw her in between dresses, was white and long and slender, her skin like pearls in the moonlight. The brunette was more my type, I reflected, but only for the barest moment. That night I was too happy for comparisons or desires. I hardly knew these girls, yet I was aware of a strange and delightful feeling of intimacy with them, perhaps from seeing them dressed in so many different ways.

When the cartons were all packed, I told Natasha that I couldn't go to El Morocco with them. "Why not?" she asked.

"I can't afford it."

"You dope!" she said, with her husky laugh. "We're all invited. Did you think I'd let you spend all that money?"

I felt like a bit of a gigolo, but her way of including me in the invitation gave me a pleasant sense of complicity. I tagged right along, overwhelmed with gratitude at the way this day was ending. At El Morocco a Viennese was singing German songs. There were quite a few Army officers in the room, and they didn't seem to mind. But by that time nothing could surprise me. I only knew that in Germany this would not have been possible. I fingered the fifty dollars in my pocket, prepared to part with my whole fortune if anyone had asked for it. But of course no one did. This is peace, I thought, the peace I have never known, the carefree life I could never have. I felt no envy. It was enough for me that such things still existed. These strangers I was with were friendlier and seemed closer to me than a good many others whom I knew well. I was sitting next to a beautiful woman whose borrowed tiara glittered in the candlelight. Here I was, a petty parasite drinking other people's champagne, and it seemed to me that for one evening I had borrowed another life, which I would have to give back the next day.

VII

"It won't be hard to find you a job in an art gallery," said Lowy Senior. "You're lucky there's a war on. Everybody's shorthanded."

"I'm beginning to feel like a war profiteer," I said ruefully. "People keep telling me I'd be sunk without the war."

"Well, isn't it the truth?" Lowy scratched his scalp with the sword of a spurious figurine of St. Michael. "You wouldn't even be here if it weren't for the war."

"That's a fact. But if it weren't for the war, the Germans wouldn't be in France."

"Wouldn't you rather be here than in France?"

"That, Mr. Lowy, is a pointless question. In both countries I feel like a parasite."

Lowy beamed. "Funny your saying that! You see, I've decided to introduce you to a certain parasite."

I laughed. "Birds of a feather, you mean."

"Not exactly," he said. "Let me explain. With your status, you can't get a regular job in a gallery. You can only be employed on the q.t., the way you've been here. I've just been talking with a man who might be able to use you. Now he's a real parasite. A rich parasite. An art dealer."

"Does he sell phony paintings?"

"God forbid!" Lowy put down the spurious St. Michael and seated himself in a much-repaired Savonarola chair, the upper part of which was authentic. I could see he was warming up for a lecture. "An art dealer," he began, "is by definition a crook. The money he makes is the money some artist should have made. With antiques it's not so bad. With modern art it's a different story. Take Van Gogh. He never sold a picture and he never had enough to eat; today the dealers make millions on his works. The artist goes hungry; the dealer buys castles."

"In other words," I said, "art dealers are parasites."

"No," he said. "Not exactly. It's a question of degree. Take the gallery owners. Of course they're exploiters, but at least they do something for their artists—the living ones, that is. They give them exhibitions, they support unknown artists in the hope that something will come of it, they take risks. I don't say they do it out of kindness of heart; their motives are a mixture of business and snobbery. They're not artists themselves, but they like to feel that they belong to the art world. The fact remains, though, that they do something for the artist—so they're not complete parasites."

He paused for effect and thrust a cigar into his mouth without removing the band. "The real gilt-edged parasites," he went on, "are the dealers who have no shops or galleries. With no risk or expense to themselves, they cash in on the interest aroused by the galleries. They operate in their own apartments. Their only expense is a secretary. They even deduct their apartment rent from their tax declarations—on the ground that it's their place of business. And the life they lead! You've been around here long enough to know what a headache it is to run a shop. And the worst of it is that we've got to be here from morning to night. Now take a look at the parasite's day. He sleeps until ten or eleven and then he dictates a couple of letters. The rest of the time he waits for customers like a spider waiting for flies."

"Don't you wait for customers?"

"Not in luxurious idleness like a spider. We have to work."

"Then why don't you turn parasite, Mr. Lowy?"

He looked at me with a frown. I saw I had put my foot in it. "For ethical reasons?" I asked.

"Worse," he said. "For financial reasons. You need money to be an art parasite. And good merchandise. A-1 merchandise."

"Does the parasite sell cheaper?"

Lowy stubbed out his cigar in a Renaissance mortar, but a moment later picked it up again and relit it. "No!" he bellowed. "That's what you might think, because he has no overhead. Actually, he gets higher prices. The rich fools fall for his game; they think they're getting a bargain. Hardheaded businessmen fall for it. They think it's classy to buy from a 'private collector.' Tell one of these fresh-baked millionaires to buy a Renoir, and he'll laugh at you. He'll think it's a bicycle. But tell him a Renoir will improve his social standing, and he'll take half a dozen!"

I listened with keen interest. Now and then Lowy gave me these free lectures on the realities of life, usually in the slack hours after lunch.

"Do you know why I'm giving you this course in the higher art trade?" he asked.

"To prepare me for a business career, I suppose."

"In a way," he said. "You see, I've mentioned you to one of those parasites. He can use an assistant who knows something about pictures. A fellow like you who doesn't talk too much. I've arranged for you to see him at five-thirty today. Okay?"

"Thanks a lot," I said. "I'm really grateful."

"You won't be making much at first, but, as my father used to say, it's the prospects. Here . . ." He made a sweeping gesture, taking in the whole shop. "Here you haven't got any prospects."

"I'm thankful for the time I've spent here. And I'm thankful to you for helping me now. What makes you want to help me?"

Lowy smiled. "It is funny," he said. "Because we're not exactly philanthropists. I suppose it's because you seem so helpless."

"What!" I wasn't too pleased.

"Yes, that's what it must be. You don't look helpless. But somehow you make a helpless impression. My brother noticed it first. He said you must be lucky with women."

The parasite's name was Silvers. He lived in a private house with no name plate on the door. I had expected some sort of two-legged barracuda. Instead, I saw a slender, exceedingly well-dressed man, who seemed gentle to the point of timidity. He poured me a drink and questioned me tactfully. Then he brought two drawings from another room and set them on an easel. "Which do you prefer?"

I pointed to the one on the right. "Why?" Silvers asked.

"Must I give a reason?"

"It would interest me. Do you know whom they're by?"

"Degas," I said. "Anyone can see that."

"A lot of people wouldn't," said Silvers, with a strangely diffident smile. "Some of my customers, for instance."

"Then why would they buy them?"

"Because it's high class to have a Degas in your living room."

I remembered Lowy Senior's lecture. He seemed to know what was what.

"Pictures," said Silvers, "are refugees like yourself. You refugees often end up in strange places. Whether you're happy about it is another question."

He left the room and came back with two water colors. "Can you identify these?" he asked.

"Cézanne water colors," I said.

Silvers was surprised. "Can you tell me which one is better?"

"All Cézanne water colors are good," I said. "The one on the left is probably the more expensive."

"Why? Because it's bigger?"

"No. Because it's from his late period, and the style is almost Cubist. It's a very beautiful landscape. Mont Sainte-Victoire in Provence. There's one like it in the Brussels Museum."

Silvers' face had changed. Suddenly he was on his guard. He stood up. "Where have you been working?" he asked.

I remembered the Balenciaga incident with Natasha. "I haven't been working anywhere," I said calmly. "I don't know any of your competitors and I'm not a spy. I was in the Brussels Museum for a while."

"When?"

"During the German occupation. I was hidden there. And that's where I learned what little I know."

Silvers sat down again. "We can't be too careful in this business," he muttered.

"Why?" I asked.

Silvers hesitated for a moment. "Pictures," he said then, "are like living creatures. Like women. If they've been exposed to too many eyes, they lose their magic. And their value."

"But that's what they're made for."

"Maybe. I'm not so sure. It's important for a dealer that they shouldn't be too well known."

"That's odd. I'd think that would raise the price."

"Not always. Far from it. Pictures that have been shown too much are 'burned out,' as we say in the trade. Pictures that have always belonged to the same private owner and that next to no one has seen are known as 'virgins.' They bring higher prices. Not because they're better, but because the connoisseur and collector feels that he's made a discovery."

"And he's willing to pay for it?"

Silvers nodded. "Unfortunately, there are ten times as many collectors as connoisseurs today. It takes time, patience, and love to become a connoisseur."

I listened to him. The room, with its gray velvet hangings, seemed to have captured the silence of a peaceful past. "Do you know this one?"

"Monet. One of his poppy fields."

"Do you like it?"

"It's magnificent. What peace! And that sun! The sun of France."

Silvers cast a quick look in my direction. "I often sit here in the morning with my pictures," he said. "Alone. But with paintings one is never alone. One can talk with them. Or, rather, listen to them."

I wasn't entirely convinced. His little speech sounded a bit too glib, rather like a come-on for his customers. And why should he be saying this to me? I had come here only to see about a temporary job. But since I was sentimental about peace and anything that could induce a feeling of peace, I banished the thought that Silvers' mornings might be devoted more to reckoning up his profits than to "listening" to his beautiful paintings.

"We can give it a try," he said finally. "You don't need to know much here. Reliability and discretion are more important. How does eight dollars a day strike you?"

At that I awoke from my dreams of peace. "For how many hours? Morning or afternoon?"

"Morning and afternoon. But you'll have plenty of time to yourself in between."

"That's about what a high-class errand boy makes."

I expected Silvers to tell me that was what my job amounted to. Instead, he told me exactly what a high-class errand boy made. It was less.

"I can't do it for less than twelve," I said. "I have debts to pay off."

"So soon?"

"I've got to pay the lawyer who's working on my residence permit."

I knew Lowy had told Silvers that, but he pretended to be hearing it for the first time—a drawback that obliged him to reconsider the whole deal. The pirate was finally showing his true colors.

With his diffident smile, Silvers pointed out to me that since my job was not legal, I wouldn't have to pay taxes. And besides, he added, my English wasn't fluent. I countered that by remarking that my French would come in very handy. In the end we settled for ten. He even held out the prospect of a raise if my work proved satisfactory. I knew that was hot air, but I had no choice.

VIII

That night Kahn and I went to Betty Stein's. In Berlin she'd had open house on Thursdays, and she did the same in New York. Anyone who could afford it brought something—a bottle of wine, a few packs of cigarettes, a pound of frankfurters. Old records were played: lieder sung by Tauber, operettas by Kálmán, Lehár, and Walter Kollo. Now and then a writer would read a passage from his works. Most of the time we just talked.

"She means well," said Kahn, "but the place is a morgue: the living dead reminiscing about the dead dead."

Betty was wearing a lavender silk dress from the pre-Hitler years. Its flounces rustled and it smelled faintly of moth balls. It didn't go very well with her red cheeks, ice-gray hair, and sparkling dark eyes. She welcomed us with plump outstretched arms. She was so touchingly warmhearted that you could only smile helplessly and love her. She acted as if the years after 1933 had never existed. They might exist on other days, but not on Thursdays. On Thursdays she was still in Berlin under the Weimar Republic.

In the large room with the photographs of the dead, a circle of admirers had formed around an actor by the name of Otto Wieler. "He has conquered Hollywood!" said Betty with pride. "He's made it!"

Wieler lapped it up. "What's the part?" I asked Betty. "Othello? The Brothers Karamazov?"

"I don't know, but it's something big. He'll show them. He's a future Clark Gable."

"Or Charles Laughton," said Betty's niece, a shriveled old maid, who was serving coffee. "More like Laughton, I'd say. He's a character actor."

I had never heard of Wieler, but that didn't mean a thing. I hadn't had much time for the theater in my last few years in Europe. The only actors I really knew were those of the preoccupation days.

Kahn gave me a sardonic look. "It's not much of a part," he said. "And Wieler wasn't much of an actor in Europe either. Do you know the story about the man who takes his dachshund to a White Russian night club in Paris? The owner wants to impress him. 'Our doorman,' he says, 'used to be a general'; the waiter was a count, the singer a grand duke, and so on. Finally the customer, who is getting rather bored, interrupts him. He points to his dachshund and asks: 'I bet you don't know who this little fellow used to be? All right, I'll tell you. He's come down in the world, but he used to be a Saint Bernard.' " Kahn smiled sadly. "Wieler really hasn't got much of a part. He's playing a Nazi in a class-B picture. An S.S. man."

"But isn't he Jewish?"

"What has that got to do with it? The ways of Hollywood are strange. A Jewish-looking S.S. man doesn't bother them in the least. This is the fourth case I've heard of. There's a kind of poetic justice in it. The Gestapo has saved these Jews from starvation."

The next arrival was a timid little man with a black goatee. "That's Dr. Gräfenheim," Kahn informed me. The name was well known. He had been a leading gynecologist in Berlin and had developed a contraceptive that bore his name. A few minutes later he came over to Kahn and me.

"Living in New York?" Kahn asked him.

"No, in Philadelphia."

"And how's your practice?"

"No practice," said Gräfenheim. "I haven't taken my examination yet. It's hard. How would you feel about taking your examinations all over again? And in English."

"But you're a famous man. They must have heard of you here."

Gräfenheim shrugged his shoulders. "That has nothing to do with it. The Medical Association over here thinks we refugee doctors are a threat to the American profession. They make it as hard as they can for us. That's why we have to take examinations. It's no joke in a foreign language. I'm over sixty." Gräfenheim smiled apologetically. "I should have studied languages. But we're all in the same boat. I'll have to do a year of internship, too. But at least they'll give me board and lodging in the hospital."

Betty interrupted him. "Tell them what happened to you," she said.

Gräfenheim shrugged. "I didn't come here to talk about my troubles."

But Betty would not be discouraged. "Then I'll tell about them. He was robbed. Robbed by a no-good refugee."

It seemed that Gräfenheim had owned a valuable stamp collection. He had entrusted a part of it to a friend who left Germany before he did. But when Gräfenheim arrived in New York, the friend wasn't a friend any more. He said Gräfenheim had never given him anything.

"Didn't you have a receipt?" Kahn asked.

"No," said Gräfenheim. "That was impossible. If the Gestapo had found a receipt, they'd have locked me up for sending valuables abroad."

"And that swine is living on the fat of the land," Betty fumed. "While Gräfenheim has been starving."

"Not exactly starving. But I was counting on my stamps to see me through my second education."

"How much could you have got for them?" Betty asked.

Gräfenheim squirmed. "Quite a lot," he admitted. "They were my rarest stamps. At least six or seven thousand dollars."

"A fortune!" Betty exclaimed. "Imagine what you could have done with all that money!"

Gräfenheim tried to mollify her. "It's better than if the Nazis had got it."

"What a way to talk!" cried Betty in a rage. "Why are refugees always so resigned? If I were you, I'd curse the day I was born."

"What good would that do, Betty?"

"Such talk makes me ashamed of being a Jew. So understanding, so forgiving. A Nazi would have more spunk. He'd find that crook and crack his skull."

With her lavender neck frills, Betty looked like an angry tropical bird. Kahn looked at her with affectionate amusement. "Sweetie pie," he said. "You're the last of the Maccabees!"

"Don't laugh! You at least showed those barbarians what a Jew can do. If there's one thing I can't stand, it's resignation!" She turned angrily to me. "What about you? Do you just put up with everything that happens?"

I said nothing. What could I have said? Betty gave herself a shake, laughed at herself, and joined another group.

I went back to the hotel. Betty's party had made me sad. I thought of Gräfenheim trying to build a new life. What for? He had left his wife in Germany. She wasn't Jewish. For five years she had resisted the pressure of the Gestapo and refused to divorce him. Those five years had made a nervous wreck of her. Every few weeks they had taken Gräfenheim away for "questioning." Every morning from four to eight he and his wife had trembled; that was the time when they usually came for him.

When they took him away, he was thrown into a cell with other Jews and usually held for several days. They huddled together, bathed in the cold sweat of terror. They whispered to each other but no one heard what the others were saying. They were too busy listening for steps in the corridor. The steps meant that one of their number was being called for questioning. Minutes or hours later a bleeding mass of flesh would be heaved into the cell. Without a word the others would do what they could to help. After the first few times, Gräfenheim was careful to have two or three handkerchiefs in his pocket. If bandages had been found on him, he would have been sent to a concentration camp for believing atrocity stories. It took a good deal of courage even to tie up a man's wounds with a handkerchief. If you were caught, you could be beaten to death for "obstructionism."

Gräfenheim had been obliged to cede his practice to another doctor. His successor had offered him thirty thousand marks for it and actually paid him a thousand—it was worth three hundred thousand. One day his successor's brother-in-law, an S.S. Sturmführer, had come to his house and given him his choice of being sent to a camp for practicing illegally or of accepting a thousand marks and signing a receipt for thirty thousand. Gräfenheim knew the score; he had accepted the thousand. His wife was on the verge of madness, but she still refused to divorce him until he had left the country, because she was convinced that he owed his relative safety to having an Aryan wife.

And then Gräfenheim had a little luck. One night the Sturmführer, who had been promoted to Obersturmführer in the meantime, came to see him. He was wearing civilian clothes. After some beating about the bush he stated his business. He wanted Gräfenheim to perform an abortion on his girl friend. Suspecting a trap, Gräfenheim refused. He pointed out that his successor was not only the Obersturmführer's brother-in-law, but also under obligation to him. "The stinker won't do it," said the Obersturmführer. "All I could get out of him was a National Socialist speech about elite stock and genetic duty and crimes against the nation—all that rubbish. That's how the bastard thanks me for getting him his practice!" All this without a trace of irony. "With you it's different," he went on. "And you can be trusted with a secret. If my brother-in-law did it, he could blackmail me for the rest of my life. I wouldn't put it past him. But with you it's a cut-and-dried bargain. We're both illegal, so it's sure that neither of us will talk. I'll bring the girl tonight and take her home tomorrow. Is it a deal?"

"No!" cried Frau Gräfenheim from the doorway. Trembling with fear, she had overheard the whole conversation. "Listen to me," she said to her husband. "You're getting an exit visa out of this, and you won't lift a finger before you have it." She turned to the Obersturmführer. "That's the price." He tried to tell her that visas weren't in his department. He started to leave. She threatened to report him to his superiors. He only laughed: who'd take the word of a Jewess against that of an S.S. officer? "I'm as much an Aryan as you are!" she told him—the first time Gräfenheim had ever heard her use that preposterous word. And besides, she pointed out, it wasn't his word against hers; the authorities would investigate and find that his girl friend was indeed pregnant. In the end the Obersturmführer gave in. The abortion was performed two weeks later. When it was all over, the young Nordic admitted to Gräfenheim that he had had still another reason for coming to him; he had more confidence in a Jewish doctor than in his imbecile brother-in-law. He seemed to be really in love with the girl. To the very end Gräfenheim suspected a trap. The Obersturmführer offered him a fee of two hundred marks. When Gräfenheim refused it, the Obersturmführer stuffed it in Gräfenheim's pocket. "It will come in handy, Doctor." Gräfenheim was so suspicious that he didn't say good-by to his wife. Soon after his departure, the war had broken out, and he had never heard from her. If only he had kissed her good-by!

Outside the Hotel Reuben stood a Rolls-Royce with a chauffeur. I heard Melikov's voice from the lobby: "I'm sorry. I haven't got time. Here comes your escort now."

I saw Natasha in the corner. "Is that your buggy outside?" I asked.

"Borrowed!" she said. "Borrowed like my evening gowns and jewelry. Nothing genuine about me."

"The voice is genuine. And so's the Rolls."

"She needs an escort," Melikov explained. "She's only got the car for this evening. She has to return it tomorrow."

I did a little mental arithmetic. I had enough money for a good dinner, even at the Pavillon if we didn't take more than one bottle of champagne.

"We've even got an English chauffeur," said Natasha.

"Do I have to change?"

"Of course not. Look at me."

I don't know what I would have changed into. I only had one other suit, and it was shabbier than the one I had on.

"Let's go!" she said.

"It's my lucky day," I said. "I've just given myself a three-day vacation, but I wasn't expecting a surprise like this."

"Can you give yourself a vacation?" she asked. "I'm not so badly off, but I can't do that."

"Neither can I. I'm between jobs. In three days I start work for an art dealer. Porter, framer, and handyman."

"Won't you be selling, too?"

"Heaven forbid! Mr. Silvers does that."

Natasha looked at me for a moment. "But why can't you sell?"

"I don't know enough."

"You don't have to know anything about what you're selling. You make out better if you don't. You feel freer if you don't know what's wrong with the merchandise."

I laughed. "How do you know all that?"

"I do a bit of selling now and then. Dresses and hats. I get a commission. So should you."

"I doubt if I'll get a commission for sweeping and for serving drinks."

We drove slowly through the streets. Natasha pressed a button. A small table detached itself from the mahogany panel in front of us and sprang into place. "Cocktails," she announced. She opened a door and produced two glasses and an assortment of bottles. "Ice-cooled," she said proudly. "What will it be? Vodka, whisky, mineral water? Vodka, I suspect."

"Right you are!"

I looked at the bottle. Genuine Russian vodka. "Good Lord," I said. "Where did this come from?"

"The man the car belongs to has something to do with the State Department. He's always going to Washington. The Russians have an embassy, and they're our allies."

The vodka was first-rate. Nothing like Melikov's rubbing alcohol. "One more?" she asked.

"Why not? I seem to be fated to live as a war profiteer. They let me into America because there's a war on; I found work because there's a war on; and now I'm drinking vodka because there's a war on. I'm an involuntary parasite."

Natasha laughed. "Make it voluntary," she said. "It's much more fun."

We drove up Fifth Avenue, along Central Park. The roaring of the lions could be heard from the zoo. It was summer and they were still out of doors.

"We're coming to your territory," said Natasha a little later. We had turned into Eighty-sixth Street. The pastry shops, beer halls, and displays of delicatessen made me think of the main street of some small town in Germany.

"Do they still speak German here?" I asked.

"As much as they please. The Americans are open-minded. They don't lock anybody up for the language he speaks. They're not like the Germans."

"Or the Russians," I reminded her. "Not to mention the French."

"I suppose it's always the wrong people that get locked up."

"Maybe so. One thing is sure. The Nazis on this street are free to run around loose. Can't we go somewhere else? Why should I have to look at all these Nazis? How about Central Park?"

Natasha looked at me for a moment in silence. "I'm not usually like this," she said. Then, thoughtfully, "But there's something about you that irritates me."

"Isn't that lovely! I feel the same about you."

She ignored my answer. "A kind of secret smugness," she said. "As if you owned some truth that nobody else could touch. I can't quite put my finger on it, but it gets on my nerves. Do you see what I mean?"

"Perfectly. It gets on my nerves, too. But why are you saying all this?"

"To annoy you," said Natasha. "But let's turn the tables. What impression do I make on you?"

I laughed. "No impression," I said.

She gasped. I already regretted what I had said, but it was too late. Her face had gone pale. "You lousy Boche!" she said between clenched teeth.

"It may interest you to know," I said, "that the Germans don't regard me as one of them. They've taken away my citizenship."

"I don't blame them," said Natasha, and tapped on the glass partition. "To the Hotel Reuben."

"Yes, ma'am."

"You don't have to take me home," I said. "I can get out here. There are plenty of buses."

"As you wish. You're at home around here anyway."

"Stop, please," I said to the chauffeur, and got out. "Thanks for the ride," I said to Natasha, and received no reply. I stood on the sidewalk staring at the Café Hindenburg and listening to the band music that welled from within. German coffee rings were on display in the window of the Café Geiger. Next door hung strings of blood sausage. German was being spoken all around me. Many times over the years I had wondered what it would be like to go back—but I had never thought it would be like this.

IX

At first my work for Silvers consisted in drawing up a catalogue of everything he had ever sold, giving a detailed history of each work since it had left the painter's easel. It wasn't difficult; most of the information could be found in catalogues and in books or monographs on painters.

"The trouble with old paintings," Silvers explained, "is their pedigree. You can't always be sure of their origin. Pictures are like nobility; you've got to be able to follow their genealogy back to the man who painted them. It has to be an unbroken line—from X Church to Cardinal A, from Prince Z's collection down to Rabinowitz, the rubber magnate, or Ford, the automobile king. No morganatic escapades allowed."

"But why do we need all that if we know the picture?"

"We may think we know it, but photography wasn't introduced until the nineteenth century. Sometimes we have contemporary engravings to go by, but not too often. Without a basis for comparison, we're reduced to conjecture." Silvers smiled diabolically. "Or to the judgment of art historians."

I was classifying a pile of photographs. On top lay some color photographs of Manets. Small paintings of flowers, peonies in a water glass. You could feel the blooms and the water. They breathed a wonderful sense of repose and an energy that was pure creation—as though the painter had created those flowers *ex nihilo*.

"Do you like them?" Silvers asked.

"They're magnificent."

"Better than Renoir's roses on the wall over there?"

"Different," I said. "You can't speak of better and worse in a case like this."

"Oh yes you can, if you're a dealer."

"These Manets are a moment of Creation. The Renoir is a moment of life in all its fullness."

Silvers wagged his head. "Not bad. Were you a writer before you came here?"

"Only a lousy journalist."

"I believe you could write very well about pictures."

"I'm afraid I don't know enough."

Again Silvers put on his diabolical smile. "Do you think the people who write about painting know any more? I'll let you in on a secret: nobody can write about paintings, or about art in general. Everything that's been written on the subject has only one purpose: to make lowbrows think they know something. Nobody can write about art. One can only feel it."

I made no reply. "And sell it," said Silvers. "Isn't that what you were thinking?"

"No," I said truthfully. "But why do you think I'd be capable of writing about it? Because there's nothing to say?"

"Maybe it's better than being a lousy journalist."

"And maybe not. Maybe it's better to be a lousy but honest journalist than a pretentious phrase-monger writing about art."

Silvers laughed. "Like many Europeans," he said, "you think in extremes. But between your two extremes there are thousands of variants and shadings. Besides, your premises are false. Take me. I wanted to be a painter. I started out as a painter. A lousy one, full of enthusiasm. Now I'm a dealer. Full of the cynicism that characterizes all art dealers. Has anything changed? Did I betray art when I stopped painting bad pictures, or am I betraying art by selling it?"

Silvers offered me a cigar. "Thoughts on a summer afternoon in New York," he said. "Try this cigar. It's the lightest Havana in existence. Are you a cigar smoker?"

"I've never learned to make distinctions. I've smoked whatever I could lay my hands on."

"You're a lucky man!"

I looked up in surprise. "That's a new one on me. Why does that make me lucky?"

"Because you have everything ahead of you—refinement of taste, enjoyment, and weariness. The end is always weariness. The lower down you start, the longer it takes you to get there."

"Then you think it's best to start as a barbarian?"

"If you can."

I felt suddenly irritated. I had seen too many barbarians. What good was this drawing-room aestheticism to me? That was for peaceful times. I was sick of this perfumed chitchat, even if I was being paid ten dollars a day for it. To change the subject I pointed to a pile of photographs. "With these," I said, "the pedigree is simpler than with Renaissance paintings. Several centuries less to worry about. Degas and Renoir died only thirty years ago."

"Even so, there are plenty of phony Degas and Renoirs floating around."

"Is an unbroken pedigree the only guarantee?"

Silvers smiled. "That and feeling. You've got to look at hundreds of pictures. Over and over again. For years and years. And study. And compare. And look at them some more."

"That sounds fine," I said, "but how is it that so many museum curators give worthless certificates of authenticity?"

"Some do it against their better knowledge. But that gets around very quickly. Usually they're just mistaken. Why do they make mistakes? That brings us to the difference between a curator and a dealer. The curator buys occasionally—with the museum's money. The dealer buys often, and always with his own money. Believe me, that makes a difference. When the dealer makes a mistake, he loses his money. The curator doesn't lose a cent. His interest in a picture is academic; the dealer's interest is financial. The dealer is more careful."

"True," I said, looking at a Sisley landscape, a flooded countryside.

Silvers followed my eyes. "If you had money," he said, "I'd advise you to buy that Sisley. Sisley is coming up. Still a lot cheaper than Monet. For the moment he's even cheaper than Pissarro. Paintings are the best possible investment. You've seen the little Manets. Ten years ago one of them cost three thousand. Today the price is thirty thousand. In ten years it'll be fifty. Or more. Show me the stocks you can do better with. Do you know what my policy is? To sell as little as possible. What I don't sell increases in value."

That was a little too much. "Then why do you sell at all?"

I was expecting him to tell me that he had to live. But that wasn't his style. With a disarming smile he answered: "Because it amuses me."

I looked at this fashion plate of a man. His suits and shoes were from London, his shirts from Paris. His nails were nicely manicured, and he smelled of French cologne. I saw him and listened to him as though he were sitting behind a glass pane; he seemed to live in a muffled world—a world of bandits and cutthroats, I was sure, but fashionable, well-groomed bandits and cutthroats. Everything he said was true, and then again nothing was true. His whole world seemed strangely unreal. He seemed serene to the point of indifference, but I had the feeling that he could change at any moment into a ruthless businessman, ready to make his way over corpses. He was a lover of frothy, mellifluous phrases; he spent half his time talking about art and he seemed to know a great deal about it, even to understand it; but perhaps, it suddenly struck me, all he really understood about his art works was their prices, because if he really loved them he wouldn't sell them. And by selling them he was enabled to live a life of luxury unknown to the painters who had made it possible. All this fascinated and troubled me; there was something wrong, almost evil, about it—though actually his activities were not too different from other supposedly honest, reputable businesses. The only difference was that he didn't deal in beans or brassières. And wasn't it more refined, more spiritual to deal in art? No, I said to myself, the exact opposite. What he sold was the very life and soul of other men. And yet by buying their works for a song, dealers had often saved poor artists from going hungry. Everything about this business was so ambiguous, so misty and unclear. There was no way of proving that he had ever wronged anyone. It was all perfectly legal. If his stock in trade had been something else than works of art, I wouldn't have given it a thought.

Silvers looked at his watch. "Let's knock off for today. I've got to go to my club."

His having to go to a club didn't surprise me in the least. That was part of the unreal showcase existence that he seemed to be displaying for my benefit. "We'll make out all right together," he said, smoothing the crease in his trousers. I looked at his shoes. Everything he had on was just a shade too elegant. His shoes were a little too pointed and a little too light in color. The cut of his suit was a little too perfect, and his tie just a little too expensive-looking. He glanced at my suit. "Isn't that rather heavy for summer in New York?"

"I can take off the jacket when it's too hot."

"Not here. Buy yourself a tropical worsted. American ready-to-wear is very good. Even millionaires seldom have their suits made to order. Go to Brooks Brothers; or if that's too expensive, to Browning, King. For sixty dollars you'll get something very decent."

He drew a wad of bills from his pocket. I had noticed before that he didn't use a wallet. "Here," he said, peeling off a hundred-dollar bill. "Call it an advance."

I felt as if that hundred-dollar bill would burn a hole in my pocket. It wasn't too late to go to Browning, King. I raced down Fifth Avenue, saying a silent prayer for Silvers. I would have kept the money and gone on wearing my old suit, but I knew that was impossible. In a few days Silvers would start asking questions.

I turned into Fifty-fourth Street. A little way from the corner there was a small flower shop where I had seen some low-priced orchids. Maybe they weren't too fresh, but that wasn't noticeable. The day before, Melikov had given me the address of the shop where Natasha worked. I had been mulling the matter over and hadn't made up my mind. One moment I decided she was a hysterical chauvinistic fool, and the next that she was a charming, if somewhat high-strung, young lady whom I had needlessly offended. But now I had a hundred dollars, and that settled it. I bought two orchids and sent them to Natasha's address. They cost only five dollars, but they looked more expensive, and that, too, seemed somehow fitting. Then with a load off my mind I went back to Fifth Avenue, happy in the feeling that I had done something silly.

At Browning, King I selected a lightweight gray suit. It fitted me perfectly except that the trousers had to be shortened. "We'll have it for you tomorrow evening," the salesman said.

"Couldn't I have it today?"

"It's pretty late."

"But I need it this evening," I pleaded. "It's urgent."

Of course I didn't need it, but suddenly I was all eagerness. I hadn't bought a suit in years, and all at once a new suit struck me as a sign that my days as a wandering Jew were over, that I would now be able to settle down to a quiet bourgeois existence.

"I'll ask the tailor," said the salesman.

I stood between long rows of suits and waited. The suits seemed to bear down on me from all sides like an army of automatons, bent on the total elimination of man. The salesman looked strangely anachronistic when he reappeared in their midst. "The tailor says he can do it," he reported. "You can call for it in half an hour."

I walked up Second Avenue. Lowy Senior was decorating his window. I stopped outside in all the splendor of my tropical worsted. He stared at me like an owl in the night and motioned to me with a twentieth-century candlestick to come in. "Beautiful," he said. "Is that the first fruits of your activity as a high-class crook?"

"It's the first fruits of my collaboration with the gentleman you recommended."

Lowy grinned. "A whole suit. I can't believe it. You look like a con man."

"Thanks for the compliment. But I'm a beginner, you know."

"You seem to be doing pretty well," he grumbled, while pinning a freshly painted eighteenth-century angel to a square of Genoa velvet. "It's a wonder you even talk to small fry like us."

I was speechless with amazement. The little man was jealous, though he himself had sent me to Silvers. "Would you rather I'd robbed Silvers?" I asked.

"I didn't tell you to rob him. But I didn't tell you to kiss his ass either!" Lowy adjusted a French chair, half of one leg of which was genuine period. A feeling of warmth rose in me. It was a long time since I had felt that someone with nothing to gain by it was really fond of me. Well, on second thought, it hadn't actually been so long. The world was full of good people. You didn't notice it until you were in trouble, and it was a kind of compensation to you for being in trouble.

"What are you gaping at?" Lowy asked.

"You're a good, kind man," I said in all sincerity. "Like a father."

"What?"

"It sounds funny, but I mean it."

"In other words," said Lowy, "you're happy. To talk such ba-

loney you've got to be happy. So the parasite's life appeals to you?"
He wiped the dust off his hands. "None of this dirty work for you,
eh?" He tossed the soiled towel onto a pile of framed Japanese
woodcuts. "Better than here, eh?"

"No," I said.

"Don't give me that."

"Different, Mr. Lowy. What does all that matter when the paintings are so beautiful? They're not parasites."

"No," he said. "They're victims. Imagine how they'd feel if they
were alive. Being sold like African slaves, to soap manufacturers,
soup manufacturers, armaments manufacturers . . ." He broke off
sharp, looking as if he had seen a ghost. "My God! If it isn't Julius.
In a dinner jacket! All is lost!"

Lowy Junior appeared in the dingy honey-colored light, amid
the exhaust fumes of a late afternoon in New York. He wasn't
wearing a dinner jacket, but his attire was festive enough: black
jacket, striped trousers, and, to my amazement, the light-gray spats
of another generation.

I looked at the spats with a feeling of nostalgia. I hadn't seen
spats since before Hitler.

"Julius!" cried Lowy Senior. "Come in! Don't go! One last
word! Think of your poor mother!"

Julius stepped slowly across the threshold. "I have thought of
Mother," he said. "And you can't intimidate me, you Jewish fascist!"

"Julius! Don't talk like that! Haven't I always done all I could
for you? Watched over you as only an elder brother can, cared for
you when you were sick! And now . . ."

"We're twins," Julius explained to me, as though I hadn't
known it. "My brother is three hours older."

"Three hours can mean more than a lifetime! You were dreamy
and impractical, a poet. I always had to look out for you, Julius;
you know that. I always had your welfare in mind, and now you
treat me like your worst enemy. . . ."

"Because I want to get married."

"Because you want to marry a shicksah! Look at him standing
there, Mr. Ross. It's pathetic. Like a goy on his way to the races!
Julius, Julius, pull yourself together! All dressed up to propose,

like J. P. Morgan! They've given you a love potion. Think of Tristan and Isolde—a lot of good their love potions did them! Already you're calling your own brother a fascist because he's trying to save your life. I'm only asking you to take a nice Jewish girl!"

"Don't pay any attention to my brother," said Julius. "I'm an American. I'm sick of his old-fashioned prejudices."

"Prejudices!" In his agitation, Lowy Senior knocked a porcelain shepherd off its stand, but caught it just in time.

"My God!" cried Julius in spite of himself. "Was that the genuine old Meissen?"

"No, it's the phony we got from Rosenthal." Lowy Senior held up the figure. "Unharmed!"

The incident had a calming effect on them. Julius took back the "Jewish fascist," toning it down to "Zionist." Lowy Senior made one tactical blunder. He brought me into it. "Would *you* marry a Jewish girl?" he asked me.

"Why not?" I said. "When I was sixteen, my father even advised me to. He said I wouldn't amount to anything if I didn't."

"See!" said Julius.

The discussion went on, with rising and falling intensity. Little by little, by sheer persistence, Lowy Senior gained ground. I had expected as much. If Julius' mind had really been made up, he wouldn't have shown himself on Second Avenue in his proposal costume. He finally agreed, not too reluctantly, to wait a little while.

"You've got nothing to lose," his brother assured him. "Just take your time."

"But suppose somebody else shows up?"

"Nobody else will show up. Hasn't thirty years in business taught you anything? Haven't we said a hundred times that another customer was waiting to snap up some white elephant? And wasn't it always a cheap trick? And now, take off that monkey jacket."

"No," said Julius. "I've got it on and I'm going out."

"Fine. We'll go out to dinner. To a first-class restaurant. We'll start with an appetizer! Chopped chicken liver. And we'll wind up with peach Melba. Wherever you like; the sky's the limit!"

"Voisin," said Julius firmly.

Lowy Senior gulped. "Okay. Voisin it is." And, turning to me, "Come along, Mr. Ross, seeing you're all dressed up. What have you got in the package?"

"My old suit."

"Leave it here. You can pick it up after dinner."

I was full of admiration for Lowy Senior. Julius had dealt him quite a blow in insisting on Voisin. Voisin was very expensive, and the poetic brother, far from contenting himself with chopped chicken liver, would order the finest *pâté de foie gras*. But the elder twin didn't bat an eyelash. He had agreed without hesitation and invited me to boot. All the same, I decided to order *pâté de foie gras*. In some remote way I felt I owed it to Julius and the racial problem.

It was about ten when I got back to the hotel. "There's a package for you," said Melikov. "It seems to be a bottle."

I removed the wrapping. "Good God!" cried Melikov. "Real Russian vodka!"

I rummaged through the wrapping paper. There was no message. "I wish to point out," Melikov said, "that the bottle is not quite full. It wasn't me. It came that way."

"I know," I said. "There are two glassfuls missing. Be my guest. What a day!"

X

I called for Kahn, who was taking me to a party at the Vriesländers'. "A kind of *bar mitzvah*," he explained. "They've just become American citizens."

"So quickly? Doesn't it take five years?"

"The Vriesländers took out their first papers five years ago. They came over with the 'smart wave' before the war started."

"They were smart, all right," I said. "Why didn't we think of it?"

Vriesländer had been lucky. Long before the Nazis came to power he had invested heavily in American securities, mostly AT&T, which had almost doubled in value over the years. Even so, he had made a big mistake. The greater part of his capital had been tied up in his business—silks and furs. He had thought there would be plenty of time to liquidate if the situation became critical. But trouble came from an unexpected quarter two years before the Nazis seized power. It suddenly became known that one of the leading German banks was threatened with bankruptcy. For fear of a general panic—the Germans had not forgotten the terrible inflation of ten years before, when the mark had dropped to one-billionth of its normal value—the democratic government had imposed currency control and blocked all foreign transfers, thereby unwittingly signing the death sentence of innumerable Jews and anti-Nazis. This measure was never rescinded, and consequently, when the Nazis became a real threat, hardly anyone was able to take his money out of the country. The National Socialists thought it was the world's best joke.

At that point Vriesländer had hesitated. He had no desire to leave everything behind, and like many Jews of his class he thought the storm would pass over, that once the Nazis were in power they would put down the hotheads in their ranks and a respectable, law-abiding government would emerge. Vriesländer was an ardent patriot. He didn't trust the Nazis, but he revered the aged President, Field Marshal von Hindenburg, who, to his mind, symbolized all the old Prussian virtues. It was Hindenburg who had appointed Hitler to the chancellorship, so everything must be all right.

Vriesländer didn't wake from his dream until he found himself threatened with prosecution by the Nazi authorities for a long list of offenses ranging from fraudulent business dealings to the rape of an underage female apprentice whom he had never even seen. Confident in the proverbial integrity of the German courts, Vriesländer had sent the girl's mother packing when she tried to blackmail him for fifty thousand marks, whereupon both the girl and her mother had sworn out a complaint. Then a police official, accompanied by a high party leader, had come to him with a new blackmailing proposition, and he knew he had no choice but to accept. They demanded no less than the whole of his capital in return for an opportunity to leave the country with his wife and daughter. The commanding officer of one of the crossing points on the Dutch border was to be given secret instructions. Vriesländer didn't believe a word of it, but signed on the dotted line. Wonder of wonders, the Nazis carried out their part of the agreement. Vriesländer's wife and daughter went first; when he received a post-card from Utrecht, he handed over the deed to his house and his remaining stocks. Three days later he, too, was in Holland.

Then began the second act of the tragicomedy. His passport expired before he could apply for an American visa. He tried unsuccessfully to get other papers. A small sum of money was sent him from America, but the bank would send no more because he himself had stipulated that funds were to be delivered only to him in person. He was a destitute millionaire without a passport. He managed to cross over into France. By that time the French authorities were suspicious of everybody and treated him like one of the many less fortunate refugees who told the most fanciful stories for fear of being sent back to Germany. In the end some relatives in America sent affidavits, and he was given a visa on his expired passport. When his pile of securities was handed to him, he kissed the topmost certificate and decided to change his name.

This was the last day of Vriesländer and the first day of Daniel Warwick—though his refugee friends continued to call him Vriesländer. He had availed himself of the right to change his name on acquiring citizenship.

We stepped into a large, brightly lighted drawing room. One could see at a glance that Vriesländer had made good use of his time in America. The whole place reeked of money. An enormous buffet had been set up in the dining room. On a separate table there were two immense layer cakes, one with "Vriesländer," the other with "Warwick" inscribed in icing. The Vriesländer cake was edged with black chocolate in guise of mourning, the other with a pink floral design. "My cook's idea," said Vriesländer proudly. "What do you think of it?"

His broad florid face glowed with pleasure. "The Vriesländer cake will be cut and eaten tonight," he explained. "The other will be preserved intact. It's symbolic."

"What gave you the idea of Warwick?" Kahn asked. "Isn't that an illustrious English family?"

Vriesländer nodded. "Exactly. When I get a chance to pick my name, I'm going to pick something good. Did you expect me to call myself Levi or Cohn?"

Kahn gave him a dirty look, and Vriesländer was flustered. "I'm sorry, Mr. Kahn," he stammered. "It had nothing to do with you. It just slipped out of me. Just a manner of speaking. You know how it is. . . ."

"Yes," said Kahn. "I know how it is, Mr. Warwick."

"Tomorrow," said Vriesländer. "Not until tomorrow. To tell you the truth, I did it for my wife. Like this whole layout. She deserves it after all she's been through." He looked anxiously at Kahn, still afraid of having offended him. "Let's have a drink, Mr. Kahn. What will it be?"

"Champagne," said Kahn without hesitation. "Dom Pérignon! You owe it to your name."

"I'm sorry," said Vriesländer, "there isn't any." For a moment he was visibly embarrassed, but then he brightened. "I can offer you a good American champagne though."

"American champagne? In that case, give me a glass of Bordeaux."

"That's the ticket. We have an excellent American Bordeaux!"

"Mr. Vriesländer," said Kahn patiently, "aren't you carrying your new patriotism a little too far?"

"It's not that," said Vriesländer, "but, you see, this is a very special day." His shirt front seemed to swell with pride. "On a day like this we can't have anything that reminds us of the past. We could have had Holland gin, and even Rhine wine is still to be had for a price. We decided against it. We suffered too much in those countries. And in France, too. That's why we didn't order any French wine. And between you and me, they're not so much better. It's all in the advertising."

Kahn and I repaired to the buffet. I helped myself to a piece of chicken in jellied port wine sauce. "The food here is all right," I said. "Is it all from their own kitchen?"

"Every bit of it. Vriesländer has had this Hungarian cook for years. A few months after he left Germany, she managed to join him in France, via Switzerland. She even brought Mrs. Vriesländer's jewels out with her. Before crossing the border she wrapped them in cake dough and swallowed them."

I looked around. The crowd was two or three deep around the buffet.

"All refugees?" I asked.

"No, not all. Mrs. Vriesländer cultivates American connections. As you've heard, they speak nothing but English now in the family. With a German accent, but English."

"Very sensible. How else would they learn?"

Kahn laughed. "Whenever I hear such English, it makes me think of an old lady I know, another refugee. After she had been here a few months, she fell sick. She had no money, and there was no one to help her. She decided to kill herself. But just as she was going into the kitchen to turn on the gas, she thought of how hard she had been working on her English, and it occurred to her that in the last few weeks she had begun to understand what people were saying. Wouldn't it be a shame, she thought, to give up now? That did it. She went back to bed and decided to get well. I always think of her when I hear these people struggling with their new language. There's something touching about them—even the Vriesländers."

My eyes lit on Kahn's enormous portion of roast pork and red cabbage. "I'm a freethinker," he said when he sensed the direction of my thoughts. "And red cabbage is one of my . . ."

"I know," I interrupted him. "One of your innumerable weaknesses."

"A man can't have too many," he said. "Especially if he lives dangerously. You'll never commit suicide if you have plenty of weaknesses."

"Have you ever had such ideas?"

"Yes. Once. Everything was going wrong and I was desperate. You know what saved me? The smell of liver and onions coming out of a restaurant. I decided to have some before committing suicide. I went in and drank beer while I was waiting for my liver and onions. Somebody involved me in a conversation, one thing led to another, and here I am. You think I made it up, but it's true."

"I believe you," I said, helping myself to some liver and mushrooms. "I'm taking my precautions," I explained.

"Another of my weaknesses," Kahn said, "is beautiful women. What do you think of that girl over there, eating strudel and whipped cream? Isn't she beautiful?"

"More than beautiful," I said. "She's tragically beautiful." And I took another look. "If she weren't eating that strudel with such dedication, I'd feel like getting down on my knees to her. But what's wrong with her? Has she a hump? Or piano legs? Something must be wrong with her. Why would a goddess be wasting her time at the Vriesländers'?"

"Wait till she stands up," said Kahn with enthusiasm. "She's perfect. Legs like a gazelle. A figure like Diana. Not too thin. Flawless skin. Full, firm breasts."

I gave him a suspicious look.

"You don't believe me?" he said. "I know all about her. And to crown her perfections, her name is Carmen. Unfortunately . . ."

"Aha! So there is something wrong with her."

Kahn sighed. "She's dumb. Not middling average dumb but spectacularly dumb. Cutting that strudel and getting the pieces into her mouth will exhaust her mental powers. She'll be very tired when she's through. She'd take a nap if she could."

"Too bad," I said. I didn't believe him.

"Not at all. It's fascinating."

"How can such stupidity be fascinating?"

"Because it's so unexpected."

"A statue is even dumber."

"A statue doesn't talk. She talks."

"What does she say?"

"The most incredible idiocies. I knew her in France. Her stupidity was legendary; it protected her like a magic cloak. In the end I found out the Gestapo were after her and I took her away with me. When I came to get her, she insisted on taking a bath. Then she had to pack; she refused to leave without her clothes. It wouldn't have surprised me if she'd wanted a permanent; luckily, it was too early in the morning. Of course she wouldn't leave without breakfast. I was expecting the Gestapo any minute, but she just sat there eating bread and jam. There were some rolls left, and she wanted to take them with her. She was still looking for paper to wrap them in when we heard the tramp of boots. Then finally, but still without haste, she got into my car. That morning I fell in love with her."

"On the spot?"

"As soon as we were safe. She never noticed it. I'm afraid she's even too stupid for love."

"That's saying a lot," I said.

"I heard from her off and on. She was in incredible situations. Nothing ever happened to her. Murderers were disarmed by her guilelessness. I don't think she was ever even raped. And then she turned up here on one of the last ships."

"What's she doing now?"

"Still the same fool's luck. She was hardly off the boat when Vriesländer took her on as a receptionist. She didn't even look for the job. That would have been too much of a strain. It fell into her lap."

"Why isn't she in the movies?"

"Even for that she's too stupid."

"Is that possible?"

"It's not just her stupidity. She's lazy. No ambition. No energy. No complexes. A wonderful woman."

Our plates were empty. We strolled over to the Vriesländer cake. Half of it was gone, but one could still read the letters VRIES. "Couldn't he just have called himself Lander?" Kahn remarked.

"He wanted something brand new," I said. "How could he start a new life with the rear end of his old name?"

"What will you call yourself when you get your citizenship?"

"That's easy. I'll just take my old name, my real one. What could be newer than that?"

"I knew a dentist in France. They'd let him out of Germany. The day before he was to leave, he was told to report to the Gestapo. He said good-by to everybody he knew; they all thought he was done for. But it was only a formality: his name. How could they let a Jew leave the country with such a name? Guess what it was. Adolf Deutschland. He changed it to Land, and they let him go."

"There is dancing in the next room," Mrs. Vriesländer announced. "I know we shouldn't because of the war, but a day like this only comes once. A nice little dance can't do any harm. And our soldiers here are looking forward to it."

Sure enough, she had rounded up some American soldiers. The living-room carpet was rolled back, and Miss Vrieslånder, in a flaming-red dress, pounced on a young lieutenant who was eating ice cream with two fellow officers. A moment later they in turn were snapped up by two pretty girls who looked startlingly alike.

"Those are the Koller twins," Kahn informed me. "Hungarians. One of them arrived in New York two years ago. She took a cab straight from the ship to a private hospital run by a well-known plastic surgeon. When she emerged six weeks later, her nose was twice as small and her bosom twice as big. Someone on shipboard had given her the address. When her sister arrived, she met her on the dock, threw a veil over her face, and hurried her to the same surgeon. Anyway, two months later, she turned up with the same improvements. Now they say a third sister has arrived but refuses to be operated on. The rumor is that the twins have sequestered her somewhere and are putting pressure on her."

"Did they have their names remodeled, too?" I asked.

"No. They claim to have been film stars in Budapest. And they've already made a start in the movies here. With all the improvements, they've still got the old paprika in their blood."

"I think it's marvelous," I said. "Anything you don't like about yourself, when you get to America you change it: face, bosom, name, anything. I'm all for it. Long live the Kollers and the Warwicks."

Vrieslånder came in to announce that there would be goulash later on. "Rosy's getting it ready now. About eleven."

Then he spied Kahn and joined us. "I try to be cheerful," he said. "But it's not easy."

"I wouldn't expect to hear that from you, Mr. Vrieslånder."

"It's true. It's kind of a sinking feeling. I just can't get rid of it. Just between you and me, Mr. Kahn, do you think I did right, changing my name? Sometimes that gives me a sinking feeling, too."

"Why not, if it gives you pleasure," said Kahn. His tone was one of sincere warmth. "You're not harming anyone. And later on, if you find it doesn't suit you, you can change it again."

"Really?"

"It's very simple in this blessed land. It's almost like Java. When a Javanese is bored with his personality, he just takes another name. Some people do it half a dozen times. Why drag the old Adam around with you if you're sick of him?"

Vriesländer smiled. "You're very kind, Mr. Kahn. You've really cheered me up." And he waddled away.

"There's Carmen dancing," said Kahn.

She hardly moved. Quite oblivious of her partner, a gangling, red-haired young sergeant, she seemed to be dreaming of faraway worlds beyond the stars. While all eyes feasted on her, she, if Kahn was to be believed, was inwardly feasting on strudel and whipped cream.

"The cow!" breathed Kahn in a voice husky with emotion. "I adore her."

I made no reply. As I watched Carmen and Mrs. Vriesländer and the Koller twins with their new bosoms and Mr. Vriesländer-Warwick, whose trousers were a little too short, I felt lighter than I had for years. Perhaps, I thought, this really was the Promised Land; maybe Kahn was right and you really could change everything in this country, not only your name and face but your personality as well. Maybe you didn't have to forget; maybe you could sublimate and transform your memories until they ceased to give pain—yet without loss, without betrayal, without desertion.

XI

When I got back to the hotel after work the next day, I found a letter from the lawyer: I had been granted a six months' extension on my residence permit. He asked me to phone the following afternoon. I could imagine why.

I decided to go and see Kahn. He had a small room over the shop where he worked. It was very noisy; the traffic went on all night. And any number of neon signs cast their light on his walls and ceiling. He didn't mind; he hated quiet and darkness, and the room was cheap.

Natasha was sitting in the lobby. I felt rather awkward. "Waiting for Melikov?" I asked.

"No. For you." She laughed. "Isn't it exciting," she said. "We know each other so little and we already have so much to forgive each other for. What kind of terms are we on?"

"The best," I said. "At least we don't seem to be bored with each other."

"Have you eaten?"

I counted up my money mentally. "No. Shall we go to the Pavillon?"

She looked me over. I had on my new suit. Silvers insisted on my wearing it to work. "New," I said. "New shoes, too. Do you think I can show myself at the Pavillon?"

"I was at the Pavillon yesterday. It was boring. You ought to be able to eat out of doors in the summer. They haven't discovered that yet in America."

"I've got a pot of the best Hungarian goulash in my room," I said. "Enough for six hungry people. It was marvelous last night and it should be even better today."

"Where did you get it?"

"I went to a party last night."

"And they gave you goulash to take home? Where was this party? Was it . . ."

I flashed her a warning glance. "No, it wasn't in a German beer hall. Goulash isn't German; it's Hungarian. This was a private party. With dancing," I added, to punish her for her thoughts.

"Oh, with dancing. You seem to get around."

"They also gave me dill pickles and strudel," I said. "A meal for the gods. Only unfortunately the goulash is cold."

"Can't it be warmed up?"

"Where? All I've got in my room is an electric coffeepot."

Natasha laughed. "What? No etchings for the ladies?"

"I'm afraid not. I'll have to get some. Shouldn't we try the Pavillon after all?"

"No. You've made the goulash sound too tempting. Melikov will be back soon. He'll help us. Let's take a little walk. I haven't been out yet today. We'll work up an appetite for your goulash."

———

Natasha warned me about her shoe complex. She couldn't pass a shoe store without looking in the window. And if she came back the same way an hour later, she had to look at the same window again. "Crazy, isn't it?"

"No. Why?"

"Because I've just seen them all. There hasn't been any time for changes."

"Maybe you've overlooked something. Or the window may have been redecorated."

"Then you don't mind looking at a few shoes?"

"Not at all. I'm crazy about shoes."

We seemed to be strolling aimlessly, but I had a destination in mind. Half an hour and two or three shoe stores later, we approached Kahn's shop. To my surprise he was still there. "Just a minute," I said to Natasha. "I think I've found a solution to our goulash problem."

I opened the door. Kahn looked past me and saw Natasha. "Won't you bring the lady in?"

"I wouldn't think of it," I said. "I only wanted to borrow your electric hot plate."

"Now?"

"Yes, now."

"I'm sorry. I need it myself. I'm expecting Carmen for dinner and then we're listening to the fight. She ought to be here any minute; she's three-quarters of an hour late already. Luckily, it doesn't matter with warmed-over goulash."

"Carmen . . ." I said, and looked out at Natasha, who suddenly seemed very remote and desirable on the other side of the window-pane. "Carmen . . ." I repeated.

"Yes. Why don't you stay? Then we'll all listen to the fight."

"Great," I said. "But where will we eat? Your room's too small."

"Right here in the shop."

I hurried out to Natasha, and she seemed very close to me.

"We're invited to dinner," I said.

"But what about my goulash?"

"A goulash dinner," I said.

"What do you mean?"

"You'll see."

"Have you hidden pots of goulash all over town?"

"Only at strategic points."

I saw Carmen coming. She was wearing a light-colored raincoat and no hat. Kahn came out to meet her. Natasha gave her a quick once-over. Carmen showed no surprise at our presence, nor did she react in any way. Her hair was a henna-colored cloud in the evening light. "I'm a little late," she said blandly. "But it doesn't matter with goulash, does it? Did they give you some of the strudel, too?"

"Cherry strudel, cheese strudel, and apple strudel," answered Kahn.

The goulash really was better than the day before. We ate it to the sound of organ music. Kahn had switched on his six radios, for fear of missing the fight. Strange to say, Bach went well with Hungarian goulash, though Liszt might have been more appropriate. We ate the pickles with our fingers, and the goulash with spoons.

There was a violent knocking at the door. Kahn and I thought it was the police, but it was only a waiter from the bar across the street, bearing four enormous drinks. "Who ordered these?" Kahn asked.

"A gentleman. It seems he was looking out the window. He saw you drinking vodka, and then he saw the bottle was empty."

"Where is he?"

The waiter shrugged. "The drinks are paid for. I'll come back for the glasses."

"Bring four more when you do."

"Yes, sir."

The six organs faded out. Kahn distributed strudel and apologized for not making coffee. If he ran upstairs for the coffeepot, he might miss the beginning of the fight.

After the fight Kahn seemed as exhausted as if he himself had been in the ring. Carmen was sleeping peacefully.

"What did I tell you?" said Kahn.

"Let her sleep," Natasha whispered. "I must be going now. Thanks for everything. Good night."

We went out into the damp street. "He must want to be alone with his girl friend," she said.

"I'm not so sure."

"Why not? She's so beautiful." She laughed. "Beautiful enough to give me an inferiority complex."

"Is that why you left?"

"No, that's why I stayed. I like beautiful people. Though sometimes they make me sad."

"Why?"

"Because they can't be beautiful forever. Old age isn't becoming to most people. That seems to call for more than beauty."

We passed sleeping shop windows full of cheap jewelry. A few delicatessen stores were still open. "Strange," I said. "I've never thought about growing old. I guess I was too busy keeping alive."

Natasha laughed. "I think about it all the time."

"Melikov says it's impossible for young people to understand such things."

"Melikov has always been old."

"Always?"

"Well, too old to be interested in women. Isn't that what old age means?"

"That's a simplification, but I suppose it's true. In that case Melikov is right."

"What do you mean?"

"I mean that at this present moment such a thing is beyond my comprehension."

She gave me one of her quick glances. "Bravo," she said with a smile, and took my arm.

I pointed across the street. "A shoe store," I said. "Shall we look at the window?"

"I couldn't live without it."

We crossed over. "How enormous this city is!" she said. "It never ends. Do you like it here?"

"Yes."

"Why?"

"Because they let me stay here. Simple, isn't it?"

She looked at me thoughtfully. "Is that enough?"

"It's a modest, primitive kind of happiness: enough to eat and a place to sleep."

"But is it enough?"

"What more can I ask for? Adventures get to be very tedious as daily fare."

Natasha laughed. "Happiness in a quiet corner. Is that it? You know what? I don't believe you."

"Neither do I, but it comforts me to say such things from time to time."

She laughed again. "Your remedy for despair? I know exactly how you feel."

"Where do we go now?" I asked.

"That's the big problem in this town. The night spots are all so boring after you've been there once or twice."

"How about El Morocco?"

"You and your millions!" she said. The tone was ironic, but I detected a trace of affection.

"I've got to show off my new suit."

"Don't you want to show me off?"

"That is an indiscreet question."

At El Morocco we went to the little side room.

"What will it be?" I asked.

"A Moscow mule."

"What on earth is that?"

"Vodka, root beer, and lime juice. Very refreshing."

"I'll try it."

Natasha pulled up her feet on the banquette, leaving her shoes on the floor. "I don't go in for sports like the Americans," she said. "I can't ride or swim or play tennis. I'm a lounge lizard and a chatterbox."

"What else are you?"

"Sentimental and romantic and unbearable. What I like best is sleazy romance. The sleazier the better. How's the Moscow mule?"

"Great."

"And the Viennese songs?"

"Great."

She leaned back contentedly in her corner of the banquette. "Sometimes I feel like plunging into a great big wave of sentimentality that washes away every shred of good sense and good taste. Afterward I can shake myself dry and laugh at myself. How about it?"

"I'm plunging."

There was something about her that made me think of a playful but melancholy cat. She looked like it, too, with her little face, abundant hair, and large eyes. "All right," she said. "Then I'll tell you about myself. I'm unhappy in love, dreadfully disillusioned, lonely, and sick of it all. I don't even know why I go on living."

I thought it over. "Why," I asked, "should you want to know that? If you know why you're living, it means you've got a purpose. That reduces life to a job."

She gaped at me. "Do you really mean that?"

"Of course not. We're talking nonsense. Isn't that what we wanted?"

"Not entirely. Half and half."

The pianist came over to our table and bade Natasha good evening. "Karl," she said. "Could you sing the song from the *Count of Luxemburg?*"

"I'll be glad to."

He sang well. *"Lieber Freund, man greift nicht nach den Sternen / die für uns in nebelhaften Fernen . . ."*

Natasha listened in a state of rapture. It was a pretty tune, the popular music of another day. The words, as usual, were idiotic.

"How do you like it?"

"Petit bourgeois."

"What!" She glared at me. I expected our little war to break out again and hastened to mollify her.

"You'd say the same thing if you understood the words. The idea is that it's no use reaching for the stars, because we have everything we need in this cunning little cottage."

She thought it over for a second. "Then you ought to like it. Isn't that the quiet corner you were talking about?"

The bitch is quick on the draw, I thought.

"Why do you have to criticize everything to death?" she asked, grown suddenly gentle. "Can't you let yourself go? Are you so afraid?"

Another of those questions in the dim light of a New York night club. I was annoyed with myself, because she was right. I couldn't help talking like the typical German I detested. I wouldn't have been surprised to hear myself delivering a lecture on places of entertainment from the dawn of history down to the most recent times, with special emphasis on cabarets and night clubs since the First World War. "That song," I burst out, "reminds me of a time long before the war. It's a very old song; my father sang it, I think. He was a frail man with a love for old things, old gardens. I often heard it sung in the garden cafés outside Vienna, where you go to drink the new wine. It's sentimental slop from an operetta; but at night in those gardens under the leafy chestnut trees, it didn't seem like slop. In the flickering light of the lanterns, to the soft music of the fiddles and accordions, it just sounded nostalgic. Not *petit bourgeois* at all—that just slipped out of me. I hadn't heard it in a long time. I remember another: 'When music and wine are gone / How then will life go on / Then shall we too be gone—' That was the last song to be heard in Vienna."

"Karl must know it."

"I'd rather not hear it. It was the last song before the Nazis marched into Austria. After that, there was nothing but marching songs."

Natasha was silent for a while. "If you like, I'll tell Karl not to sing the other song again."

"But he's just sung it."

"He knows I like it. When I'm here, he sings it over and over."

"He didn't sing it the last time we were here."

"That was his night off. Somebody else was singing."

"Never mind. I enjoy it as much as you."

"Really? It doesn't bring back sad memories?"

"All memories are sad, because the past will never come back."

She pondered that one a moment. Then she found the right answer: "I think it's time for another Moscow mule."

"You're full of good ideas." I looked at her. She had none of Carmen's tragic beauty, or, rather, her beauty was not of the tragic type. Her little face was too much alive, reflecting by turns a keen intelligence, quick, malicious humor, and a sudden startling gentleness.

"Why are you looking at me like that?" she asked, grown suddenly suspicious. "Is my nose shiny?"

"No. I'm wondering why you're so friendly to waiters and piano players and so aggressive with your friends."

"Because the waiters are defenseless." She looked at me. "Am I really so aggressive? Or are you hypersensitive?"

"I think I'm hypersensitive."

She laughed. "You don't believe that for a minute. People who are never think so. Do you believe that?"

"I believe everything you say."

Karl started on the *Count of Luxemburg* again. "I warned you," said Natasha.

Some people came in and waved to her. She seemed to know everybody. Two men came over to our table and talked to her. I stood up and suddenly had the feeling you get in a small plane when it drops into an air pocket. Everything began to rise and fall and sway, the green-and-blue-striped walls, the many faces, and the beastly music. What was wrong with me? It couldn't have been the vodka or the goulash. The goulash had been too good, and there hadn't been enough vodka. Probably, I thought bitterly, it was the memory of Vienna and my dead father, who hadn't left the country in time, because my mother couldn't bear to leave her home and furniture, which had come down to her from her parents. I stared at the piano and at Karl. I saw his hands on the piano but heard scarcely a sound. Then the walls began to calm down. I took a deep breath and felt as if I had returned from a long journey.

"It's getting too crowded," said Natasha. "The theaters are out. Shall we go?"

The theaters are out, I thought; at midnight the night clubs fill up with millionaires and gigolos; the world is at war, and I'm somewhere in between. A silly thought, and unfair as well, because a good many of the men at the tables were in uniform, and some of them had wound stripes—but just then I was choking with helpless rage and in no mood to be fair.

The air outside was warm and humid. A taxi drove up, and the porter opened the door for us.

"No, thanks," said Natasha. "We don't need a cab. I live in the neighborhood."

At the next corner we left the neon signs behind us. The street grew darker. We came to the house she lived in, and she stretched like a cat. "I love these conversations about everything and nothing," she said. "Especially at night. Of course you mustn't believe anything I said."

The street light shone full in her face. "Of course not," I said. Still feeling helpless and furious with myself for my self-pity, I took her in my arms and kissed her. I expected her to repulse me in anger, but she didn't. She only looked at me with strangely quiet eyes, stood there for a moment, and then went inside without a word.

XII

Betty Stein had given me a hundred dollars for the lawyer's first installment. With my eyes on the cuckoo clock, I tried to bargain; but the lawyer was adamant. I even went so far as to tell him a little about the last few years of my life. Five hundred dollars was a big debt for me to be saddled with. "Give him a sob story," Betty had advised me. "Maybe it will do some good. And besides, it will be the truth." It didn't do any good. The lawyer told me that he had already made a sacrifice, that his usual fee was a good deal higher. When I tried the destitute refugee ploy, he only laughed. "A hundred and fifty thousand refugees like you come to America every year. There's nothing so heart-rending about your case. You're young and healthy. Most of our millionaires started out just like you. You've passed the dishwashing stage; they tell me you've got a decent job. Your situation isn't so bad. You know what's bad? To be poor and old and sick and a Jew in Germany. That's bad. And now good-by. I have more important things to do. And don't be late with the next installment."

In the end I was glad he hadn't demanded an extra fee for listening to me. Slowly I sauntered through the city. The morning sun shone from behind glittering clouds. The freshly washed cars sparkled; whichever way I looked there were blue patches in the sky. Central Park was alive with children's shouts. My annoyance with the lawyer had evaporated; now I was only annoyed with myself for the pathetic act I had put on. He had seen through me and he had been right. I couldn't even blame Betty for her advice. It was my fault for taking it.

I went to see the seals in their pool; they glistened like polished bronzes in the sunlight. The lions and tigers, with their transparent beryl-colored eyes, were in their outdoor cages, striding restlessly back and forth. The monkeys were playing and throwing banana peels at each other. I repressed any thought of sentimental sympathy; these animals, who might have been hungry hunters tormented by vermin and disease, looked like well-fed retired businessmen taking their morning walk. True, there was a certain monotony in their lives, but at least they were free from hunger and thirst. And how was anyone to know which they would have preferred if they had had their choice? Animals, like people, get attached to their habits, and it's only a short step from habits to boredom. I couldn't help thinking of my conversation with Natasha and my theory of happiness in a quiet corner.

I sat down on the terrace and ordered a cup of coffee. I had forty dollars to my name and I owed four hundred. But I was free and in good health, and, as the lawyer had told me, on the first rung of the millionaire's ladder. I took another cup of coffee and thought of the summer mornings in the Jardins du Luxembourg in Paris when I had impersonated a *flâneur,* so as not to attract the attention of the police. Today I asked a passing policeman for a light, which he gave me. The Luxembourg reminded me of the *Count of Luxemburg* song and its effect on me. But that had been at night, and now it was bright wind-swept day. Everything is different in the daytime.

"Where in God's name have you been?" Silvers asked. "Does it take all day to pay a lawyer?"

"It takes longer when you're broke," I explained.

"Never mind the jokes," he said. "We have work to do."

I hardly recognized the man. The suave, effete art lover—a pose I had never taken seriously—had given way to the jungle beast. It was clear that he had scented a prey.

We went into the room with the easels. Silvers brought in two pictures and set them up. "I'm going to ask you a question," he said, "and I want a quick answer. Which one would you buy?"

Both were Degas dancing girls. Both unframed. "Quick!" said Silvers. "Don't stop to think."

I pointed to the one on the left. "This one."

"Why? It's less finished."

I shrugged. "I like it better. I can't give you reasons so quickly. You know the reasons yourself."

"Of course I know the reasons. I'm not asking you for a dissertation. I only want to know why you like it better. In two words."

"Why do you want to know?"

"Because I want the naïve impression of somebody who doesn't know much about art."

I didn't flinch, but he saw the look in my eyes. Was putting up with his insults part of my job?

He laughed, and suddenly he was the old charmer again. "Don't feel offended," he said. "Didn't I tell you not to think? I'm interested in your first impression because it might help me to predict the customer's reaction. I know how much the pictures are worth. But the customer's opinion is always an unknown quantity. Now do you understand?"

"Yes. But why is it so important to know his preference in advance? Show him both."

Silvers gave me an amused look. "That would be very unwise. He wouldn't be able to make up his mind." He lit a cigarette and exhaled a great cloud of smoke. "You see," he said, "there's more to this trade than meets the eye. Anybody can own pictures, but selling them, for a good price, that is, is something else again. All right, I'll let myself be guided by your impression. The one on the right is the more valuable—not the one you like. Get moving now. We've got to frame them before the customer gets here."

He led me to the next room and showed me a number of empty frames. "Standard sizes," he mumbled. "These will fit. No time for adjustments."

It was amazing how the frames changed the pictures. Unframed, they had seemed dispersed, as though ready to flutter off into space. The frames held them together, defined them as self-contained worlds, and made them look more finished.

"Pictures should never be shown unframed," Silvers explained. "Only dealers can judge them without frames. Which one would you choose?"

"This one."

Silvers gave me a look of approval. "Your taste is all right. However, we'll take another. This one."

He put the dancing girls into a broad, heavily ornamented frame. "Isn't that a little too rich for a picture that isn't quite finished?" I asked.

Both paintings bore a red stamp: "From the studio of Degas." The painter hadn't signed them because he didn't regard them as finished. They had been sold by his estate.

"On the contrary; it has to be rich precisely because the picture is unfinished."

"I understand. It masks the unfinished quality."

"It enhances the picture. The frame is so finished that it makes the picture look finished." He took his professorial stance. "Frames are very important things. Some dealers scrimp on frames. They think the customer won't notice. They say gilded plaster looks just like the genuine article. And it does at first sight. But only at first sight."

I fitted the first Degas carefully into the frame, while Silvers selected a frame for the other. "Have you decided to show them both?" I asked.

He smiled. "No. I'm holding the other one in reserve. You never can tell. They're both absolute virgins. Never been shown. I wasn't expecting this man until tomorrow. He just rang up and said he was coming this morning. We can't paste the backs, no time. Just bend the nails back to make them stay on."

I brought in the second frame. "Isn't it a beauty?" said Silvers. "Louis Quinze. Sumptuous. Adds five thousand dollars to the value. At least! Even Van Gogh wanted first-class frames. Degas framed most of his in white-painted lath. Maybe he was stingy."

Or maybe he had no money, I thought. Van Gogh certainly had none. "How much is a Van Gogh worth today?" I asked.

"It all depends," said Silvers, smacking his lips. "The Dutch period from ten to thirty thousand, the Paris period from twenty-five to fifty thousand. A really good one from the Arles period will bring as much as a hundred thousand. Ten years ago you could buy them for a quarter as much. In another ten years they'll have tripled in value."

I thought of Lowy Senior's tirades about parasites; but wouldn't the Lowys have gladly turned themselves into just such parasites if they could? Wouldn't I myself if I had a chance?

The pictures were framed. Silvers told me to put one of them back in its old place. "And take the other up to my wife's bedroom."

I looked at him in amazement. "You heard right," he told me. "I'll go with you. Come on." Mrs. Silvers' bedroom was pretty and very feminine. The walls were adorned with drawings and pastels. "We'll take down that Renoir drawing and put the Degas in its place. Put the Renoir over there above the dresser, and we'll remove the Berthe Morisot. Now close the curtain on the right. No, not all the way. Fine, now the light is right."

He knew what he was doing. The muted light gave the painting sweetness and warmth.

We went downstairs, and he told me which pictures he had decided to show. I was to wait in the adjoining room. When he wanted a picture, he would ring for me. After the fourth or fifth he would ask for the Degas, and I was to remind him that it was in his wife's bedroom. "Talk as much French as you like," he said. "But when I ask for the Degas, answer in English so the customer can understand."

The doorbell rang. "There he is," said Silvers.

I went into the room where the pictures were lined up on wooden racks, and sat down. Silvers went downstairs to receive his visitor. The room had a small frosted-glass window with heavy bars over it. I had the feeling that I was sitting in a prison cell which a philanthropic warden had furnished with several hundred thousand dollars' worth of paintings. The milky light reminded me of a cell in Switzerland where I had once spent two weeks for illegal entry. It had been just as neat and clean, and I would gladly have stayed more than two weeks—the food was good and the cell was heated—but one stormy night I was taken to the French border near Annemasse. There I was given a cigarette and a powerful shove: "Now you're in France. And don't show your face in Switzerland again."

I must have dozed off. Suddenly I heard the bell. I heard Silvers' voice in the next room. I went in. A heavily built man with big red ears and little pig's eyes was sitting there. "Monsieur Ross," said Silvers in his suavest tones, "kindly bring in the Sisley landscape."

I brought it in and set it down on one of the easels. For a long while Silvers said nothing, but stood at the window watching the clouds. "Do you like it?" he finally asked in a bored tone. "A Sisley from the best period. A flood. No one would be ashamed to own it."

"Junk," said the customer in a tone of still-greater boredom.

I waited for a moment for Silvers to tell me what to bring in next. When he failed to do so, I went out with the Sisley. As I was leaving I heard him say: "You're not in the mood, Mr. Cooper. Why don't you come another day?"

Not bad, I thought in my prison cell. Now the next move was up to Cooper. When I was called again a few minutes later, they were both smoking Silvers' special-for-customers Havanas. I brought in the other paintings one by one. And then I heard my cue: "Degas."

"It's not here, Mr. Silvers," I said.

"Of course it is. Where else would it be?"

I came over to him, leaned down, and said in a stage whisper: "It's upstairs. In Mrs. Silvers' bedroom."

"Where?"

I said it again in French.

Silvers slapped his forehead. "That's right! I'd forgotten. Well, in that case, I'm sorry . . ."

I was overcome with admiration; it was Cooper's play again. Silvers didn't tell me to get the picture and he didn't say the picture belonged to his wife. He just dropped the subject and waited.

I went back to my cell and waited, too. It was as though Silvers had a shark on the hook, and I wasn't so sure he would land him. This shark was no babe in arms. There was nothing to stop him from biting off the line and swimming away. One thing was certain: Silvers wouldn't sell for less than he intended. I had inadvertently left the door ajar and I heard the shark making interesting attempts to get the price down. The conversation turned to the economic situation and the war. The shark predicted the worst: more government spending, staggering public debt, stock-market crash, social unrest, the threat of Communism. Prices would collapse. The only thing that would have any value was hard cash. He reminded Silvers of the crash of 1929. The man with cash was a king; he could buy what he wanted at half price—no, for a third or a quarter of the old price. And he added, with a look of profound concern: "Especially luxuries like furniture, rugs, and paintings."

Silvers poured brandy imperturbably. "Then after a while," he countered, "the prices went up, and money went down. It lost fifty per cent of its value and it never went up again. I don't have to tell you that. Paintings, on the other hand, are worth five times as much as they were then. Or more." He gave a soft, absolutely artificial laugh. "Ha, inflation! It began two thousand years ago, and we'll never see the end of it. Real values go up, money goes down. There you have it."

"If that's the case," the shark parried, "we shouldn't ever sell anything."

"If only we didn't have to," said Silvers blandly. "I sell as little as possible. But I need operating capital. Just ask my customers. To them I'm a benefactor. Five years ago I sold a Degas dancing girl, and only the other day I bought it back for twice as much."

"From whom?" asked the shark.

"I can't tell you that. Would you like me to go around telling people how much I sold you a picture for?"

"Why not?" The shark was a shrewd article.

"Most of my customers wouldn't like it one bit, and their wish is my law." Silvers made sounds suggesting that he was about to rise. "I'm sorry you haven't found anything, Mr. Cooper. Perhaps another time. Of course I can't hold the prices very long. You know that."

The shark stood up. "Didn't you have another Degas you wanted to show me?" he asked offhandedly.

"Oh, you mean the one in my wife's room?" Silvers hesitated. Then I heard the bell. "Is my wife in her room?"

"She went out half an hour ago."

"Then bring down the Degas. It's hanging beside the mirror."

"It will take a few minutes, Mr. Silvers," I said. "I had to put in a dowel because the wall isn't very solid, and the picture is screwed to the dowel."

"Never mind," said Silvers. "We'll just go upstairs. Do you mind, Mr. Cooper?"

"It's all right with me."

Again I huddled in my cell, feeling like Fafnir amid the treasure of the Rhine. Some minutes later the two of them came down again, and I was sent up for the picture. Since there was nothing to be unfastened, I simply waited for five minutes. I looked through one of the windows, which opened out onto the court, and saw Mrs. Silvers in the kitchen window across the way. She made a questioning gesture. I shook my head; the coast wasn't clear yet, she should stay in the kitchen for the present.

I took the picture to the easel room and left. This time Silvers closed the door, and I could hear no more of the conversation. It would have amused me to hear Silvers intimating that his wife would have liked to keep the picture for her private collection. I was sure he did it subtly enough not to arouse the shark's suspicions.

The interview lasted about half an hour; then Silvers appeared in person to release me from my gilded cage. "No need to hang the Degas," he said. "You're to deliver it to Mr. Cooper tomorrow."

"Congratulations."

He made a face. "You see what I go through to sell a picture! And in two years the price will have doubled, and the bastard will be laughing up his sleeve."

I repeated Cooper's question. "Then why do you sell?"

"Because I can't stop. I'm a born gambler. Besides, I've got to make money. By the way, the gag with the dowel wasn't bad. You're developing."

"Maybe I ought to have a raise."

Silvers' eyes narrowed. "You're developing a little too fast. Don't forget that I'm giving you a free education that a good many museum directors would envy."

In the evening I went to Betty Stein's to thank her for the money she had loaned me. I found her with eyes red from weeping. A few friends were there, apparently to comfort her. "I can come again tomorrow," I said. "I only wanted to thank you."

"What for?" asked Betty with a dazed look.

"For the money," I said. "And getting me a lawyer. They've given me an extension. I don't have to leave the country."

She burst into tears. Rabinowitz, an actor, put his arm around her and tried to comfort her. "What's happened?" I asked him.

"Don't you know? Moller is dead. It happened the day before yesterday."

He helped her over to a sofa and came back to me. Rabinowitz was one of the gentlest souls I have ever known. He, too, played the parts of brutal Nazis in class-B pictures. "He hanged himself. Lipschütz found him. He must have been dead for a day or two. He was hanging from the chandelier in his room. All the lights were on. Maybe he couldn't stand the idea of dying in the dark."

I wanted to leave. "Don't go," said Rabinowitz. "The more people Betty has around her the better. We mustn't leave her alone."

The room was hot and stuffy. Betty refused to open the windows. She had a strange superstitious belief that to let your grief escape into the open air was to betray the dead. I had heard of opening windows to release a dead man's soul, but never of closing them to preserve one's grief.

"I'm so stupid," said Betty, and blew her nose with determination. "But now I'm going to pull myself together and make you some coffee." She stood up. "Or would you prefer something else?"

"Nothing, Betty. Really, nothing at all."

"All right then, coffee."

She rustled into the kitchen with her rumpled dress.

"Does anyone know why he did it?" I asked Rabinowitz.

"Does there have to be a reason?"

"No," I admitted.

"He wasn't destitute. It can't have been that. And he wasn't sick. Lipschütz here saw him only two weeks ago."

"Was he able to work?"

"He was able to write. But not to publish. He hadn't been able to publish for years. But that's true of so many writers. It can't have been just that."

"Did he leave a note?"

"No. His face was blue, his tongue was all swollen, and the flies were crawling over his eyeballs. Horrible . . ." Lipschütz gave himself a shake. "The worst of it is that Betty wants to see him."

"Where is he now?"

"At a funeral home, as they call it here. They try to make the bodies presentable. Were you ever in such an establishment? Well, stay away. The Americans are a young people; they don't acknowledge death. The dead are made up to look as if they were sleeping. Some are even embalmed."

"Maybe if they put on plenty of make-up . . ." I suggested.

"That's what we thought. But in the shape he's in they'd have to lay it on an inch thick. Besides, it's too expensive. It's very expensive to die in America."

"Not in Germany," I said.

"Well, in America it's expensive. We found the cheapest place we could, but even so it's going to cost several hundred dollars."

I saw that Betty's photographs had been rearranged. Moller's picture was no longer among the living. It was still in its gilt frame, but a piece of tulle had been looped around one corner of it. The face was youthful and smiling; the picture had been taken fifteen years before.

Betty brought in cups and saucers and poured coffee from a china pot with little flowers on it. Cream and sugar were passed around.

"The funeral is tomorrow," she said. "Will you come?"

"If I can. I had to take off a few hours today."

Betty was beside herself. "You've got to come. Everybody who knew him must be there. It's tomorrow at half past twelve. We chose the lunch hour so everybody could come."

"I'll be there. Where is it?"

"Asher's Funeral Home on Fourteenth Street," said Lipschütz.

"And where is he being buried?" Rabinowitz asked.

"He's being cremated. It's cheaper."

"What?"

"He's being cremated."

"Cremated," I repeated mechanically.

"Yes. The funeral home takes care of it."

"To think of him lying there among total strangers," Betty wailed. "Why couldn't we have had him here with us until the funeral?" She turned to me. "What was it you wanted to know? Who advanced the money for the lawyer? Vriesländer."

"Vriesländer?"

"Of course. Who else has any money? But you'll definitely be there tomorrow?"

"Definitely." What else could I have said?

Rabinowitz took me to the door. "We have to keep stalling Betty," he whispered. "She mustn't see Moller. What's left of him, that is. There's been an autopsy—there always is in cases of suicide. Betty doesn't know. And it's not easy to stop her once she gets an idea. Luckily, Lipschütz managed to slip a sleeping pill into her coffee. We tried to give her tranquilizers, but she wouldn't take them. She thinks it would be betraying Moller. The same as opening the windows. We'll try to smuggle a pill into her breakfast coffee. The early morning is the worst time. You'll be there?"

"Yes. At the funeral home. And then they're cremating him?"

Rabinowitz nodded.

"Where?" I asked. "At the funeral home?"

"I don't think so. Why?"

"What are you talking about so long?" Betty called out to us.

"Good night," Rabinowitz whispered.

XIII

I slept very little that night and left the hotel early in the morning —too early to go to Silvers'. I took the Fifth Avenue bus to the Metropolitan Museum, but it wasn't open. I strolled through Central Park to the Shakespeare Garden, then around the lake to the statue of Schiller. I had seen it once before, but it still seemed an odd thing to find in the middle of New York. No doubt some prosperous German-American had donated it years ago. At the moment it was embellished by a drawing in red chalk: a luxuriant female posterior being raped from behind by a gentleman in glasses. I retraced my steps, and by then the museum was open.

I had been there several times. It reminded me of my days in the Brussels Museum, and most of all, strangely enough, of the stillness. The endless tortured boredom of my first months there, my constant fear of being discovered, which had only gradually turned to fatalistic resignation—all that seemed to have left me. What remained was my memory of the eerie silence, the sense of being removed from all reality, as though living in the windless center of a tornado.

On my first visit to the Metropolitan I was afraid that other memories would rise up in me, but this museum seemed to enfold me in the same sheltering stillness. Even the furious battle scenes on the walls seemed to emanate peace, a peace that had something metaphysical about it, a peace removed from time. Here in these rooms I suddenly had the pure and boundless feeling of life that the Hindus call "samadhi," a feeling one never quite loses once one has known it. One knows forever after that life is eternal and that we, too, can partake of eternal life if only we succeed in sloughing off the snakeskin of the ego and in understanding that death is transformation. I had had this insight while looking at El Greco's sublimely somber view of Toledo, which hangs directly beside his much larger portrait of the Grand Inquisitor, that prototype of the Gestapo and of all the torturers in the world. I did not know whether there was any connection between the two; in that luminous moment I felt that all things were at once connected and unconnected, and that connections, coherence, were nothing but a human crutch, half lie and half imponderable truth. But what was the difference between an imponderable truth and an imponderable lie?

I had not come to the museum by accident. Moller's death had shaken me more than I would have expected. At first it had not touched me deeply; so many of my friends and acquaintances had killed themselves in the last few years. Hasenclever, held by idiotic bureaucrats in a French internment camp when it was known that the Germans would be there any moment, had preferred to take his own life rather than fall into their hands. That was easy enough to understand. This was different. Moller was not in danger; he was saved. Yet he had not wished to go on living. I tried to tell myself that his motives must have been purely personal, but I knew that this voluntary death concerned us all. The thought of Moller pursued me and left me no peace. That was why I was here, going from picture to picture until I came to the El Grecos.

Today the painting of Toledo seemed dull and lifeless. It may have been the light, but more likely it was my own state of mind. When I had first seen this picture, I had not been looking for it; today I had come to it for comfort, and that is no way to approach a work of art. Works of art are not nurses. The picture did not speak; it revealed nothing, neither of eternal nor of temporal life. It was beautiful, self-contained in its repose, but when I looked for life in it in order to shake off the thought of death, there was a funereal quality in its spectral light. By contrast, the enormous picture of the Grand Inquisitor, with its cool reds and obsessive eyes, seemed radiant as never before, as though it had suddenly come to life after all the centuries. It dominated the room with its power. It was not dead; it would never die. Torture was eternal. Fear was undying. No one was ever saved. Then I knew what had killed Moller.

I went on through endless rooms till I came to the Chinese bronzes. There was one piece I was especially fond of, a robin's-egg-blue bowl. It was not polished like the jagged green Chou pieces belonging to the magnificent altar in the center of the room. I would have liked to hold it in my hands for a few minutes, but all these bronzes were enclosed in glass cases, and for good reason, for even the barest trace of sweat on one's hands would have damaged them a little. I stood there awhile, imagining that I was holding it. The effect on me was strangely soothing.

This was a low-priced funeral home, but regardless of the price all such places breathe the same false pathos. I felt so crushed by the atmosphere of refined solemnity—the festoons of crepe, the bereaved glances, the potted plants and canned organ music—that it came almost as a relief when Betty burst into loud, uncontrollable sobs.

I knew I was being unreasonable. How would it be possible to avoid false pathos at a funeral? For how can a group of people be expected to react with natural dignity to so shocking and inconceivable an event as death, or to dispel, though they themselves despise it, a feeling of secret satisfaction that someone else, not they, is lying in that hideous polished casket. And besides, I was obsessed by the thought of the crematorium. It left me no peace. I decided that if the funeral party was driving to the crematorium after the ceremony—as was the custom in Europe—I would decline to go. Or, rather, I would just disappear.

Lipschütz delivered the funeral address. I didn't listen. The air was close, and my head was swimming with the smell of the flowers on the casket. I saw Vriesländer and Rabinowitz. Some thirty people had come, half of them unknown to me. I recognized several writers and actors. The Koller sisters, with their flamboyant hair, were sitting with the Vriesländers. Kahn and Carmen were there, but not together. I had the impression that she slept through Lipschütz's address.

When it was all over, two men in black gloves appeared at either end of the casket, lifted it up with a dexterity suggestive of executioner's helpers, and, walking silently on rubber soles, carried it down the aisle. They passed close to me, my stomach nearly turned over, and then to my surprise I felt that there were tears in my eyes.

We filed out. I looked around; the casket had disappeared. In the doorway I found myself next to Vriesländer. I wondered if this was the right time to thank him for the loan.

"Won't you come with us?" he asked. "I've got my car."

"Where to?" I asked in a panic.

"To Betty's. She's made us a bite to eat."

"I haven't got too much time."

"It's lunch hour. You don't have to stay long. Just so she sees you've come. It means a great deal to her."

Rabinowitz, the Koller twins, Kahn, and Carmen rode along with us. "It was the only way to prevent her from seeing Moller," said Rabinowitz. "We invited ourselves to her place after the ceremony. It was Meyer's idea, and she fell for it. Her hospitality won out. She got up at six o'clock to cook for us. That kept her busy until an hour ago, thank goodness."

Betty opened the door for us, and the Koller twins disappeared into the kitchen with her. The china and cutlery were laid out in neat piles, and Betty had brought out her best linen tablecloth. It was as though she had thrown the full force of her grief into her preparations for this buffet lunch. Rabinowitz took refuge in his always latent academicism. "The funeral repast," he informed me, "is a strange custom, harking back to the earliest times. . . ."

What a German! I thought, listening to his lecture with half an ear and looking for a chance to get away. The twins appeared with enormous platters of sardines, tuna-fish salad, and chopped chicken liver. I saw Meyer slyly pinching one of them in her very alluring rear end. Life had begun to stir again. It was marvelous or revolting, depending on how you looked at it.

I spent the afternoon being educated by Silvers. We rehearsed a little maneuver. I was to come in and announce that a picture, which was actually in the adjoining room, had been sent out, that one of the Rockefellers, Fords, or Mellons had wanted to look at it. I had to repeat my little speech until it sounded absolutely convincing. "You can't imagine," said Silvers, "how effective that is. Snobbery and envy are an art dealer's most reliable allies. The mere fact that a multimillionaire is interested in a picture makes it more desirable to common mortals."

"But what about the buyers who really love paintings?"

"Real collectors? They're a dying race. Today people collect as an investment or as a status symbol."

"Suppose somebody who didn't have much money wanted to buy a picture because he sincerely loved it—would you come down on the price?"

Silvers stroked his beard. "It would be easy for me to lie. But the truth is no. Your poor man can go to the Metropolitan every day and look at great paintings to his heart's content."

"That might not satisfy him," I objected. "He might want to have it in his own home so he can worship it at any time, day or night."

"Then he should buy a print," said Silvers, unmoved. "The offset prints they make today are so good that even collectors have been known to take them for originals."

Of course there was no point to this discussion. I was only trying to keep my mind off something else. Just as I was leaving Betty's, Carmen had suddenly blurted out: "Poor Mr. Moller, now he's burning in the crematorium." My first reaction had been irritation at the idiocy of referring to a corpse as "Mister." But what stayed with me like a toothache was the thought of the crematorium. To me, a crematorium was no vague image. I knew. I knew how on contact with the fire the body was convulsed as though in a last terrible access of pain, how the hair burst into a flaming aureole, and the face turned into a final, hideous grimace. I knew how eyes looked in the fire.

"Let me tell you a story," said Silvers. "Old Oppenheimer had a fine collection, but all he got out of it was trouble. Two of his best pictures were stolen. He got them back, but then he was so worried that he doubled his insurance, and that comes to a lot of money. Besides, he really loved his pictures, and wouldn't have felt compensated by the insurance money. He was so afraid of burglary that he didn't dare to leave the house. In the end he hit on a solution: he sold the whole collection to a museum here in New York. All at once he felt free, he could travel as much as he pleased, he had money in the bank, and when he wanted to see his pictures he went to the museum. He was always making jokes about collectors. Prisoners, he called them, free men who didn't know any better than to lock themselves up." Silvers laughed. "He had something there."

I burned with envy as I contemplated Silvers. What a comfortable existence! He had turned the agonizing flame of artistic creation into a cozy chimney fire, to be enjoyed with irony and cynicism. And whenever he grew bored with his life of sybaritic ease, he could find excitement in the heady battle of buying and selling. Ordinarily I had my doubts: would I really want to live like that? But that day I envied him. I was afraid of going back to my gray hotel room.

The moment I turned the corner I saw the Rolls-Royce outside the hotel and hastened my step for fear of missing Natasha.

"Here he comes," she said as I entered the lobby. "Should we give him some vodka?"

"Too hot," I said. "This town is a Turkish bath."

"Then let's go somewhere and cool off. I've got the Rolls again until eleven."

As usual, I reckoned up my finances. "Where do we go?"

She laughed. "Not to the Pavillon. How about a hamburger in the park?"

"With Coca-Cola?"

"The European gentleman can have beer."

"She wanted me to come along," said Melikov. "But I've been invited to Leopold's."

"For a wedding or a funeral?" Natasha asked.

"A business conference. One of our guests wants to leave and move into an apartment. I'm supposed to talk him out of it. Boss's orders."

"What boss?" I asked.

"The owner of this hotel."

"You make it sound like the Ritz. Who is this mysterious boss? Have I ever seen him?"

"No," said Melikov curtly.

"A gangster," said Natasha.

Melikov looked around. "You shouldn't talk like that, Natasha. It's unhealthy."

"I know him. I used to live here. He's fat and greasy, and his suits are too tight, and he wanted to sleep with me."

"Natasha!"

"All right, Vladimir. We'll change the subject, but he did want to sleep with me."

"Who doesn't?" Melikov was smiling again.

"Always the wrong ones, Vladimir, that's the hell of it. Give me another drop of vodka." She turned to me. "You know why the vodka here is so good? Because the boss is part owner of a distillery. That's why they sell it so cheap, too. Also because the boss hasn't entirely given up the idea of sleeping with me. He's very patient. That's his strong point."

"Natasha!" Melikov protested.

"All right. All right. We're going."

The chauffeur was standing beside the car, smoking. "Would you like to drive, sir?" he asked me.

"A Rolls-Royce? I wouldn't dare. I haven't got a license and I haven't driven for years."

"How wonderful!" said Natasha. "There's nothing more boring than an amateur racing driver."

I looked at her. Boredom seemed to be the one thing she was afraid of. I loved Natasha. She gave me a sense of security. On the other hand, she probably loved adventure, which I detested.

"Do you really want to go to the park?"

"Why not? The restaurant is still open. You sit outside and watch the seals. The tigers are just going to bed. The pigeons light on your table. Even squirrels turn up now and then. Where can you be nearer to paradise?"

"Will our fancy chauffeur want hamburger and mineral water for dinner? I suppose he's not allowed to drink."

"Don't make me laugh. He drinks like a fish. Not today though. He's got to pick up his lord and master at the theater. Anyway, hamburgers are his passion. Mine, too."

There were few people at the zoo, and it was very quiet. Night was falling, and the brown bears were lying down to sleep. Only the polar bears were still swimming restlessly back and forth in their little pool. The chauffeur had settled himself at another table. He ordered three large hamburgers—which he proceeded to drown in ketchup—dill pickles, and coffee.

"What have you been doing today?" Natasha asked.

"Oh, my boss has been telling me how to live."

"Isn't it funny how much advice people dish out? Everybody wants to arrange my life for me. And they're always so sure of themselves. They all have such good ideas—for other people."

"It seems to me," I said, "that you can manage very well without advice."

"Not at all. I need all I can get. But it doesn't help. Everything I do is wrong. I don't want to be unhappy, but I am. I don't want to be alone, but I always am. That makes you laugh. You think I know so many people. It's true, but the other is true, too."

She looked very sweet, talking this childish nonsense in the gathering dusk amid the last roars of the wild animals. I listened, feeling very much as I had with Silvers that afternoon: how incomprehensibly remote these lives seemed from mine! Their emotions were so simple, nothing more distressing than a childlike dismay at discovering that happiness is not a secure possession but a wave in the water; neither was tormented by an Orestean obligation, a mission of vengeance, a dark innocence and involvement in guilt. How enviably happy they were with their success, their tired cynicism, their witticisms and little misfortunes that never went beyond a loss of money or love. They twittered like the ornamental birds of another century. How glad I would have been to be like them, to forget, and to twitter with them.

"They say you get used to disappointments," said Natasha. "It's not true. Each new disappointment hurts more than the last. And each time it takes longer to heal. You're afraid of being burned again, and that makes you afraid to live." She propped her head in her hand. "I don't want to be burned again."

"How will you manage that?" I asked. "Go into a nunnery?"

She made an impatient gesture. "Nobody can run away from himself."

"Oh yes they can. Once. But then there's no coming back," I said, thinking of Moller hanging from the chandelier on a hot night in New York. As Lipschütz had told me, he was wearing his good suit and a clean shirt. He had even put on a necktie, on the theory that it would strangle him more quickly. I found that hard to believe. It was like walking up and down the corridor in a train in order to get there faster.

"You told me a few days ago that you were unhappy," I said. "Then later you said it wasn't true. Do your feelings change as fast as that? How lucky you are!"

"Neither one was true. Are you really so naïve? Or are you making fun of me?"

"I've learned never to make fun of anybody," I said. "And I've learned to believe what people tell me. It's so much simpler."

Natasha looked at me incredulously. "You're funny," she said. "You talk like an old man. Did you ever want to be a priest?"

I laughed. "Never."

"Sometimes you seem like a priest. Why shouldn't you make fun of people? You're so ponderous. You could use a little humor. But the Germans . . ."

I stopped her with a gesture. "I know. The Germans have no sense of humor. Actually, it's true."

"What have they got to take its place?"

"*Schadenfreude.* That's an untranslatable German word, meaning malicious pleasure in other people's misfortunes. It's the same as what you call humor—making fun of people."

"*Touché,* Professor. How thorough you are!"

"German thoroughness," I said, laughing.

"But I am unhappy. Or empty. Or sentimental. Or burned. Don't you understand?"

"I do. I do."

"Do the Germans ever feel that way?"

"They used to."

"You, too?"

I had no answer to that.

"Every word has to be dragged out of you," said Natasha impatiently. "Can't we ever have a sensible conversation? Are you unhappy, too?"

"I don't know. Unhappiness is such a tame word."

She looked at me in consternation. Her eyes had grown brighter in the failing light. "In that case nothing can happen to us," she said finally. "We're both in the soup."

"Nothing can happen," I agreed. "We're both burned children and very very cautious."

The waiter brought the check. "I think they're closing," said Natasha.

Again I felt a moment of panic. I didn't want to be alone that evening and I was afraid Natasha wanted to go home. "Haven't you got the car until the theaters are out?" I asked.

"Yes. Shall we drive around till then?"

"That would be lovely."

We stood up. The terrace and the zoo were deserted. She took my arm. I felt an almost anonymous tenderness, a tenderness that still had no name and was attached to no one. Yet it was not pure, but a mixture of different feelings; there was fear in it, fear that the past might rise up again, and fear that something might yet go wrong in this mysterious interval of helplessness between peril and salvation; there was a blind groping for anything that would give promise of security. I felt ashamed to be dissecting my emotions and ashamed of what the dissection revealed, but I consoled myself rather lamely with the thought that Natasha's feelings could not be far different, that she, too, was a tendril clinging to the nearest support, without even asking herself to what extent her heart was in it. She didn't want to be alone in a troubled period of her existence, and neither did I. But for all our hidden motives we were caught up in that light, warm tenderness, which seemed to involve no danger or threat of pain because it still had no name. "I worship you," I said suddenly, much to my own surprise, as we were following the broad shadow of the chauffeur along the leafy path leading to Fifth Avenue. "I don't know you and I worship you, Natasha."

She turned toward me. "It's not true," she said. "You're a liar. But go on saying it. I like it."

It was some time before I realized that I had been dreaming. Little by little I recognized the dark contours of my room, the lighter outline of the window, and the reddish glow of the New York night. It was a slow, difficult awakening, a struggle—like pulling myself out of a swamp.

I dreamed that I had murdered someone and buried the body in an abandoned garden beside a brook. Years later the body had been found, and now doom was creeping up on me. I couldn't remember whether I had killed a man or a woman, or why. Nothing was really clear to me but my terror, which stayed with me long after I was awake. The night and my sudden awakening had swept away the barriers I had built around my memories. I saw before me the whitewashed room in the crematorium. I saw the hooks for hanging, I saw the spots under them where quivering flesh had effaced the whitewash. I saw the bony hand moving on the floor and heard a guttural voice commanding: "Step on it! Step on it, you shit-ass, or I'll brain you. And we'll hang you, too, you swine!" I heard the voice and saw the cold contemptuous eyes, and I told myself for the hundredth time that he would have killed me like a fly, as he had killed hundreds of other prisoners, if I hadn't complied. He was only waiting for a pretext. Nevertheless, I felt the sweat trickling from my armpits, as I always did when this memory hit me. I retched and groaned in my helplessness. That guttural voice and those cruel eyes had to be extinguished. März, I thought, Egon März. Later on I was released—that happened now and then. It wasn't far to the Dutch border, and I knew the country. Soon I was in relative safety, but I knew that I would have to see that face again before I died.

I sat up in bed, clutching my knees, as though frozen from within on that sultry summer night. I thought of everything I had wanted to forget, and once again it came to me that this new life was impossible, that I had to go back, that I must not put an end to myself out of despair and disgust, as Moller had done. I had to preserve my life. I knew that we lose all sense of proportion at night, but I was powerless to dispel my remorse and helpless rage and grief. I sat there shivering, the night turned gray, and I spoke to myself as I might have spoken to a child. I waited for daylight, and when it came I was as broken as if I had spent the whole night driving a knife into an endless wall of black cotton wool.

XIV

Silvers sent me to deliver the Degas to Cooper and help him to hang it. Cooper lived on the eighteenth floor of an apartment house on Park Avenue. I expected a butler to open the door, but Cooper himself received me in his shirt sleeves. "Come in," he said. "Care for some whisky? Or would you rather have coffee?"

"Thank you, I'd like a cup of coffee."

"I'll have whisky. It's the only thing in this heat."

His face glowed like a ripe tomato though the apartment was air-conditioned and very cool. I felt as if I had stepped into a mausoleum. The furniture was mostly French, Louis Quinze, delicate gilded pieces, with a few small Italian chairs and a magnificent little yellow Venetian dresser. French Impressionists hung on the damask-covered walls.

Cooper removed the wrapping from the Degas and set it down on a chair. "There's something I'd like to ask you," he said. "Silvers gave me a song and dance about this little lady being a present to his wife, said she'd raise hell when she got home. Now tell me: wasn't that just a trick?"

"Is that why you bought it?" I asked.

"Of course not. I bought it because I wanted it. Do you know what Silvers made me pay for it?"

"I haven't the faintest idea."

"Thirty thousand."

Cooper gave me a questioning look. I knew he was lying and was trying to pump me. "Well?" he said. "That's a lot of money, isn't it?"

"For me it would be a lot of money."

"What's that? How much would you be willing to pay for it?"

"Not a cent," I said.

"What do you mean?" asked Cooper almost angrily.

"I mean that I haven't got that kind of money. Right now I have all of thirty-five dollars to my name."

Cooper refused to be diverted. "How much would you be willing to pay if you had the money?"

It seemed to me that I'd answered enough questions for a cup of coffee. "Everything I owned," I said. "You know as well as I do that a passion for painting is good business. There's none better. I bet Silvers would buy it back from you and let you have a good profit."

"The crook! And offer it to me a week later for fifty per cent more."

This little exchange, for reasons unknown to me, seemed to put Cooper in a good humor. "Well," he said. "Where will we hang our little lady?"

Cooper was called to the phone. "Just look around," he called out to me as he was disappearing into his study. "Maybe you'll find a place."

A maid appeared from nowhere and offered to guide me. The apartment was furnished in excellent taste. Cooper must have known his stuff or had good advisers. Probably both. The maid took me to Cooper's bedroom. "This might be a good place," she said.

The center of attraction was a broad bed in the worst art-nouveau style. Above it, in a gilt frame, hung a forest landscape showing a stag and several does, with a spring in the background. I stared at this hideous kitsch in speechless amazement. "Did Mr. Cooper paint this?" I asked. "Or did he inherit it from his parents?"

"I don't know. It was here when I came. Isn't it beautiful? So true to nature."

"It certainly is. You can see the stag's breath. Is Mr. Cooper a hunter?"

"Not that I know of."

The next thing that met my eye was a view of Venice by Ziem. I realized that I had discovered Cooper's secret, and somehow it moved me. Here in his bedroom he was his own true self. This was what he really liked. All the rest was pretense and business, with perhaps a little lukewarm inclination thrown in. But this amorous stag was passion; this sentimental study of Venice was romance.

"Let's go on," I said to the maid. "Everything is so right in this room it would only jar. Are there more rooms upstairs?"

"Only a terrace and a small drawing room."

She led me up the stairs. I could hear Cooper in his study bellowing orders into the phone. I was curious to see whether the study was furnished like the bedroom. A second amorous stag would not have surprised me.

I stopped in the doorway leading to the terrace. Down below lay New York in the summer heat, like an African city with skyscrapers. One could see at a glance that this city of steel had not grown slowly and organically, taking on the patina of the centuries, but had been built quickly and heedlessly by determined men unencumbered by traditions. And because their aim had been not beauty but efficiency, they had created a new and daring beauty that was neither classical nor romantic.

I heard Cooper puffing up the stairs. "Have you found a place?"

"Here," I said, pointing to the terrace. "But the sun wouldn't be good for it. A ballet dancer above the city! That would be something. Maybe in the drawing room. On the wall away from the sun."

We went in. The drawing room was very bright, with white walls and chintz-covered furniture. On a table there were three Chinese bronzes and a pair of Tang dancing girls. I looked at Cooper, wondering if he wouldn't have preferred three beer mugs to the Chou bronzes and a set of porcelain dwarves to the terracotta dancers. "Over there," I said. "On the wall behind the bronzes. The greenish-blue patina matches the color of the dancer's tutu."

Cooper was still panting. I held the picture up in the place I had decided on. "We'd have to make a hole in the wall," he said finally. "If we take the picture away later on, the hole will still be there."

I looked at him in amazement. "You can hang something else in the same place," I said. "Or you can have the hole plastered over." What a penny pincher! But that was probably how he had made his millions. Strangely enough, I didn't hold it against him; the stag in the bedroom redeemed him in my eyes. For Cooper, everything else in the apartment must have been vaguely hostile; I felt sure that he didn't understand it, any more than he understood why he had spent so much money on it. That was why he had tried to pump me. He was suspicious because, though he knew there was some connection between art and money, it didn't quite make sense to him.

"All right," Cooper finally decided. "Put it there. But don't make a big hole."

"I'll make it as small as possible. You see these patent hooks. They only need a thin nail and they'll support a big picture."

It didn't take me long. Cooper looked on suspiciously. When I had finished, I looked again at the Chinese bronzes and held them in my hand. I felt the gentle warmth of the patina. They were very fine bronzes and gave me a strange sense of being at home; they were so perfect that they communicated no other thought than that of perfection.

"Do you know anything about them?" Cooper asked.

"A little."

"What are they worth?" he asked. I could have hugged him for being so frank and predictable.

"They're priceless."

"What do you mean by that? Are they a better investment than paintings?"

"No," I said, grown suddenly cautious for fear of contradicting Silvers. "But they're very beautiful. There's nothing better in the Metropolitan."

"Really? I can't believe it. Some crook palmed them off on me."

"Then you're just lucky."

"Think so?" He laughed uproariously and gave me an appraising look. I think he was wondering whether he could offer me a tip; if so, he decided against it. "Would you care for some more coffee?"

"No, thank you."

I went back to Silvers and reported. "The old cutthroat," he said. "Whenever I send anybody over to his place, he tries the same dodge. He's a born bargain hunter. He started out with a cart full of junk. Pretty soon he was selling whole trainloads of scrap. Then he went into armaments. Sold arms and scrap to the Japanese. When we went to war, he transferred the account to the U.S. Do you realize that for every Degas he buys, a few thousand people die?"

I had never seen Silvers so angry. "Then why do you sell to him?" I asked. "Doesn't that make you an accomplice?"

Silvers burst into an angry laugh. "Why do I sell to him? Because selling's my business. I can't operate like a Quaker. What do you mean an accomplice? In what? In the war? That's ridiculous!"

I had quite a time calming him down—that was my punishment for trying to be logical.

"I can't stand these merchants of death," said Silvers, but in a gentler tone. "I got five thousand more out of him than the valuation I'd put on the picture; I should have tacked on another five thousand."

He poured himself a whisky-and-soda. "Have some?" he asked.

"No, thanks. I've had too much coffee."

That's the way to take revenge, I thought. With money. If I could do that, I'd be able to escape from my past. "Maybe you'll get another chance," I said. "I wouldn't be surprised if he came back soon. I told him the other Degas would make a marvelous pair with the one he bought and that I personally—though of course it was all a matter of taste—found the other Degas almost more interesting and beautiful."

Silvers looked at me thoughtfully. "You're developing!" he said. "Tell you what I'll do. If Cooper comes back for the other Degas within a month, I'll give you a hundred-dollar bonus."

I caught sight of Natasha outside the Plaza. She was crossing the square to Fifty-ninth Street. She seemed deep in thought and didn't see me.

"Natasha," I said, hurrying over to her. "What are you thinking about so hard?"

She was quick on the draw. "That's easy," she said. "I was thinking about taking you to lunch."

"Alas," I said. "I'm too old for a gigolo. And I haven't enough charm."

"You have none at all, but it doesn't matter. Forget your old-fashioned principles. We all eat together on credit. Nobody pays until the end of the month. So you won't be embarrassed. Besides, there's somebody I want you to meet. An old lady. She wants to buy some paintings, and I've told her about you."

"But Natasha! I don't sell paintings."

"No, but Silvers does. And if you bring him customers, he'll pay you a commission."

"What?"

"A commission. It's customary. Didn't you know that half the people in New York live on the commissions they get out of each other?"

"No."

"Then it's time you found out. Come along. I'm hungry. Or are you scared?"

She gave me a challenging look. "You're very beautiful," I said.

"Bravo!"

"If anything comes of the commission, you're having champagne and caviar on me."

"Bravo! *D'accord.*"

The restaurant was rather crowded. I had the impression of being in a cage full of butterflies and assorted birds. Waiters were dashing about. As usual, Natasha seemed to know everybody.

"You know half New York," I said.

"Nonsense. Just a few people in advertising and fashion."

"What do we eat?" I asked.

"For the sake of your puritanical principles, I suggest the summer menu."

"What's that?"

"A polite name for a diet menu. Mostly rabbit food. Everybody's on a diet in this country."

"Why? They look healthy enough to me."

"It's the youth cult. Skinny people are supposed to look

younger." She lit a cigarette and gave me a glance of mock severity. "All right, I know half the world is starving, but let's not talk about it right now. You were going to, weren't you?"

"Not really."

"Who do you think you're kidding?"

"Well, I was thinking of Europe. They're not dieting over there. You can't diet with a food shortage."

She peered at me out of half-closed eyes. "It seems to me," she said, "that you think about Europe too much."

I was amazed at her perspicacity. "I try not to."

She laughed. "Here comes our old lady."

I had expected a corpulent harridan, a feminine version of Cooper. Instead, I saw a tidy little woman with crisply curled silvery hair and red cheeks. She was about seventy and looked no more than fifty. One could see at a glance that she had led a very sheltered life. Her skin, fragile but scarcely wrinkled, had the quality of tissue paper. Only her hands had aged, and her neck, a good part of which was concealed by a pearl choker.

She questioned me about Paris, of which she had fond memories. I was careful to say nothing about the life I had led there. I talked as if the war did not exist. With my eyes on Natasha, I spoke of the Seine, the Ile Saint-Louis and the Quai des Grands-Augustins, of summer afternoons in the Luxembourg and evenings on the Champs-Elysées or in the Bois. A nostalgic look came into Natasha's eyes, and that made it easier for me.

The luncheon was served with dispatch, and in less than an hour Mrs. Whymper rose to go. "Perhaps you could take me to see the Silvers collection," she said. "Would you call for me tomorrow at five?"

"I'll be glad to," I said. I was about to add certain explanations, but Natasha kicked me under the table.

"That was painless," said Natasha when she had gone. Then she laughed. "Weren't you going to tell her you only swept the floor and opened crates? Quite unnecessary. There are lots of people here who make a business of advising the helpless rich and taking them around to galleries."

"Touts!" I said.

"Advisers," Natasha corrected me. "Honest young men who protect poor helpless millionaires from thieving art dealers. Are you going to do it?"

"Yes," I said.

"Bravo!"

"For your sake."

"Double bravo!"

"To tell you the truth, I'm more corruptible than you think."

She clapped her hands discreetly. "In a minute you'll be almost human. The statue is beginning to move."

"But weren't you surprised to see it come off so smoothly? After all, Mrs. Whymper doesn't know me from Adam."

"It was because you spoke about things she loves: Paris, summer in the Bois, the Seine, the quais, the book stalls . . ."

"But not a word about paintings."

"Exactly. That was very clever of you."

We walked along Fiftieth Street. I felt light and happy. We passed the Savoy auction rooms. A load of rugs was being carried out. The street was alive, and my black night seemed far behind me.

"Will I be seeing you tonight?" I asked.

She nodded.

"At the hotel?"

"Yes."

I retraced my steps. The sun was covered with a film of dust. The air was hot and smelled of exhaust fumes. I stopped outside the Savoy auction rooms and after some hesitation went in. The place was half empty, and everyone seemed half asleep. The auctioneer, looking down from a sort of pulpit, was trying to arouse interest in some figures of saints. One by one they were brought in and set down on a platform. Nobody wanted them very much, and they were going for a song. What can you do with saints in wartime, except put them in jail? I went out again and studied the windows. In among the heavy Renaissance furniture there were two Chinese bronzes. One was obviously a Ming copy, but something told me that the other might be authentic. The patina was poor and may even have been tampered with, but even so . . . My guess was that some ignoramus had taken it for a copy and tried to improve on it. I went back in and consulted the catalogue. The bronzes were listed without dates, in among pewter pitchers, brass candlesticks, and other miscellaneous objects. I felt sure they would go for very little—none of the big dealers was likely to go out of his way for such an assortment of junk.

Why shouldn't I buy this bronze and sell it to Lowy Senior, who couldn't possibly have noticed it? Then, as I strolled on, I started to think of Natasha and the night she had brought me back to the hotel in the Rolls. I had been silent during the latter part of the drive and had left her with unseemly haste. For a ridiculous reason: an urgent need to empty my bladder. Once relieved, I had been very angry with myself, certain that Natasha must be furious; maybe it was all over between us. Next day I changed my mind. Of course my behavior had been silly. But hadn't it been romantic of me to suffer in silence rather than exhibit my mortality, have the chauffeur stop at the nearest hotel, and keep Natasha waiting in the car? Besides, I reflected, I wouldn't have acted so foolishly if I hadn't been fond of Natasha, and the thought gave me a delicious feeling of tenderness.

Deep in my tender musings, I paid no attention to where I was going. Then suddenly I was outside the Lowys' shop and saw Lowy Junior standing in the center of a group of white Louis Seize chairs, gazing dreamily at the street.

"How are you, Mr. Lowy?" I asked.

"So-so. My brother's still at lunch. We go separately, you know. Somebody has to mind the shop. And besides, he eats kosher, whereas I—I eat American."

The Lowy brothers reminded me of the original Siamese twins, one of whom had been a drinker, the other a teetotaler. Since they had the same blood stream, the unfortunate teetotaler was forced to share his brother's spells of drunkenness and the ensuing hangovers as well. Proving that virtue is its own reward.

"I've found a bronze," I said. "It's up for sale at a third-class auction."

Lowy Junior made a disparaging gesture. "Tell my fascist brother about it. I'm not in the mood for business right now. I've got my life to think about." He paused for a moment, then decided to speak. "Tell me the honest truth—what do you advise? Should I get married or shouldn't I?"

A ticklish question. A yes or a no could be equally disastrous.

"In Catholic Italy," I ventured, "I'd say no. In America it's simpler: here you can get divorced."

"Who's talking about divorce? I'm talking about marriage."

It was clear to me that when a man really wants to get married he doesn't ask for advice, but I was saved from having to say so by the appearance of Lowy Senior, floating in well-being after a copious meal.

He beamed at me. "Well, how's the old parasite?"

"Silvers? He's just given me a raise of his own free will."

"He can afford it. How much? A dollar a month?"

"A hundred."

"What!"

They both gaped at me. Lowy Senior was first to recover his composure. "He should have made it two hundred."

"He did, he did," I replied. "But I turned it down. I don't think I'm worth that much yet. Maybe in another year."

"The trouble with you," Lowy Senior grumbled, "is that you can't be serious."

"Oh yes I can," I said. "I can be serious about bronzes."

I told him about my discovery. "I advise you to bid on it. Everybody else will think it's a fake."

"But what if it is a fake?"

"I don't think it is. I suppose you want me to insure you against error and loss?"

"Why not?" Lowy grinned. "With your income."

"If that's how you feel about it," I said, "I'll buy it myself." I was disappointed. I had expected a little more gratitude for the tip. "How was the lentil soup?" I asked.

"Lentil soup? How do you know I had lentil soup?"

I pointed to the crushed lentil on his lapel. "Too heavy for this time of year, Mr. Lowy. Watch out, or you'll have a stroke. Good afternoon, gentlemen."

"My goodness, Mr. Ross! Can't you take a joke? You've been a good friend. It's all settled. How high should I go?"

"Let me take another look at it first."

"Good idea. I can't do it myself. If they see me poking around, they'll smell a rat. They know me. Then you'll come back and tell me about it?"

"Of course."

I felt strangely buoyant as I walked away. I had been so pleased with the idea of doing a little business on my own, and then without a thought I had turned it over to Lowy. But now I knew why. Something was changing in my life. For the first time in years I was looking forward to something. But because this feeling was so utterly new, my uncertainty was as great as my hopes. It was to propitiate a fate that might still turn against me that I had called Lowy's attention to the bronze. That was why my tender thoughts of Natasha had led me to his door. Call it superstition.

XV

Next morning when I announced Mrs. Whymper's projected visit to Silvers, he reacted with indifference. "Whymper? Whymper? When's she coming? At five? I'm not sure I'll have time for her."

I was well aware that the lazy crocodile had nothing else to do but wait for customers and drink whisky. "All right," I said. "Let's put it off until you have time."

"No," he said wearily. "Better bring her. It's always best to get these things over with."

Good, I thought. That will give me another chance to look at the bronze.

"How did you like Cooper's setup?" Silvers asked.

"Very much. He must have good advisers."

"He does. He himself doesn't know a thing."

It occurred to me that Silvers himself didn't know very much outside the limited field of French Impressionism. He had nothing to be so arrogant about; the Impressionists were his business, just as munitions and scrap iron were Cooper's. In a way Cooper came off better—in addition to his paintings he had magnificent furniture, whereas Silvers had nothing but upholstered sofas and armchairs and mass-produced functional modern furniture.

He must have guessed my thoughts. "It would be easy to furnish my house with eighteenth-century pieces," he said. "If I don't, it's because of the pictures. All that baroque and rococo rubbish only distracts the attention. Bric-a-brac from the dead past. What sense does it make in a modern house?"

"It's different with Cooper," I said. "He doesn't have to sell his pictures. He can fit them into his own setting."

Silvers laughed. "If he really wanted to put them in his own setting, he should furnish the house with mortars and machine guns."

He often displayed such animosity toward his customers. But in expressing his contempt for them, he only showed me that in reality he envied them. He persuaded himself that his cynicism preserved his freedom; but it was a cheap freedom, comparable to an employee's freedom to run down his boss behind his back. Like many half-educated people, Silvers was given to ridiculing everything he did not understand—a convenient defense mechanism, except that it didn't quite work because he himself remained dimly aware of what he was doing. All in all, I came to the conclusion that the man was a desperate neurotic, and as far as I was concerned, that was the one thing that made him interesting. Once the novelty had worn off, I found his lectures on art and life rather tedious.

During the lunch hour I went to the auction rooms. They were not at all crowded, for there was to be no auction that day. For a few minutes I pretended to be looking at the Renaissance furniture, then at the clutter of antique weaponry—swords, spears, and breastplates. Finally I asked to be shown the bronze. Now that I had ceased to be an indifferent onlooker and had become a prospective buyer, I found myself looking with hostility at the other customers. These people had never struck me before as particularly objectionable; today I detested them as potential competitors. Holding the bronze in my hand, I stood by the window with my back to the enormous showroom. Fondling the bronze, I looked out at the street, knowing that Natasha might appear at any moment like a naiad amidst a flock of penguins. I was seized by the vague agitation that had made me unfair to Silvers and would no doubt make me unfair to others. I felt it in the palms of my hands. I wanted this bronze and I knew that I somehow identified it with Natasha. At last, after all these years, I wanted something that had nothing to do with survival.

I put the bronze back in the window. "It's not old," I remarked to the man who had brought it in for me, an elderly employee who was chewing gum and seemed totally indifferent to my opinion. Slowly I left the auction rooms and crossed the street to the restaurant where I had eaten with Natasha. I didn't go in, but I could have sworn that a kind of aura set this entrance apart from all the other doorways on the street.

Mrs. Whymper lived on Fifth Avenue, across from the park. I arrived punctually at five. She seemed to be in no hurry. The only paintings in sight were a few Romneys and a Ruisdael. "Is it too early for a Martini?" she asked me.

She had one in front of her, a very dry one, as I could see by the color. It looked like vodka. "Is that a vodka Martini?" I asked.

"Vodka Martini? What on earth is that? This one is gin with a dash of vermouth."

Displaying my newly acquired knowledge, I told her that vodka could be used instead of gin.

"Isn't that amusing? We must try it." She rang for the butler. "John," she asked him, "is there any vodka in the house?"

"Yes, madam."

"Then make Mr. Ross a Martini with vodka instead of gin." She turned to me. "French or Italian vermouth? With or without an olive?"

"French vermouth, I think. And yes please, an olive. But don't go to any trouble—gin will be perfectly all right."

"No, no. We must always be willing to learn. Make one for me, too, John. I'll give it a try."

I saw that my sheltered old lady was a drinker and only hoped she wouldn't be too far gone when we got to Silvers'.

John served the Martinis. "Chin-chin," said Mrs. Whymper merrily.

She emptied half the glass at one gulp. "Good!" she said. "We'll have to include that in our repertory, John. It's excellent."

"Certainly, madam."

"Who gave you the recipe?" she asked me.

"A man who claims that vodka can't be smelled on the breath."

"Really? How amusing! Have you ever experimented? Is it true?"

"I don't know. It doesn't matter to me."

"Really? Haven't you someone who might care?"

I laughed. "No. All the people I know are drinkers."

Mrs. Whymper eyed me, tilting her head like a bird. "It's good for the heart," she said out of a clear sky. "And it clears the head. Shall we each have another little one for the road?"

"I'd be glad to," I said reluctantly, foreseeing an interminable series of little ones for the road. But I was wrong. After the first, Mrs. Whymper stood up and rang.

"Is the car outside, John?"

"Yes, madam."

"Splendid. Then we shall call on Mr. Silvers."

Transformed into a chauffeur, John opened the door of the Cadillac for us. It seemed to me that I wasn't doing so badly in the car department—a Rolls and a Cadillac, both with chauffeurs, in so short a time. My eye lit on a portable bar similar to the one in the Rolls. I fully expected Mrs. Whymper to offer more refreshment, but she didn't. Instead, she struck up a conversation about Paris and the provinces in rather halting French. I replied in the same language, partly to please her and partly because it gave me a certain advantage over her. I thought that might come in handy later on.

I expected Silvers to send me away after the first few moments, so as to have an open field for his own charm. But Mrs. Whymper kept addressing her remarks to me, as often as not in French. After a while I asked her if she would care for a vodka Martini. She clapped her hands. Silvers looked at me disapprovingly; he wouldn't have minded serving Scotch, but everything else struck him as barbarous. I said Mrs. Whymper's physician had forbidden Scotch and went to the kitchen, where, with the cook's help, I finally located a bottle of vodka.

"You drink this stuff in the afternoon?" she asked me.

"Not me. The customers."

"You ought to be ashamed of yourself."

It was apparently my fate to be held responsible for other people's failings. I stood by the kitchen window and sent the cook in with the two Martinis and Scotch for Silvers. Some pigeons had settled on the window ledge. New York was as full of pigeons as Venice. I felt the coolness of the windowpane against my forehead. When the cook came back, I went to my observation post in the storeroom. Silvers had brought in some small Renoirs. That surprised me. Ordinarily he liked to make it clear that he had an assistant to perform these menial tasks.

A few minutes later he came to me. "You've forgotten your cocktail," he said. "Come in."

Mrs. Whymper had drained her glass. "Ah, there you are," she said. "Unfaithful so soon? Or are you afraid of your own Martinis?"

She sat straight as a die, looking very much like a doll. But there was nothing soft or doll-like about her hands. They were thin, hard, and bony. "What do you think of the little Renoir?" she asked.

It was a still life with flowers, done about 1880. "It's wonderful," I said. "We'll have a hard time finding anything comparable when it's sold."

Mrs. Whymper nodded. "Shall we have one more for the road?" I went back to the kitchen.

"You've made them so big," she said when I returned with the two Martinis, and downed hers at one gulp. "Mr. Silvers tells me you would like to hang the picture for me. Thank you so much. See you tomorrow at five."

The Martinis had had no visible effect on her. I saw her to the car. The air was still hot but there was an evening breeze, and the sound of rustling leaves in the park made me think of palm trees.

I went back in. "Why didn't you tell me who it was?" said Silvers in his tone of deepest boredom. "Of course I know Mrs. Whymper."

I bit my lip. "I did tell you."

"There are so many Whympers. You didn't tell me it was Mrs. André Whymper. I've known her for years. Oh well, it doesn't matter."

"I hope you won't hold it against me," I said, mustering all my sarcasm.

"Why should I hold it against you?"

"Anyway," I said, "she seems to have bought something."

Silvers made a gesture as though chasing a fly. "That's not so certain," he said. "These old ladies are always returning things—it ruins the frames, and in the end they don't buy. This business isn't as simple as you think." Silvers yawned. "Let's call it a day. This heat is fatiguing. See you tomorrow. Put the pictures away before you go."

And off he went. I stood dumbfounded. The scoundrel! I thought. Trying to cheat me out of my commission by saying he'd known her all along! I took the three Renoirs he had shown back to the storeroom. Two were portraits of young women. I could see that Mrs. Whymper, who made such frantic efforts to look like a youthful mummy, wouldn't have wanted them in the house. I locked the doors and brought the keys to Mrs. Silvers.

"Is the coast clear?" she asked.

"All clear," I said.

"Then I can finally take a bath."

When I turned the corner, there was the Rolls-Royce outside the hotel. I had been wondering where to take Natasha that evening. Every place I could think of seemed too hot. The Rolls was the solution.

"Have you got it till after theater?" I asked.

"Longer. Until midnight. At midnight it must be outside El Morocco."

"You, too?"

"Both of us. How did it go with Mrs. Whymper?"

"Fine. She bought a nice little Renoir that will look very well in her doll's house."

"Doll's house," said Natasha, laughing. "That doll, who looks as if she could only open and close her china-blue eyes and smile helplessly at the world, is president of two important corporations. And nothing honorary about it. She knows her stuff."

"Really?"

"You have a lot to learn about women in America."

"Natasha," I said, "the only woman I want to know anything about is right here beside me."

To my surprise she blushed to the roots of her hair. "Mrs. Whymper seems to have had a good effect on you," she said. "I'll have to find some more like her."

———

"Let's drive up the Hudson past the George Washington Bridge," said Natasha. "Maybe there'll be a place where we can sit outside in the moonlight and watch the boats go by."

She pressed close to me. I felt her hair and her cool warmth. Even on these hot days she never seemed to perspire.

"Were you a good journalist?" she asked.

"No, strictly second-rate."

"And now you can't write any more?"

"Who would I write for? My English isn't good enough. I haven't been able to write in a long time."

"Then you're like a pianist without a piano?"

"You could put it that way. Has your unknown patron left you something to drink?"

"We'll take a look. You don't like to talk about yourself, do you?"

"Not especially."

"I can understand that. Not even about your present job?"

"As a tout and errand boy?"

Natasha opened the bottle compartment. "You see," she said. "We're shadows. Strange shadows of the past. Will it ever be different? This is Polish vodka. I wonder how it got here. Poland doesn't even exist any more."

"No," I said bitterly. "Poland doesn't exist, but Polish vodka has survived. Should we laugh about it or cry?"

"We should drink it, darling."

She produced two glasses and filled them. The vodka was cold and very good.

"Could you enlist," she asked, "if you wanted to?"

"No," I said. "Nobody wants me. You're right. I'm neither fish nor flesh, but it was the same in Europe. Next to Europe this is paradise. The paradise of an involuntary spectator. Oh, Natasha, let's not talk about what we've lost but about what we have left. Look at the moon."

For a time we were silent. I cursed myself for being so idiotically ponderous. I was behaving like a man I had met at El Morocco. He had wept bitter tears over the fate of France; he even seemed to be sincere, but that didn't prevent him from being ridiculous.

Suddenly Natasha turned to me. Her eyes were shining. We were approaching the bridge. "How beautiful it is!"

She had completely forgotten our gloomy conversation. I had seen that a number of times. She was quick to understand and quick to forget, which was lucky for an elephant like me with a long memory for misfortune and a very short one for happiness.

"I worship you," I said. "Here, now, under this moon and beside this river that flows into the sea and reflects hundreds and thousands of shattered moons. I worship you and no fear of platitudes can stop me from saying that the George Washington Bridge shines like a diadem over the restless Hudson and that I wish it were really a diadem and I were Rockefeller or Napoleon to make you a present of it. I know it's childish of me, but I had to say it."

"Why childish? Can't you just let yourself go? And if it is childish, don't you know that women lap such childishness up?"

"I'm a born coward. I have to say these things to keep up my courage."

I kissed her. "I wish I had a driver's license. Then we could drop our chaperon off at a bar. It's like being in Madrid with a *dueña* always trailing along behind us, except that this one is in front of us."

She laughed. "He's not in our way. He doesn't know a word of French, except 'Madame.' "

"You think he's not in our way?"

"Darling," she murmured, "that's the misery of a big city. One is practically never alone."

"How do people make children in this town?"

"God only knows."

I tapped on the partition. "Please stop over there by the park," I said to the chauffeur and handed him a five-dollar bill. "Go and get yourself some dinner. And pick us up in an hour."

"Yes, sir."

"You see!" said Natasha.

The car vanished into the darkness. Hundreds of radios blared at us from the open windows beyond the park. It was a very small park, littered with Coca-Cola bottles, beer cans, and ice-cream wrappers, and alive with howling children.

"Good God," said Natasha. "And the driver won't be back for an hour."

"We could take a walk by the river."

"But look at the crowds. And how can I walk in these shoes?"

In the light of a street lamp I saw the foursquare radiator of a Rolls-Royce. I ran out and waved my arms like a windmill. Sure enough, it was our driver, who had miraculously turned back. A friend and savior—I would never have mean thoughts about him again. Like so many idealists, I loved humanity but was much less fond of people. Natasha's eyes sparkled with repressed laughter. "Now what?" she asked. "Where can we eat?"

"How about the Blue Ribbon?" the chauffeur suggested. "It's cool and the sauerbraten is first-rate."

"Sauerbraten?" I said.

"Sauerbraten," he repeated. "First-rate."

"I'm damned if I've crossed the ocean to eat sauerbraten or sauerkraut," I said to Natasha. "Let's go to Third Avenue; there are lots of places there."

"What would you say to the King of the Sea, sir?" The chauffeur knew his way around.

"That sounds cool," I said. "Good. The King of the Sea it is."

When we arrived, we flung ourselves into our seats as if we had had a long journey behind us. I decided not to go to El Morocco with Natasha. I wasn't eager to meet any more of her friends.

XVI

I had a lunch date with Kahn, and he took me to a Chinese restaurant. He had acquired a taste for Chinese food in Paris, but, he assured me, the restaurants in Chinatown surpassed his wildest dreams.

We took the bus to Mott Street. The restaurant was in a basement. "Isn't it odd," said Kahn, "how few Chinese women you see in New York? Either the men keep them locked up or they've solved the problem of spontaneous reproduction. Children all over the place, but no women. Too bad, because they're the most wonderful women in the world."

"In novels?"

"In China."

"Have you been there?" I asked.

"Yes, for two years. From 1928 to 1930."

"Why did you come back?"

Kahn laughed. "Homesickness. The Jews have always been such German patriots."

We ordered fried shrimp. "How's Carmen?" I asked. "She looks like a cross between a Polynesian and a Chinese. Tropical and tragic."

"She was born in Pomerania. You wouldn't know it because, luckily, she's Jewish."

"She looks as if she came from Timbuctoo, Hong Kong, and Papeete."

"Mentally she's from Dogpatch. A fascinating mixture. Real stupidity is so fascinating because it's unpredictable. I can more or less imagine how you would react in a given situation. With Carmen it's out of the question. She's not, as you suppose, a romantic mixture from Yokohama, Canton, and the Spice Islands. Her origins are much more remote: maybe the craters of the moon —anyway some archetypal home of pure timeless stupidity, a place to which you and I can never find our way back. Every moment is as fresh and new to her as the first day of the Creation, and she herself is always fresh and new. Nothing troubles her, doubts are unknown to her, she is what she is, and *basta*. Won't you have another portion of shrimp? They're marvelous. To make up for it, we can go without dessert. It's no good anyway—litchi nuts and those silly cookies with the fortunes inside."

"Fine."

"Stupidity is a precious possession," Kahn went on. "Once lost, it can never be recovered. It protects you; you don't see the shoals that intelligence comes to grief on. I once gave myself a course in stupidity. I worked hard at it and made good progress—without it some of my little tricks in France would have turned out very badly for me. But obviously, acquired stupidity is only a pathetic substitute for the genuine article, especially the genuine article combined with a face that might have been made for Duse. And, what's more, in a Jewess. Really stupid Jews are as rare as spotted zebras."

"I wouldn't say that. The Jews are a sentimental, trusting people with a gift for business and the arts. They're clever, but not always intelligent. Far from it."

Kahn grinned. *"Really* stupid, I said. I'm speaking of a Parsifalian, almost saintly stupidity."

I gulped. His identification of Carmen with Parsifal or Lohengrin was so incongruous that I felt there must be some truth in it. I had a weakness for abstruse allusions and had spent a good deal of my time in Brussels thinking them up. They still had the power to put me in a good humor. They were like the sacred flash of enlightenment in the Zen religion. "How are you otherwise?" I asked. "How's business?"

"I'm bored," said Kahn, looking around. There were no Chinese except for the waiters. Stout perspiring businessmen were making clumsy attempts to eat with chopsticks. Kahn handled his with the elegance of a mandarin. "I'm hopelessly bored," he said. "Business is good. In a few years I could be sales manager; later on I might buy into the business, and even end up owning it. Beautiful prospect, isn't it?"

"In France we'd have found the idea very attractive."

"Because it was only an idea. In France security looked like the most beautiful thing on earth. But there's an enormous difference between an idea and its realization. Once you've got security, you see it for what it really is: boredom. Do you know what I think? That living like gypsies for all those years ruined us for bourgeois ideals."

I laughed. "Not all of us. For a lot of refugees the gypsy life was something to be endured and got over with. They were like bank clerks who'd been forced to perform on the flying trapeze. As soon as they could climb down, they went back to their ledgers."

Kahn shook his head. "Not all of them. The life unhinged them more than you think."

"Then they'll be unhinged bank clerks."

"And what about the artists? The writers and actors who can't work. And now they're ten years older. How old will they be before they can go back and work again?"

I thought about it for a moment. What would become of me? I couldn't imagine. I was stuck so deep in my past that I couldn't think ahead.

The waiter asked us if we wanted more tea. I looked into his impassive Asiatic face. He was a wanderer like ourselves.

"We won't know what we've lost until it's all over."

"Our imaginary fatherland, you mean?"

"The fatherland in ourselves."

"My dear Kahn," I said, "that, I think, is something I'll be able to bear."

His face changed. "What phrases I've been making," he said. "It must be the heat. Would you care for some rice wine?"

"Too hot," I said. "Besides, I'm afraid I'll have to drink vodka Martinis this afternoon."

Mrs. Whymper was waiting and so were the Martinis. This time, in fact, there was a whole pitcher of them. My heart sank. I estimated that the pitcher must hold at least six to eight big ones.

I attempted a crisp, businesslike tone in hopes of getting away quickly. "Where would you like me to hang the Renoir?" I asked. "I've brought everything with me; it won't take two minutes."

"Let's think it over." Mrs. Whymper, who was all in pink, motioned toward the pitcher. "Your recipe. It's very good. I think we're in need of refreshment. Such a hot day!"

"Aren't Martinis too strong in this heat?"

She laughed. "I don't think so. And something tells me you don't either."

I looked around. "Shall we hang it in this room?" I asked. "There behind the sofa would be a good place."

She wagged her head gravely, indicating that she was giving the matter due thought. "When were you in Paris last?" she asked.

I resigned myself to my fate. After the second Martini I stood up. "Now I must really get to work. Have you come to a decision?"

"I'm not quite sure. What do you think?"

Again I suggested the place over the sofa. "Just right, I should say. It fits in with the surroundings, and the light is perfect."

Mrs. Whymper arose, a small slender figure with blue-tinted silver hair, took a few steps this way and that, appeared to be studying the walls, and finally proceeded to the next room, which was dominated by an oil painting of a man whose face consisted mostly of jutting chin. "My husband," she informed me as we passed through. "Died in 1935. He worked too hard, poor man.

Never had a moment's time. Now he has plenty." She laughed melodiously. "American men are like that; they don't work to live, they work to die. Wouldn't you say that European men were different?"

"Plenty of them are dying right now."

She turned around. "You're referring to the war? Let's not think about that."

We passed through two more rooms and then mounted a stairway decorated with Guys illustrations. I had taken the Renoir and my equipment with me and looked for a place. "Maybe in my bedroom," said Mrs. Whymper languidly, and went on ahead.

I was beginning to have a definitely sticky feeling. The bedroom was all gold and cream. A broad cream-colored Louis Seize bed with a brocade coverlet, fine chairs, and a black lacquer Louis Quinze dresser with gilt *chinoiseries* and bronze shoes. For a moment I forgot my sticky feeling. The dresser was magnificent. Standing by itself some distance from the wall, it spoke with the authority of a true work of art.

"Here," I said. "Here and nowhere else. Over the dresser."

Mrs. Whymper said nothing. She turned to me with a veiled, almost absent look. "Don't you agree?" I asked, holding the little Renoir over the dresser.

Still looking at me, she smiled. "I need a chair to stand on," I said.

"Take one."

"But these are Louis Seize!"

Still the same smile. "Think nothing of it."

I tested one of the chairs, and it didn't seem to wobble. Cautiously I climbed up and took measurements. Behind me not a sound. When I had found the right spot, I held the hook in place with my left hand. Before hammering I looked around. Mrs. Whymper was still standing there, holding a cigarette and gazing at me with a dreamy smile that made me feel very uncomfortable. I hammered in the nail. The hook held. I took the picture, which I had set down on the dresser, and hung it. Then I climbed down and put the chair back where it had been. Mrs. Whymper hadn't stirred from the spot.

"All right?" I asked.

She nodded. I followed her to the stairs with a sigh of relief. She went back to the drawing room and picked up the pitcher. "One for the road?" she asked.

"With pleasure," I said, determined to announce after the second drink that I was late for a funeral. It wasn't necessary. Mrs. Whymper continued to look at me without seeming to see me. There was a faint smile on her face, and, as a confirmed masochist, I suspected that she was inwardly laughing at me. "The check hasn't been made out yet," she said. "Won't you come and pick it up in a day or two?"

"Certainly. I'll give you a ring first."

"There's no need to. I'm always home at five. And thank you for the Martini recipe."

My head was in a whirl as I stepped out into the hot street. I had thought this woman was making a fool of herself, and she had only been making a fool of me. She had put on that languid look for the sole purpose of laughing at my discomfiture. Oh well, I consoled myself, I wouldn't have to go again; Silvers would insist on picking up the check, for fear of letting me in on his prices.

"No car?" I asked Natasha.

"No car, no driver, no vodka, and no courage. It's too hot. This hotel ought to put in air conditioning."

"But we've got the makings of Moscow mules. Root beer, limes, vodka, and ice."

She looked at me affectionately. "You shopped for all that?"

"Certainly. And I've already got two Martinis under my belt."

She laughed. "At Mrs. Whymper's?"

"Right. How did you know?"

"She's famous."

"For what? Her Martinis?"

"For the Martinis, too."

"She's an old lush. I'm amazed that it all went off so smoothly."

"Has she paid?"

"Not yet," I said with alarm. "Why? Do you think she'll return the picture?"

"I doubt it. She's too fond of young men."

"What?"

"She's taken a shine to you."

"Natasha," I said, "are you serious? Were you trying to match me up with that old booze hound?"

She laughed. "Forget it," she said. "Give me a Moscow mule."

"Not a drop. Answer me first."

"Did you like her?"

I stared at her.

"Ha!" she said. "She likes young men and she likes you. Has she invited you to one of her parties?"

"Not yet. So far she's only asked me to pick up the check," I said angrily. "But maybe she will."

"She will, all right." Natasha was watching me. "And she'll invite me, too."

"Are you so sure? Or have you gone through this routine before? Should she have assaulted me?"

"No," said Natasha dryly. "Give me some vodka."

"Why not a vodka Martini?"

"Because I don't drink Martinis. Any more questions?"

"Several. I'm not used to being palmed off as a gigolo." The vodka was in my face before I saw her throw it. It was dripping down my chin. Livid and wide-eyed, she reached for the bottle. I was quicker. I grabbed it, made sure the cork was secure, and tossed it onto the nearest plush sofa, out of her reach. She made a leap, but I held her fast. Imprisoning her two hands in one of mine, I pushed her into a corner and tugged at her skirt. "Don't touch me," she hissed. "I'm not only going to touch you, you she-devil, I'm going to fuck you on the spot." She spat in my face and kicked me. I forced her backward. Struggling to free herself, she stumbled and fell. I pushed her down on the sofa, thrust my knee between her legs, and pulled up her skirt. "Let me go, you fool," she whispered in a high, strange voice, "let me go or I'll scream." "Scream away," I snarled. "You she-devil, you're going to get fucked." "Somebody's coming. Can't you see somebody's coming? Let me go, you beast, you monster, let me . . ."

She lay stiff on the sofa, arching her back to keep me at a distance. I felt the hard flesh of her legs against mine. She had nothing on under her skirt, and I felt the skin of her belly. I pushed her away and tore open my fly. Her face was close to mine, and I could see her staring eyes. "Let me go," she whispered. "Not here, not here, let me go, not here . . . not here . . ."

"Where else, you damn bitch," I snarled. "Take your hand away or I'll pull it off. . . ."

"Not here, not here," she whispered in the same high, strange voice.

"Where else, you . . . you . . ."

"In your room, not here, in your room . . ."

"So you can run away and have a good laugh."

"I won't run away, I won't run away, but not here. I promise I won't run away, dearest, but not here, dearest. . . ."

"What?"

"Let me go. I promise, I won't run away, but let me go. Somebody's coming. . . ."

I let her go. I stood up. I expected her to push me aside and run. She didn't. She pulled down her skirt. "Put that away," she whispered. "What?" "That!" I put it away. I watched her. Maybe she'd run for it, but I could still stop her. "Come along," she said. "Where to?" "Your room." I followed her, then passed her and went ahead, first hurrying, then more cautiously. The squeaky steps, the green runner, the THINK! sign, the second flight of stairs to the third floor, where my room was. I stopped at the door. "You can go away if you like," I said. "Come on in," she said. I followed her and closed the door. I didn't lock it. I felt a sudden letdown; I leaned against the wall with the sinking feeling you get in a descending express elevator. I steadied myself against the wall.

I saw Natasha lying on the bed. "Come on," she said.

"I can't."

"What do you mean?"

"I can't. Those damn stairs."

"What have the stairs got to do with it?"

"I don't know. I can't, that's all. Throw me out if you want to."

"Out of your own room?"

"Then laugh at me."

"Why should I laugh?"

"I don't know. It's traditional for women to laugh when this happens."

"It never happened to me."

"All the more reason to laugh."

"No," said Natasha.

"Why don't you go away?"

"Do you want me to?"

"No."

She hadn't moved. Now she propped her head on her arm and looked at me. "I feel lousy," I said.

"I feel fine," she said.

"It was your calling me 'dearest,' " I said. "That's what murdered me."

"I thought it was the stairs."

"No, it was your wanting to all of a sudden."

"Didn't you want me to want to?"

"Don't try to get me mixed up."

"Where's the bathroom?" she asked.

"Outside. Three doors down."

She stood up slowly, ran her hand through her hair, and went to the door. She grazed me in passing. I let go of the wall and reached for her. She tried to break away. I felt the touch of her body as keenly as if she had been naked. In that moment I recovered. I held her fast. "But you don't want me," she whispered, averting her face and holding her elbows close to her body. I picked her up and carried her back to the bed. She was heavier than I had thought. "I want you," I said. "I want you and nothing but you, I want you more than myself, I want to be inside you, all of me inside you." My face was directly over hers. Her eyes were very brilliant and rigid. I felt her breasts and I felt myself going into her, I felt it in my neck and hands and member. "Then take me," she hissed, her eyes still open. "Take me and crush me and crash through me, break me to pieces, do it, do it, deeper, deeper, pierce me, fuck me, the fountain is gushing, my ears are full of it, I'm coming, I'm bursting, the rain, the rain, the swishing of the rain . . ." Her voice dwindled to an incomprehensible, disjointed murmur, and then died away altogether.

She opened her eyes, stretched, mumbled something, then closed them again. "Has it rained?" she asked.

I burst out laughing. "Not yet. Maybe tonight."

"It's cooler. Where did you say the bathroom was?"

"Three doors down."

"Can I use your bathrobe?"

I gave it to her. Slowly and deliberately, without looking at me, she took everything off but her shoes. She showed no sign of embarrassment. She wasn't as thin as I had thought. "You're beautiful," I said.

She looked up. "Not too fat?"

"Good God, no."

"That's lucky," she said. "Then there's hope for our future. Because I like to eat and in my job I'm not allowed to be fat."

"We'll go out to dinner later on. You can eat as much as you like—mountains of hors d'oeuvres, roast goose, and a nice gooey dessert."

She took my soap and her handbag, saluted in the doorway, and went out. I lay still, thinking of nothing. I, too, had the feeling that rain had fallen. I knew it wasn't true, but I nevertheless went to the window and looked out. A wave of sultry garbage-scented air rose from the court. It had rained only in our room. I lay down again and stared at the bare light bulb that hung from the ceiling. Natasha came back. "I went into the wrong room," she said.

"Was anybody in it?"

"No. It was dark. Don't the people lock their doors here?"

"Some of them don't. They have nothing worth stealing."

She smelled of soap and cologne. "Mrs. Whymper likes young men," she said, "but that's as far as it goes. She likes to talk with them, that's all. Can't you get that into your thick head?"

"Yes," I said, not quite convinced.

Natasha looked into the tarnished mirror over the washbasin and brushed her hair in the bleak light. "Her husband died of syphilis," she added. "He probably infected her."

"Besides, she has cancer and athlete's foot and bathes in Martinis," I countered.

She laughed. "You don't believe me. Why should you?"

I stood up, took the brush out of her hand, and kissed her. "What would you think," I asked, "if I told you that it makes me tremble to touch you?"

"It didn't always look that way."

"Never mind. That's how it is now."

She pressed close to me. "I'd kill you if it weren't," she said.

I slipped the bathrobe off her and let it fall to the ground. "You have the longest legs I've ever seen," I said, and turned out the light. I put my arm around her and groped my way to the bed. She took my hands and pressed them to her breasts. In the darkness I could see nothing but her pale skin and the black hollows of her mouth and eyes. "Slowly," she whispered. "I want to come very slowly."

We held each other close and felt the dark wave rising and surging over us. Afterward we lay still, breathing gently and feeling the lesser waves ebb within us until we could no longer distinguish them from our breath.

Natasha came to life first. "Got a cigarette?"

"Yes." Her face was serene and innocent in the glow of the match. "Would you like something to drink?" I asked.

The motion of her cigarette told me that she was nodding. "But no vodka."

"I haven't got a refrigerator; everything is warm. But I can get something downstairs."

"Can't someone bring it up?"

"There's only Melikov."

I heard Natasha laugh in the darkness. "He'll see us anyway when we go down," she said.

"But then we'll have some clothes on," I said.

Natasha kissed me. "All right," she said. "We'll get dressed. I'm hungry anyway. Let's go to the King of the Sea."

"Again? Wouldn't you rather go somewhere else?"

"Have you got your commission for the Whymper sale?"

"Not yet."

"Then we'll go to the King of the Sea."

She jumped out of bed and switched on the light. She crossed the room naked and picked up my bathrobe. "Three doors down," I said.

"Those are the things one never forgets."

I got up and dressed. Then I sat down on the bed and waited for her to come back.

XVII

"Actually," said Silvers, "I'm a public benefactor." He lit a cigarette and looked at me contentedly.

We were expecting Mr. and Mrs. Lasky. Lasky was a fresh-baked millionaire. "The man is a vulgarian," Silvers explained. "By selling him pictures I shall be transforming him into a member of polite society." He stubbed out his cigarette and looked at his watch. "He'll be here in fifteen minutes. This is our ploy. You come in with two pictures, anything you please, and I ask you for the Sisley. You bring it in and put it down with its face to the wall. Then you come over and whisper something in my ear. I don't understand you and tell you to speak more plainly. You whisper—audibly this time—that the Sisley is being reserved for Mr. Rockefeller. Okay?"

"Okay!"

It worked. "What are you whispering for?" Silvers growled at me. "We have no secrets." I said my piece. "Wasn't that the Monet?" he said. "You must be mistaken. It's the Monet he reserved."

"I beg your pardon, Mr. Silvers, but I'm afraid you've got it wrong. I made a note of it. Here . . ." I pulled out a little notebook and showed him.

"He's right," said Silvers. "I'm afraid there's nothing we can do about it. Reserved is reserved."

Mr. Lasky was a frail little man in a blue suit and brown shoes. A few long strands of hair had been carefully plastered over his bald crown. Mrs. Lasky was a head taller and twice as broad. It looked to me as if she might gobble him up any minute.

I stood there for a moment in indecision, holding the picture in one hand so that part of it could be seen upside down. When I turned around, Mrs. Lasky bit. "Couldn't we look at it?" she asked in a hoarse, squeaky voice. "Or is that reserved, too?"

Silvers turned on his charm. "Why, of course, madam. I beg

your pardon. Why don't you put the picture down, Monsieur Ross," he snarled at me in atrocious French. *"Allez, vite, vite!"*

With a display of embarrassment I set the picture on one of the easels. Then I disappeared into the storeroom, which still reminded me of Brussels, and immersed myself in a monograph on Delacroix, listening occasionally to the conversation next door. I bet on Mrs. Lasky. She looked like the kind of woman who always thinks she is under attack and doesn't take it lying down. Her battle, I gathered, was with the old-established socialites, who looked down on the Laskys as parvenus. She was determined to gain admittance to their ranks, so as to be able to treat other newcomers with equal scorn. I closed my book and picked up a small Manet still life, a peony in a water glass.

I heard sounds of departure next door. Carefully I put the wonderful little painting back on its rack. The afternoon heat, which had retreated before the dewdrops on the white peony and the shimmering water in the glass, returned. Suddenly a profound joy rose up in me; for a moment the past and present, the cellar in Brussels and the room where I was sitting, receded, and all that remained was the feeling that I was still alive. For an instant the wall of obligations that hemmed in my life fell away, as the walls of Jericho had fallen before the trumpets of the chosen people, and I was as free as a bird, with a freedom that took my breath away for it opened up to me the possibility of a life whose existence I had never so much as suspected.

Then Silvers was standing there, shrouded in the fragrance of his Partagas. "Would you care for a cigar?" he asked genially.

I declined. I was suspicious of such generosity from people who owed me money. In my experience, they tend to think that a good cigar cancels out their debt. What I wanted of Silvers was not a cigar but my commission for the sale to Mrs. Whymper.

"The Laskys bit," said the public benefactor. "I told them Rockefeller had a week's option, but that he'd left town on business and had probably forgotten all about it. Mrs. Lasky was out of her mind at the thought of snatching something away from him."

"The old shell game," I said. "What always amazes me is that these cheap tricks work."

"Why shouldn't they?"

"Because it's hard to see how these bandits, who certainly haven't piled up a fortune by being guileless, can fall for such stuff."

"It's very simple. In their own business it wouldn't take; they'd laugh at me. But in the art world they're like sharks in fresh water; it's not their element. It undermines their self-assurance and muddles their wits. And when they bring their social-climbing wives, they're really sunk."

"I've got to go to the photographer's," said Natasha. "Come along with me. It won't be long."

"How long?"

"An hour. Not much more. Why? Does it bore you?"

"Not at all. I only wanted to know if we should eat before or after."

"After. Then we'll have plenty of time. Is eating so important? Or have you already got the commission for Mrs. Whymper?"

"Not yet. But I've got ten dollars from the Lowy brothers for a tip. I'm dying to blow it with you."

She looked at me tenderly. "Don't worry, we'll blow it. To-night."

It was cool at the photographer's; the windows were closed and the air conditioning was working. It was like sitting in a submarine. The others didn't seem to notice; they were used to it. "It gets even hotter in August," said Nicky the photographer by way of consolation.

The spotlights were turned on. The only models were Natasha and the brunette. The pale, dark-haired specialist in Lyons silks remembered me. "The war is doing all right," he said with a weary attempt at enthusiasm. "It'll be over in a year."

"You think so?"

"I've had inside dope from Europe."

"Really?"

In the unreal white light I was ready to believe that this man really knew more than anyone else. I took a deep breath. I knew the war was going badly for the Germans, but I could no more conceive of peace than I could of death; it was outside my frame of reference.

"Really," he said. "Take my word for it. Next year we'll be importing silks from Lyons again."

The effect of this remark on me was magical: suddenly a jumble of objects and sounds came tumbling into the timeless vacuum of my refugee world, ushered in by a bolt of Lyons silk; then clocks began to tick and bells to peal. A film that had stopped dead began to move, faster and faster, backward and forward in an incomprehensible sequence. I realized that in spite of all the encouraging news in the papers I had never seriously believed that the war could end. But now, precisely because of his idiocy, the opinion of this pale little man, to whom the end of the war meant neither more nor less than the possibility of importing silk from Lyons, had carried more weight with me than that of half a dozen field marshals.

Natasha appeared in a tight-fitting white evening dress that left one shoulder bare, long white gloves, and the Empress Eugénie's tiara. My heart turned over. Everything struck me at once: the contrast between the Natasha of the night before and this unreal, starkly illumined apparition with the cool bare shoulder in this artificially cooled room; the tumult into which the thought of the war's end had thrown me, and even the tiara in Natasha's hair that gleamed like the crown of the Statue of Liberty. "Lyons silk," said the pale man beside me. "Our last bolt."

"Really?"

He nodded. "But next year we'll have all we need."

I looked at Natasha. She was standing very still in the white light, a charming slender copy, I thought, of the bronze giantess holding out her torch over the Atlantic, equally unafraid, but not, like the statue, a mixture of Brünhilde and a resolute French market woman, but, rather, a Diana emerging from the forest, too dangerous for all her charm, ready to fight in defense of her freedom.

"How do you like the Rolls?" asked a man who had sat down beside me.

I looked around. "Are you the owner?"

He nodded. He was a tall, dark man, younger than I had imagined. "Fraser," he said. "I was hoping to meet you a few days ago."

"I'm sorry," I said. "I was busy."

"Let's make up for it tonight. I've already spoken to Natasha. We're going to Lüchow's. You know the place?"

"No," I said in surprise. I had been looking forward to the King of the Sea and, above all, to being alone with her. But if Natasha had accepted, I couldn't very well say no without being rude. Of course I wasn't sure she had accepted, but . . .

"Glad to have you with us," he said. "See you later."

That seemed to make it a joint invitation, from him and Natasha.

I found Natasha packing up her things.

"I hear we're going to Lüchow's," I said. I was pretty well steamed up.

"Yes, of course. That's what you wanted, wasn't it?"

"What I wanted? I wanted to blow in my ten dollars with you at the King of the Sea. But then you accepted this invitation from Mr. Rolls-Royce."

"Nothing of the kind. He said he'd consulted you."

"He did, but only after he'd asked you."

She laughed. "What an operator!"

I stood open-mouthed. I didn't know whether to believe her or not. If she was telling the truth, I had fallen for the oldest dodge in the world, as though my life with Silvers had taught me nothing. But somehow Fraser didn't seem like that kind of a man.

"Nothing we can do about it now," said Natasha. "We'll have our party tomorrow."

The Rolls was waiting outside. The heat was sickening after the cool studio. "I'll have the car air-conditioned next year," said Fraser. "The machines are all ready, but they're not on the market yet. You know how it is—war priorities."

"The war will be over next summer," I said.

"You think so?" said Fraser. "In that case you know more than Eisenhower. Vodka?" He opened the famous refrigerator.

"No, thanks," I said glumly. "It's really too hot."

It wouldn't have surprised me to hear that Eisenhower would not have thought it too hot. "It's Polish vodka," said Fraser instead.

I didn't tell him that I was well aware of it. "I'll have one, Jack," said Natasha.

"Good!"

Luckily it wasn't far to Lüchow's. I prepared to be tormented by Natasha as well as Fraser, of whom I had by now developed a low opinion. To my astonishment, Lüchow's proved to be a German restaurant.

"How about roast venison with *Kronsbeeren?*" Fraser suggested. "And some of those little potato pancakes."

"You have *Kronsbeeren* in America?"

"Something of the sort. Cranberries. But Lüchow's still has the genuine preserves from Germany. They are called *Preiselbeeren* in Bavaria, aren't they?"

"I think so," I said. "I haven't been there in a long time. They've changed a good many things. Maybe *Preiselbeeren* didn't sound Aryan enough for them."

"What do we drink, Jack?" asked Natasha.

"Whatever you like. Maybe Mr. Ross would like beer? Or Rhine wine. They still have some."

"Beer wouldn't be bad," I said. "It goes with the atmosphere here. Or strawberry punch, if they've got some."

"With the meat course?" Natasha asked. "Isn't it kind of dessert-ish?"

"We're in America now," I said. "Here they even drink coffee with the meat course."

She gave me a quick amused glance. "Or ice water," she said.

"Or Coca-Cola."

"Maybe they do have strawberry punch," said Fraser, without batting an eyelash. "May punch they call it, I think. Would you like some?"

"I've never tasted it," I said. "And I have no desire to. I'm not all that homesick. Beer will do. What I'd really like is a glass of Bordeaux, but I suppose they wouldn't have that."

"But they do. They do."

Fraser conferred with the waiter. I looked around. The place was a cross between a Bavarian beer cellar and a Rhenish wine tavern, with a shot of Haus Vaterland thrown in. It was jam-packed. A small band was playing dinner music and folk songs. I had a feeling that Fraser hadn't chosen Lüchow's at random. Sheer dignity would oblige me to defend some of the more harmless aspects of my detested fatherland against this American, and in so doing I would expose myself as just another German. A none-too-subtle way of killing off a rival.

"How about Matjes herring to begin with?" Fraser asked. "It's really good here. With a drop of genuine Steinhäger."

"Sounds wonderful," I said. "Unfortunately, I can't have it. Doctor's orders."

As I expected, Natasha joined the conspiracy against me and ordered herring with beet salad, another German specialty. The band played sentimental slop from the banks of the Rhine. What amazed me about the place was that a good many of the guests seemed to take the old-country atmosphere seriously and think it poetic. Soldiers in uniform were happily joining in the German songs. Fraser didn't sing, but only beat time with his knife and watched me. I decided to get the jump on him when it came time for dessert by ordering apple pie and cheese, an American monstrosity, before he could offer me *rote Grütze,* a loathsome German fruit pudding.

The Bordeaux pacified me, and I began to consider Fraser with benign irony. He asked if there was anything he could do to help me, thereby presenting himself in the flattering posture of a friendly god from Washington who was not above putting himself out for an insignificant refugee. I replied with fulsome praises of America and assured him that everything was all right. Aside from not wanting to be helped by Fraser, I was none too eager for him to get interested in my papers. I didn't trust him.

The roast venison was excellent and so were the potato pancakes. Now I understood why the place was so crowded. I knew my sense of humor was unequal to the situation and hated myself for it. Natasha didn't seem to notice anything. She ordered the German fruit pudding. I wouldn't have been surprised if she had asked to run up to Eighty-sixth Street after dinner for coffee and cake at the Café Hindenburg. Fraser kept making remarks with no other point than to show that Natasha had gone out with him before. But what irked me most was his lofty way of implying that I owed him personally a debt of gratitude for the privilege of staying in his country. I was grateful to the government—not to Fraser, who hadn't done a thing for me.

"How about a nightcap at El Morocco?"

That was all I needed! I rather expected Natasha to say yes; she liked El Morocco. But she didn't. "I'm tired, Jack," she said. "I've had a hard day."

We stepped out into the torrid night. "Shall we walk?" I asked Natasha.

"Of course not," said Fraser. "I'll take you home."

Just what I expected. He would drop me off and then persuade Natasha to go on with him—to El Morocco or his apartment. How did I know? And what business was it of mine? Had I any rights over Natasha? If anyone had, maybe it was Fraser.

"Won't you come, too?" Fraser asked me in a tone that seemed none too friendly.

"I live in the neighborhood. I can walk," I said reluctantly. It seemed the only way of avoiding further humiliation.

"Nonsense," said Natasha. "You can't walk in this heat. Let us off at my place, Jack. From there he has only a few steps."

"Very well."

Jack made no attempt to let me off first. He was smart enough to know that Natasha wouldn't stand for it. Outside Natasha's house he bade us a friendly good-by. "It's been very nice. We'll have to do it again soon."

"Many thanks. With pleasure."

Not in a thousand years, I thought, and looked on as Fraser kissed Natasha on the cheek. "Good night, Jack," she said. "I'm sorry I can't come along. I'm just too tired."

"Another time. Good night, darling."

That was his parting shot. Darling, I thought: in America that meant everything and nothing. You said darling to a telephone operator, and you said it to the woman you couldn't live without. Fraser had dropped a little time bomb in leaving.

We stood face to face. I knew that all was lost if I showed any anger now. "A delightful fellow," I said. "Are you really so tired, Natasha?"

She nodded. "Yes, really. It was boring, and Fraser's a louse."

"I didn't think so. It was charming of him to pick a German restaurant on my account. You seldom find such delicacy."

Natasha looked at me. "Darling," she said, and the word gave me a pang like a sudden toothache, "you don't have to be a gentle-man. I've often been terribly bored by gentlemen."

"This evening, for instance?"

"This evening especially. Why on earth did you accept that stupid invitation?"

"Me?"

"Yes, you. I suppose you're going to say it was my fault."

I had been on the verge of saying just that.

"It was all my fault," I said, boiling inwardly. "Can you ever forgive such an idiot?"

She looked at me suspiciously. "Do you really mean that? Or are you just pretending?"

"Both, Natasha."

"Both?"

"What else would you expect? I'm all mixed up and I act like an idiot because I worship you."

"I haven't noticed very much of that."

"It doesn't have to be noticeable. Visible adoration is like a slob-bering bulldog. My adoration takes the form of distraction, unrea-soning hate, and plain obstinacy. You've turned me all topsy-turvy."

Her expression changed. "You poor thing," she said. "I can't take you up to my place. The lady next door would faint. And when she came to, she'd listen at the door."

I'd have given anything to be with her, and yet I was suddenly glad it was impossible. I held her by the shoulders. "We have so much time," she said. "Tomorrow, the day after, and the day after, weeks and months, and yet with this one botched evening we feel that we've lost a lifetime."

"As far as I'm concerned," I said, "you're still wearing that won-derful tiara. Again, I mean. Not so much at Lüchow's. Then it was lusterless lead."

She laughed. "Did you think I was unbearable?"

"Yes."

"Same here. We'll never do that kind of thing again. We're too close to hate."

"Isn't it always like that?"

"Yes, thank God. What a syrupy life it would be otherwise!"

It seemed to me that the world could do nicely with a bit more syrup, but I didn't say so. "Honey is better," I said. "You smell like honey. Today you've been good and bad and good again, and you smell like honey."

She pulled me into the doorway. "Kiss me," she murmured. "And love me. I need plenty of love. And now beat it. Beat it or I'll rip my dress off."

"Go ahead. Nobody'll see us here."

She shut the door behind me. I walked slowly through the sultry night to the subway station. The train came roaring out of the darkness. The car was almost empty. An elderly woman was sitting in one corner. Obliquely across from her sat a man. I settled myself in the middle of the car.

"You pig!" the woman suddenly screamed. "You dirty pig!"

She stood up and rushed over to me. "You saw it! You're a witness! He can't get away with it. You're my witness!"

"Witness? To what?"

"Don't play dumb! You saw the stinker. Exhibiting his slimy no-good prick!"

"What!"

"You're my witness. I'm going to have him arrested. Police! Police!"

The man arose and came over to us slowly and deliberately. "My dear lady, you're dreaming. You fell asleep and you dreamed it. You better be careful who you insult or I'll call the police."

"What's that? You bastard!"

"Take a good look at me. What do you see? A happily married man. A family man. The police would laugh at you."

"I've got a witness." And, turning to me like a fighting fury, "You're my witness!"

"Me?"

I had been in America long enough to know that the best way to keep healthy is to see nothing. Then you won't be shot by gangsters or arrested as an accomplice. It's cowardly, but in my situation I couldn't afford much courage. Besides, I really hadn't seen anything.

"You see?" the man gloated, revealing a set of bad teeth. "It's hysteria. The police know all about it. They don't think much of

146

hysterical women. Just watch your step or they'll pull you in for defamation of character and fine you. Can you afford it? I've a good mind to call the police myself. This gentleman hasn't seen a thing; he's not your witness, he's mine. He can testify that you made it all up!" He spoke fast, making chattering sounds like an angry squirrel.

The woman moved her lips but no words came out. "Behind his paper," she said finally. "Pretended to be reading the paper, the stinker! You must have seen him!"

"I can't help you," I said. "I didn't see a thing."

The man grinned. "There you have it, lady. Just watch your step. You're lucky I'm a good-natured man."

The woman moved her lips again as though chewing inaudible words. "You're both stinkers!" she said finally.

The train pulled into a deserted station. The doors opened. The woman spat and got out. The man was still making chattering sounds. "Now you can fuck each other!" the woman called out to us. The automatic doors closed. The man mopped his forehead with a dirty handkerchief. "Women, women!" he muttered. Then he turned to me. "Thank you, sir."

"Shut up!" I said.

XVIII

Kahn asked me to come along. "It's a raid," he explained. "The victim is a certain Hirsch."

"The one who swindled Dr. Gräfenheim?"

"That's the man," said Kahn grimly. "The one who claims he never received anything from Gräfenheim. That's why it's a raid. If Gräfenheim had a receipt, a lawyer could handle it. Now he's run out of money. We've got to help him or he'll have to stop studying. He wrote to Hirsch and received no answer. He even called once in person. Hirsch threatened to have him prosecuted for blackmail if he ever came back."

"How do you know all this?"

"From Betty."

"Does Gräfenheim know of your plan?"

Kahn bared his teeth. "No," he said, laughing. "He'd be outside Hirsch's door, barring the way. He's scared to death."

"Does Hirsch know we're coming?"

Kahn nodded. "I've prepared him. Two phone calls."

"He'll throw us out. Or he won't be home."

Kahn bared his teeth again. You might have called it a laugh, but I wouldn't have cared to be up against him. The whole man had changed. He walked faster, with longer steps, and his face had grown tense. That's how he must have looked in France, I thought.

"He'll be home."

"With his lawyer, to threaten *us* with a blackmail suit."

"I don't think so," said Kahn, and stopped still. "This is where the stinker lives. Pretty nice, eh?"

It was an apartment house on Fifty-fourth Street. Red carpets, steel engravings on the walls, doorman dressed like an admiral, paneled elevator. "Fifteenth floor," said Kahn. "Hirsch."

We shot upward. "I don't think he'll have a lawyer with him," said Kahn. "I threatened him with new documents. Since he knows what he's done, he'll want to see them; he's not an American citizen yet, and there must still be a bit of the good old refugee's fear in him. He'll want to know what's cooking before taking a lawyer into his confidence."

He rang. A maid opened and showed us into a drawing room furnished with copies of Louis Quinze chairs, some of them gilded. "Mr. Hirsch will be with you in a moment."

Mr. Hirsch seemed to be in his fifties, a stout man of medium height. A German shepherd dog followed at his heels. Kahn smiled at the sight. "The last time I saw one of those, Herr Hirsch, it was with the Gestapo. They were used for man hunts."

"Quiet, Harro!" Hirsch stroked the dog's head. "You wished to speak to me. You didn't tell me there would be two of you. I haven't got much time."

"This is Mr. Ross. I won't keep you very long, Herr Hirsch. We've come in behalf of Dr. Gräfenheim. He's sick, he has no money, and he's going to have to drop his studies. You know him, I believe?"

No answer. Hirsch stroked the dog, who growled softly.

"You know him, all right," said Kahn. "I don't know whether you know me. There are lots of Kahns, just as there are lots of Hirsches. I'm Gestapo Kahn. Maybe you've heard of me. I spent a good deal of my time in France duping the Gestapo. As you can imagine, Herr Hirsch, no kid gloves were worn on either side. What I'm getting at is that the protection of a German shepherd would have made me laugh. It still makes me laugh. Before your animal so much as touched me, Herr Hirsch, he'd be dead. And you, too, in all likelihood. But we're not interested in hurting either of you. We've come to collect money for Dr. Gräfenheim. I assume that you wish to help him. How much are you prepared to contribute?"

Hirsch stared at Kahn. "Why should I?"

"For a number of reasons. One is known as compassion."

Hirsch seemed to be chewing his cud for a time. Then he drew a brown alligator billfold from his pocket and took out two bills. "Here's twenty dollars. I can't give you any more. Too many people come to me with such troubles. If a hundred refugees give you comparable sums, you'll have enough to see Dr. Gräfenheim through his studies."

I expected Kahn to throw the money back at him, but he took it and put it in his pocket. "Very well, Herr Hirsch," he said. "Now all we need from you is another nine hundred and eighty dollars. That's about what Dr. Gräfenheim needs if he lives very modestly, without smoking or drinking."

"You're joking. I'm sorry, I have no time. . . ."

"Don't say that, Herr Hirsch. You have plenty of time. And don't tell me your lawyer is sitting in the next room, because he isn't. I believe you'll be interested in what I have to tell you. You're not an American citizen yet but hope to become one next year. You can't afford any black marks against you. The United States authorities are very particular about these things. My friend Ross here is a well-known journalist. We would like to protect you from such a possibility."

"What would you say to my notifying the police?" Hirsch asked.

"I wouldn't advise it. We'd simply hand our documents over to them."

"Documents. Blackmail is a very serious offense in this country. And now get out!"

Kahn sat down in one of the gilt chairs. "You thought you were being very clever, Hirsch," he said in a changed tone. "You weren't. You should have given Gräfenheim his money. Here in my pocket I have a petition to the immigration authorities signed by a hundred refugees requesting that you be refused American citizenship. Here is another petition to the same effect, signed by six persons and attesting your collaboration with the Gestapo in Germany; it tells why you were able to take more money out of Germany than other refugees and even gives the name of the Nazi who brought your money to Switzerland for you. Further, I have here a newspaper clipping from Lyons, telling the story of the Jew Hirsch who under questioning by the Gestapo revealed the names of two fugitives who were both shot immediately afterward. Don't protest, Herr Hirsch. It may not have been you, but I'm ready to say it was."

"What?"

"I'll testify that it was you. Everybody here knows what I did in France. They'll believe me sooner than you."

Hirsch stood open-mouthed. "You'd give false evidence?"

"False perhaps from the standpoint of civil law, but sanctioned by Biblical law, the law of our forefathers, an eye for an eye and a tooth for a tooth. You ruined Gräfenheim; we'll ruin you. It makes no difference to us whether it's true or not. I've told you that I learned something from my experience with the Nazis."

"And you claim to be a Jew?"

"Yes, I have that much in common with you, I'm ashamed to say."

"And you'd be willing to persecute a Jew?"

For a moment Kahn was flabbergasted. "Yes," he said finally. "I told you that I've learned from the Gestapo."

"The American police . . ."

"We've learned from the American police, too," Kahn interrupted. "But we don't even need the police. The papers in my pocket are enough to take care of you. I don't insist on sending you to jail. An internment camp will be good enough."

Hirsch raised his hand. "It will take a better man than you to do that, Herr Kahn. And better proofs than your false accusations."

"Think so?" said Kahn. "In wartime? For an alleged refugee born in Germany? They don't have to convict you of anything to intern you. Suspicion is regarded as reason enough. And even if they don't, what about your citizenship? When in doubt, they turn you down."

Hirsch clutched at his dog's collar. "What about you?" he said in an undertone. "Suppose they get wind of this little incident. Where would you stand? Blackmail, false accusations . . ."

"I know all that," said Kahn, "and I couldn't care less. You're a scoundrel with dreams of respectability. I don't give a damn about respectability, or even about the comfort and security that mean so much to people like you. Even in France I didn't care. Do you think I could have done what I did if I cared? In short, I'm a desperado. And get this straight, Hirsch, if you do make trouble for me in any way, I won't go to the police. I'll take care of you myself. And it won't be the first time. But why all these dramatics? I'm not out for your blood. I'm only asking you to pay back a small part of the money you owe."

Again Hirsch seemed to be chewing silently. "I haven't any money here," he said finally.

"I'll take a check."

Hirsch suddenly released the dog. "Go lie down, Harro!" He opened a door, and the dog disappeared. Hirsch closed the door behind him.

"You know I can't give you a check," said Hirsch. "I'll pay cash."

I hadn't expected him to give in so quickly. Maybe Kahn had been right: the anonymous terror common to refugees must have joined forces with Hirsch's guilty conscience to shatter his morale.

"I'll be back for the cash tomorrow," said Kahn.

"And the papers?"

"I'll destroy them tomorrow before your eyes."

"I'll only give you the money in exchange for the papers."

Kahn shook his head. "And let you know the names of all the people who are prepared to testify against you? Oh no!"

"But how do I know the papers are genuine?"

"Because I say so."

Hirsch chewed some more in silence. "All right," he said finally. "Tomorrow at the same time." Kahn stood up from his gilt chair.

Hirsch nodded. He was bathed in sweat. "My son is sick," he

whispered. "My only son! And you . . . you ought to be ashamed of yourself! I'm desperate, and you . . ."

"I hope your son will be well soon," said Kahn calmly. "Perhaps you ought to consult Dr. Gräfenheim."

Hirsch made no answer. There was hatred in his face, but also suffering. He seemed more stooped than before. Maybe he's superstitious, I thought. Maybe he thinks his son's illness was brought on by his betrayal of Gräfenheim, and that's why he gave in so easily. Strangely enough, I felt almost sorry for him.

"I'm not so sure his son is really sick," said Kahn in the elevator.

"He must be," I said. "A Jew doesn't tempt fate where members of his family are concerned."

Kahn gave me an amused look. "I bet he hasn't even got a son," he said.

We stepped out into the torrid street. "Do you expect any trouble with Hirsch tomorrow?" I asked.

"I don't think so. He's worried about his naturalization."

"Why did you take me along?" I asked. "I was only in the way. Without a witness he mightn't have been so cautious."

Kahn laughed. "No. Your exterior was a big help."

"Why?"

"Because you look like such a big wholesome goy. A real Aryan. Two Jews understand each other too well—they don't take each other quite seriously. But a big Aryan bruiser—that's something else again. I'm sure you scared Hirsch out of his wits."

I knew I didn't have much sense of humor, but for this kind of thing I had none at all. I felt as if he had emptied a chamber pot over my head.

Kahn was quite unaware of my thoughts. He strode through the glassy noonday heat with the resilient step of a hunter who had sighted game. "At last a break in the boredom," he said. "It was getting unbearable. I'm not used to all this security."

"Why don't you enlist?" I asked dryly.

"I've tried. You know they don't take us. We're 'enemy aliens.' "

"But you must be a special case. The people in Washington must know what you did in France."

"They know, all right. As far as they're concerned, it's just one more reason for not trusting me. They think I was probably a double agent. I wouldn't be surprised if they locked me up."

"Have you really got those signatures?"

"Of course not. That's why I asked for a thousand instead of the whole amount. This way Hirsch will think he got off easy."

"You mean he'll think it was good business?"

"Yes, my poor Ross," he answered in a tone of commiseration. "That's the kind of world it is."

"I wish we could drive out someplace where it's quiet," I said to Natasha. "To some little European village, or to a lake. Where we could stop sweating for a while."

"No car. Do you want me to call Fraser?"

"Certainly not."

"He wouldn't have to come along. He could lend us his car."

"No, I don't even want his car. I'd rather take the subway or a bus."

"Where to?"

"That's the question, where to? There seem to be twice as many people in this city in the summer."

"And it's so hot. Poor Ross!"

That irritated me. It was the second time that day I had been called "poor Ross." "Couldn't we go to the Cloisters? I've never been there. Have you?"

"Yes. But the museums are closed in the evening. Even for refugees."

"Sometimes I get pretty sick of being a refugee," I said with mounting irritation. "I've been one all day. First with Silvers, then with Kahn. Couldn't you and I try to be plain people?"

She laughed. "As soon as people stop having to worry about food and lodging, they stop being plain people, my dear Rousseau. Even with love, complications set in."

"Not if we take it the way we do."

"How do we take it?"

"Universally. Not individually."

"Good grief!" said Natasha.

"Like the sea. Not like a single wave. Isn't that the way you feel about it?"

"Me?"

"Yes, you. With so many boy friends."

"Do you think a drink of vodka would kill me?" she asked.

"No," I said. "Not even in this ghastly lounge. You look as cool as the Alpine snow."

Melikov was on duty. "Vodka?" he exclaimed. "In this heat?" But he produced a bottle and two glasses. "There's a storm in the air, and that makes it worse," he commented as I was walking away. "These damn fans only churn up the hot air."

"Before we start fighting," I suggested to Natasha, "let's decide where to go. We'll be able to fight much better in a cool place. I'll drop the European village and the lake. Besides, I've got money. Silvers has given me a bonus."

"How much?"

"Two fifty."

"Shabby," said Natasha. "It should have been five hundred."

"Nonsense. The part I didn't like was his saying he really didn't owe me anything because he'd known Mrs. Whymper all along. As though he were making me a present. That went against my grain."

Natasha put down her glass. "Would it always have gone against your grain?"

The question surprised me. "I don't know," I said. "Probably not. Why?"

She watched me closely. "I don't think you'd have minded a few weeks ago."

"Think so? I have no sense of humor. That must be it."

"Your sense of humor is all right. Maybe you haven't any today."

"Who has a sense of humor in such heat?"

"Fraser," said Natasha. "He bubbles over in this kind of weather."

Several thoughts came to me at once, but I was careful not to express them. "I thought he was very nice," I said instead. "I'm willing to believe that he bubbles over. He was very amusing the other evening."

"Give me two fingers more," said Natasha, laughing.

I poured the vodka in silence. "Won't you have some?" she asked.

"Why not? I've heard that liquor is as cooling as coffee in hot weather. Only the first glass heats you up. After that it dilates the blood vessels and makes you feel cool."

"There's a scientific explanation for everything," said Natasha. "But is it necessary?"

"No. But it responds to the noblest of human aspirations: the desire to know why."

"How German!"

"This seems to be my German day. I only hope it will be a short one."

"Short and universal. Not individual."

I looked up. "You're right, Natasha. That was tactless German nonsense. Forgive me."

She stood up and came close to me. I could feel that she had practically nothing on under her dress. "I worship you," I murmured.

"Where do you want to go?" she asked.

"I can't drag you up to my room. Too many people."

"Drag me to a cool restaurant."

"Good. I know a little French place on Third Avenue. The Bistro."

"Expensive?"

"Not for a man with two hundred and fifty dollars. Even if it was a present, it belongs to me."

Her eyes grew tender. "That's the way to talk, darling. To hell with morality."

I nodded. I had a feeling that I had narrowly escaped a wide range of perils.

Melikov had been right about the storm. When we left the restaurant, the wind was whipping up dust and papers, and flashes of lightning shot across the sky. "We'd better grab a taxi," I said.

"What for? The cabs stink of sweat. Let's walk."

"It's going to pour. You're not dressed for it."

"Who cares? I was going to wash my hair tonight anyway."

"But you'll be soaked through."

"It won't hurt this dress. It was too cold in the restaurant. Let's walk. If it gets bad, we can duck into a doorway. Oh, the wind! It's so exciting!"

We walked close to the house fronts. Great streaks of lightning seemed to shoot down from the tops of the skyscrapers, followed by claps of thunder that drowned out the sound of the traffic. Then came the raindrops, big dark spots scattered over the sidewalk, and a moment later the deluge.

Natasha held out her face into the rain. Her mouth was half open, and her eyes were closed. "Hold me tight," she said.

People scurried into doorways, and in an instant the sidewalks were deserted. The street was transformed into a dark frothing lake.

"My God!" cried Natasha. "You've got your new suit on."

"Too late," I said.

"I only thought of myself. I'm stark naked." She lifted up her skirt to the waist, revealing nothing but bare skin and her infinitesimal white panties. "But you! Your beautiful new suit!"

"Too late," I said. "Anyway, a little water won't hurt it. It'll just need pressing. So let's rejoice in the elements. How about a swim in the Plaza fountain?"

She laughed and pulled me into a doorway. "Come on. It's no good to get the lining wet. We can rejoice in the elements right here. Look at the lightning! And it's so blissfully cool! We're lucky our stomachs are full of good food and wine!"

How practical she is, for all her enthusiasm, I thought, and kissed her warm little face. We were standing between two shop windows; on one side, corsets for corpulent matrons quivered in the lightning flashes; on the other, tropical fish were swimming lazily about in the silky green light of their tanks. I had kept such fish in my childhood and recognized some of the varieties: the viviparous cyprinodonts, the guppies that sparkle like jewels, the king cichlids, the crescent-shaped, silver-and-black-striped scalares making their way like tall exotic sails through the forests of Vallisneria. There amid the phantasmagoric lightnings lay a bit of my childhood, unchanged by the intervening years and events. I held Natasha in my arms and felt her warmth; yet a part of me was far away, crouched over a forgotten spring that had long ceased to flow, harking to a past that entranced me all the more because it had grown so strange to me. Days spent in the woods, or on the lake, as dragonflies with quivering wings hovered motionless in mid-air; evenings in gardens amid the fragrance and freshness of the lilacs. All this passed before my eyes like swift silent film as I peered into the transparent gold and green of the little submarine universe, which to me meant supreme peace, though actually murder and cannibalism were just as prevalent here as anywhere else.

"What would you say if I had an ass like that?" asked Natasha. I turned around. She was looking into the window of the corset shop at a black dressmaker's dummy built like a Valkyrie and girded in an apparatus that looked like armor plate. "You have a magnificent ass," I said, "and you'll never need a corset, even if you're not one of those giraffes you see running around nowadays with buttocks like coffee beans and concave thighs. God bless you. You're the most beautiful *fausse maigre* in the world. God bless every pound of you."

She nodded happily. "Then I don't need to diet for your sake?"

"Never."

"It's almost stopped raining. Let's go." I turned back for a nostalgic glance at the fish. "Look at the monkeys," said Natasha, pointing into the interior of the shop. In a large cage two excited long-tailed monkeys were doing gymnastics.

"Those are real refugees," she said. "In a cage. You people haven't come to that yet."

"Is that what you think?"

Natasha looked at me. "I don't know anything about you," she answered. "And I don't want to know. It's boring for two people to tell each other the whole story of their lives." She cast a last glance at the Brünhilde corset. "Life passes so quickly. One of these days I'll be like that. Maybe I'll even join a women's club. Sometimes I wake up at night in a cold sweat. You, too?"

"Me, too."

"Really? You don't look it."

"Neither do you, Natasha."

"Let's get as much out of it as we can."

"Isn't that what we're doing?"

She pressed close to me. I could feel her from her legs to her shoulders. Her dress was like a bathing suit. Her hair hung down in strands, and her face was very pale.

"In a few days I'll have a different apartment," she murmured. "I'll be able to bring you in; we won't have to sit around in hotels and bars any more." She laughed. "And it's air conditioned."

"Are you moving?"

"No. It belongs to some friends who are going to Canada for the summer."

"Fraser?" I asked with foreboding.

"No, not Fraser." She laughed again. "Somebody you wouldn't mind."

A sprinkling of stars could be seen between the clouds. The asphalt glittered like black ice under the headlights of the passing cars. We passed the Lowy brothers' shop: two cloisonné roosters were standing on a Louis Philippe table which, I suspected, Lowy Senior would represent as Directoire, if not Louis Quinze or Seize.

The rain had stopped entirely when I left her outside her door. I walked back to the hotel, savoring the cool air and mulling over the events of the day. I had a sense of danger, but not from outside; no, this danger was inside me. It was as though unsuspectingly I had crossed a mysterious boundary line and now found myself in a region whose values and way of life were very different from those to which I was accustomed. Many things that had been indifferent to me had taken on a new importance. I had ceased to be a total outsider. What is happening to me, I asked myself. Can I be in love? I knew that even an outsider can fall in love, because, perhaps more than others, he is so desperately in need of love. But I also knew that in so doing he is risking his status as an outsider, and, for all the misery it entailed, that status meant a great deal to me.

XIX

"Betty's being operated on tomorrow," said Kahn over the phone. "Go and see her, will you? She's scared."

"Of course. What's the matter with her?"

"They're not sure. Gräfenheim and Ravic have examined her. Some kind of tumor. The operation will show whether it's benign or not. Ravic is in charge. He's an assistant at Mount Sinai Hospital now."

"Will he operate?"

"He'll be there. I don't know if he himself is allowed to operate yet. When will you go to see her?"

"At six, when I'm through here. Have you heard from Hirsch?"

"I've seen him. Everything's all right. Gräfenheim already has the money. It was harder for me to give it to him than to get it out of Hirsch. Decent people can be a pain; with crooks you know where you stand."

"Will you be at Betty's?"

"No. I've just been. I had to argue with Gräfenheim for a whole hour. He didn't want to accept his own money from that stinker. And he's on the ragged edge. Talk German to Betty. This is her German day. It's bad enough to be sick, she says, without having to talk English."

It was a warm, gray day. The sky was the color of white ashes. I found Betty sitting up in bed in a Chinese salmon-colored wrapper, no doubt described by the Brooklyn manufacturer as a mandarin coat.

"You're just in time to share my execution supper," said Betty. "Tomorrow the guillotine!"

"My goodness, Betty," said Gräfenheim. "It's a little routine examination. A precaution."

"The guillotine is the guillotine," said Betty, with forced merriment, "regardless of whether it cuts off your toenails or your head."

I looked around. There were about ten people, most of whom I knew. Ravic was sitting by the window, gazing out at the street. It was very hot, but the windows were closed. Betty was afraid that opening them would bring in still more heat. An electric fan was buzzing like a large tired fly. The door to the next room was open. The Koller twins brought in coffee and apple strudel. They had turned blond, and I didn't recognize them at first. They were wearing short, tight-fitting skirts and striped, short-sleeved cotton sweaters.

"Cute, aren't they?" Tannenbaum asked. "Look at those cunning rear ends!"

"Definitely," I said. "It must be pretty upsetting," I went on, "to get interested in a twin—especially if they look as much alike as these do."

"Double guarantee," said Tannenbaum, cutting into a piece of strudel. "If one dies, you can marry the other."

"That's a dismal thought." I glanced at Betty. Luckily, she hadn't heard. She was busy looking at some engravings of Berlin.

"I wasn't really thinking of marrying the Koller twins," I said. "To tell the truth, I wasn't even thinking of death."

Tannenbaum wagged his head. Its bald crown encased in shaggy black tufts suggested the rear end of a baboon. "What else is there to think of? If a man's in love, he's bound to think: one of us will die first and the other will be left alone. If you don't think that, you're not really in love."

Tannenbaum licked the powdered sugar from the strudel off his fingers. "If a man is really in love, what he dreads isn't so much the thought of dying first. What he really dreads is that the loved one should die first and leave him alone. Obviously the best solution is twins. Especially if they're as pretty as the Koller girls."

"How would you know which one to marry?" I asked. "You can't even tell them apart. Or would you toss a coin?"

He looked at me over his pince-nez. "All right. Make fun of a man who's poor, sick, bald, and Jewish, you Aryan monster—sitting there like a white raven cackling at people whose culture was at its height when your ancestors were swinging from trees on both sides of the Rhine and shitting into their fur."

"A magnificent image," I said. "But let's stick to our twins. Why don't you forget your inferiority complex and court one of them?"

Tannenbaum gave me a grieved look. "Those chicks are for movie directors," he said. "They wouldn't even look at me."

"Aren't you an actor?"

"What kind of parts do I get? Nazi underlings. I have no glamour."

"What would interest me is to live with twins, not to wait for somebody to die. If you quarreled with one, you'd have the other. If one of them ran away, the other would still be there. Not to mention more tempting possibilities."

Tannenbaum looked at me in disgust. "Is that what you've gone through these last terrible ten years for? Is that all the greatest war in history has taught you?"

"But, Tannenbaum," I protested, "you're the one who started talking about cunning rear ends."

"I meant it metaphysically, as a cosmic dilemma, not in the vulgar sense, like you, you late offshoot of the Nibelungs."

One of the Koller girls came to us with a fresh platter of strudel, and when the twin's free hand was occupied with putting it on his plate, he gave her well-rounded behind a tiny little pinch. "Why, Mr. Tannenbaum!" she protested, and went off laughing. Tannenbaum was delighted with himself.

"Hm," I said. "Some metaphysician you turned out to be, you late bloom from the dry cactus of the Talmud!"

"You put me up to it," said Tannenbaum in some confusion.

"Sure, sure. It's always the other fellow. Never take any responsibility, you, you German!"

"But I thank you for it. She didn't seem to mind. What do you think?"

Tannenbaum was radiant. His face had turned rust-red.

"You made one mistake," I said. "You should have made a little chalk mark on her skirt. Then you'd know which one of the twins had tolerated your vulgar advances. Because, you see, the other one might not feel the same way about it. In fact, I wouldn't be surprised if she upset the whole plate of strudel, plus hot coffee, on your head. As you can see, both twins are serving strudel at the moment. Do you know which one it was? I don't."

"I . . . it was . . . no . . ." There was hatred in the glance that Tannenbaum darted at me. He stared at the twins as though dazed. Then with superhuman determination he forced a sweet smile, thinking no doubt that the pinched twin would smile back. Instead, they both smiled. Tannenbaum uttered a muffled curse. I left him and went back to Betty's room.

I wanted to leave. I detested this atmosphere of nostalgia, which no amount of hate or revulsion could stifle. I had heard too many conversations beginning with "The Germans aren't all like that"— in itself an unquestionable truth, but invariably leading to reminiscences of the good old days in Germany, before the Nazis came and spoiled everything. I understood Betty, I loved her for her naïve, kind heart, but still I couldn't bear to listen. Her tearful eyes, the pictures of Berlin, the language of her homeland, to which she reverted in her fear—all this moved me to tears and at the same time turned my stomach. I detested this prison without walls, this living in memory, this shadowy hatred that strikes out at the void. I looked around; I felt like a deserter because, though I knew this atmosphere was heavy with real suffering, with irretrievable loss, I didn't want to live in it. Suddenly I knew why I wanted to get away. I was afraid that I myself would sink into this sort of helpless shadow rebellion and shadow resignation. For one led to the other. I didn't want to wake up one day after years of waiting and find that all the waiting and useless shadowboxing had sapped my strength. I was determined to take real revenge, to exact real retribution with my own hands, not to content myself with lamentations and protests, and I realized that this meant keeping my distance from the Wailing Wall and the rivers of Babylon.

I looked around, as though fearing that someone had read my thoughts. "Ross," said Betty, "I'm so glad you've come. It's wonderful to have so many friends."

"You're our mother, Betty. We refugees would be lost without you."

"How are you getting along in your job?"

"Fine, Betty. I'll be able to return some money to Vriesländer pretty soon."

She raised her head. "Take your time about it," she said. "Vriesländer is a very wealthy man. He doesn't need the money. You can pay him back when the war is over." She laughed. "I'm glad you're doing well, Ross. So few of us are. I mustn't be sick long. The others need me. Don't you think so?"

"We wouldn't know what to do without you, Betty."

"I've got to get back home soon. I mustn't be sick now that things are going so well."

It was a moment before I understood that she meant the war.

"Of course not, Betty," I said. "We'll keep our fingers crossed. Especially me. If it weren't for you, I'd probably be in an internment camp."

"Tomorrow you can all talk broken English again. Today I wanted to feel at home. With my own people. You understand, don't you? Kahn understood."

"We all understand, Betty."

"I've got to be brave."

"You're the bravest of the lot. Good-by, Betty. We'll all come and see you."

She nodded. "Good-by, Ross."

I left the room with Ravic. Tannenbaum was standing by the door looking perplexedly from one twin to the other. I could see by his expression that he hated me again. "Have you quarreled with him?" Ravic asked.

"Just a bit of frivolous byplay to take my mind off the sick-room. I'm no good at visiting sick people. It makes me impatient and irritable. I hate myself for it, but I can't help it."

"Almost everybody is like that. We feel guilty because of our good health."

I asked him about Betty's condition.

"We won't know until we've opened her up."

"Have you finished with your examinations?"

"Yes."

"Are you performing the operation?"

"Yes. In collaboration with an American colleague."

"Well, good-by, Ravic."

"My name is Fresenberg now. My real name."

"Mine is still Ross. Not my real name."

He laughed and walked away quickly. I had wanted to ask him if we could see each other again; but then it occurred to me that he had no more desire to speak of the past than I did. We would have nothing to say to each other.

"You're looking around as if you'd hidden a corpse somewhere," said Natasha.

"It's an old habit," I said. "A hard one to get rid of."

"Did you often have to hide?"

I looked at her in surprise. It was a silly question, as silly as asking me if I had to breathe. Then it occurred to me that she knew next to nothing of the life I had led. That gave me a strange feeling of pleasant warmth. Thank God that she doesn't know, I thought.

She stood there, dark against the brightness of the window, and I had no need to give her any explanations or to feel like a refugee. I took her in my arms and kissed her.

"I've stocked the icebox," she informed me. "We can order anything else we need from the delicatessen and stay in all day. It's Sunday, in case you've forgotten."

"I haven't forgotten. Is there something to drink in the icebox?"

"Two bottles of vodka. Two bottles of milk and some beer."

"Can you cook?"

"Sort of. I can broil steaks and I'm pretty good with a can opener. We have plenty of fruit and salad and two radios. We're ready to set up housekeeping."

She laughed. I held her in my arms, and I didn't laugh. I felt as if I had been struck by a dozen rubber bolts, the kind that children shoot from air pistols. They don't hurt, but you feel them. "I guess it's too tame for you," said Natasha. "Too *petit-bourgeois.*"

"It's the greatest adventure possible in these times," I said, breathing the fragrance of her hair.

I looked around. It was a small apartment on the fifteenth floor, consisting of living room, bedroom, kitchen, and bath. Maybe Fraser would have turned up his nose at it, but to me it was the height of luxury. The living room and bedroom had broad windows, from which one could see all the way to Wall Street.

"What do you think of it?" Natasha asked.

"This is the way to live in New York. You're right; we'd be crazy to set foot outside today."

"Just get us the Sunday papers. There's a newsstand right on the corner. Then we'll have everything we need. In the meantime I'll try to make some coffee."

I bought the *Times* and the *Herald Tribune,* about two hundred pages in all. I wondered whether people had been happier in the eighteenth century, when only the wealthy and educated read newspapers, and foreign correspondents were unknown, but came to no more significant conclusion than that what people don't know won't hurt them. A plane was circling in the fresh morning sky. I looked up and shook off my thoughts like fleas. I walked a little way on Second Avenue looking at the shops. The first two I saw were a German butcher shop and, right beside it, the Stern Brothers' delicatessen. It was comforting to know that the German butcher didn't spend his time massacring the three Stern Brothers, but that all four of them, as Eddie, the news dealer, had informed me, had gone fishing together.

I retraced my steps and rode up to the fifteenth floor with a redheaded queer in a checked sports jacket who introduced himself as Jasper. He was accompanied by a white poodle named René.

Jasper invited me to breakfast, but I managed to shake him off.

Natasha opened the door, her head done up in a turban and she had a towel around her waist; otherwise she was naked. "Marvelous!" I said, dropping the papers on a chair. "It fits in with what I've heard about this fifteenth floor."

"What have you heard?"

"The news dealer at the corner tells me it used to be a whorehouse."

"I've been taking a bath," said Natasha. "You were gone so long. Did you go all the way to Times Square for the papers?"

"No, just roaming around. Did you know this place was alive with fags?"

She nodded and threw off her towel. "I know. To tell you the truth, this apartment belongs to one. But I have another confession to make."

"A confession? So soon?"

"Well . . ." she said. "Can you make coffee?"

"I'll make coffee later," I said.

I brought Natasha her coffee in bed. When we were hungry, an hour or two later, I called up Stern Brothers, which was open despite the absence of the owners, and had them send up pastrami, salami, butter, cheese, and pumpernickel.

"I worship you, Natasha," I said. I had just refused to put on a pair of red pajamas belonging to the anonymous owner of the apartment. "I worship you, but I will not put these things on, though the size seems to be right."

"Of course it is. You're built just like Jeremiah . . ."

"Who?"

"Jeremiah!"

"I don't care if it's the prophet in person; I won't wear them."

"Be reasonable, Robert. They're washed and ironed, and Jerry is very clean."

"Who?"

"Jerry. Don't you sleep between sheets that have been used by other people?"

"At the hotel? Yes, but I don't know them."

"You don't know Jerry either."

"I know him through you. It's like a chicken. If a chicken's a total stranger to me, I'm willing to eat it, but if I've raised it from the cradle and call it by name . . ."

"Too bad! I'd have loved to see you in red pajamas. But pajamas or no pajamas, I'm sleepy. Would you let me sleep for an hour? I'm so full of pastrami and beer and love. You can read the paper."

"I wouldn't dream of it. I'll lie down beside you."

"Do you think I'll be able to sleep? I don't. I'm not used to it."

"We can try. Maybe I'll drop off, too."

"All right."

A few minutes later she was sound asleep. The air conditioner hummed almost inaudibly. I could hear the muffled notes of a piano from somewhere down below. Someone who played very badly was practicing. I was carried back to my childhood and the hot summer days when just such slow, shaky piano playing was wafted down from a higher story and the chestnut trees outside the window rustled lazily in the breeze. I saw my father's tired, friendly face as he shuffled, slightly stooped, about the apartment —not his last, frightened, heartbreakingly brave face, but his peacetime face of years before.

I woke with a start. I had fallen asleep myself. Cautiously I rose and went into the other room to dress. I gathered my scattered clothes and stood by the window, looking out at the strange glistening city, which knew nothing of memories or traditions. The piano started up again, but this time it was a blues. I went to the middle of the room, from where I could see Natasha. She lay naked, with her head to one side and one hand in her hair. I loved her dearly. I loved her for her wholeheartedness. When she was with me, she was all there, but her presence never weighed on me, and then before I knew it she was gone. I went back to the window and looked again at the white, almost oriental landscape, a cross between Algiers and the moon. I listened to the steady hum of the traffic and watched the long row of traffic lights on Second Avenue as, section after section, they shifted from green to red and red to green. There was something comforting and at the same time inhuman about the regularity of it, as though this city were already controlled by robots, but not unfriendly ones. I went back to the middle of the room and discovered that when I turned around I could see Natasha in the mirror.

She sighed and turned over. I thought of taking the tray with the beer cans and leftovers to the kitchen, but decided against it. I had no desire to impress her with my domestic virtues. I didn't even put the vodka bottle back in the icebox, though I might have if I hadn't known there was another ice-cold bottle waiting. I thought of how strangely this rather normal situation had moved me—suddenly coming home and finding someone waiting for me, someone who had now dropped trustingly off to sleep.

I looked at Natasha. I loved her dearly, but without sentimentality. As long as this remained true, I knew I was relatively safe; I could break off without being hurt. I gazed at her lovely shoulders and arms, and moved my arms in a gesture of silent prayer: Stay with me! Don't leave me before I leave you!

"What on earth are you doing?" said Natasha.

I dropped my hands. "How can you see me, lying on your belly like that?"

She pointed to a small mirror beside the radio on the bedside table. "Are you trying to hex me?" she asked. "Or have you had enough of domestic life?"

"Neither. I've never been so happy as here among the ghosts of old-time whores and new-time queers. And we're not going to budge. Maybe in the late afternoon we can take a little stroll on Fifth Avenue. But then we'll hurry back to grilled steak and love."

We didn't even go out in the afternoon. Instead, we opened the windows wide for an hour and let the hot air into the room. Then we set the air conditioning at top speed so as not to sweat while making love. By the end of the day I felt as though we had spent almost a year of weightless peace in a vacuum.

XX

"I'm giving a little party," said Silvers. "You're invited."

"Thanks," I said without enthusiasm. "I'm afraid I can't make it. No dinner jacket."

"You don't need one. This is a summer party. You can wear what you like."

I saw no way out. "All right," I said.

"Could you bring Mrs. Whymper?"

"Have you invited her?"

"Not yet. But she's your friend."

The hypocrite! "I'm not so sure she'd come," I said. "And besides, she's been your friend much longer than mine. You told me so yourself."

"Oh well, it was just an idea. Some very interesting people will be coming."

I could imagine his interesting people. The applied psychology of the merchant class is very simple. Anyone you can make money out of is interesting. Anyone who makes you lose money is a dog. All the rest are extras. Silvers observed this rule fanatically.

The Rockefellers, Fords, and Mellons, whom Silvers had told me so much about that I couldn't help thinking they were his best friends, were absent. But there were other millionaires, mostly of the self-made variety. They were hearty, rather loud-mouthed, and lovable in a way, because it was plain that they felt as insecure in the world of art as they felt secure in the world of business. They all regarded themselves as collectors, not as purchasers of a few pictures. That was Silvers' big trick; he made them into collectors, seeing to it that a museum borrowed one of their paintings for an exhibition now and then. For these rich men, the little notice in the catalogue—"From the collection of Mr. and Mrs. X"—was a significant rung in the social ladder. It put them into the class of the great robber barons, the old-established plutocrats. Silvers took a very generous view: as far as he was concerned, anyone who had bought two small pictures was a collector; he advised him as though the outcome of the war depended on it and, perhaps even more important, affected to consult him: Here at last was a man on whose taste he could count.

Suddenly I found myself face to face with Mrs. Whymper. "What are you doing with these sharks?" she asked me. "Dreadful people! Shall we go?"

"Where?"

"Anywhere. To El Morocco. Or come home with me."

"I'd be glad to," I said. "But I can't leave. I'm sort of on duty."

"Sort of! What about me? Haven't you an obligation to me? You've got to get me out of here. It's your fault I was invited."

Her reasoning was pretty good, I thought.

"Are you Russian by any chance?" I asked.

"No. Why?"

"Your logic. An irresistible argument based on false premises and false deductions. Very charming, very feminine, and most irritating."

She laughed. "Have you known so many Russian women?"

"A few. They have a real genius for accusing men unjustly. They think it keeps us on our toes."

"You know such interesting things," said Mrs. Whymper, with a long sultry look. "When can we go? I'm sick of listening to those Little Red Riding Hood speeches."

"Little Red Riding Hood?"

"That's right. A wolf in sheep's clothing."

"That's not in Little Red Riding Hood. It's in the Bible."

"Thank you, professor, but there's a wolf in both. Don't these hyenas with their Renoirs and their big mouths make you sick?"

"Not really. I like to hear a man pontificating on a subject he knows nothing about. It's so refreshingly childlike. Experts are always a bore."

"And what about your high priest, who talks about his pictures with tears in his eyes, as if they were his children, and then goes out and sells them at a good profit? What do you think of a man who sells his children?"

I couldn't help laughing. She seemed to know the score.

"Well then," she said. "Are you taking me home?"

"I can take you home, but I'll have to come back."

"Very well."

I ought to have known that her car would be waiting outside, but I was taken by surprise, and she saw it. "Never mind. Take me home. I won't eat you. My chauffeur will drive you back. You can't imagine how empty a house can be."

"I know all about it," I said.

"How's your beautiful girl friend?" she asked.

I gave her a disapproving look and said nothing.

She burst out laughing. "You don't have to tell me if it's a secret."

I saw she was trying to provoke me and controlled myself. "Have you been married very often?" I asked.

"Once. My husband died five years ago." Suddenly there were tears in her eyes.

I said nothing more. It seemed to me that we were quits.

The driver stopped and opened the door for us. She went straight to the house without waiting for me, and I followed with a feeling of annoyance. "I'm sorry," I said when I had caught up with her. "I've got to go back. You understand that I have no choice."

"I understand," she said coldly. "But perhaps you don't. Good night. John, drive Mr. . . . What was the name again?"

"Dimwit," I said without hesitation.

She didn't bat an eyelash. "Mr. Dimwit," she said.

I thought of declining, but then I got in. "Drive me to the nearest taxi stand," I said to the driver.

He drove off. "Stop here," I said, two blocks farther on. "I see a cab."

The chauffeur turned around. "Why take a cab? What difference does it make?"

"Plenty."

He shrugged his shoulders. I gave him a tip. He shook his head but took it. Then I shook my head. What an ass I am, I thought. "Fifty-seventh Street and Second Avenue," I said to the driver. "Not Sixty-second."

"Why would I want to go to Sixty-second Street?" he said. "They're all the same to me."

"Not to me," I said.

I stopped at Stern Brothers. The place was full of queens buying cold cuts for supper. I called Natasha. She wasn't expecting me until three hours later, and I didn't want any surprises.

She was there. "Where are you?" she asked. "Taking a breather from your collectors?"

"No, I'm at Stern Brothers."

"Bring home half a pound of salami and a loaf of pumpernickel."

"Butter?"

"We've got butter, but we could do with some cheese."

Suddenly I felt very happy. There were three poodles in the shop when I stepped out of the phone booth. I recognized René and his master, the red-haired Jasper. "Hiya, pardner," said Jasper. "Long time no see."

I bought salami, cheese, bread, and a chocolate cake. "Shopping for a late supper, eh?" Jasper asked.

I looked at him in silence. If he had said anything about supper with my girl friend, I would have crowned him with the cake.

He didn't. But he followed me into the street.

"Going for a little stroll?" he asked. I looked around. It must have been the evening parade hour. Fifty-seventh Street was alive with queers, with and without dogs. Most of the dogs were poodles of varying sizes, but there was also a sprinkling of dachshunds. The atmosphere was festive. Greetings and jokes were exchanged, and conversations struck up as the dogs relieved themselves at the curb. I could see I was attracting attention; Jasper strode along beside me, waving to friends and preening himself as if I were his latest conquest. That was too much. I did an abrupt about-face. "What's the hurry?" said Jasper.

"I take communion every morning. I have to go home and get ready. Good-by!"

His scornful laughter followed me in my withdrawal. I stopped at the newsstand. "Quite a crowd!" said Eddie, with disgust.

"Is it always like this?"

"Every evening. Fags' Walk, we call it. More and more of them. I'm getting worried about the birth rate."

I rode up to Natasha's apartment.

"I need a bath," I said. "I worship you, but I've got to take a bath."

"Go ahead. Take some of the bath oil, if you want it. Mary Chess carnation."

"I'd better not." I didn't want to smell of carnation if I met Jasper in the elevator.

I turned on the water and undressed. "Vodka?" she asked.

"Sure."

She brought me my vodka and sat down on the edge of the bathtub. "How come you got away so soon?"

"I took Mrs. Whymper home. Silvers invited her without telling me."

"And she let you go so quickly? Bravo!"

I sat up in the hot water. "She didn't want to let me go. How do you know that it's not so easy?"

She laughed. "Everybody knows."

"What? That she's a nympho?"

"Not at all. She likes to sit around with younger men, that's all. I told you."

"Are you so sure?"

"Everybody knows that."

"Who's everybody?"

"Everybody who knows her. She's lonely, bored with men of her own age, likes Martinis, and is quite harmless. Poor Robert! Were you afraid?"

I grabbed her and tried to pull her into the bathtub. "Let me go!" she screamed. "This dress doesn't belong to me. It's a model."

I let her go. "What does belong to us anyway? Borrowed apartment, borrowed dress, borrowed jewelry, borrowed . . ."

"Isn't it wonderful? No responsibility. Isn't that what you wanted?"

"Have pity on me," I said. "I've had a bad day."

"And you wanted to raise hell with me about Elisa Whymper. You and your famous pact."

"What pact?"

"Not to hurt each other. To help each other recover from old sorrows. To keep our love reasonable and moderate."

She danced around the bathroom. I looked at her in amazement.

I sensed that she was building up to an outburst. I was sure I had never said anything of the sort; I couldn't have been that stupid. But I was also dimly aware that she had seen through me and that there was some truth in what she said.

"Give me another drink," I said.

"Admit that we've just been kidding each other," she said.

"Isn't it always that way?"

"I don't know. I keep forgetting."

"Keep? Has it happened to you so often?"

"I've forgotten that, too. You may be an adding machine, but I'm not."

"I'm lying in the bathtub, Natasha. Defenseless. Let's make peace."

"Peace!" she said scornfully. "Who wants peace?"

"The whole world right now. Including Hitler."

"I knew you'd drag that in. Whenever you Huns are in a jam, you fall back on the state of the world."

"Holding up my former nationality to me is like kicking a defenseless man on the ground."

Natasha laughed. Her eyes glittered. "Defenseless men are made to be kicked. That's what they're on the ground for."

"Nietzsche!" I said. "Misinterpreted Nietzsche. What's wrong with you today?"

I stood up and reached for a towel. If I had known this was going to happen, I would have avoided the bathtub like the plague. I could tell by Natasha's eyes and quick movements that what had started out as a joke had become serious.

"That's a marvelous dress," I said. "Imagine my wanting to pull you into the bathtub with it."

"Why didn't you?"

"The water was too hot and the tub too narrow."

I was careful not to remind her that she had screamed and begged me not to; this was no time to be logical. I decided to dress and clear out. Maybe tomorrow would be a better day.

"What are you dressing for?" Natasha asked.

"I'm cold."

"We can turn off the air conditioning."

"Don't bother. Then you'd be too hot."

She looked at me with suspicion. "You coward! Are you running out on me?"

"I wouldn't think of running out on all that nice salami."

Somehow that infuriated her. "Go to hell!" she screamed. "Go back to your flea-bitten hotel! That's where you belong."

She was trembling with rage. I raised my hands to ward off the ash trays I expected her to start throwing. I was sure she was a dead shot. She looked magnificent. Far from disfiguring her, anger made her more beautiful than ever. She quivered not only with anger, but also with life. I wanted to take her, but something warned me not to. In a lucid moment I realized that it wouldn't have helped; it wouldn't have solved the problem, but only postponed it. The best solution was flight. "As you wish," I said, and dashed out of the apartment.

I had to wait for the elevator. I listened, but heard nothing. Maybe she was expecting me to come back. When the elevator door opened, two poodles rushed out. One was René. "Hiya, pardner," said Jasper. "Supper over so soon? How about a spot of brandy on the terrace?"

"Too hot," I said. "Besides, I'm on my way to church."

"At this time of night?"

"Midnight mass. I'm the acolyte."

"Acolyte?" Jasper asked. "With a censer and all that snazzy lace? Why, that's charming!"

I stepped on René's paw. He yelped and ran up the hallway, pursued by Jasper. I took advantage of the diversion to close the elevator door and press the button. The elevator smelled of Chevalier d'Orsay. Once outside, I had a moment's hesitation, but quickly decided it would be a mistake to go back. In front of the Lowy brothers' window I stopped again and gazed at some French brass candlesticks and porcelain flowers. Unfortunately, they reminded me of that evening with Natasha after the storm.

Melikov was on duty. *"Cafard?"* he asked.

I nodded. "How did you know?"

"One look at your face. Do you want a drink?"

I shook my head. "Liquor only makes it worse in the first stage."

"What's the first stage?"

"When I realize that I've behaved like a humorless fool."

"And the second?"

"When I realize that it's all over and that I'm to blame."

While Melikov was busy with his room service, I sank into deep gloom. "Good evening," said a voice behind me.

Lachmann! I wanted to get up and run. "You're all I needed," I said.

He pushed me back into my chair. "I won't tell you any troubles," he whispered. "The days of my misery are over. You see before you a happy man!"

"You mean you've made her?"

"Who?"

I raised my head. "Who? You shake the whole hotel with your lamentations, and now you have the nerve to ask who?"

"That's water under the bridge," said Lachmann. "I'm a quick forgetter."

"You really do seem cheerful," I said, with a certain envy.

"I've found a jewel," Lachmann whispered. "A jewel without a Mexican."

Melikov called me from the desk. "Robert. Telephone."

"Who is it?"

"Natasha."

I picked up the receiver. "Where are you?" she asked.

"At Silvers' party."

"Don't be silly. You're drinking Melikov's vodka."

"I'm down on my knees to the chair you last sat in, worshiping you and cursing my fate. I'm crushed."

She laughed. "Come back, Robert."

"Armed?"

"Unarmed, you fool. How can you leave me alone like this?"

"I'm spending the night here," I announced to Natasha. "I want to sleep with you and wake up with you. In the morning I'll go out for milk and eggs, and if I meet René and Jasper in the elevator, *tant pis*. It will be our first waking-up together. We're not together enough—that's why we have these misunderstandings. We've got to get used to each other."

She stretched. "I've always thought life was too long to be together all the time."

I couldn't help laughing. "There's probably something in that," I said. "I've never had a chance to find out."

For a time we lay on the bed in silence.

"I feel as if we were in a balloon," I said finally. "Not on a plane, but in a silent balloon, just high enough not to hear anything but to see the streets, the toy cars, and the city lights. God bless the unknown benefactor who brought this big bed up here, and that wall mirror. When you walk around the room, it turns you into twins, and one of them is mute."

"Which one is nicer? The mute one, I suppose?"

"No."

She patted my head. "That was the right answer."

"You're very beautiful," I said. "Usually the first thing I look at in a woman is her legs, and then her ass. The face comes last. With you the order was reversed. First your face and then your legs. I didn't start thinking about your ass until I'd fallen in love. I was worried at first. You were so slender, I thought it might be flat, bony, nonexistent."

"When did you stop worrying?"

"Very soon. There are simple ways of finding out. The funny part was that it took me so long to get interested in it."

"Tell me some more."

She lay sprawled on the bed like a lazy cat. I almost fancied that I could hear her purring. "Go on talking."

"I used to think sunburned women would be my dish," I said. "Creatures who splash around in the water and lie in the sun all summer. And now my dream girl turns out to be white, as though the sun had never touched her skin. There's a good deal of the moon about you—those transparent gray eyes, for instance. Except, of course, for your peppery temperament. An explosive nymph, that's what you are: rockets, firecrackers, Roman candles, gunfire. But somehow they don't seem to make any noise."

"Tell me some more. Do you want a drink?"

I shook my head. "I've never really faced up to my emotions before. I treated them like a side issue, they glanced off me, I never let myself feel their full impact. I don't know why. Maybe I was afraid. With you it's different. With you I have no fears. Everything is open and aboveboard. It's wonderful to make love to you, and it's just as wonderful to be with you afterward, like now."

176

"Tell me some more."

I looked into the dimly lit living room. "It's wonderful to be with you and imagine that we're immortal," I said. "Sometimes I really believe it, and so do you, I think; we're so much a part of each other that even now when we're as close together as two bodies can be, we want to be even closer, and that's why we cry out; that's the meaning of the crude, primitive, obscene words that burst out of us."

Natasha stretched voluptuously, and a few minutes later she was fast asleep. I spread the sheet over her and lay awake for a long time, listening to her breathing.

XXI

Betty Stein was back. "Nobody tells me the truth," she wailed. "Neither my friends nor my enemies."

"You have no enemies, Betty."

"You're an angel. But why don't they tell me the truth? I could bear it. Not knowing is much worse."

I cast a questioning glance at Gräfenheim, who was sitting on the other side of her. "We've told you the truth, Betty. What makes you insist on believing the worst?"

She smiled like a child. "Then I'd be able to adjust myself," she said. "If I'm all right, I'll just drift along as usual; I know myself. But if I know my life is in danger, I'll fight. I'll fight like a madwoman for the time I have left. And maybe, by fighting, I can make it last longer. Otherwise I'll waste it. Don't you understand?"

"I understand perfectly. But if Dr. Gräfenheim says you're all right, you ought to believe him. Why would he lie to you?"

"Because they always do. A doctor never tells the truth."

"Not even when he's an old friend?"

"Especially when he's an old friend."

She had been home for three days, and for three days she had been tormenting herself and her friends with such questions. Her face still had the softness of an immature young girl's; all her suffering and anxiety were revealed in her restless, intense eyes. Now and then someone thought of something to say that put her mind at rest for a while, and she was all childlike gratitude; but an hour or two later her doubts revived. She was sitting in an old armchair she had bought from the Lowy brothers because it reminded her of Europe, surrounded by her engravings of Berlin. The news of the almost daily bombing of Berlin threw her into such a turmoil that at the hospital Gräfenheim had given orders that she was not to see the papers. It had done no good. The next day he found her in tears by the radio. What made it worse was that her grief over Berlin conflicted with her hatred of the murderers who had killed several members of her family, and that she was obliged to hide her feelings about Berlin from other refugees, who because they were unable to dispel such feelings in themselves were only too ready to condemn them in others.

"How are you getting along, Ross?" she asked me.

"Very well, Betty."

"That's good to hear." My little bit of good fortune was a message of hope to her. If someone else was getting along, why wouldn't she, too, be all right? "I'm so glad," she said. "Very well, did you say?"

"Yes, Betty, very well."

She nodded with satisfaction. "They've bombed Olivaer Platz in Berlin," she whispered. "Did you know?"

"They're bombing the whole city," I said.

"I know. But Olivaer Platz—that's where we lived." She looked diffidently around. "Most people get angry when I talk about it. Our beautiful old Berlin."

"It's not really so beautiful," I said cautiously. "Compared with Paris or Rome. As architecture, I mean."

"Do you think I'll live long enough to see it again?"

"Of course you will. Why not?"

"It would be so awful if I didn't. I've waited so long."

"It will be rather different from what we remember," I said.

She thought that over. "But something will be left. And they weren't all Nazis."

"No," I said, and stood up. I couldn't stand this kind of conversation for long. "We'll be able to think about that later on."

I went into the other room. Tannenbaum was sitting there with a sheet of paper. Kahn had just come in.

"It's my blood list," said Tannenbaum.

"What's that?"

"A list of Germans who've got to be shot." Tannenbaum helped himself to a piece of strudel.

Kahn glanced at the list. "Not bad," he said.

"More names will be added, of course."

"By whom?" Kahn asked.

"Suggestions are accepted from all."

"And who's going to do the shooting?"

"A committee. We'll have to set up a committee, but that's easy."

"Are you going to head it?"

Tannenbaum considered for a moment. "If I'm elected."

"I have a suggestion," said Kahn. "You shoot the first man on the list, and I'll take care of the rest. Okay?"

Tannenbaum thought about it. Gräfenheim and Ravic were watching him. "I mean you yourself," said Kahn. "Not through an anonymous committee, but with your own hand. Okay?"

Tannenbaum said nothing. "It's lucky for you," said Kahn, "that you didn't answer that one. If you had said okay, I'd have socked you in the jaw. I'm fed up with this bloodthirsty drawing-room chitchat. Stick to the movies."

He went in to see Betty. "He's got the manners of a Nazi," Tannenbaum muttered behind him.

I left with Gräfenheim. He was living in New York now, interning at one of the hospitals, for which he received sixty dollars a month, board, and lodging. "Let's go up to my place," he suggested.

"Glad to," I said. It was a pleasant evening; the heat had let up. "What about Betty?" I asked. "Or aren't you allowed to say?"

"Ask Ravic."

"He'll tell me to ask you."

He hesitated.

"They cut her open and sewed her up again," I said. "Is that it?"

No answer.

"Had she been operated on before?"

"Yes," he said.

"Poor Betty," I said. "How long do you think . . ."

"We don't know. Maybe weeks, maybe years."

Gräfenheim's room at the hospital was small and simple. The only conspicuous object was a large heated aquarium. "An extravagance," he said. "I treated myself to it when Kahn brought me that money. In Berlin my waiting room was full of decorative fish." He looked at me apologetically out of his nearsighted eyes. "We all have our hobbies."

"When the war is over," I asked, "would you like to go back to Berlin?"

"My wife is still there."

"Have you heard from her?"

"We agreed not to write. They open all the mail. I hope she managed to get out of Berlin. Do you think they've locked her up?"

"Why should they?"

"Do you think they need reasons?"

"Some of them, yes. The Germans are bureaucrats even in their crimes."

"It's hard to wait so long," he said. "Do you think they've let her go to the country? To some place that's not being bombed?"

"I should think so."

The irony of the situation did not escape me—Gräfenheim deceiving Betty, and me deceiving Gräfenheim. "The worst part of it is sitting here with my hands tied," he said. "Not being able to do anything."

"That's true," I said. "We're nothing but onlookers. A lot of people must envy us because we're not allowed to do anything. That's what makes our existence here so shadowy and almost obscene. In part, the Allies are fighting for us, but they don't want our help. Except in very special cases."

"In France they let us volunteer for the Foreign Legion," said Gräfenheim.

"Did you try?"

"No."

"You didn't want to shoot at Germans. Is that it?"

"I didn't want to shoot, period."

I shrugged my shoulders. "Sometimes we have no choice. We have to shoot somebody."

"Why not ourselves?"

"Nonsense. But it's true that a lot of us didn't want to shoot Germans. They knew that the people they wanted to kill were not at the front. At the front there were only obedient law-abiding citizens. Cannon fodder."

Gräfenheim nodded. "They don't trust us. They don't trust our hatred. We're like Tannenbaum. He draws up lists, but he'd never shoot anybody."

"They wouldn't even take Kahn. And I think they were right."

"An apartment!" I said. "Lamps! Furniture! A bed! A woman! A glass of vodka! The bright side of my unfortunate life. I'll never get used to it, and that's all to the good. Whenever I come here, I enjoy it as much as the first time. I'm Robinson Crusoe, and every time I come here I see Friday's footprints in the sand. You're my woman Friday. The first woman."

"What have you been drinking?"

"Nothing. Coffee and sadness."

"Are you sad?"

"A man with my kind of life can't be sad for very long. Sadness is only a background; the joy of life stands out more clearly against it. Sadness sinks to the bottom like a stone, and the water level of life rises. Am I telling the truth? No, not exactly, but I want it to be true, and actually there is some truth in it."

"It's good you're not sad," said Natasha. "I don't need your reasons. Reasons are always suspect."

"I worship you. Is that suspect?"

She laughed. "It is rather sinister. You wouldn't have these exaggerated reactions unless you had something to hide."

I looked at her in consternation. "What makes you think that?"

"Just so."

"Do you really believe it?"

"Why not? Aren't you Robinson Crusoe, who keeps having to convince himself that he's seen footprints in the sand?"

I didn't answer. Her words had touched me deeply. Was it possible that where I hoped to find solid ground there were only loose pebbles that would slip out from under my feet at the first shock? Did I exaggerate in order to convince myself?

I tried to shake off my thoughts. "Natasha," I said, "I don't know. All I know is that I worship you, even if you find it suspect."

She sat down beside me. "There's something awfully elusive about you," she said.

"I'm afraid so."

"And something tells me you enjoy it."

I shook my head. "No, Natasha. I only kid myself."

"You do a good job of it."

"Like Kahn, you mean? There are active and passive refugees. Kahn and I prefer to be active. In France we were active. We had to be. Instead of bewailing our lot, we tried, whenever possible, to call it an adventure. A pretty desperate adventure it was, too. Couldn't we stop talking about it now?"

"Why?"

"Because it's not over yet."

"You can say that again. One of these days you'll just disappear."

I opened the window and looked out. "It's cooled off, Natasha," I announced. "For the first time in weeks. You can breathe."

She joined me at the window. "The fall is coming," she said.

"Thank goodness!"

"Don't say that. You mustn't wish the time away."

I laughed. "You talk as if you were eighty."

"It's no good wishing the time away. It's like wishing your life away. And that's what you're doing."

"Not any more," I said, but I knew I was lying.

"Where do you want to run off to? I know. You want to go back."

"Don't be silly, Natasha. I've just got here. Why should I think of going back?"

"Don't try to kid me. You think of nothing else."

I shook my head. "I've stopped thinking ahead. It will be fall and winter and spring and summer and then fall again, and we'll laugh and we'll still be together."

She pressed close to me. "Don't leave me. I can't bear to be alone. I'm not a heroic woman."

"Who wants you to be? Instead of regretting the turn of the seasons, let's just switch off the air conditioning and go out for some real air."

"That's a very good idea."

We rode down, meeting no one. The poodles and their masters seemed to have settled in for the night.

"The summer's over," Eddie called out to us from his stand.

"Thank goodness," said Natasha.

"Don't gloat too soon," I said. "It will be back again."

"Nothing ever comes back," said Eddie. "Except trouble and those lousy poodles that keep pissing on my magazines. Paper?"

"We'll pick it up on the way back."

These little neighborhood chats always gave me the same thrill, the thrill of a man who no longer has to hide. True, my presence in this country was tolerated, rather than accepted, but at least I was not hunted.

"Shall we do the Tour des Grands Ducs?" I asked.

Natasha nodded. "Yes. Let's have plenty of light. The days are getting shorter."

We went to Fifth Avenue, past the Sherry-Netherland, toward Central Park. We could hear the roaring of the lions through the hum of the traffic. We stopped outside La Vieille Russie to look at the icons and the onyx-and-gold Easter eggs that Fabergé had fashioned for the family of the Tsar. The White Russian refugees still seemed to have these things to sell.

We stopped across from the park. The trees were groaning in the wind, and the first leaves were falling. "It looks too sad," said Natasha. "Let's go down the Avenue."

The fall fashions were being shown in the shop windows. "That's ancient history to me," said Natasha. "We photographed those things in June. I'm always a season in advance. Tomorrow we'll be doing furs. Maybe that's what makes me feel that life is passing so quickly. While other people are still enjoying the summer, I've got the fall in my blood."

I stopped and kissed her. "How we talk!" I said. "Like characters in Turgenev or Flaubert. Natasha, harbinger of the seasons. Now I

183

suppose you've got the winter in your blood, with snowstorms, furs, and chimney corners."

"What about you?"

"Me? I don't know. I don't know anything about autumn and winter in America. I only know this country in the spring and summer. I don't know what skyscrapers look like in the snow."

We turned east on Forty-second Street and walked back on Second Avenue. "Here time is asleep," I said. "These antique shops know nothing of autumn and winter. To them one century is as good as another. Nineteenth-century chandeliers make their peace with twentieth-century electricity. In those mirrors the eighteenth century reflects the light of the present. If we could only be as wise as those inanimate objects and stop worrying about time!"

"Will you be spending the night with me?" Natasha asked.

"May I?"

"You certainly may. I don't want to be alone tonight. It's going to be windy. If the wind wakes me up, I want you to be there to comfort me. I want to be very sentimental and to let myself be comforted and to fall back asleep in your arms and be reminded of the autumn and forget it and remember it again."

"I'll stay."

"Then let's go to bed. Let's look at ourselves making love in the mirror and listen to the storm. And then you'll hold me tight and tell me about Florence and Paris and Venice and all the places we'll never go to together."

"I've never been in Venice or Florence."

"Never mind. You can tell me about them; it will be the same as if you'd been there. Maybe I'll cry and look terrible. Crying doesn't become me. You'll forgive me and forgive my sentimentality. We've got to be sentimental once in a while; it's like a fresh-flowing stream that washes off the protective coating of cynicism we wear in our everyday lives. Can you bear it?"

"Yes."

"Then come and tell me you'll always love me and that we'll never be any older."

XXII

"I've got some interesting news for you," said Silvers. "We're going west—to conquer Hollywood. How does that strike you?"

"As actors?"

"As art dealers. I've thought about it a long time, and now I've made up my mind to go."

"With me?"

"With you," said Silvers in his expansive tone. "You've learned the trade very nicely, and I can use your help."

"When?"

"In about two weeks. That gives us time to get ready."

"For how long?"

"Two weeks is my present idea. Maybe longer. Los Angeles is virgin soil. Paved with gold."

"Gold?"

"Thousand-dollar bills. Why these niggling questions? Anybody else would be jumping with joy. Or don't you want to go? Then I'd have to look for another companion."

"And fire me?"

"What's the matter with you?" he asked angrily. "Of course I'd have to fire you. But why shouldn't you want to go?" He paused for a moment. "Maybe you think you haven't the right clothes for it? I can advance you the money."

"For the clothes I'm to wear while slaving for you? My business equipment, so to speak? And you'd expect me to pay it back?"

He laughed. "Well, that's one way of looking at it."

I was stalling. I wasn't too eager to leave New York. I didn't know a soul in California, and the prospect of being dependent on Silvers for company didn't exactly thrill me.

"Where will we stay?" I was thinking of those interminable evenings together in some hotel lobby.

"I'll be staying at the Beverly Hills Hotel and you at the Garden of Allah."

I looked up. "Lovely name. Sounds like Rudolph Valentino. So we won't be staying at the same hotel?"

"Too expensive. They tell me the Garden of Allah is very nice. And it's right nearby."

"And how do we handle our accounts? My hotel bill and so on?"

"I'll pick up the tab."

"You mean I'm supposed to take all my meals at the hotel?"

Silvers threw up his hands. "You're being awfully difficult. You can eat where you please. Any more questions?"

"Yes," I said. "I need a raise. A man in my position has to dress properly."

"How much?"

"A hundred a month."

Silvers jumped. "That's ridiculous. What's the matter with your suit? It looks good to me."

"It's not good enough for Mr. Silvers' right-hand man. And maybe I'll need a dinner jacket."

"We're not going to Hollywood for the night life."

"You never can tell. It mightn't be a bad idea. Night clubs are a good place for softening up millionaires. For persuading them to improve their social position by buying paintings."

Silvers gave me an angry look. "You are not to repeat my business secrets, not even to me. Anyway, we'll need a different approach with those Hollywood millionaires. They regard themselves as cultural leaders and they're not worried about their social position. However, I'll give you a twenty-dollar raise."

"A hundred," I said.

"Don't forget that I'm employing you illegally. I'm taking a big risk on your account."

"Not any more," I said. I looked at a Monet on the wall across from me: a white-clad woman in a field of poppies. "They've extended my residence permit for another three months," I said. "And the next extension will be automatic."

Silvers bit his lip. "So what?"

"So I'm allowed to work." This wasn't true, but the authorities were not being very strict just then.

"You mean you're considering a different job?"

"Of course not. Why should I? At Wildenstein's I'd probably be standing around the gallery all day. I'm happier with you."

I could see that Silvers was reckoning, trying to figure out how much what I knew about him was worth—to him and to Wildenstein. He was probably kicking himself for having initiated me into so many of his tricks. "You ought to compensate me," I said, "for what you've done to my morals. Why, only the other day you made me palm myself off as a former assistant curator of the Louvre. Not to mention my knowledge of languages; that ought to be worth something."

He finally agreed to a seventy-five-dollar raise. I had counted on thirty. All the same, I decided, I wasn't going to buy a dinner jacket.

Silvers seemed to have guessed my thoughts. "You've done all right for yourself," he said. "But forget about the dinner jacket. If you need one, you can rent it."

I went to see Vriesländer to pay back a hundred dollars of the money I owed him. "Sit down," he said, absently slipping the bills into his wallet. "Have you had dinner?"

"No," I said without hesitation, remembering that the Vriesländers ate very well.

"Then stick around," he said. "There'll be a few more guests. I don't know who they are. Ask my wife. Can I offer you some Scotch?"

Since his naturalization, Vriesländer drank only whisky. I would have expected the contrary—that he would have drunk whisky beforehand, to demonstrate his intention of becoming a good American, and then gone back to Steinhäger and kümmel. But Vriesländer had his quirks. Before naturalization, on the other hand, he had refused to speak anything but broken English and insisted on the whole family doing the same. Malicious tongues even claimed that he enforced this ruling in bed. Once naturalized, however, the family reverted to Babylonian—a mixture of German, English, and Yiddish.

"Tell me," he said, "are you homesick?"

"For what?"

"Germany."

"No. I'm not a Jew."

Vriesländer laughed. "You've got something there."

I thought of Betty Stein. "Yes," I said. "The Jews were the most sentimental patriots of all."

"Do you know why? Because we were well off in Germany until

1933. The last Kaiser ennobled any number of Jews. He even received Jews at court. He had Jewish friends. The Crown Prince had a Jewish mistress."

"Under His Majesty you might have become a baron," I said.

"That was a long time ago," he said sadly.

I was ashamed of my insolence, but Vriesländer hadn't even noticed it. For a moment the conservatism of a man who had owned a villa on Tiergartenstrasse had regained possession of him. "You were still a child in those days, my dear Ross. But one thing you can't deny: under the Kaiser we wouldn't have had this mess."

"He lost a war, too."

"I'm not talking about the war. I mean the Nazis."

Where am I? I thought. In New York, in the Black Forest hunted by the S.S., in Brussels, or in some never-never land? I felt as I often did at night, when I woke up in the dark. I gave myself a jolt and looked into Vriesländer's watery eyes.

"A drop of vodka would hit the spot," I said.

"Excellent. Suppose we join the ladies."

The "ladies" consisted of Tannenbaum and Ravic, the surgeon. "How are the twins?" I asked Tannenbaum. "Have you pinched the wrong one in the ass yet?"

"I never pinch young ladies in the ass. But while we're on the subject, do you think it's only their faces that are alike or . . ."

"You mean their temperaments?"

"Yes, call it their temperaments."

"Well, there are two schools."

"But wouldn't it be terrible to take the wrong one. Suppose one were a cold fish and the other a sex fiend."

"It's been known to happen," I said. "Even in Siamese twins. They both have the same smile, but one turns out to be a nun and the other a whore."

Mrs. Vriesländer appeared in a high-waisted Empire gown, as bulky as Madame de Staël. She was wearing a sapphire bracelet with stones the size of hazelnuts. "Cocktails, gentlemen?"

The remaining guests arrived, the twins, an actor by the name of Vesel, and Carmen, who was munching a chocolate bar. I wondered whether it would spoil her appetite for the inevitable herring. It didn't.

"I'm leaving for Hollywood in two weeks," Tannenbaum announced as the goulash was being served. Preening himself like a peacock, he leered in the general direction of the twins.

"What will you be doing there?" Vriesländer asked.

"Acting, of course. The usual S.S. man. A Gruppenführer, in fact."

"I suppose they picked you for your name?" I suggested.

"I act under the name of Gordon T. Crane. T is for Tannenbaum."

"A Gruppenführer?" said Vriesländer. "Isn't that the equivalent of a general? Have you had military experience?"

"I don't need military experience. All I need is hatred. Naturally the guy is a stinker. If he weren't, I'd have to turn down the part."

"Gruppenführer," said Mrs. Vriesländer. "That's very impressive. I'd have expected one of the big American actors to play a part like that."

"American actors refuse to play Nazis," said Vesel. "It's bad for their image. We have to or we'd starve."

"Art is art," said Tannenbaum loftily. "Wouldn't you do Rasputin or Genghis Khan or Ivan the Terrible if they asked you?"

"Don't quarrel," said Vriesländer. "You ought to be helping each other. What have we got for dessert?"

"Sachertorte."

We ate till we were foaming at the mouth. After the Sachertorte the cook brought in an enormous dish of Salzburger Nockerl, as light as an angel's nightgown. "Nobody eats in this crazy country," she complained. "They're all dieting. They live on raw carrots and celery. It's pathetic."

As usual there was plenty of goulash left over, and the guests were offered jars of it to take home. Ravic and Carmen declined, he because of his dignity, she because she was too lazy to carry it. The cook, who had a special liking for me, perhaps because I made no secret of my admiration for her talents, gave me two jars of goulash and a whole box of cake.

Natasha was working that night. She had given me the keys to her apartment. I deposited my goulash and cake and went back down for beer.

It gave me a strange feeling to let myself into the empty apartment. As far as I could remember, this had never happened to me before. It was like having an apartment of my own. The place was cool. I heard the hum of the air conditioning and of the icebox, and they seemed like friendly guardian spirits. I turned on the light, put the beer in the icebox, emptied the goulash into a saucepan, and put it on a low gas flame. Then I switched off the light and opened the windows. A wave of warm air poured in. The little blue flame of the stove diffused a faint magical glow. I turned on the radio and tuned in on a program of Debussy preludes. I sat down in a chair by the window and looked out at the glittering city. It was the first time I had waited for Natasha like this. I felt deliciously calm and relaxed. I hadn't told her yet that I was going to California with Silvers.

About an hour later I heard the key in the lock. For an instant I thought the owner of the apartment had come back unexpectedly —then I heard Natasha's step. "Is that you, Robert? Why are you sitting in the dark?"

She flung down her suitcase. "I'm dirty and very hungry. What should I do first?"

"Take a bath. And while you're in the tub, I'll serve you a dish of goulash. I've got it on the stove. And there's Sachertorte for dessert."

"Have you been visiting that wonderful cook again?"

"Yes, and like a good mother bird I've brought home plenty for the family. We won't have to shop for three days."

Natasha had already thrown her clothes off. The bathroom was full of steam and smelled of Mary Chess carnation. I brought in the goulash. For a moment the world was at peace.

"I was Anna Karenina this evening. All done up in furs. When I came out I was surprised not to see any snow on the ground."

"You look like Anna Karenina."

She laughed. "Everybody has his private Anna Karenina. I'm afraid the original was a good deal stouter than the women of today. That was the style. Built like a Rubens, long whalebone corset, floor-length skirt. You wouldn't have been likely to see her in a bathtub. But why were you sitting in the dark?"

"Because you'd left the newspaper on the table and I didn't want to look at it."

"Why not?"

"Because there's nothing I can do about it."

"Who can? Except the soldiers."

"Yes," I said. "Except the soldiers."

Natasha handed me her empty plate. "Would you like to be one?"

"No. It wouldn't change anything."

She watched me for a minute or two. Then she asked me: "Are you very unhappy?"

"I'd never admit that. And besides, what difference does my unhappiness make when other people are dying?"

She shook her head. "What is it you really want, Robert?"

I looked at her in surprise. "What I want? That's a funny question." I was stalling for time.

"What do you want to do later on? What's your aim in life?"

"You can't ask questions like that in the bathtub," I said. "Come on out."

She stood up but refused to be diverted. "What do you really want out of life?" she asked.

"Nobody knows that. Do you?"

"I don't need to know. I'm only a reflection."

"A reflection?"

"Don't try to sidetrack me. What do you want? What do you live for?"

"Who knows that? And if I did know, it probably wouldn't be true any more. For the present I travel light and I don't think about such things."

"You really don't know?"

"I really don't know. Not the way a banker or a priest knows. And in that sense I never will." I kissed her wet shoulders. "You've got to remember, Natasha, that for years my whole life was a struggle for survival. It kept me so busy that I never got around to asking what I wanted to survive for. Satisfied?"

"That's not true and you know it. You don't want to tell me. Or maybe you don't want to admit it to yourself. I've heard you screaming."

"What?"

She nodded. "In your sleep."

191

"What did I scream?"

"I don't remember. I was asleep myself. Your screaming woke me."

Thank God she didn't remember. "Everybody has bad dreams now and then."

For a time she was silent. Then she said thoughtfully: "I don't really know anything about you."

"You know too much already. It's not good for love."

I pushed her gently out of the bathroom. "You have the most beautiful knees in the world."

"You're trying to change the subject."

"Why should I want to do that? Haven't we got our pact? You reminded me of it yourself not so long ago."

"Forget about our pact. That was only a pretext. We both wanted to forget something. Did you succeed?"

Suddenly I felt a cold pang in my heart. Not the violent blow I would have expected—more like the touch of a shadowy hand. It lasted for only a moment but the chill remained. "I had nothing to forget," I said. "I was lying."

"I shouldn't ask you such stupid questions," she said. "I don't know what got into me. Maybe it's because I was Anna Karenina all evening, wrapped in furs. It made me feel so romantic and sentimental, I saw myself riding through the snow in a troika. Maybe the fall has hit me harder than you. In the fall all pacts are suspended. In the fall people only want . . . What do we want in the fall?"

"Love," I said.

She laughed. "What would you do right now if you had your choice?"

"Make love to you."

"Why don't you then? Can't you see that's what I've been waiting for the whole time?"

XXIII

The dream came more than a week later. I had expected it sooner and then I had started thinking it wouldn't come. Very cautiously I had toyed with the hope that it was gone forever, and tried to persuade myself that the attacks of sudden faintness, which made me feel as if the earth were trembling, were mere aftereffects.

I was mistaken. It was the same sticky, dense black dream as before. It began in the musty darkness of the cellar in Brussels. The walls were moving in on me to crush me. I screamed and gasped for air. I thought I was awake but, still in my dream, the sticky mud had come. I was being hunted. I had secretly crossed the border. I was in the Black Forest, and the S.S. were hunting me with police dogs, led by the man with the cruel smile. They had caught me, and I was back in the crematorium. The breath had gone out of me. They had just taken me down unconscious from one of the meat hooks on the wall. I smelled perfume, I saw the smiling face. The man with the face was speaking to me. He said that he wouldn't kill me just yet; maybe later, much later, when I begged him on my knees, he'd burn me alive. He told me what would happen to my eyes. And my dream ended as it always did: I had buried someone in a garden and almost forgotten about it. But then the police had found the body, and I wondered why I hadn't chosen a better hiding place.

It was a long time before I realized that I was in America and that I had been dreaming. I was too exhausted to move. I lay there staring at the reddish glow of the New York night. Finally, I summoned the strength to get up and dress. I was afraid the dream would attack again if I let myself fall asleep. That had already happened to me, and the second time was even worse than the first.

I went down to the dimly lit lobby. Melikov's replacement was snoring in the corner. With his furrowed lifeless face and his open groaning mouth, he himself looked like a torture victim who had just been taken down unconscious from the meat hook.

I'm one of them, I thought; I belong to that horde of murderers. Regardless of what I tell myself in the daytime, they were my people—even if they did hunt me and drive me out of the country and take away my citizenship. I was born among them and that was why I tried to make myself believe that an honest, kindly, innocent people had been hypnotized by invading demons from Mars. How absurd! The evil had grown from the very heart of the people, a people who had elected to be ruled by drill sergeants and classroom martinets. Those tens of thousands of wide-open, roaring mouths in the newsreels—those were the people; they had cast off their thin coating of civilization and reverted to barbarism. *Furor Teutonicus!*

I went out into the street and headed for Broadway in quest of light. Here and there an all-night cafeteria cast its cold neon glow over the street. A few weary customers sat livid and motionless at the counters. The street was deserted. Light without people was even eerier than darkness; it was something useless in a utilitarian world, and made me think of the moon, as though the streets were craters between buildings.

I stopped outside a delicatessen. The sausages in the window seemed to be in mourning. A sign told me that the owner's name was Chaim Finkelstein, a man who no doubt had left Europe at the right time. I stared at the name. I didn't even have that excuse. I couldn't claim to be a Jew, I couldn't say I had nothing in common with the Teutons, I was one of them, and in that spectral foggy dawn I wouldn't have been surprised if Mr. Chaim Finkelstein had suddenly appeared with a knife and attacked me as one of the murderers of his people.

I plodded down Broadway through the theater district, past Macy's, and on to Twenty-third Street, where I turned back north on Fifth Avenue. There was little traffic, but the traffic lights kept changing obstinately from red to green and green to red, as though playing some game of their own, unrelated to human purposes. I trudged on, knowing that my only salvation lay in walking and breathing. On this avenue of luxury I felt rather more secure, as though its imposing walls protected me from the dark chaos that seemed to threaten from both sides. The light paled; time seemed suspended between night and morning. Then suddenly the new day appeared, tender and virginal, clad in pink and silvery-gray, and the first rays of the sun struck the uppermost stories of the taller buildings. The night was over, I thought, and felt relieved of a great weight. I stopped outside one of the windows of Saks Fifth Avenue, where a group of fur-clad ladies had been struck motionless by a fairy wand—a dozen Anna Kareninas congealed by the Russian winter. Then I was very hungry and I stopped at the nearest cafeteria for breakfast.

By now Betty knew she had cancer. No one had told her, everyone had tried to set her mind at rest, but, suspicious from the first, she had taken note of every troubling indication and gradually pieced the picture together—very much like a general who, disregarding the official optimism of his entourage, carefully coordinates the scraps of information that pour in from all sides and concludes that the battle is lost. But instead of resigning herself, instead of surrendering, she had thrown herself into a heroic struggle for every single day. She didn't want to die. Death had stood by her bedside during her period of doubt, but now by a supreme effort of the will she banished it. She would live to see Berlin and her cherished Olivaer Platz again. That was where she came from, and she was determined to go back, just as a salmon finds its way from the ocean to the mountain brook where it was spawned.

She studied the newspapers feverishly. She bought a map of Germany and fastened it to her bedroom wall. Every morning after reading the news dispatches she would mark the positions of the advancing Allied armies with colored pins. The Third Reich was dying, and she had made up her mind to outlast it.

Betty had always been the soul of kindness, and for her friends she remained unchanged. She could not see an unhappy face without trying to help. But she hardened her heart to the suffering of the German people and the mass death that foreshadowed the end of the war, a catastrophe which to her frenzied mind had ceased to be human and become mathematical. Why didn't the Germans just surrender? Not for their own sake, but for hers. According to Kahn, she took it as a personal insult.

Actually, Germany had ceased to exist for her; only Berlin was left. In connection with Berlin she saw the human reality of the war, the blood and horror. She marked the bombings on a large map of the city and suffered. She wept and raged because children had been put into uniform and sent out to fight. Like a melancholy owl she stared at us out of great horror-stricken eyes, unable to understand why her Berlin and her Berliners wouldn't surrender and drive out the parasites who were sucking their blood.

"How long will you be away?" she asked me.

"I'm not sure. Two weeks, maybe more."

"I'll miss you."

"I'll miss you, too, Betty. You're my guardian angel."

"A guardian angel with a cancer in her belly."

"You haven't got cancer, Betty."

"I can feel it," she whispered. "I feel it gnawing at night. I hear it. Like a silkworm gnawing mulberry leaves. I've got to stuff myself, or it will eat me away too quickly. I eat five meals a day now. I mustn't lose weight. I've got to have reserves. How do I look?"

"Well, Betty. Flourishing."

"Do you think I'll make it?"

"What, Betty?"

"That I'll make it back to Berlin."

"Why not?"

She looked at me with her hungry sunken eyes. "Will they let us in?"

"Who? The Germans?"

Betty nodded. "I was thinking about it last night. Maybe they'll arrest us at the border and send us to a camp."

"That's impossible, Betty. They won't be giving the orders any more. The Americans and the English and the Russians will be there. They'll be giving the orders."

"The Russians? But haven't they got concentration camps, too? And they'll be in Berlin. Won't they send us to the mines in Siberia? Or to their death camps?"

Her lips trembled. "I wouldn't think about all that now, Betty," I said. "Wait till the war is over. Then we'll see what happens. Maybe it will be entirely different from anything we can imagine now."

"What do you mean?" asked Betty anxiously. "Do you think the war will go on after Berlin is taken? In the Alps? In Berchtes-gaden?"

She thought of the war only in relation to her quickly ebbing life. I saw she was watching me and I knew I had to be careful. Sick people are very keen-sighted. "You think the same as Kahn," she said accusingly. "That I only think of Olivaer Platz, instead of worrying about victories and defeats like other people."

"Why shouldn't you, Betty? You've suffered enough. You have a perfect right to concentrate on Olivaer Platz."

"I know. But . . ."

"Don't listen to those people, Betty. Our refugee friends are a lot of armchair generals. Do you think the war will be won any sooner because of their grand strategy, or that our own General Tannen-baum is doing any good with his blood list? Just be your own self."

Great raindrops splashed against the windowpanes, and the room darkened. Suddenly Betty giggled. "That Tannenbaum! He says if he ever has to play Hitler in a movie, he'll play him as a cheap seducer out to bamboozle elderly widows. He says that's what he looks like, with his Napoleon hairdo and the little brush under his nose."

I nodded. I was sick of these cheap refugee jokes. When a man had come so close to destroying the world, you couldn't dispose of him with a joke. "Tannenbaum is a card," I said.

I stood up. "Good-by, Betty. I'll be back soon. By then you'll have forgotten all your black thoughts—it's just your imagination. You should have been a writer. I wish I had half your imagina-tion."

She took this as the compliment I had intended. Her eyes lit up. "That's a good idea, Ross. But what should I write about? Nothing interesting has ever happened to me."

"About your life, Betty. The full life that you've lived for us all."

"Do you know what, Ross? I think I might actually try."

"You really should."

"But who would read what I write? And who would publish it? That was the trouble with Moller. He was desperate because no one would publish him in America. That's why he hanged him-self."

"I don't think so, Betty," I said quickly. "I believe it was because he couldn't write over here. He had no more ideas. The first year he was still full of indignation and protest and he did write. But he had nothing to say. The danger was over, his indignation had no new personal experience to back it up, it turned into rebellious boredom and impotent resignation. Most of us are satisfied to have saved our lives; he wasn't. He wanted more, and that destroyed him."

Betty had listened attentively. "Like Kahn?" she asked.

"Kahn? What has it got to do with Kahn?"

"I don't know. Just a hunch."

"Kahn isn't a writer. He's a man of action."

"Exactly," said Betty hesitantly. "But maybe I'm mistaken."

"I'm sure you are, Betty."

I wasn't so sure as I descended the dark stairs. In the doorway I met Gräfenheim. "How is she?" he asked.

"Not so good," I said. "Are you giving her sedatives?"

"Not yet. She'll need them soon enough."

The rain had stopped, but the sidewalk was still wet. I headed for Fifty-seventh Street, but after a few blocks I decided to look in on Kahn.

I found him in his shop. He was reading *Grimm's Fairy-Tales*. "Amazing how bloodthirsty German fairy tales are," he said. "Have you ever thought about it?"

"No. I haven't read them since I was a child."

"They drip with blood. Knives, poison, torture. No wonder the Germans are a people of executioners, growing up with such stuff."

He slammed the book shut. "You might say that the Bible isn't exactly a tea party either, but that's history! Fairy tales are imagination. Some imagination! When are you off to Hollywood?"

"In two days."

"You may see Carmen turning up there."

"Carmen?"

Kahn laughed. "Some little assistant director has given her a contract. Three months at a hundred dollars a week. She'll be back again before you know it. No talent whatever."

"Did she want to go?"

"No, she's too lazy. I had to persuade her."

"Why did you want to do that?"

"So she won't think she's missed something. She'd never have forgiven me. Let her find out for herself. Wasn't I right?"

I said nothing. He was uneasy. "Wasn't I right?" he asked again.

"I hope so. She's very beautiful. I wouldn't have risked it."

He laughed again; it sounded rather forced. "Why not? There are thousands of beautiful women in Hollywood. Some of them even have talent. She hardly knows a word of English. I hope you'll kind of keep an eye on her after she arrives. You will, won't you?"

"Of course. Insofar as it's possible to look after a beautiful girl."

"With Carmen it's easy. She sleeps most of the time."

"I'll be glad to. But I don't know anybody myself. Except maybe Tannenbaum."

"Just take her out to dinner now and then. And when the time is ripe, persuade her to come back to New York."

"All right. What will you do while she's away?"

"The same as usual."

"What's that?"

"Nothing. Sell radios. What else can I do? Enthusiasm over being alive is like champagne. Once the cork is drawn, it goes stale. Luckily, most people don't notice. Good luck, Ross. Don't turn into an actor. You're one already."

"When you get back," said Natasha, "this little love nest will again be the home of a melancholy homosexual. I had a letter from him this morning on the loveliest stationery. It smelled of Jockey Club."

"Where from?"

"Does that suddenly interest you?"

"No. Just an idiotic question to hide my confusion."

"From Mexico. Where one more great love has come to an end."

"What do you mean, one more?"

"Is that another idiotic question to hide your confusion?"

"No, this time I'm interested."

She propped herself up on one arm and looked into the mirror, so that our eyes met. "Why do we find unhappiness so much more interesting than happiness? Are we such envious animals?"

"That, too. But mostly because happiness is boring."

She laughed. "There's something in that. It would be hard to talk five minutes about happiness. What can a happy person say except that he's happy? About unhappiness we can talk day and night."

"That's true of trivial unhappiness," I said hesitantly. "Not of the real thing."

She was still looking straight at me. The light from the living room shone into her eyes, making them strangely bright and transparent. "Are you very unhappy, Robert?" she asked.

"No," I said, after a while.

"I'm glad you didn't say you were happy. Usually I don't object to lies. I'm a pretty good liar myself. But sometimes I can't stand a lie."

"I wish very much that I were happy," I said.

"You're not, though. Not the way other people are happy."

We were still looking at each other in the mirror. It seemed easier than to face each other directly. "You asked me the same question a few days ago," I said.

"That time you lied. You thought I was going to make a scene and you were trying to head me off. I wasn't going to make a scene."

"I wasn't lying," I said almost automatically, and immediately regretted it. Sad to say, I had acquired certain principles that had helped me to survive but were of no use at all in my private life; one of them was never to confess a lie. It was axiomatic in my battle with the police but sadly out of place in my dealings with the woman I loved.

"I wasn't lying," I said. "I only expressed myself clumsily. We have taken over certain terms from a more romantic century. One of them is 'happiness.' When a romantic was happy in love, he was completely happy, and the universe with him: the birds sang madrigals, the heavens kissed the sea, even the most distant stars celebrated. Today things, or maybe I should say people, are a little more complicated. We're never more than partly happy, maybe a third, maybe half, and I suppose the part of us that isn't happy is unhappy."

"Thank you, professor," said Natasha, releasing my eyes and lying back on the pillow. "But don't you think the old way was better—anyway, simpler?"

"Probably. The old total happiness was a lie, but it was easier to live with."

"No," she said. "Why must you always be so reasonable? In those days people had imagination. They took their fantasies seriously, and nobody thought of calling them lies. What counted was feeling, and feeling was measured by its intensity, not by ethical standards. The trouble with you is that you've lost faith in feeling, but you're still ready to fall for high-sounding phrases. Well, you'll hear plenty of those in Hollywood."

"How do you know? Have you been there?"

"Yes. Luckily, I wasn't photogenic."

"You not photogenic!"

"Not for the movies, or so they said."

"Would you have stayed there if you had been?"

She kissed me. "You poor innocent. Any woman who says different is lying. Do you think I'm so in love with the work I do now? Persuading a lot of rich fat cows that they can wear dresses designed for nymphs!"

"I wish you could come along," I said without thinking.

"I can't. The winter season is starting. And we have no money."

"Will you be unfaithful to me?"

"Naturally."

"You think it's natural?"

"I'm not unfaithful to you when you're here."

I looked at her. I didn't know whether she meant it or not. "When somebody's not here," she said, "it's as though he were never coming back. It won't hit me right away—later on . . ."

"How soon?"

"How do I know? Don't leave me alone and you'll never have to ask such questions."

"That's a funny way to look at it," I said.

"It's the simplest way. If somebody's here, I don't need anybody else. If he's not here, I'm alone. And who can stand being alone? I can't."

"Does it happen so quickly?" I asked, beginning to feel alarmed. "You just exchange one for another?"

She laughed. "Of course not. It's not one for another; it's being alone for not being alone. Maybe men can stand being alone. Women can't. The ones who say they can are kidding you, or kidding themselves."

"So you can't stand being alone?"

"Not very well, Robert. I'm a clinging vine. When there's no one to cling to, I lie on the ground and rot."

"In two weeks?"

"How do I know how long you'll be gone? I never believe in dates. Especially coming-back dates."

"That's a lovely prospect."

She took me in her arms and kissed me. "Would you rather have a weeping willow who went into a nunnery?"

"Not while I'm here. Only when I'm away."

"You can't have everything."

"That's the saddest sentence in the world."

"Not the saddest, the wisest."

I knew we were playing, but not with blunted arrows. "I'd stay here if I could," I said. "But in a week I'd have nothing to eat. Silvers would take on another assistant."

I hated myself for explaining. I hadn't wanted to put myself in a situation that required me to make explanations like some wishy-washy husband. She was a sly one, I thought angrily, she had forced a change of terrain. I was no longer fighting her on her territory, but on mine, and that meant danger. A bullfighter had once taught me that. "I'll just have to get used to it," I said with a laugh.

This displeased her, but she didn't react. "It's fall," she said, with one of her abrupt changes of mood. "It's a hard season to live through even without being alone."

"But for you it's already winter, Natasha. You told me you were always a season in advance."

"You can worm your way out of everything," she said angrily. "You ought to be a lawyer."

"There's one thing I can't worm myself out of," I said. "My love for you."

Her face changed. "I wish you wouldn't lie," she said.

"I'm not lying," I said. "Why should I?"

"You're always so full of plans. You never let anything take you by surprise. I always do. Why don't you?"

"I have. To my regret. You're my first pleasant surprise. A surprise that can never become a habit."

"Are you spending the night here?"

"I'll stay here until I have to double-time to the station."

"I wouldn't do that. Take a cab."

We slept very little that night. We woke up and made love and fell asleep in each other's arms and woke up and talked and made love again, or merely felt each other's warmth and the mystery of two bodies, united and yet forever separate. We wore ourselves out in an attempt to overcome that separation, emitting frantic, senseless cries that welled up from the unconscious. We hated each other and loved each other. We shouted at each other like truck drivers in an effort to penetrate each other even more deeply, to efface all artificial limits from our minds and fathom the secret of the wind and the sea. Exhausted, we waited for the profound brown-and-gold stillness of the final letdown, when even words are too much trouble and there is no need of them, when all words are far away, dispersed like pebbles after a heavy rain; we waited, and the stillness came, and it was in us and we felt it: the stillness in which one is nothing more than a soft breath that scarcely stirs the lungs—we waited for it, we sank into it, and through it Natasha sank into sleep, but I lay awake, watching her, and it was a long while before I, too, fell asleep. I looked at her with the secret curiosity I have always felt toward sleepers, as though they knew something that was forever hidden from me. I saw her relaxed face, which, carried away from me by the magic of sleep, knew nothing of me, that face for which all the cries, oaths, and raptures of an hour past had ceased to exist, beside which I could die without its taking notice; with a fascination akin to horror I looked at this stranger next to me, this stranger who was closer to me than anyone else in the world, and I suddenly realized that the only beings we can possess entirely are the dead, because they cannot escape. All others change with every heartbeat; they go away and when they come back they are not the same. Only the dead were faithful. That was their power.

I listened to the wind. I was afraid to fall asleep, I shooed away the past and looked at Natasha's face. A slight crease had appeared in the forehead. I stared at it, and for a short while it seemed to me that I was on the point of discovering something I had never before suspected. I was conscious of a peace so deep as to be almost ecstatic, a feeling of infinite space. And the ultimate revelation was like a secret compartment, so close to me that I had only to stretch out my hand to open it. Cautiously, with bated breath, I moved toward it, I moved, and then I knew nothing: I had fallen asleep.

XXIV

The Garden of Allah had a swimming pool. The living quarters consisted of one-, two-, and three-room cabins. I was assigned to a two-room cabin with an actor; we each had our own bedroom and shared the bathroom. The general effect of the place was that of a gypsy encampment with modern comfort. This came as a surprise to me, and I took to it from the start. The first evening, the actor invited me to his room for a drink. There was whisky and California wine. Some of his friends dropped in. The atmosphere was quite free and easy. If anyone felt like a swim, he jumped into the green-and-blue swimming pool and cooled off. I represented myself as a former assistant curator of the Louvre; suspecting that gossip got around rather quickly in this community, I thought it best to stick to the role I would have to play in my work for Silvers.

The first few days I had nothing to do. The paintings Silvers had shipped from New York hadn't arrived yet. I hung around the Garden of Allah or drove to the beach with John Scott, the actor, and questioned him about life in Hollywood. Even in New York it had amazed me, and given me a strange sense of unreality, that though the country was at war one saw no sign of it. Here in Hollywood the war was a purely literary conception.

"There's one thing you've got to understand here in California," said Scott. "The first land beyond the horizon is Japan."

We were sitting on the Santa Monica beach, looking out over the gray-green waves of the Pacific. All around us children were screaming. In a wooden shack behind us lobsters were being cooked. Unemployed extras were strutting about, hoping to be discovered by a talent scout. The waitresses in the restaurants and snack bars were all waiting for the great moment, meanwhile consuming lavish quantities of make-up, tight-fitting pants, and short skirts. The whole place was one giant lottery: who would pick the winning number? Who would be discovered for the movies?

"Can it be Tannenbaum?" I asked incredulously, gaping at an apparition in an incredible sports jacket, who suddenly formed a dark spot against the sun.

"In person," said the Gruppenführer with dignity. "I hear you're staying at the Garden of Allah."

"How did you know?"

"It's the refugee actors' haven."

"Curses. I was hoping to get away from all that. Do you live there, too?"

"Moved in after lunch."

"After lunch? And barely two hours later you're running around on the beach in that ghastly getup. My compliments."

"A man's got to move fast around here. I see you're with Scott."

"You already know Scott?"

"Of course. I've been here twice before. Started out as a Scharführer. Then I was promoted to Sturmführer."

"And now you're a Gruppenführer. You're getting ahead fast."

"Obergruppenführer."

"Have you started shooting?" Scott asked.

"Not yet. We're starting next week. Now we're trying on costumes."

Trying on costumes, I thought. What I hadn't dared to think of and had tried to banish from my dreams had here been reduced to a pageant. For a moment I stood dumbfounded; then I had a feeling of wonderful release. I looked at the silver-gray ocean, the vast surge of quicksilver and lead crowding against the horizon, and in front of it this ridiculous little man for whom the catastrophes of the world had already reduced themselves to a matter of make-up and costumes, and I felt as though a ceiling of black clouds had parted. Maybe it's possible, I thought. Maybe a time comes when one stops taking it seriously. Even if I never get to the movie-actor stage, maybe a time will come when the nightmare stops hanging over me like a glacier waiting to bury me in ice.

"Tannenbaum," I said, "when did you leave Germany?"

"Thirty-four."

I should have liked to ask him some more questions. I was curious to know if he had suffered personal losses, if any of his relatives or close friends had been murdered or sent to concentration camps. Probably, almost certainly, but those were questions one couldn't ask. What I really wanted to know was whether he had put all that far enough behind him to be able to play such parts—the parts of men who had murdered his friends and relatives—without an acute inner crisis. But there was no need to ask. He did play them, and that was answer enough.

"It's been a pleasure running into you, Tannenbaum," I said.

He squinted at me suspiciously. "I wasn't expecting any compliments from you," he said.

"I meant it," I assured him.

His face lit up. "We must see more of each other," he said. "I'll have plenty of time in the next few days."

"I'll be glad to see you, Tannenbaum. Really glad."

Silvers called up producers and directors he had met in New York, and invited them to come and look at his paintings. But the usual thing happened: people who in New York had begged him almost with tears in their eyes to drop in on them if he ever came to Los Angeles had just about forgotten his existence; at all events, they were too busy to look at his pictures.

"Barbarians!" he growled. "If this keeps on, we'll just have to go back to New York. What kind of people are staying at the Garden of Allah?"

"No customers," I said. "In a pinch you might sell them a small drawing or a lithograph. Nothing bigger."

"Little fish are also welcome. We've got two small Degas drawings and two Picasso charcoal sketches. Take them home and hang them up in your room. And throw a cocktail party."

"Out of my own pocket?"

"On me, of course. Do you ever think about anything but money?"

"If I had any, I wouldn't have to think about it."

Silvers made a disparaging gesture. He was in no mood for jokes. "Give it a try. If there are no salmon to be had, maybe we'll catch a sardine."

I invited Scott, Tannenbaum, and a few of their friends. The Garden of Allah was famous for its cocktail parties. Scott told me they often lasted till noon the next day. To be on the safe side, but also because the irony of it appealed to me, I invited Silvers. He declined with good-humored condescension; it was beneath his dignity to attend a party for small fry.

It started out promisingly. By nine o'clock there were ten more people than had been invited; by ten there were dozens. My liquor gave out, and we moved to one of the other bungalows, belonging to a white-haired, red-faced man, who proceeded to order sandwiches, hamburgers, and tons of hot dogs. By eleven half of these total strangers were my bosom friends. Around midnight a few of the company fell into the swimming pool and others were pushed in. This was thought to be very funny. In the blue-green light I could see girls swimming around in panties and bras. They were young and pretty, and it all seemed very innocent. Much later we stood around the piano singing sentimental cowboy songs.

Little by little I lost track of what was going on. The world began to reel, and I made no attempt to straighten it out; what was the use of being sober? I hated those nights when I woke up alone and didn't know where I was; they were dense with dreams that were impossible to shake off. I sank into a deep, not unpleasant stupor, punctuated here and there by brown and golden lights. In the morning I couldn't recollect where I had been or how I had got back to my room.

Scott filled me in. "Remember those two drawings you had hanging here?" he said. "Well, you sold them. Did they belong to you?"

I looked around. I had a splitting headache. The two Degas drawings were gone. "Who did I sell them to?" I asked.

"Holt, I think. The director of Tannenbaum's picture."

"Holt? Never heard of him. I must have been pretty far gone."

"So was everybody else. Wonderful party! You were great, Bob."

I looked at him suspiciously. "Did I make an ass of myself?"

"No, that was Jimmy. He always cries his heart out when he's drunk. You were okay. Then you were drunk when you sold the drawings? You didn't look it."

"I must have been. I don't remember a thing."

"Not even the check?"

"What check?"

"Holt gave you a check on the spot."

I stood up, rummaged through my pockets, and actually found a neatly folded check. I stared at it. "Holt was stewed to the gills," said Scott. "You talked about art. You were brilliant. Holt was so impressed that he took the pictures right with him."

I held the check up to the light. Then I laughed. I had sold the drawings for five hundred dollars more than the price set by Silvers. "Hell!" I said to Scott. "I sold them too cheap."

"Really? Say, that's too bad. I don't think Holt will want to part with them."

"It doesn't matter," I said. "It serves me right."

"Does it make a big difference to you?"

"Forget it. It's my punishment. Did I sell the Picassos, too?"

"The what?"

"The two other pictures."

"I don't know. How about jumping into the pool? Best thing for a hangover."

"I haven't any trunks."

Scott produced four pairs from his room. "Take your pick. Do you want to eat breakfast or lunch? It's one o'clock."

I stood up. A vision of peace awaited me outside. The water sparkled; a few girls were swimming about; comfortably dressed men were sitting in deck chairs reading the papers, drinking orange juice or whisky, and chatting lazily. I recognized the white-haired man in whose bungalow we had been the night before. He waved at me. Three others, whom I did not remember, waved, too. I seemed to have friends all over—if only I knew who they were. Liquor was a more effective social catalyst than ideas: life seemed to be without problems, the sky was cloudless, and this was a privileged spot, a paradise far removed from the realities of the world and the black night of Europe. That was the illusion of a first impression; this, too, undoubtedly was a world of snakes and not of butterflies. But the mere illusion was a miracle. It was as though I had suddenly been wafted away to a South Sea idyll in Tahiti. Here I would be able to forget the past and my acquired guilt-ridden self, and revert to an original, primordial self, preceding all experience and unpolluted by the years. Perhaps, I thought, as I emerged from the artificially blue-green water, perhaps this time no memory will pursue me, perhaps I shall be able to start afresh and cast off the obligation to vengeance that I had been carrying about with me like a knapsack full of lead.

Silvers' irritation evaporated when I handed him the check. "You should have asked a thousand more," he said.

"I asked and received five hundred more than you told me. If you like, I can return the check and get the pictures back."

"That's not my style. A sale is a sale. Even at a loss."

He was sprawled out on a light-blue leather chaise longue by a window overlooking the hotel swimming pool. "I had some offers for the Picasso sketches," I said. "But I thought I'd better let you sell them yourself. I wouldn't want to bankrupt you by misinterpreting your figures."

Suddenly a smile lit up his face. "Ross," he said, "you have no sense of humor. Go ahead and sell them. Can't you see that I'm eaten by professional jealousy? You've sold something—I haven't."

I looked at him. His attire was already more Californian than Tannenbaum's, which was no small order. Silvers, of course, was wearing a tailor-made English sports jacket, while Tannenbaum's was ready-to-wear. But Silvers' shoes were too yellow, his silk ascot scarf was too wide and too outrageously turkey red. I knew what he was getting at; he didn't want to pay me a commission on my sale. Actually, I hadn't expected one, and I wasn't at all surprised when he asked me to bring him the bill for the cocktail party as soon as possible.

In the afternoon Tannenbaum called for me. "You promised Holt to drop in at the studio," he said.

"I did? What else did I say?"

"You were in top form. You sold Holt two drawings and you promised to tell him how to frame them."

"But they're already framed."

"You told him those were shop frames. You advised him to get eighteenth-century frames, said they'd make the pictures three times as valuable. Come on. The studio is worth seeing."

"All right."

My head was still in pretty bad shape. Tannenbaum led me to an ancient Chevrolet. "Where did you learn to drive?" I asked.

"In California. You need a car here. The distances are too great. You can buy a used car for peanuts."

We drove through a Moorish gate guarded by policemen. "Is this a prison?" I asked when we were stopped.

"Good God, no. That's the studio police. Without them the whole place would be flooded with sight-seers and job hunters."

We drove past a gold miners' village. Then down a street lined with Wild West saloons. It was strange to see these sets against the blue sky. Since most of them consisted only of house fronts, they looked as if they had been shelled and bombed in a neat, methodical war.

"This is where they shoot the outdoor scenes," Tannenbaum explained. "Hundreds of Westerns have been made here, all with the same plots. Sometimes they don't even change the actors. Nobody seems to mind."

We stopped outside an enormous shed, divided into several studios. The red light over the door of Studio 5 was on.

"We'll have to wait a moment," said Tannenbaum. "They're shooting. What do you think of all this?"

"I love it," I said. "It makes me think of a circus or a gypsy camp."

Outside Studio 4 I saw a few cowboys standing around and some men and women dressed like early settlers, the women in long skirts, the men in frock coats, beards, and slouch hats. They were almost all made up, which looked weird in the sunlight. There were also horses and a sheriff who was drinking Coca-Cola.

The red light over the door of Studio 5 went out. Blinded by the glare outside, I could see nothing for a moment. Then I froze. Some twenty S.S. men were coming toward me. Automatically, I turned to run and bumped into Tannenbaum. "Look pretty good, don't they?" he said.

"What!"

"I mean authentic. Good job, I mean."

"Yes," I mumbled. For a moment I didn't know if I was going to smack him in the jaw or not. Looking past the S.S. men I saw a watchtower and at the foot of it a barbed-wire fence. I noticed that my breath was coming in a high wheeze.

"What's the matter?" Tannenbaum asked. "Did they scare you? Didn't you know I was in an anti-Nazi picture?"

I nodded and tried to calm myself. "I'd forgotten," I said. "After last night. My head isn't quite clear yet."

"Of course. I should have reminded you."

"What for?" I said, still falteringly. "I know I'm in California. It was only the first moment."

"Sure. I understand. It was the same with me the first time. Now, of course, I'm used to it."

"What?"

"I mean you get used to it," said Tannenbaum.

"Really?"

"Sure."

I turned around again and looked at the detested uniforms. I was very close to vomiting. I was choking with rage, but there was nothing to vent it on. These S.S. men were chatting peacefully in English. But I was still in a state of shock. My fear and rage evaporated, but they left me aching in every muscle.

"There's Holt," said Tannenbaum.

"Yes," I said, staring at the barbed-wire fence.

"Hi, Bob." Holt was wearing a hunter's cap and leggings. I wouldn't have been surprised if he had had a swastika on his chest or a Star of David.

"I didn't know you'd started shooting," said Tannenbaum.

"Only a couple of hours this afternoon. We're through now. What do you say to a drink, Bob?"

I raised my hand. "Not just yet. After last night."

"That's just when you need it most."

"Really?" I asked absently.

"It's an old recipe! Fighting fire with firewater, we call it." Holt slapped me on the back.

"Maybe," I said. "Okay, in fact."

"That's the stuff."

We went out past a group of chattering S.S. men. Costumed actors, I thought, but I still didn't fully believe it. I gave myself a jolt. "That man's cap isn't right," I said, pointing at a Scharführer.

"Really?" asked Holt with dismay. "Are you sure?"

"Yes, I regret to say, I'm sure."

"We'll have to look into it," said Holt to a young man in green sunglasses. "Where's the costume consultant?"

"I'll get him."

Costume consultant, I thought. Over there they're still murdering people and here they've turned into extras. But then, what was Nazism but a revolt of the extras, who wanted to play the parts of heroes for once in their lives and only managed to turn into a gang of vulgar butchers? "Who is this consultant?" I asked. "A real Nazi?"

"I don't really know," said Holt. "Anyway, he's a specialist. Christ! If we have to shoot the whole scene over again on account of one lousy cap!"

We went to the bar. Holt ordered whisky and soda. "There's something I want to ask you about those drawings," Holt said after a while. "Don't be offended, but I've been told there are so many forgeries. They are authentic, aren't they?"

"There's nothing to be offended about. You're entitled to know. Those drawings were not signed by the artist; there's only a red stamp with his name. That's what bothers you, isn't it?"

Holt nodded.

"The stamp is his studio stamp," I explained. "Those drawings were authenticated after Degas' death. Mr. Silvers, my employer, has books containing descriptions and reproductions of all these posthumously authenticated works. He'll be glad to show them to you. Why not drop over to see him now? Are you through here?"

"I'll be through in an hour. But I believe you, Bob."

"Sometimes I don't believe myself, Joe. Let's meet at six at the Beverly Hills Hotel. Then you can convince yourself. Besides, Silvers will want to give you a bill of sale and a guarantee."

"Okay."

Silvers was sprawled on his light-blue chaise longue when we came in, a picture of benign self-satisfaction. No one could have guessed that so far his trip to Hollywood had been a total flop. He had me make out a guarantee, to which he appended photographs of the drawings. "You could almost call those drawings a gift," he said blandly. "Mr. Ross here came to me from the Louvre; he's a scholar; the financial end just isn't his line. He thought he knew the prices. What he failed to realize was that those were the prices I paid for the drawings a year ago. If I wanted to buy them back, they'd cost me at least fifty per cent more."

"Would you like to cancel the sale?" Holt asked.

"I wouldn't dream of it," said Silvers. "A sale is a sale. I only wanted to congratulate you. You've made a good buy. Pictures are the best investment there is. Every year they go up thirty to forty per cent. What do you think of that?"

Silvers grew more and more amiable and ordered coffee and brandy. "I'll make you a proposition," he said. "I'll buy back the drawings for twenty per cent more than you paid. This minute." He reached for his checkbook.

I waited eagerly to see how Holt would react to this booby trap. He reacted as Silvers had expected, saying that he had bought the drawings because he liked them. Not only did he mean to keep them, but he also wished to take up the option I had given him the night before on the two Picassos.

I looked at him in amazement. I had no recollection of any option and thought I detected a glint in Holt's eye, the look of a man who was on to a good piece of business. He had thought fast.

"An option?" Silvers asked me. "Did you give Mr. Holt an option?"

It was my turn to think fast. I knew nothing of any option; Holt had probably made it up. I only hoped he didn't know too much about the prices. "Yes," I said. "A twenty-four-hour option."

"And the price?"

"Six thousand."

"For one?" Silvers asked.

"For both," said Holt.

"Is that right?" Silvers snapped at me.

I hung my head. It was two thousand more than the price Silvers had fixed. "That's right," I said.

"Mr. Ross," said Silvers with surprising gentleness, "you're ruining me."

"I had quite a lot to drink," I said. "I'm not used to it."

Holt laughed. "One time when I was drunk," he said, "I lost twelve thousand bucks at backgammon. Taught me a lesson."

At the words "twelve thousand bucks" the same glint as I had seen in Holt's eyes came into Silvers'. "Let this be a lesson to you, too, Ross," he said. "We'll have to face it: you're a scholar, not a businessman."

I put on my best hangdog look. "Maybe you've got something there," I said, gazing out the window at the last white-clad tennis players disporting themselves under the wide afternoon sky. The swimming pool was deserted, but people were drinking at little round tables, and muffled music could be heard from the bar. Suddenly I felt a yearning for Natasha, for my childhood, and for long-forgotten dreams, a yearning so poignant that I thought it impossible to bear, and I realized to my despair that I would never be free. There was no salvation; the most I could hope for was to enjoy this oasis of calm that had opened up to me while in the world outside the avalanche of catastrophes rolled on unabated, to savor it with all my senses, for it was a brief gift. And the irony of it was that my brief moment of peace would be over when the world outside began to breathe again and to celebrate the triumph of peace. For then it would be time for me to embark on the lonely expedition that would lead me to inevitable destruction.

"Well then," said Silvers, pocketing the second check as nonchalantly as the first, "let me congratulate you again. You've laid the foundations of a fine collection. Four drawings by two of the greatest masters! One of these days I'll show you some Degas and Picasso pastels. I haven't time right now; I've been invited out to dinner. My arrival has been bruited about. Or if we don't get around to it while I'm here, perhaps you'll be coming to New York."

I applauded him in silence. I knew he had no dinner date; but I also knew that Holt was expecting him to try to palm off a larger picture. Silvers knew it, too, which is why he did nothing of the sort. Now Holt was certain that he had done a good piece of business. He was, as Silvers would have put it, ripe.

"Chin up, Bob," Joe consoled me. "I'll call for the pictures tomorrow."

"Sure thing, Joe."

XXV

A week later Tannenbaum came to see me. "We've checked up on that consultant of ours, Bob, and he's not reliable. He knows a certain amount, but Holt has lost confidence in him. He doesn't trust the guy who wrote the script either. He's never been in Germany. A stinking mess."

I was sitting by the swimming pool, reading the paper. In this blessed country the impending divorce of some movie star was featured on the front page; the war news was tucked away inside. A man could eat his breakfast without choking with impotent rage.

I looked at the palms, at two girls in the water, and then at the agitated Tannenbaum. "It's no skin off my ass," I said and went back to the Hollywood gossip in the paper: who had been seen with whom the night before, who might be having an affair with whom, and who might be playing what part.

"Oh, so it's no skin off your ass?" said Tannenbaum grimly. "Hell, the whole thing is your fault. Why did you have to notice that Scharführer's cap? That's what got Holt started."

"I'm sorry. Forget what I said."

"How can I? Our consultant has been fired."

"Find another."

"That's what I'm here for. Holt sent me. He wants to talk to you."

"Nonsense. I'm not a consultant for anti-Nazi movies."

"Oh yes you are. You're the only man in Hollywood who's seen the inside of a concentration camp."

I looked up. "What are you talking about?"

"Everybody knows that. Everybody in New York, I mean. Your friends, to be exact."

"So what?"

"Listen to me, Bob. Holt needs help. He wants to take you on as his consultant."

"Tannenbaum, you're nuts."

"He pays well. And after all, it's an anti-Nazi picture. That ought to interest you."

I saw that the only way I could make myself halfway clear to Tannenbaum was to tell him something about myself, and that I had no desire to do. He wouldn't have understood. He saw the world from a different angle. He was waiting for peace so as to be able to live a quiet life in Germany or America; I was waiting for peace in order to take my revenge. "I am not interested in movies about Nazis," I blurted out. "You don't write film scripts about those people; you kill them. So don't bother me. Have you seen Carmen?"

"Carmen? You mean Kahn's girl friend?"

"I mean Carmen."

"What do I care about Carmen? I'm thinking about our picture. Won't you at least talk to Holt?"

"No."

That afternoon I received a letter from Kahn. "Dear Robert," he wrote. "First the bad news. Gräfenheim is dead, an overdose of sleeping pills. He had heard via Switzerland that his wife had been killed in Berlin. In an American air raid. That was too much for him. American planes—he couldn't see that such things were inevitable under the circumstances; to him it was a cruel irony. And so he quietly and discreetly put an end to his life. Maybe you remember our last conversation about suicide. Gräfenheim pointed out that suicide was unknown to animals, because no animal was capable of total despair. He also thought that the possibility of suicide was one of God's greatest gifts to man, because it could put an end to hell, as Christians call the torment of the mind. He took his life. There is nothing more to be said about it. He has it behind him. We are still alive; we still have it ahead of us, regardless of whether we envisage it in the form of old age, natural death, or suicide.

"I have heard nothing from Carmen. She is too lazy to write. I enclose her address. Tell her she had better come back.

"Good-by, Robert. Come back soon. Our hardest time is yet to come. When we find ourselves staring into the void and even our illusions of revenge collapse. Prepare yourself for it gradually or the shock will be too great. We don't stand up very well under shocks, especially shocks that come from an entirely different direction than we expected. The impact of death, like that of happiness, is a question of degree. Sometimes I think of Tannenbaum, the Gruppenführer of the silver screen. Maybe that simpleton is the wisest of us all. *Salut,* Robert."

I went to the address Kahn had given me. It was a small shabby bungalow in Westwood with a couple of orange trees out in front. In a garden behind the house, surrounded by cackling chickens, Carmen was sleeping in a deck chair. She had on a very brief bathing suit, and it was beyond me how Kahn could think she couldn't get anywhere in Hollywood. She was the most beautiful girl I had ever seen. Not an insipid doll, but a tragic figure that made the heart throb.

She showed no surprise at seeing me. "Well, if it isn't Robert! What are you doing here?"

"Selling pictures. And you?"

"Some dope gave me a contract. I don't do a thing. It's lovely."

I asked her out to dinner. She wasn't enthusiastic. Her landlady, she said, was a first-class cook. I had my doubts when I saw the blowsy red-haired landlady. She looked more like hot dogs, hamburgers, and canned vegetables. "Fresh eggs," said Carmen, pointing at the hens. "Marvelous omelets."

Nevertheless, she finally agreed to have dinner with me at the Brown Derby. "They say it's full of movie stars," I said, to arouse her interest.

"Even a movie star can't eat more than one meal at a time" was her answer.

Carmen went inside to dress. She walked as if she had carried baskets on her head all her life, with Biblical dignity and easy grace. I couldn't understand Kahn; anybody in his right mind would have married her long ago and headed north to sell radios to the Eskimos, who, I had read somewhere, were attracted by a different type of woman.

When the taxi stopped outside the Brown Derby, my conscience began to trouble me. I saw men in raw-silk suits smitten with awe at the sight of Carmen. "Just a minute," I said. "I'll go in and see if they have room for us."

Carmen waited outside. The Brown Derby was full of seducers, but there were still a few free tables. "Not a table to be had," I announced when I came out. "I'm sorry. Do you mind if we go to a smaller place?"

"Not at all. To tell the truth, I'd rather."

We went to a restaurant that was small, dark, and empty. "How do you like it in Hollywood?" I asked. "Don't you find it rather tiresome after New York?"

She raised her wonderful eyes. "I haven't thought about it yet," she said.

"I hate it," I lied. "Never been so bored in my life. I can't wait to get back."

"It all depends," she said. "In New York I had no real friends. Here I've got my landlady. We get along beautifully. We talk about everything. And I'm crazy about chickens. They're not as dumb as most people think. I never saw a live chicken in New York, did you? I know their names, and they come when I call them. And the oranges! Isn't it wonderful just to go out and pick them off the trees?"

I suddenly understood the reason for Kahn's attachment to her. It was something more than the fascination of her unpredictable stupidity for a man of active, penetrating mind. It was also, though Kahn probably didn't know it, the miracle of such sheer untrammeled innocence in conjunction with such a body.

"How did you get my address?" she asked, picking up a drumstick and nibbling at it.

"I had a letter from Kahn. Hasn't he written you?"

"Oh yes," she said, busily chewing. "I never know what to write him. He's so complicated."

"Write him about the chickens."

"He wouldn't understand."

"Give it a try. Or write about something else. He'd be awfully glad to hear from you."

She shook her head. "I'd know what to write my landlady. But Kahn is so difficult. I don't understand him."

"Tell me about your movie career."

"Isn't it marvelous? They pay me my salary and I don't have to do a thing. A hundred a week! Where do they get all that money? At Vriesländer's I only got sixty, and I had to work all day. Besides, he was so mean and nervous, he always yelled at me when I forgot something. And Mrs. Vriesländer hated me. No, I like it here."

"But what about Kahn?" I asked, though I knew I wasn't getting anywhere.

"Kahn? He doesn't need me."

"Maybe he does."

"What for? I never know what to say to him."

"He needs you all the same, Carmen. Don't you want to go back?"

She looked at me out of her tragic eyes. "Back to Vriesländer? He's got a new secretary to bully. I'd be crazy. No, I'll stay here as long as the studio is dumb enough to pay me for doing nothing."

"Who is this director of yours?" I asked her. I was getting suspicious.

"Silvio Coleman. I'd never seen him before I got here. And then it was only for five minutes. Isn't it crazy?"

That reassured me. "I'm told it's the custom out here," I said.

Kahn's letter upset me. I lay awake, expecting my nightmare to drag me under. I had expected it after seeing the S.S. men in the studio, but that night, to my surprise, I had slept like a baby. Perhaps, it occurred to me now, my initial shock had been dispelled by the absurdity of the scene; perhaps my unconscious refused to be set in motion by a group of English-speaking, Coca-Cola-drinking S.S. men. In his letter Kahn had warned me of another, more serious kind of shock—the shock of a new and unexpected reality—and I realized that I had better steel myself against it. A hysterical wreck, who trembled at the sight of a uniform, would never be able to perform the task I had set myself. Why not take advantage of the unusual opportunity that Hollywood offered? It would do me a world of good, I decided, to get used to these comic-opera Nazis.

I got up early and strolled around the swimming pool in my pajamas. The palm trees rustled in the breeze, and the high foreign sky was not unfriendly. My mind was made up: yes, that would be the best solution.

Tannenbaum dropped in before lunch. "Tell me," I said, "how did you feel the first time you played the part of a Nazi?"

"I couldn't sleep at night. But then I got used to it. You get used to anything."

"Yes," I said. "I suppose you do."

"A pro-Nazi picture would be different. Naturally I couldn't do it. But who's going to make a pro-Nazi picture?" Tannenbaum fiddled with the corners of his ornate pocket handkerchief. "Holt spoke to Silvers this morning. Silvers has no objection to your taking on another job in the morning. He says he needs you mostly in the afternoon and evening."

"You mean he's already sold me to Holt?" I asked. "The way they buy and sell stars, or so I'm told."

"Of course not. He only inquired, because he needs you badly. I told you, there's nobody else around here who has actually been in a concentration camp."

"Hm. I bet Holt bought a painting in exchange for Silvers' benevolence."

"I don't know. Holt looked at Silvers' pictures yesterday. He was very enthusiastic."

The little Renoir, I thought. The one he's been trying to unload for three years. The cadaver with the eels. He's palmed it off on him, for sure. That gangster, selling my soul! It's lucky I'd decided to sell it anyway, for my own good.

In the noonday glare I saw Holt in green slacks circling the swimming pool on his way to join us. He was wearing a Hawaiian shirt, printed with a South Sea landscape. He waved both hands at me from the distance. I remembered just in time that he had ostensibly put one over on me with the Picasso sketches. "Hi, Bob."

"How do you do, Mr. Holt."

He slapped me on the back, something I detest. "Still sore about those little drawings? Don't let it get you down. I've just bought a still life from your boss; that ought to make us quits."

"The one with the eels?"

"That's right. Has he already told you?"

"No. But I could imagine. The best picture he's got."

"Glad to hear it."

He beat about the bush for a while, then he came to the point. He wanted me to check the script for mistakes and also act as a consultant on costumes and the Nazi background in general. "Those are two entirely different jobs," I said. "What do we do if the script is impossible?"

"Rewrite it. But first, take a look at it." Holt was sweating perceptibly. "We'll have to work fast. We want to start shooting the big scenes tomorrow. Could you take a quick look at the script today?"

I didn't answer. Holt opened his dispatch case and took out a bright-yellow binder. "A hundred and seventy pages," he said. "Take you two or three hours."

I looked at the binder. Would I? Wouldn't I? But actually my decision had been made. "Five hundred dollars," said Holt. "For a thousand-word report."

"That's fair enough," said Tannenbaum.

"Two thousand," I said. If I was going to sell myself, at least I wanted to be able to pay my debts and put a few dollars aside.

Holt was almost in tears. "That's out of the question," he said.

"Okay," I said. "I wasn't too keen on it anyway. It's no joke having to think of those things."

"A thousand," said Holt. "Because it's you."

"Two thousand. What's two thousand dollars to a man with a collection of Impressionists?"

"That's hitting below the belt, Bob. It's not my money. It's the studio's."

"So much the better."

"Fifteen hundred," said Holt, gnashing his teeth. "And three hundred a week as a consultant."

"Okay," I said. "Of course you'll put a car at my disposal. And it's understood that I'm to be free in the afternoon."

Holt bore it like a man. "Okay, Bob. I'll leave the script. Start right in; we're in a hurry."

"Sure thing, Joe," I said amiably. "I'll want a thousand in advance. Then I'll start right in."

"What do you mean? Don't you trust me?"

"I had my fingers burned with those Picasso drawings. Same as you with that game of backgammon."

"You don't forget anything, do you?"

"I can't afford to."

"Okay. You'll get your check this afternoon. I need your report on the script at eight in the morning. I expect you to be on time."

Holt stood up. He had come to plead for help, but now he was my boss. I had often experienced that sort of transformation; it takes place in a twinkling. In coming, the green slacks had sauntered around the pool; in leaving, they marched. It wouldn't have surprised me if they had grown top boots.

"Naturally," said Silvers, "if you can only work for me part time, I'll have to reduce your salary. Fifty per cent would be fair, don't you think?"

"That's the second time in one day," I said, "that I've heard the word 'fair' taken in vain."

Silvers pulled up his feet on the light-blue chaise longue. "It seems to me that my offer is not only fair, but exceedingly generous. I'm giving you a chance to make a lot of money in another job. Instead of firing you, I let you work for me when it suits your convenience. You ought to be thankful."

"Sorry, I can't manage that."

The Renoir with the eels was still hanging on his wall. Which meant that Holt could still back out. I had no intention of influencing him, but I made a note of the possibility. "I'd have expected you to give me a raise," I said. "Or at least a bonus for the things I sell for you. If you like, you can cut my salary and put me on a commission basis."

Silvers examined me as if I were a rare insect. "Do you know the first thing about selling pictures? You'd starve on a commission basis."

Silvers liked to believe that selling pictures required no less genius than painting them. He was thoroughly exasperated with me for implying the contrary. "Here I persuade Mr. Holt to employ you in the movies and you . . ."

"Don't give me that, Mr. Silvers," I said calmly. "You're not trying to sell me anything; Mr. Holt is your customer. You've given him the impression that you're doing him a big favor. That's fine. I'm sure he'll show his gratitude by buying more pictures from you. But don't try to make *me* feel grateful, when the benefit is all yours. It was very nice of you to teach me that the mark of a great dealer is that he doesn't just fleece the customer, but makes him feel grateful for being fleeced. I recognize your mastery, but you don't have to practice it on me."

All at once Silvers' face collapsed; in half a second he had aged twenty years. "Oh," he said. "I don't have to practice it on you. Think it over. What do I get out of life? You throw cocktail parties on my money, you're twenty-five years younger than I am. I sit around this hotel waiting for customers like an old spider; I train you as if you were my own son, and you get sore if I try to sharpen my tired claws on you. Can't I have any fun at all?"

I watched him closely. I knew his tricks. One of them was to be sick in bed, at death's door, as it were, when a customer called. Since a dying man couldn't take even the tiniest picture with him, he preferred to sell, even at a loss, to someone he had taken a shine to. I had arranged the medicine bottles myself. His wife made him up to look like a ghost. Thus reclining in a blue dressing gown— the blue dressing gown was my idea; it accentuated his pallor beautifully—he had sold the most hideous monstrosity, an enormous jockey lying dead beside his horse, to a Texas oil millionaire, "at a loss." I had even interrupted the negotiations twice to bring Silvers his medicine, consisting not of whisky, as Silvers wished, but of vodka—also my idea, because vodka was odorless, whereas a good Texan nose would have smelled whisky a mile off. In a dying voice Silvers had finally dictated the sales contract, giving himself a net profit of twenty thousand dollars. I knew this trick and a dozen more—his own special brand of artistic expression, Silvers called them—but this note of petulance was new to me. And the look of weariness that had come over him seemed genuine.

"What's the matter?" I asked. "Doesn't the climate agree with you?"

"Climate, hell! I'm dying of boredom."

I looked at Renoir's eels. I was sure he had made a profit of eight thousand dollars on them, not a fortune, but nothing to despair about either.

"All right," he said. "I'll tell you my troubles. From sheer boredom I pick up a girl by the swimming pool, a pretty, insignificant little blonde. I invite her to dinner, and she accepts. Champagne, shrimps with Thousand Island dressing, sirloin steak, and so on, all served here in my pretty little dinette. I cheer up, I forget my miserable life, we go to the bedroom, and what happens?"

"She leans out the window and starts shouting 'Rape! Police!' "

Silvers let that sink in for a second. "Does that happen?" he asked.

"Sure. So my neighbor Scott tells me. Seems to be the standard way for a girl to pick up some easy change."

"Interesting. No, it wasn't that. I wish it had been. This was worse. She asked for money."

"Yes," I said, "that's very depressing for a man who's used to being loved for his own sake. How much? A hundred?"

"Worse."

"A thousand? She had her nerve with her."

Silvers made a disparaging gesture. "She asked for a certain sum, but it wasn't that." He stood up, bared his teeth, and spoke in a high, girlish voice. " 'What will you give me if I climb into bed . . .' " and then, exploding: " 'Daddy!' "

I had watched his performance with admiration. The bared teeth gave it a touch of virtuosity. "Daddy," I said. "Yes, that's quite a blow for a man over fifty. But it doesn't mean very much. It's just a term of endearment. Like darling. It has nothing to do with age."

Silvers looked at me eagerly, trying to find comfort in my words. But then he shook his head. "No, this was different. I could have kicked myself for not holding my tongue. But I was too upset. Not by the money. I'd have made her a present anyway. It was her calling me 'daddy.' To me it sounded like 'grandfather.' I asked her what she meant. She thought it was the money I minded. 'Well,' she says, in that tinny little doll's voice of hers, 'if I'm going to shack up with an old man, I expect to get something out of it. I saw this genuine camel's-hair coat at Bullock's Wilshire and . . .' "

Silvers' voice failed him. "What did you do?" I asked.

"What any gentleman would do. I paid her and threw her out."

"The full price?"

"All I could lay hands on."

"Painful but understandable."

"You don't understand a thing," said Silvers. "The money didn't bother me; it was the psychological shock. That little tart calling me an old goat. But you wouldn't understand. You're unfeeling, that's what you are."

"That's a fact. Besides, there are some things that can be understood only between people of the same age. And it seems that the gap between age groups increases as we grow older. I once heard a man of eighty refer to a seventy-seven-year-old friend as a young whippersnapper, still wet behind the ears. A strange phenomenon."

"A strange phenomenon! Is that all you have to say?"

"Yes," I said firmly, "that's all I have to say. You can't expect me to take this nonsense seriously."

He was going to flare up, but then a spark of hope appeared in his art-dealer's eyes—as though a dubious Pieter de Hooch in his possession had just been declared authentic by a leading expert. "You mean . . ."

"Why, of course. It's absurd for a man like you to worry about such nonsense."

He thought it over. "But what if I think of it next time? It'll make me impotent. I felt as if a bucket of ice had been . . ." He paused.

"Dashed over your head," I completed.

"Not my head—my cock," he said, with a shamefaced look. "Now I've got this fear hanging over me. What can I do?"

I pondered the problem for a while. Then I said: "One way is to get drunk and forget all your fears and inhibitions. The only trouble is that drinking makes some people impotent. Or you could do what a racing driver does after an accident. Before shock has had time to set in, he hops into another car and steps on the gas."

"Yes, but in my case shock has already set in."

"Pure imagination, Mr. Silvers. You've read about it, you know what's supposed to happen, so you imagine it's happened to you."

A look of relief, almost of gratitude, crept over his face.

"You really think so?"

"Definitely."

He was clearly on the road to recovery. "Strange," he said after a while, "how a silly little word spoken by a silly little tart can take the soul out of everything—money, success, social standing. As though the whole world were secretly Communist."

"What!"

"I mean, as though, when you come right down to it, all men were equal—without exception."

"Time is a Communist," I said. "Regardless of money or social standing, regardless of whether you're a saint or a stinker, it just adds day to day and year to year. An interesting idea, Mr. Silvers, though not exactly new."

"An antiquarian has no use for new ideas."

A faint smile spread over his face. "I guess no one believes that he's getting old. He knows it, but he doesn't believe it." I could see he was his old self again.

"What about this cut in my salary?" I asked.

"Forget it. Just so you're available in the evening."

"With time and a half for overtime after seven."

"At your normal salary. No extra pay for overtime. Right now you're making more than I am."

"I see you've recovered from your shock, Mr. Silvers."

XXVI

I spent a few hours studying the script. A third of the situations were impossible. The rest could be straightened out. I worked until one in the morning. A good many of the scenes had been taken over from Westerns. The script-writer had undoubtedly picked the cruelest, most violent incidents he could find, but compared with what was really happening in Germany they looked like sugar candy and harmless fireworks. The strangest borrowing from the Westerns was their code of honor: the two adversaries always reached for their guns at the same time. This was obviously an experienced writer, who had done gangster pictures as well as Westerns, but the reality of the Third Reich was quite beyond the scope of his imagination.

Luckily, Scott was giving one of his all-night parties. As usual, it had drifted out to the swimming pool. I went down and joined the merrymakers. "Knocking off?" Scott asked me.

"Yes, for today. I need a drink."

"There's Russian vodka and every known brand of whisky."

"A short whisky," I said. "I don't want to get drunk."

Scott laughed. "No pictures to sell, eh?"

Silvers had given me two Renoir drawings, one in pencil, the other in sanguine. He had forced them on me with the observation that small fry shit, too.

"I've got two Renoirs," I said. "You're just in time."

"Renoirs?" asked Scott. "Real ones?"

"Yes," I said. "That seems to be unusual in Hollywood."

"What kind of a character is this Silvers?"

"A public benefactor in spite of himself. His customers are always happy, because even if they've been overcharged, their pictures keep increasing in value. The best investment in the world."

"Better than stocks?"

I laughed. "That's what Silvers always says, though he doesn't really believe it himself. The funny part of it is that it's true. It's like the crook who sold worthless land in Florida, claiming there was oil on it. Years later, he bumped into a group of his victims. He expected to be skinned alive. Not at all. They welcomed him as their benefactor. They really had found oil; they were millionaires."

Scott filled my glass. "Do you know, Bob, I wish you'd taken vodka, a big tall glass. Maybe I'll buy a drawing myself tonight. I've just received my check."

"Take the sanguine. It's better."

I stretched out in a deck chair and put my glass down on the ground. I closed my eyes and listened to the music of the little radio someone had brought with him. It was a pretty tune, something called "Sunrise Serenade." I opened my eyes again and looked up into the California sky. For a moment I felt as though I were swimming in a soft transparent ocean without a horizon. Then I heard Holt's voice beside me. "Is it eight o'clock already?" I asked.

"No. I just thought I'd look in and see what you were doing."

"I'm drinking whisky. Any more questions? Our contract doesn't start until tomorrow."

"Have you read the script?"

I turned around and looked into his worried face. I didn't want to discuss what I had read, I wanted to forget it. "Tomorrow," I said. "I'll tell you all about it tomorrow."

"Why not now? Then we can get everything ready. We'll be saving half a day. We're in a hurry, Bob."

I saw there was no chance of getting rid of him. Why not now? I thought finally. Why not here amid liquor and water and girls, under this serene night sky? Why not chew it over right here instead of going to bed with a bellyful of memories and having to take sleeping pills. "Okay, Joe. Let's just move off to one side."

An hour later I had finished showing Holt the mistakes in his script. "I wouldn't worry about the uniforms and props," I said. "Those things are easy to fix. What really bothers me is the atmosphere. It shouldn't be melodramatic, as in a Western. What's really going on over there is much worse than melodrama."

For a while Holt hemmed and hawed. Finally he said: "Don't forget that movies are a business."

"What do you mean by that?"

"The studio is investing almost a million. Which means that we need receipts of more than two million before we make our first dollar. We've got to have audiences."

"I know that. But . . ."

"Nobody would believe these things you've been telling me. Is it really like that?"

"Much worse."

Holt spat into the water. "Nobody'd believe us, Bob."

I stood up. My head ached. I had really had enough. "Then leave it the way it is, Joe. But isn't it ironic? Here's the United States at war with Germany, and you tell me that no American would believe what the Germans are doing."

Holt wrung his hands. "I believe you, Bob. But the studio wouldn't and neither would the public. Nobody would go to see the kind of picture you're suggesting. The subject is risky enough already. I'm all in favor, Bob, but I'd have to convince the big shots at the studio. What I'd like best is to do a documentary; it would be a flop. The studio wants melodrama."

"With abducted virgins, tortured movie stars, and wedding bells at the end?"

"Not exactly. But with pursuits, fighting, and excitement."

Scott came strolling over. "It sounds like you need some liquor over here."

He set down a bottle of whisky and two glasses on the rim of the pool. "We're moving over to my place. If you're hungry, come on over. There's plenty of cold chicken."

Holt grabbed me by the lapels. "Just ten minutes more, Bob. Just the practical details. We can talk about the rest tomorrow."

The ten minutes turned out to be an hour. Holt was typical of Hollywood, a man who would have liked to do something good but was willing to settle for less, though not without a soul struggle that he took very seriously. "You've got to help me, Bob," he said. "We can't put our ideas over all at once. We'll have to do it gradually, *petit à petit.*"

His French was all I needed. I left Holt in haste and went to my room. For a time I lay on the bed, wrangling with myself. Then I decided to phone Kahn next day, now that I could afford it. And I'd call Natasha, too; so far I had only written her two short letters, and even that had been hard for me. Somehow she wasn't the kind of person you wrote long letters to. Phone calls and telegrams were more her style. When she wasn't actually with me, I could think of very little to say. The feeling was there, but I couldn't put it into words. When she was there, everything was right; life was full and exciting. When she wasn't, the thought of her seemed as radiant as the northern lights, but also as remote.

It occurred to me that what with the time interval between California and New York this was a good time to call her. I asked for the number and suddenly noticed that I was tense with excitement.

She answered. Her voice seemed very far away. "Natasha," I said, "this is Robert."

"Who?"

"Robert."

"Robert? Where are you? In New York?"

"No, I'm in Hollywood."

"In Hollywood?"

"Yes, Natasha. Had you forgotten? What's the matter?"

"I was asleep."

"Asleep? At this hour?"

"It's the middle of the night. You woke me up. What is it? Are you coming back?"

Damn it, I thought. I had reckoned the time difference in reverse. "Go back to sleep, Natasha. I'll call again tomorrow."

"Okay. Are you coming back?"

"Not yet. I'll tell you all about it tomorrow. Go back to sleep."

"Okay."

This was my bad day, I thought. I shouldn't have called her. There were lots of things I shouldn't have done. I was furious with myself. What had I let myself in for? Why had I got mixed up with Holt? But what harm could it do me? I waited awhile, then I rang Kahn. This time I was making no mistake. Kahn was a light sleeper.

He answered instantly. "What's the matter, Robert? What are you calling for?"

In our attitude toward the telephone we refugees were still far from being Americans; a long-distance call still evoked the thought of disaster. "Has something happened to Carmen?" he asked.

"No. I've seen her. She seems to want to stay on."

He waited a moment. "Maybe she'll change her mind. She hasn't been there very long. Has she got somebody?"

"I don't think so. She hardly knows a soul. As far as I know, her only friend is her landlady."

He laughed. "What about you? When are you coming back?"

"Not for a while."

I told him about my work with Holt. "What do you think of it?" I asked.

"Do it, by all means. You haven't any moral scruples, I hope? That would be too absurd. Or could it be your patriotism?"

"No." I had suddenly forgotten why I had called. "I've been thinking about your letter," I said.

"The only thing that matters is to pull through," he said. "How you do it is your business. I'd say it wasn't a bad idea, learning to live with your complex in a situation without any danger. It gives you kind of a dry run. We'll all have to do it later on, but then the chips will be down and you won't have a chance to practice. You can always quit if it gets you down too much. Later on, over there, you won't be able to. Am I right?"

"That's just what I wanted to hear," I said.

"Good." He laughed. "Don't let Hollywood confuse you, Robert. In New York you wouldn't have asked me. The answer would have been obvious to you. Hollywood is corrupt; the people know it and for that reason invent ridiculous ethical standards. Don't fall for them. Even in New York it's hard enough to keep your head. Look at Gräfenheim. His suicide was unnecessary. A moment of weakness. He'd never have been able to live with his wife again."

"How's Betty?"

"Fighting. She wants to outlive the war. No doctor could have given her a better prescription. But this call must be costing you a fortune. Have you made a million?"

"Not yet."

It was a weird night. A little later Scott came in and insisted on seeing the sanguine drawing. Liquor made him stubborn, that was its only visible effect on him. "I never dreamed of owning a Renoir," he admitted. "I never had the money until recently. And now all of a sudden I've got the bug. A Renoir of my own! I want it! I want it right now!"

I took the drawing down and handed it to him. "Here you are, Scott."

He handled the picture as if it were a monstrance. "He signed it," he said. "With his own hand. And now it's mine. A poor kid from Iowa, from the wrong side of the tracks. We've got to drink to that. Come on, Bob. In my room. With the picture on the wall. I'm going to hang it this minute."

His room was a picture of desolation, littered with empty bottles, half-eaten sandwiches, and overturned ash trays. "Man is a swine," Scott observed profoundly. He removed a photograph of Rudolph Valentino as the Sheik from the wall and hung the Renoir in its place. "How does it look up there?" he asked. "Like a whisky ad?"

I stayed for an hour, and Scott told me the story of his life. He was convinced that his beginnings had been tragic, because he had been very poor and obliged to make his way by selling papers, washing dishes, and similar humiliating occupations. I listened patiently and unsmilingly, drawing no comparisons between his life and mine. In the end he got sleepy and wrote out a check. "Imagine me making out a check for a Renoir!" he sighed. "It's sort of scary."

I went back to my room. An insect with green transparent wings was buzzing around the light bulb. I watched it for a while; an unfathomable work of art, a creature throbbing with life, yet bent on immolating itself as heedlessly as an Indian widow. I caught it and carried it out into the cool night. A minute later it was back again. I realized that the only way to save it was for me to go to bed. I turned out the light and tried to sleep. When I opened my eyes again, I saw a figure in the doorway. I groped for the lamp, meaning to brandish it in self-defense, but switched it on instead. The figure proved to be a young girl in a rather rumpled dress. "Oh, excuse me," she said with a strong accent. "May I come in?"

She took a step forward. "Are you sure you've got the right room?" I asked.

She smiled. "It doesn't make much difference at this time of night, does it? I fell asleep outside. I was very tired."

"Were you at Scott's party?"

"I don't know the name. Somebody brought me. But they're all gone now. I'll have to wait till morning. Would you let me sit here? It's so damp outside."

"You're not an American, are you?" I asked idiotically.

"Mexican. From Guadalajara. Couldn't I just stay here until the buses start running?"

"I can give you a pair of pajamas and a blanket," I said. "The couch here is big enough for you. You can change in the bathroom, over there. Your dress is wet. Hang it over a chair to dry."

She looked at me with amusement. "You know all about women, don't you?"

"No. I'm just being practical. Take a hot bath if you're cold. You won't be in anybody's way."

"Thanks a lot. I'll be very quiet."

She was a pretty little thing, with black hair and delicate feet, and somehow she reminded me of the insect with the transparent wings. When she had disappeared into the bathroom, I looked to see if it had come back, but I couldn't find it. But another had flown in and made itself at home, as though it were the most natural thing in the world. And maybe it was. I listened to the gurgling of the bath water and felt strangely moved. The usual, everyday things of life often gave me this feeling. I was so used to the unusual that the usual had become an adventure to me. Nevertheless, or perhaps for that very reason, I hid Scott's check, which was made out to cash, in among my books. Even in a romantic frame of mind I knew better than to tempt fate.

It was rather late when I woke up. The girl was gone. I saw the mark of her lipstick on one of the towels. I looked for the check. It was still there. Nothing was missing. I wasn't sure whether I had made love with her or not. I only remembered that at some time or other she had stood beside my bed; I seemed to recall the smooth, cool feel of her naked body, but I had no recollection whether anything more had happened.

I drove to the studio. It was already ten o'clock, but to my way of thinking, I was only making up for the two hours I had spent with Holt the night before. I could hear the S.S. men practicing the Horst Wessel song. Holt's first question was whether I thought they should do it in English or German. I suggested German. He thought that might jar with the ensuing English dialogue. We tried both. The English dialogue was a blessing to me—without it I might have taken the S.S men seriously.

In the afternoon I delivered Scott's check to Silvers. "What about the other one?" he asked. "Haven't you sold it?"

"You know damn well I haven't," I said. "The check would be for twice as much."

"You should have sold them both—a package deal. The sanguine is the better one; I meant it as bait."

I said nothing. I only looked at him, wondering if ever in all his life he could do anything straight and simple, or whether on his deathbed he wouldn't try to set some snare for the Reaper, knowing full well that it wouldn't get him anywhere—just for the hell of it.

"We've been invited out tonight," he said finally. "At about ten."

"For dinner?"

"After dinner. At the Villa Weller. I said I couldn't make it for dinner."

"And what is my role to be? Assistant curator or Belgian art historian?"

"Assistant curator. You're to take the Gauguin over there beforehand—right now would be best. Try and find a place to hang it. A picture on the wall is easier to sell. You can take a cab."

"I won't need one," I said loftily. "I've got a car."

"What!"

"Provided by the studio." I relished the momentary superiority the car gave me over Silvers and didn't tell him it was an old Ford. At half past nine he said condescendingly that I might as well drive him to the Villa Weller. When he saw the car, he groaned and wanted to phone for a Cadillac. I persuaded him that everybody else would be coming in a Cadillac or Rolls-Royce, and that my jalopy would set him off from the common herd.

We arrived in the middle of a private showing of some movie. It was customary in Hollywood for producers and directors to try out their latest productions on their dinner guests. I was amused at the honeyed smile with which Silvers tried to mask his impatience. He was wearing a silk dinner jacket, I my blue suit. Silvers felt "overdressed." He even thought of going back to the hotel to change. Of course he held me to blame. Why hadn't I told him? It was my job to keep him informed.

It was almost two hours before the lights went on. To my surprise I found Holt and Tannenbaum among the guests. "How come we're all at the same party?" I asked. "Is it always this way in Los Angeles?"

"Hell, Bob," said Holt reproachfully, "Weller is our boss. His studio is doing our picture. Didn't you know that?"

"No. How would I?"

"Happy man! I'll tell him you're here. He'll want to meet you."

"I'm here with Silvers. For other purposes."

"I can imagine. I've seen the old ape. All dolled up, isn't he? Why didn't you come for dinner? We had stuffed turkey. Practicing up for Thanksgiving."

"My boss couldn't make it for dinner."

"Your boss wasn't invited to dinner. But you could have come. Mr. Weller knows all about you."

For a moment I savored the thought that I was one of the boys and Silvers a mere outsider. Then I turned my attention to the guests. What struck me immediately was how young and attractive many of them were. I identified half a dozen screen heroes.

"I know what you're going to say," said Holt. "You're going to ask why they're not in the Army. A lot of them are 4-F, flat feet, asthma, injuries contracted while playing football or tennis, or even at work."

"No," I said. "I was going to ask if this was a colonels' congress. I never saw so many colonels in all my life."

Holt laughed. "Those are our Hollywood colonels. None of these majors, colonels, commodores, and admirals has ever gone near an Army camp. The commodore over there has never seen a warship; and that admiral has a beautiful swivel chair in Washington. The colonels are producers, directors, or agents who've made a nest for themselves in the Army film section. You won't find anything under a major around here."

"Are you a major?"

"I have a heart defect. And besides, I make anti-Nazi pictures. Ridiculous, isn't it?"

"Not at all. It's the same all over the world. In Germany, too. You never see the fighters, only the home-front warriors. That doesn't apply to you, Holt. But I'm amazed at how many good-looking people there are."

He laughed. "Where would you expect to find good-looking people if not in Hollywood? Where looks can be sold at a high price. But here comes Mr. Weller."

He was a tubby little man in a colonel's uniform. He was all smiles, and his bearing was utterly unmilitary. He immediately drew me off to one side. Silvers couldn't get over it; he was sitting all by himself in an armchair from which he could see the Gauguin, to which no one else was paying the slightest attention. It shone like a patch of southern sunlight over the piano, around which, I feared, the usual chorus would soon form.

After a brief chat, in which he complimented me on my fine work, Weller started introducing me as a man who had been in a concentration camp. Word got around. Everyone wanted to meet me, including some of the prettiest girls I had ever laid eyes on. All at once I was a social lion—of the most gruesome variety. I broke out in a cold sweat and shot angry looks at Holt, though he was hardly to blame. In the end, Tannenbaum rescued me. All evening he had circled around me as a cat circles around a bowl of milk. Then at the first opportunity he pounced, and led me off to a corner of the bar. He had a secret to confide. "The twins have arrived," he whispered. He had wangled two small parts in Holt's picture for them. "That's fine," I said. "Now you have all the imaginary troubles you need."

He shook his head. "No more troubles," he said. "Success!"

"Really? With both of them? Congratulations."

"Not both. They wouldn't do that. They're Catholics. With one of them."

"Bravo! I'd never have expected it. With your sensitive, complicated character."

"Neither would I," he said happily. "The picture did it."

"You mean because you got them the job?"

"No, no. I'd already done that twice. Twins can always get small parts. It never did any good before. This time it was different!"

"Different?"

"My role as an Obergruppenführer! As you may know, I belong to the Stanislavsky school of acting. I've got to feel my part completely. When I play the part of a murderer, I've got to feel like a murderer. Well, as an Obergruppenführer . . ."

"I understand. But the twins are always together. That's their strength."

Tannenbaum smiled. "For Tannenbaum, not for an Obergruppenführer. I was in uniform when they arrived. The moment they stepped into my bungalow, I bellowed at them so loud they almost fainted. I had them completely intimidated. I told one of them—I ordered her, in fact—to beat it over to the clothing depot and try on some costumes. Then I locked the door, flung the other one down on the couch, and attacked her like an Obergruppenführer. And you know what? Instead of scratching my eyes out, she was as meek as Moses. That's the power of a uniform. Would you believe it?"

I remembered my first afternoon at the studio. "I believe it," I said. "But what will happen when you exchange your uniform for that stunning sports jacket?"

"I've tried it," said Tannenbaum. "The aura sticks. The charisma."

I bowed to the Obergruppenführer in the blue suit. "A small compensation for a great misfortune," I said. "It reminds me of the last eruption of Vesuvius, the survivors cooking eggs in the hot ashes."

"*C'est la vie,*" said Tannenbaum. "There's only one hitch. I don't know if I got the right twin."

"What do you mean? Aren't they identical?"

"Not in bed. Vesel told me one was a bombshell. Mine is more on the quiet side."

"Maybe that's the effect of your aura."

Tannenbaum's face brightened. "Maybe it is. I hadn't thought of that. But what should I do?"

"Wait till the next picture. Maybe you'll get the part of a pirate or a sheik."

"A sheik," said Tannenbaum. "A sheik with a harem. *A la* Stanislavsky."

It was very quiet when I returned to the Garden of Allah. It was not late, but everyone seemed to be asleep. I sat down by the swimming pool and suddenly I was overcome by an unaccountable sadness. I had often been depressed in my life, but this was a feeling I had never known before. I sat very still, half hoping that some memory, some figure from the past, would emerge to explain it. I felt no pain or anguish. This was a serene, luminous, transparent sadness, behind which a whole world became discernible. I remembered that Elijah had found God not in the wind or the earthquake but in the still, small voice. Could that voice be death, and could death be no more than a gentle, nameless extinction, in which the will and, with it, fear were reduced to nothingness? I sat there for a long while and at length I felt life returning like a slow, almost imperceptible tide. I went back to my room and stretched out on the bed. I listened to the soft rustling of the palm trees and had the feeling that this hour had given me a counterforce to my nightmares, that it had brought a kind of metaphysical balance into my life. I knew this feeling would be short-lived, but it was strangely comforting while it lasted. I was not surprised to see the transparent insect with the green wings circling around my lamp; that, too, seemed to be a part of this privileged moment. And then I noticed that there were tears in my eyes.

XXVII

Two weeks later Silvers left Hollywood. Here on the coast, where he seemed to belong, it was much harder for him to do business than in New York. Wealth and publicity went hand in hand; status was just about synonymous with publicity, or call it "fame." In New York the run-of-the-mill millionaire had no such publicity machine at his disposal; he was known only to a relatively small circle. If he wished to make a name for himself, he had to do something outside the sphere of business, and that was where art collecting came in. At the very least the New York sharks were amused at Silvers and his tricks; in their desire to become well-known collectors, they were only too glad to be taken in by him, often against their better judgment. In Hollywood no one took him seriously, because anyone with any standing at all in the movies enjoyed more fame, hence status, than the most eminent art collector.

He finally managed to sell the Gauguin to Weller, but, to his infinite disgust, he needed my help even for that. In Weller's eyes I was more important than Silvers. Weller needed me for his picture; he didn't need Silvers for anything. That was too much for Silvers, whose vanity was even greater than his passion for business. "You stay here," he said, "as my bridgehead in the land of the barbarians." He wanted to put me on a strict salary basis, but I put my foot down. I was in a strong bargaining position because I could have lived on what Weller was paying me. It was only on the day of his departure that he gave in; he cut my salary but agreed to a small commission on anything I sold. "I'm treating you like my own son," he fumed. "Anywhere else you'd have to pay for what I'm teaching you. All you care about is money, money, money! What a generation!"

I drove him to the station in Scott's Cadillac, alleging that in appreciation of my services the studio had promoted me to a better car. It almost broke Silvers' heart. In New York he drove a mere Chrysler.

In the morning I reported to the studio. My work as a consultant was simple, but trying to rescue the script was something else again. My idea was to transform this melodrama, which seemed to have been taken over almost intact from some gangster movie, into a faithful picture of a modern bureaucratic murder machine, operated not by picturesque villains or madmen, but by drab, unimaginative citizens who did their daily stint and went to bed with a clear conscience. Holt's reaction was always the same: "Nobody will believe us. There's no psychological motivation."

To his mind—and he was sure the American public agreed with him—the crimes of the Nazis could only be motivated by innate evil. Fiendish actions could be performed only by natural-born fiends. He made only one concession. He was willing to admit that even the biggest of fiends could have his human moments—this he called "subtlety of characterization." The commander of a concentration camp, for instance, could be exceedingly fond of animals; he could be shown caressing his angora rabbits and stubbornly refusing to let his cook butcher them for stew. But to his mind, this human touch merely served to set off the bestial cruelty that was the man's true nature. I simply couldn't bring him to understand the real horror of the bureaucrats of death, who administered the camps. I couldn't make him see that they were just law-abiding citizens performing their daily tasks with the same clear conscience and sense of work well done as if they had been making toys or plumbing fixtures. He wouldn't go along; the idea was distasteful to him and it didn't fit in with the notions of psychology he had acquired while directing horror movies. He refused to believe that most of these cogs in the murder machine were perfectly normal; that when it was all over, they would go back to their jobs as clerks, grocers, or hotelkeepers without a trace of repentance, without so much as suspecting that they had done any wrong. Any misgivings they might possibly have had were dispelled by the magic words "duty" and "orders." They were the first human automata of a mechanical age; they could not be understood in psychological terms because psychology as we know it is inseparable from ethical considerations, which were inapplicable to such men. They murdered without guilt or responsibility. They were good citizens doing their duty, automated citizens—the only good kind in the Third Reich.

Holt's answer was always the same: "Nobody will believe it. Nobody. We've got to make this thing human. Even if it's inhuman, it's got to have a human motivation."

I tried to put in a scene that would show inhumanity without human motivation: one of the slave camps operated for the benefit of German industry. Holt had never heard of them. I explained to him over and over again that the crimes of the German regime had not been instigated and committed by men from Mars, but by good Germans, who certainly regarded themselves as such. I told him it was absurd to suppose that all the German generals were so blind or naïve as to be unaware of the torturing and murdering that went on day after day; I told him how the leading German corporations contracted with the concentration camps for slave laborers, who worked for sixteen hours a day on a starvation diet until their strength gave out and were then fed to the crematoriums.

"That can't be true!" said Holt.

"It is true. A lot of the big corporations have even built factories near the concentration camps, so as to save on transportation."

"We can't use it," said Holt in despair. "Nobody would believe it."

"But this country is at war with Germany. Germany is the enemy."

"That makes no difference. Psychology is international. They'd say we were inventing atrocities. In 1914 you could still use German atrocities in the movies—all those women and children they were supposed to have butchered in Belgium. Not any more."

"In 1914 it wasn't true, but it was all right for the movies. Today it's true, and you can't use it in the movies because no one would believe it."

"That's the story in a nutshell."

I nodded and gave up. I saw there was no point in arguing. Holt was beginning to regard me as a fanatic; he no longer believed everything I said. I could tell by the way he looked at me and the weariness with which he repeated: "I know, Bob, but we can't use it. It would clash with the rest of the picture. Maybe later on, in another picture."

I left the studio in despair. If even here, in enemy country, no one would believe what had happened and was still happening over there, what would it be like when I got back?

In the next month I sold several drawings and an oil painting. It was Weller who bought the oil, a "Répétition de Danse" by Degas. Silvers promptly reduced my commission, on the ground that the buyer had been one of *his* customers.

Holt bought a Renoir pastel and resold it a week later at a thousand-dollar profit. Encouraged by his success, he bought another small picture and made two thousand on it. "Why couldn't we go into business together?" he asked me.

"We'd need a lot of money. Paintings are expensive."

"We could start on a small scale. I've got money in the bank."

I shook my head. I felt no particular loyalty to Silvers, but I had had about enough of California. For all the local excitement, I felt as if I were living in a strange vacuum somewhere between Japan and Europe. Besides, I realized that I couldn't stay in America forever and was eager to spend as much as possible of the time I had left in New York.

During my last few weeks on the set I was still consulted in matters of detail, but I couldn't help noticing that they wanted no more of my advice about the script. Both Holt and Weller had lost faith in me and were convinced that they knew better. When the movie was finished, I was on my own, with nothing to do but wait for the fish to bite. I had decided to stay on a couple of weeks to sell a few more pictures. I knew the money would come in handy.

"It's snowing here," Kahn wrote. "When are you coming back? I met Natasha on the street. She was wearing a fur cape and a fur cap and looked like Anna Karenina. She couldn't tell me much about you and doesn't think you'll ever come back to New York. What's Carmen doing? I haven't had any news of her."

I was sitting by the swimming pool when the letter came. The earth must be round, I thought, because my horizon was always moving. Once upon a time Germany was my home, then Austria, then France, then all Europe, then Africa—and every one of those places became my home not while I was living there, but only after I had left it. Then it became home and took its place on the horizon. Now it was suddenly New York that I saw on the horizon, and perhaps it would be California once I was in New York.

I went to see Carmen. She was still living in the same bungalow. Nothing seemed to have changed. "I'm going back to New York in two weeks," I said. "Why don't you come along?"

"I couldn't possibly, Robert! My contract has another five weeks to go."

"Have they given you something to do?"

"I've tried on some clothes. They're giving me a small part in the next picture."

"They always say that. Tell me, Carmen, do you think of yourself as an actress?"

She laughed. "Of course not. But who is?" She inspected me. "Why, Robert, you're looking marvelous."

"I've got a new suit."

"No, it's not that. Have you lost weight? Or is it your sunburn?"

"Search me. Can I take you out to lunch? I'm loaded. I can take you to Romanoff's."

"Great," she said, to my surprise.

The movie actors at Romanoff's didn't interest her; she hadn't even bothered to change. She was wearing tight-fitting white slacks, which enabled me to see for the first time that she had a magnificent rear end. It was almost too much: that tragic face that would even have reconciled one to short legs, and then suddenly that delicious, well-rounded ass. "Have you heard from Kahn?" I asked.

"He calls up now and then. But you must have heard from him or you wouldn't have come to see me."

"No," I lied. "I came to see you because I'm leaving soon."

"Why are you leaving? Don't you love it here?"

"No."

As she tried to understand, she looked like a very young Lady Macbeth. "Because of your girl friend? There are so many women. Especially here. One woman is pretty much the same as another."

"But Carmen!" I exclaimed. "That's perfect nonsense."

"Only men think it's nonsense."

I looked at her. She had changed a little. "Are men all alike, too?" I asked her. "But then, as a woman, you probably wouldn't think so."

"Men aren't the least bit alike. Kahn, for instance. He's a pest."

"What!"

"A pest," she repeated, with a tranquil smile. "First he wanted me to go to Hollywood, now he wants me back. I'm not going. It's warm here. In New York there's snow on the ground."

"Is that the only reason?"

"Isn't it enough?"

"God bless you, Carmen. But wouldn't you like to come all the same?"

She shook her head. "Kahn would only drive me crazy. I'm a simple girl, Robert. All that talk of his gives me a headache."

"He's much more than a talker, Carmen. He's what we call a hero."

"Heroes aren't fit to live with. They should die. If they come through alive, they're the biggest bores on earth."

"Who told you that?"

"Does somebody have to tell me? You think I'm abysmally stupid, don't you? That's what Kahn thinks."

"Not at all. And neither does Kahn. He worships you."

"That gives me a headache, too. Why can't you people be natural?"

"What do you mean?"

"Why can't you be natural like everybody else? Like my landlady, for instance. Everything gets so complicated with you people."

The waiter served us *macédoine de fruits.* "Same as this here," said Carmen. "Why do they have to give it such a pompous name when it's only cut-up fruit with a bit of liqueur?"

"Carmen," I said. "I worship you, too. Would you rather have some American ice cream instead of the pompous name? Unfortunately, they only have forty-five flavors here. In New York you'd have more choice."

Carmen studied the list. "Almond, frangipani, and vanilla," she decided. "When Kahn and I ate ice cream together, we got along. That's the only thing we agreed about."

"That's not to be sneezed at," I said. "Did you hear about that woman in Texas who took a potshot at her husband because he liked peppermint ice cream? She couldn't stand it; she only liked strawberry."

"You just made it up," said Carmen gravely. "American men are sweet. They're not as pigheaded as Europeans."

"But, Carmen, it wasn't the man who took the potshot. It was the woman!"

"You see!"

I brought her back to her chickens and her beloved redheaded landlady. "Why, you've even got a car," said the tragic face. "You're getting ahead, Robert, you're getting ahead."

"Kahn has a car now, too," I lied. "A better one than this. Tannenbaum told me. A Chevrolet."

"A Chevrolet with a headache," said Carmen, turning her magnificent behind in my direction. "What's your girl friend doing?" she asked me over her shoulder.

"I don't know. I haven't heard from her in some time."

"Don't you correspond?"

"We've both got writer's cramp."

Carmen laughed. "That's the way it goes. Out of sight, out of mind. That makes everything much simpler."

"A wiser word was seldom spoken. Can I take Kahn a message?"

She thought it over. "What for?"

Some chickens came fluttering out from the garden. Suddenly Carmen came to life. "Heavens! My white pants! I just ironed them! Emily! Patrick!" she screamed. "Shoo! Shoo! Oh, they've made a spot!"

"It's nice to be able to call a calamity by name," I said. "Makes it sort of cozy."

I started back to my Ford and suddenly stopped still. What had I said? For a second I felt as if someone had knifed me from behind. I turned half around. "It's not so bad," came Carmen's voice from the garden. "It will come out in the wash."

Yes, I thought, but will it?

———

I took leave of Scott. "I wish I had another of those sanguine drawings," he said. "I like things in pairs. God knows if you'll ever be back. Have you got one?"

"Nothing in sanguine. But there's a nice charcoal. Also by Renoir."

"Fine. Then I'll have two Renoirs. Who'd have thought it!"

I took the drawing out of my suitcase and handed it to him. "I'd rather you had it than anyone else I can think of," I said.

"Why? I don't know anything about art."

"You have respect for it; that's even better. Good-by, John. I feel as if we'd known each other for years."

A typical American friendship. After a few hours or even minutes people called each other by their first names. Such relationships may be superficial, but there is often a real cordiality about them. Friendship comes quickly and easily in America; in Europe, slowly and painfully. Maybe because the one continent is young, the other old. We ought always to live as though about to take leave, I thought.

Tannenbaum had been given another small part. He drove me to the station. "Have you solved all your problems?" I asked him.

"Not yet. My authority isn't what it used to be since we finished shooting the Nazi picture."

"What's your new part?"

"An English cook on a ship that gets torpedoed by a German submarine."

"Is he drowned?" I asked hopefully.

"No. He's a comic figure. He's rescued, and they put him to work as cook on the submarine."

"Does he poison the crew?"

"Not at all. He cooks plum pudding for them on Christmas Day. They all fraternize on the high seas and start singing English and German folk songs. Then under a little Christmas tree they discover that the British national anthem and the former German national anthem have the same tune, 'God Save the King' and *'Heil dir im Siegeskranz.'* That does it. They decide that when the war is over they'll never fight each other again. They have too much in common."

"Your future looks pretty dark to me," I said. "But maybe your own personality will supply a counterweight."

"I'm a fatalist," said Tannenbaum. "I'll just have to take things as they come. Maybe I've got the wrong twin."

"Can't you find out from Vesel? They say he knows them inside out."

"Even he always got their first names mixed up. Those girls are devils. It amused them to fool him. Within the limits of propriety, of course. As I say, I'm a fatalist. If my method turns me into a cook and this twin doesn't like it, there's always the other. At the moment she's gone to New York to be with Betty. Give them both my regards. Good-by, Robert. Funny how fond a man gets of people when they're going away. Even of you!"

I got into the train, with its Negro porters, its wide comfortable beds and built-in private toilets. Tannenbaum waved. For the first time in many years I had paid all my debts and had money in my pocket. My residence permit had been extended another three months.

XXVIII

"Robert," said Melikov, "I was beginning to think you'd never come back."

"You weren't the only one," I said.

Melikov nodded. He looked tired and gray. "Are you sick?" I asked.

"Why?" He laughed. "Oh, I get it. When you come in from the fresh air, everybody in New York looks as if he's just come out of the hospital. Why did you come back?"

"I'm a masochist."

"Natasha had given you up."

"Really?"

"She thought you'd get a job in the movies."

I didn't ask any more questions. It was a gloomy homecoming. The plush lobby looked dustier and shabbier than ever. Suddenly I, too, began to wonder why I had come back. The streets were filthy and a cold rain was falling. "I've got to buy a coat," I said.

"Do you want to live here?" Melikov asked.

"Yes. I could use a bigger room. Have you got one?"

"Yes. Lisa Teruel died a week ago. Overdose of sleeping pills. That's all we've got, Robert. You should have written."

"All right, I'll take it."

"I thought you would. You don't look as if you'd be afraid of ghosts. Anyway, Lisa died peacefully. She looked ten years younger when we found her."

"How old was she?"

"Forty-two. Come, I'll show you the room. It's the cleanest one in the house. We had to fumigate it. Besides, it's sunny, and that's not to be sneezed at in the winter."

The room was on the second floor. You could go up without being seen from the lobby. I unpacked. I distributed some large sea shells I had bought in Los Angeles. They had lost their deep-sea magic and looked forlorn. "The place is more cheerful when it's not raining," said Melikov. "Care for some vodka to cheer you up?"

"No thanks. I'll just sleep a couple of hours."

"Same here. We're not getting any younger. I've been on night duty. And my rheumatism comes on in the cold weather."

In the afternoon I reported to Silvers. He was much friendlier than I had expected. "Have you brought back some orders?" he asked.

"I've sold the little Renoir charcoal for five thousand."

Silvers nodded. "Not bad," he said, to my amazement.

"What's wrong?" I asked. "You usually burst into tears when we sell something."

"That's right. The best way would be to keep everything. But the war will be over soon. Germany is washed up. Well, you know what that means."

"No," I said. I knew what it meant to me, not what it meant to him.

"It means people will be able to go to Europe pretty soon. And Europe is poor. Anybody with dollars will be able to buy pictures for a song, which means hard times for American dealers. We've got to be careful and cut down on our stock."

"Even I can understand that."

"It was the same after the first war. I was new to the trade and I made some bad mistakes. That mustn't happen again. So if you've got any deals pending and the customer seems to be in doubt, come down on the prices. Tell them we need cash because we're buying a big collection."

Somehow this frankly commercial approach, unclouded by moral considerations, cheered me up, especially the cold-blooded way in which Silvers considered the world's disasters from the standpoint of profit and loss. "Of course we'll have to cut down on your commissions," he added.

I fully expected that. I'd have been disappointed if he hadn't said it. Those words were the salt in the stew. "Of course," I said cheerfully.

I hesitated to call Natasha. I put it off from hour to hour. In the last few weeks our relationship had become an abstraction; even the few postcards we exchanged had struck me as empty and false. When we weren't together, there was simply nothing to say. I had no idea what would happen if I called. I felt so shaky about it that I hadn't even informed her of my arrival, though I had meant to. As the weeks and months slipped by, Natasha had become strangely unreal in my thoughts, as though our relationship had been a mere accident and had dwindled painlessly away.

I went to see Betty and was horrified at the way she looked. She must have lost twenty pounds. Except for her great shining eyes, all life had gone out of her shrunken face.

"You're looking good, Betty."

"Not too thin?"

"Not in this day and age. It's the style."

"Betty will bury us all," said Ravic, emerging from the dark living room.

"Not Ross," said Betty with a spectral smile. "Look at him. A picture of health. So tan!"

"That will be gone in two weeks, Betty. It's winter in New York."

"I'd like to go to California myself," she said. "It must be good for the health, now in the wintertime. But it's so far from Europe."

I looked around. There was a smell of death in the room.

"It gets dark so early now," Betty complained. "It makes the nights so long."

"Leave the light on," said Ravic. "Ignore the times of day."

"I do. I'm afraid of the darkness. In Berlin I was never afraid."

"That was a long time ago, Betty. We change. I've often been afraid to wake up in the dark."

She fixed her great shining eyes on me. "Even now?"

"Yes, here in New York. Not so much in California."

"Why? What did you do? Maybe you weren't alone at night?"

"Oh yes. I forgot, Betty. I just forgot."

"That's the best way," said Ravic.

Betty threatened me with a bony finger and smiled a ghastly smile; the loose skin of her face moved as if invisible fists were at work under it. "One look at him tells the story," she said, gazing at me out of her great round eyes. "He's happy."

"Who can claim to be happy, Betty?"

"That's something I've found out. Everyone who has his health. Except that nobody knows it until he gets sick. And when they get well, they forget it."

She propped herself up. Her breasts sagged like empty sacks under her flowered bed jacket. "Everything else is nonsense," she gasped. "Believe me! The rest is talk. All this stuff about unhappiness and love and loneliness—it all evaporates when you're sick. All these memories of ours are like a lot of colored balloons. We think they're so pretty, and then someone comes along and sticks a pin in them."

"I can't believe that, Betty," I said. "You have such wonderful memories. All the people you've helped. All the friends you've made."

Betty was silent for a moment. Then she motioned me to come close. I approached reluctantly; she smelled of peppermint and decay. "I've stopped caring," she whispered. "Believe me. I just don't care any more."

The New York twin came in from the living room. "Betty is having one of her bad days," said Ravic, and stood up. "*Cafard.* Everybody gets it now and then. Sometimes mine lasts for weeks. I'll come again this afternoon."

He left. The twin spread out some photographs on the bed. "Olivaer Platz, Betty. In the days before the Nazis."

Suddenly Betty came to life. "Really? Where did you get them? Give me my glasses! My goodness! Is my house there?"

The twin brought her a magnifying glass. "My house isn't on it," said Betty. "It was taken from the wrong side. Here's Dr. Schlesinger's house. I can even read the name. Of course it's before the Nazis. Or the name plate wouldn't be there."

"Good-by, Betty," I said. "I've got to go."

"Can't you stay?"

"I've just arrived in New York. I've got to unpack."

"How's my sister?" the twin asked. "The poor thing. All alone in Hollywood."

"She's doing fine," I said.

"I hope so. We're both kind of lost without each other."

Betty had followed the conversation with visible alarm. "Oh, Lissy, you're not going away?" she pleaded. "You can't leave me here all alone. What would I do?"

"I won't go away."

Lissy—this was the first time I had heard either twin called by her individual name—took me to the door. "She's driving me crazy," she whispered. "Day after day, dying and not dying. I'm getting sick myself. Ravic wants to put her in the hospital, but she won't go; she says she'd rather die. But she won't die."

I thought of going to see Kahn, but I had nothing pleasant to tell him and I didn't want to be a bearer of bad news. I kept putting off my call to Natasha. I hadn't thought about her very much in California; we had told each other, and tried to make ourselves believe, that there was nothing sentimental about this affair of ours, that neither of us would ever be unhappy over it, and this was the picture I carried with me to California. If that was the case, it should have been perfectly simple to phone Natasha and find out where we stood. Neither of us had any obligations or ground for reproach. Nevertheless, I dreaded this phone call. It seemed to me that by my stupidity or negligence I had lost something that could never be recaptured. By the end of the day my vague forebodings had condensed into anguish: what if she were dead? I knew this absurd fear had something to do with my visit to Betty, but that did not relieve it.

In the end I rushed to the phone as though my life were at stake. I heard the ring at the other end and I knew at once that the room was empty. I tried the number every ten minutes. I knew that she often worked in the evening, that she could have gone out for any number of reasons, but that was no help. I thought of Kahn and Carmen, of Silvers and his unfortunate adventure; I thought of Betty, and how all our grandiose visions of happiness pale in the presence of sickness. I tried to remember the little Mexican girl in Hollywood and to comfort myself with the thought that the world was full of women more beautiful than Natasha. These mental exercises were small consolation, but at least they gave me the courage to call again. Finally I resorted to the old numbers game: I'd try twice more and then give up. But two turned to three and four.

Suddenly she was there. I hadn't even put the receiver to my ear, but left it lying in my lap. "Robert," she said, "where are you calling from?"

"New York. I arrived today."

After a moment's silence she asked: "Is that all?"

"No, Natasha. When can I see you? I've called twenty times and I'm desperate. Your phone has the emptiest sound I ever heard when you're not there."

She laughed softly. "I've just come in."

"Come out and eat with me," I said. "I can take you to the Pavillon. Don't say no. Or we can have a hamburger in a drugstore. We can do anything you like."

I was afraid of what she might say; I was afraid of a long discussion about why we hadn't written in so long, of all the unnecessary but understandable reproaches that can poison a meeting in advance.

"Okay," she said. "Call for me in an hour."

"I worship you, Natasha. Those are the most beautiful words I've heard since I left New York."

The moment I had said that, I foresaw her answer. I had led

with my chin. But she said nothing at all. I could hear the click as she hung up. I was relieved and disappointed. I would almost have preferred a fight. There was something suspicious about her calm.

I went back to Lisa Teruel's room to dress. The room smelled more strongly of sulphur and Lysol in the evening than in the morning; this was hardly the atmosphere to prepare me for the battle I anticipated. What I needed was perfect composure. For a moment I even thought of finding someone to make love to first; then perhaps I would be able to face Natasha without trembling.

"Are you going to a funeral?" Melikov asked. "How about some vodka?"

"No, thanks," I said. "This is too serious. Well, actually, it's not serious at all, only I mustn't make any mistakes. How does Natasha look?"

"Better than ever. I can't help it. That's the way it is."

"Are you on duty tonight?"

"Until 7:00 A.M."

"Thank God. So long, Vladimir. What an idiot I am! Why didn't I write more often? Or phone? I was actually proud of it."

"The dogs bark, but the caravan passes by."

"What's that?"

"An old Arab saying. Don't bark too much."

"Or too little."

I went out into the cold night, armed with fear, hope, good resolutions, repentance, and a new ready-to-wear overcoat. On the way I thought up an assortment of lies and tactical plans.

The light outside the elevator went on, and I heard the hum of the engine. "Natasha," I blurted out. "I was full of confusion, repentance, hope, lies, and tactical plans. The second you stepped out of the elevator I forgot them all. The one thing left in my mind is a question: how in God's name could I ever have left you?"

I took her in my arms and kissed her. I felt that she was resisting me and held her tighter. She gave in, but the moment I relaxed my hold she freed herself. "You look about as confused as a stone," she said. "And you're thinner."

"I've been living on grass and health food."

"I've been taken out to gala dinners at 21 and the Pavillon. Am I too fat?"

"I wish you were. Then there'd be more of you."

I ignored the gala dinners. Now I was really confused, torn between joy and apprehension and, now that I had held her in my arms, unable to control my trembling. She never wore very much under her dress and always seemed naked, warm, and exciting to the touch. I had stopped thinking of all that; now I could think of nothing else.

"Aren't you cold?" I asked idiotically.

"In this cape? Where are we going?"

I was careful not to suggest 21 or the Pavillon. I didn't want to be told again that she had been to those places night after night and was bored with them. "How about the Bistro?"

"The Bistro is closed," she said. "The owner sold it. He's gone back to France. He wants to be there when De Gaulle marches in."

"Really? They let him go?"

"So it seems. The French refugees have all got the itch to go back. They're afraid of being treated as deserters if they get there too late. Let's go to the Coq d'Or. It's pretty much like the Bistro."

"Fine. I hope the *patron* is still there. He's French, too, isn't he?"

"Maybe he's decided to stay here."

The *patron* was a man in his forties, with a red face and a thick black mustache. I would have liked to ask him about his plans, but those were things one didn't mention.

"I can recommend the rosé d'Anjou," he said.

"Fine."

I looked at him with envy. He was a refugee, too, but not my kind. He could go back. His country had been occupied and was being liberated. Not mine.

"You're brown," said Natasha. "What have you been doing?"

She knew I had been working for Holt, but not much more. I gave her a succinct account of myself, so as to get the tedious question period over with as quickly as possible.

"Do you have to go back?" she asked.

"No, Natasha."

"I hate the winter in New York."

"I hate it everywhere, except in Switzerland."

"Were you in the mountains?"

"No, in jail for having no papers. But it was a well-heated jail. I enjoyed every minute of it. I could see the snow without having to run around in it. It was the only heated jail I've ever been in."

She burst out laughing. "I never know whether you're kidding or not."

"That's the only way to talk about an injustice. The whole idea is obsolete. There is no such thing as injustice. There's only bad luck."

"Do you believe that?"

"No, Natasha. Not when I'm sitting beside you."

"I suppose you had lots of women in California?"

"Not a one."

"Of course not. Poor Robert."

I hated her to call me that. This conversation was taking a bad turn. I should have tried to get her into bed as quickly as possible. I should have met her at the hotel and carried her off to Lisa Teruel's room. This skirmishing was dangerous. Every one of our seemingly amiable words had a time bomb hidden in it. I knew she was expecting me to ask her the same question.

"The climate in Hollywood isn't right for it. It made me tired and listless."

"Is that why I practically never heard from you?"

"No. I can't write letters. With the kind of life I led, there was never anyone to write to. Our addresses were always changing. I lived from day to day and moment to moment. I never had a future and couldn't even imagine one. I thought you were the same."

"How do you know I'm not?"

I didn't want to answer that one. After a while I said: "You meet again, and it's the same as before."

"That's what we want, isn't it?"

I saw the trap and tried to extricate myself. "No," I said. "It's not what *I* want."

"That's not what you said a minute ago."

"It's different now. I didn't realize it before. I do now."

"What's different?"

This was a grilling. I couldn't keep my thoughts in order. They kept wandering. I ought to have gone to bed with another woman first. Then my head would be clearer. I had forgotten, or never been really aware of, the intensity of my feeling for Natasha. At the beginning of our affair it had not been so strong, and, strangely enough, it was this beginning that had remained foremost in my memory in Hollywood. Now it all came back to me. I was almost afraid to look at her for fear of revealing something—I didn't know exactly what, but I felt that I should be defeated forever if she found out. She hadn't played all her cards, not by any means. She was only waiting to crush me with the information that she was having an affair with someone else, or at least had gone to bed with somebody. I tried to stop her. I felt that I hadn't the strength to take it, though I fortified myself with the thought that if she said it, it probably wasn't true.

"Everything is different, Natasha. I can't explain it. It's hard to explain something so important and unexpected. I'm glad we're together. The time in between has vanished like smoke."

"You think so?"

"I think so."

She laughed. "That's very convenient. I've got to go home now. I'm tired. We're getting our spring collection ready."

"I know. You're always a season in advance."

Spring! I thought. What will have happened by then? I looked at the *patron*. Would he go back to Paris and be prosecuted as a deserter? And where would I be? I saw threats on all sides. I felt as if I were suffocating. What I had been waiting for so long was now within reach, and suddenly the intervening period seemed like a brief reprieve from the gallows. I looked across at Natasha, who was calmly putting on her gloves. She was infinitely far away. I wanted to say something that would cut through all our misunderstandings; I could think of nothing. I walked along beside her with hardly a word. It was very cold; a snow-charged wind swept around the corners. I found a cab. We hardly spoke. The driver predicted snow for next morning.

"Good night, Robert," said Natasha.

"Good night, Natasha."

I was glad to know that Melikov would be awake when I got back. Not for the vodka; just to be with someone who would ask no questions.

XXIX

I stood for a while looking into Lowys' window. The eighteenth-century table was still there. The repaired legs filled me with tenderness. It was surrounded by some freshly painted armchairs. There were a few small Egyptian bronzes, among them a rather good cat and a figure of the goddess Neith, finely formed, authentic, and with a good patina.

I saw Lowy Senior coming up from the cellar like Lazarus rising from his rocky grave. He seemed to have aged; but strangely enough, all my New York friends had made that impression on me, except for Natasha. She had changed but had not grown older. She seemed more independent and more desirable than before. I didn't want to think of her; the thought of her grieved me as if in a moment of blindness I had mistaken a magnificent Chou bronze for a copy and given it away.

Lowy gave a start when he saw me outside the window. He didn't recognize me at first, probably because of my tan and the splendor of my new coat.

Then he waved, I waved back, and he hobbled to the door. "Come in, Ross, come in. Why are you standing out there in the cold?"

The place smelled of age, dust, and varnish. "You've come up in the world," said Lowy. "Doing good business? Been in Florida? Congratulations!"

I told him what I had been up to, but said nothing about my work for Holt. I had no reason to make a secret of it, but that morning I was in no mood for any more explanations than absolutely necessary. I had done enough damage with my explanations to Natasha.

"How is everything?" I asked.

Lowy threw up his hands in despair. "It's happened," he said gloomily.

"What's happened?"

"He's married her. The shicksah!"

"What of it?" I said to console him. "It's so easy to get a divorce nowadays."

"That's what I thought. But this shicksah is a Catholic."

"Has your brother turned Catholic?"

"Not yet, but I wouldn't put it past him. She's working on him day and night."

"How do you know?"

"That's easy. He's always talking about religion. She keeps dinning it into him that he'll roast in hell if he doesn't turn Catholic."

"Were they married in church?"

"Naturally. She insisted. You should have seen it. My brother in a cutaway. Rented, of course. What would he do with a cutaway? His legs are too short. It was horrible."

"So now there's mourning in the house of Israel!"

Lowy gave me a sharp look. "Damn it, I'd forgotten! You're a goy yourself. You wouldn't see it the same way. Protestant?"

"Atheist. Born a Catholic."

"What? How is that possible?"

"I left the Church when they signed the concordat with Hitler. My immortal soul couldn't take it."

Lowy was interested for a moment. "You did right," he said calmly. "Love thy neighbor as thyself! Isn't that what they're always saying? And then they make a deal with those murderers. Is the concordat still in force?"

"Yes, as far as I know."

"Then my brother's in partnership with Hitler," Lowy fumed.

"Take it easy, Mr. Lowy. Your brother has nothing to do with it. He's an innocent victim of love."

"Innocent? Look over there." Lowy made a sweeping theatrical gesture. "Take a look at that, Mr. Ross! Can you believe it?"

"What?"

"What? Saints! Bishops! Madonnas! Are you blind? Graven images. We never had any of that stuff around here. Now the place is full of it."

I looked around. There were a few good pieces of religious sculpture in the corners. "Why do you put them where nobody can see them?" I asked. "They're good. Two of them even have the original paint and gilt. They're the best things in the shop right now, Mr. Lowy. What is there to complain about? Art is art!"

"Not in this situation!"

"Mr. Lowy, without religious art, most Jewish art dealers would go out of business tomorrow. You've got to be tolerant."

"I can't. Even if it brings in money, it breaks my heart. My no-good brother buys the stuff. Good pieces, I admit. But that makes it even worse. I'd be happier if the paint were new, if the gilt were made out of powdered bronze, if only one foot were genuine and the rest had worm holes made with a shotgun. I'd have a right to scream and yell. This way I've got to hold my tongue when I'm burning up inside. I can hardly eat. Even chopped chicken liver, that used to be my favorite delicacy, gives me a sour stomach. I'm wasting away. The worst part of it is that the shicksah has a head for business. Whenever we get into an argument she calls me an antichrist. I guess that's the opposite of anti-Semite. And the way she laughs. All day she laughs. It gives her the shimmies, all hundred and fifty pounds of her. I can't stand it!" Lowy raised both arms. "Mr. Ross, come back to us. With you here it would be bearable. I'll give you a raise."

"That's the first friendly offer since I've been back."

"So you'll come?"

"I can't, Mr. Lowy. I'm still with Silvers. Many thanks."

His face fell. "Not even if we specialize in bronzes? There are bronze saints, too, you know."

"Not very many. It can't be done. Silvers has put me on a commission basis, and I'm making good money."

"Naturally. The bastard has no overhead. Every time he takes a leak it's tax deductible."

"Good-by, Mr. Lowy. I'll never forget that you gave me my first job."

"What is this? You sound as if you were saying good-by. You wouldn't be going back to Europe?"

"What gives you that idea?"

"The funny way you talk. Don't do it, Mr. Ross. Even if they lose the war, those people will never change. Take it from Raoul Lowy!"

"Raoul?"

"Yes. My poor mother read novels. Raoul! Makes you laugh, doesn't it?"

"No. It gives me pleasure. I don't know why."

"Raoul," Lowy muttered darkly. "Maybe that's why I never married. A name like that does things to a man's self-confidence."

"It's never too late for a man like you. You won't have any trouble finding a good Jewess here in New York."

Raoul's eyes lit up. "Not a bad idea! I never thought of it. But now with this renegade of a brother!" He thought it over for a moment. "I wonder what the kid would say."

Suddenly he laughed. "First time I've laughed in weeks," he said. "It's a good idea. Wonderful. Even if I don't do it. It's like handing a defenseless man a club." He seized my hand in both of his and shook it. "Tell me, Mr. Ross, is there anything I can do for you? How about a saint at purchase price? A St. Sebastian from the Rhineland?"

"No, thanks. What does the cat cost?"

"The cat? That's one of the finest and rarest . . ."

"Mr. Lowy," I interrupted, "you taught me the trade. The spiel is unnecessary. How much does it cost?"

"For you personally or to sell?"

I hesitated a moment. Then a superstitious thought came to me: if I told him the truth, an unknown God would reward me and Natasha would call me up. "To sell," I said.

"That's the stuff. You're an honest man. If you'd said different, I wouldn't have believed you. All right: five hundred. Exactly what I paid for it, word of honor."

"Three fifty. My customer won't go any higher."

We settled for four twenty-five. "As long as I'm losing my shirt," I said, "I may as well lose my pants, too. How much is the Egyptian figurine? I'll give you sixty. It's for a present."

"A hundred and twenty if it's a present."

He let me have it for ninety. I gave him Natasha's address, and he promised to deliver the goddess himself during lunch hour. I took the cat with me. I knew I'd be able to sell it for six hundred and fifty dollars. That gave me the statue for Natasha for nothing and enough profit to pay for a new hat, a pair of good winter shoes, and a muffler. Thus equipped, I'd be able to take her anywhere.

She called me that evening. "You've sent me a little goddess," she said. "What's her name?"

"She's Egyptian, her name is Neith, and she's two thousand years old."

"That's pretty old for a woman. Does she bring good luck?"

"It's a funny thing about Egyptian figurines. They only bring you luck if they take a shine to you. This one ought to bring you luck because she looks like you."

"I'll take her with me wherever I go. In my handbag. She's lovely. Many thanks, Robert. How are you getting along in New York?"

"I've been buying winter clothes. I hear you have blizzards here."

"We do. Will you have dinner with me tomorrow? I'll pick you up."

A lot of thoughts can pass through a man's mind in a second. I was disappointed at her putting me off till the next day. I felt a wave of jealousy mounting from my heart into my throat. I thought of telling her that I too was busy that evening, but had sense enough not to. "That's fine," I said. "I'll be at the hotel from seven on. Come when you feel like it."

"I'm sorry I can't make it tonight. I didn't know you were coming, so I made a date. It's hard to be alone in the evening."

"That's a fact," I said. "I've got a dinner invitation myself. From the people with the wonderful goulash. I wouldn't have had to go; they always invite so many people I wouldn't have been missed."

"That's good, Robert. I'll see you tomorrow. At about eight."

I hung up. I wondered if my superstition had helped me, and decided it had, though I was disappointed not to be seeing Natasha right away. The night lay ahead of me like a black pit. I had been away from Natasha for months and hardly given the matter a thought; now this one night seemed endless.

Mrs. Vriesländer actually had invited me to dinner, and I decided to go. For the first time I would be appearing there as a free man, without debts and in all the glory of my new suit and overcoat. I had repaid Vriesländer's loan and even paid the lawyer with the cuckoo clock in full. I could eat the Vriesländers' goulash without shame. And in token of my gratitude I brought Mrs. Vriesländer an impressive bunch of dark-red gladioli. They were somewhat past their bloom, and the Italian on the corner had sold them to me cheap.

"Tell us about Hollywood," said my hostess almost at once.

That was just what I had wanted to avoid. "It's like having your head in a transparent bag," I said. "You see everything, understand nothing, and believe nothing. You hear muffled sounds and live in a kind of gelatinous dream. One day you wake up and you're four months older."

"Is that all?"

"Just about."

Lissy appeared. I thought of Tannenbaum and his doubts. "How's Betty?" I asked.

"She's not in great pain. Ravic gives her injections. She sleeps a good deal. But she still wakes up at night. And then she starts fighting for the next day."

"Is somebody with her?"

"Ravic. He sent me away; he said I had to get out once in a while." She smoothed her dress. "I'm going nuts. How can I eat goulash when Betty's dying?"

She turned to me with her pretty, rather empty face, in which Tannenbaum thought he detected a volcano of passion. "It's no use thinking about death," I said. "We just can't understand. Try and eat."

"I can't. Sometimes I feel like hanging myself. Or going into a convent. And then sometimes I want to let myself go and smash everything. You see how crazy I am."

"It's perfectly normal, Lissy. Healthy and normal. Have you a boy friend?"

"What for? To get pregnant and lose my last chance of getting anywhere?"

Tannenbaum must have got the right twin, I thought. But maybe Vesel had only been telling him stories and hadn't had any dealings with either of them. "Will the war be over soon?" Lissy asked.

"It looks like it."

"And then what?"

"I have no idea, Lissy."

Vriesländer came in. "Ah, our young capitalist!" And turning to Lissy: "Have you tasted the almond cake? No? Have some! Have some! You're getting too thin." He pinched her behind. She seemed used to it and did not react in any way. It wasn't a lascivious pinch, more like a fatherly employer checking up to see that everything was there. Vriesländer's tone to me was equally paternal. "My dear Ross," he said, "if you've made a little money, now's your big chance to invest it. Once the war is over, German stocks will be practically worthless and so will the mark. That's your big chance to get in on the ground floor. Nobody can keep the German people down. They'll build up the country in no time. Do you know who's going to help them? We Americans. And I'll tell you why. We need their help against Russia. Our alliance with Russia is like two homosexuals trying to have a baby; it's an alliance against nature. I've got friends in the government, and they know. Once the Nazis are out of the way, we'll support Germany." He tapped me on the shoulder. "Don't tell anybody. That tip is worth millions. I'm giving it to you because you're one of the few people who've paid their debts to me."

"Thank you," I said, "but I haven't any money."

Vriesländer looked at me benevolently. "You've still got time to make some. They tell me you're a first-class salesman. If you want to set yourself up in business, come and see me. I finance you, you do the selling, and we share fifty-fifty."

"That's not so simple. I'd have to buy pictures from dealers. They'd expect me to pay the prices they get from their customers."

Vriesländer laughed. "You're still a greenhorn, Ross. Give it a try. In the business world everybody gets his little cut. Otherwise every market in the world would collapse. Come and see me when you've thought it over."

He stood up and so did I. For a moment I thought he might pinch my behind in fatherly absent-mindedness.

I prepared to leave. "Don't forget the tip," said Vriesländer.

My feelings must have appeared in my face, because he burst out laughing. "You and your moral scruples," he said. "My dear Ross, there's going to be money lying around, just waiting to be picked up. Do you want to leave it for the Nazis who robbed us? I say we've got it coming to us. You should be logical about these things."

The cook handed me a jar of goulash as I was leaving. I took Lissy home in a cab. "You must be all black and blue," I said. "Working for that pinching machine. Does he chase you around the typewriter?"

"No. He only pinches me when people are looking. It's his way of showing off. He's impotent."

Lissy stood shivering in the doorway, a small forlorn figure. "Won't you come up?" she asked.

"I can't, Lissy."

"I suppose not," she said dejectedly.

"I'm sick," I said, God knows why. "Hollywood," I added.

"I don't want you to make love to me. It's just that the room seems so dead when I go in alone."

I paid the driver and went up with her. It was a dismal room, with pictures of movie actresses on the wall. The only personal note was a teddy bear and a few dolls.

"Should I make some coffee?" she asked.

"That would be lovely."

The activity revived her. Over the coffee she told me a little about her life. It went in one ear and out the other. I stood up to go. "Sleep well, Lissy," I said. "And don't do anything foolish. You're very pretty and tomorrow is another day."

She nodded. "Don't worry. It was just one of those bad moments. Take care of yourself, Robert."

It snowed next day. In the afternoon the streets were white, and the skyscrapers looked like enormous beehives covered with snow and light. The traffic sounds were muffled and the snow was still coming down.

I was playing chess with Melikov when Natasha came in. She shook the snow off her hair and the hood of her cape.

"Did you come in the Rolls-Royce?" I asked.

She was silent for a moment. "I took a cab," she said finally. "Does that make you feel better?"

"Much better," I said. "Where do you want to go?"

"Wherever you say."

I went to the door and looked out. "It's snowing hard," I said. "Your furs would be ruined. We'd better stay here till it stops."

"You don't have to give me reasons for staying here," she said. "If only we had something to eat."

I suddenly remembered the Vrieslanders' goulash. The strain in our relations had driven it from my mind.

"My goulash!" I said. "We can eat in my room."

"Can we? Won't that gangster call the police?"

"Nothing to worry about. With the room I've got now nobody can see us going in or out. Come on!"

Thanks to Lisa Teruel's good taste in lamp shades, the room looked a lot better by night than by day. Lowy's cat, which I had put on the table, seemed to welcome us. I took Natasha's cape and set about my preparations for dinner. I possessed an enamel cooking pot, an electric hot plate, a few dishes, and the most necessary cutlery. I spread out a towel on the table, poured the goulash into the pot, and switched on the hot plate. "It won't be long," I said. Natasha was still standing, leaning against the door.

"There's not much room," I said. "But there's always the bed."

"You don't mean it."

I wasn't at all sure of myself and I had intended to go slow. But once again, the moment I came close to her I felt that she was almost naked under her thin dress and I forgot my resolutions. I said nothing, and she, too, was silent. It was a long time since I had been with a woman, and I suddenly realized how indifferent everything else in the world can become when the bit of individuality we carry around with us is swept away by the nameless, faceless being that consists only of hands, burning skin, and avidly swollen member. I wanted to be inside her, to merge with her hot darkness, her quivering lungs, her heartbeat, until nothing remained of our existence but the throbbing of our blood and a panting that seemed no longer to be within us but somewhere outside us.

We lay on the bed exhausted, on the verge of sleep. I felt Natasha beside me, her breath, her hair, the gentle movement of her ribs, and the faint beating of her heart. She was not yet wholly Natasha or even a nameless woman; she was breath and heartbeat and skin. Only later did consciousness rush in, bringing with it name and feeling, a weary hand groping for a shoulder, and a mouth muttering meaningless words. Then suddenly I smelled it.

"Damn it, the goulash!"

Natasha half opened her eyes. "Throw it out the window."

"God forbid. I think I can save it."

I turned off the hot plate and carefully poured out the goulash, leaving only the burned crust that had stuck to the pot. Then I opened the window and put the pot on the outside sill. "The smell will be gone in a minute," I said. "The goulash is saved."

"The goulash is saved," Natasha repeated without moving. "Now I suppose you want me to get out of bed."

"All I want is to bring you a cigarette and a glass of vodka. You don't have to take them."

She thought it over for a moment. "I'll take them. Where did you get the lamp shades? In Hollywood?"

"They were here when I moved in."

"They're Mexican. And I'll bet they belonged to a woman."

"That may be. The woman's name was Lisa Teruel. She's moved out."

"No woman would leave such nice lamp shades behind."

"Sometimes people leave more than that behind, Natasha."

"Only if the police are after them." She sat up. "I don't know why, but all of a sudden I'm ravenous."

"I knew it. So am I."

I filled the plates.

"Do you know, Robert, I didn't believe you when you said you were having dinner with your goulash family. I see it was true."

"I lie as little as possible. It's simpler."

"So it is. For instance, I'd never tell you that I hadn't been unfaithful to you."

"Unfaithful! What a preposterous word!"

"Why is it preposterous?"

"Because it implies a pact we never made, a kind of ownership. If you go to bed with other men, you may be unfaithful to yourself, but not to me."

"That sounds pretty silly to me, but if it makes you feel better. . . ."

I laughed. "Natasha," I said, "horrible as it may sound, something tells me that I love you. And we tried so hard not to."

"Did we?" She gave me a strange look. "All the same I've been unfaithful to you."

"And I love you all the same. What has the one got to do with the other? They're two separate things, like wind and water; they move each other, but they don't mix."

"I don't get it."

265

"Neither do I. Do we always have to understand everything?"

I didn't believe her. Or even if I did, what did it matter? She was there, she was with me; anything more was for people who knew what the future held in store for them.

XXX

I sold the Egyptian cat to a Dutchman. The day I received the check I asked Kahn to have dinner with me at Voisin. "Are you as rich as all that?" he asked.

"When the ancients were getting ready to drink," I explained, "they used to pour a little wine on the ground as an offering to the gods. I go to a good restaurant for the same reason. Which reminds me that they've still got some beautiful Cheval Blanc in their cellar. We'll have a bottle. Okay?"

"Okay. We can pour out the dregs on our plates to keep the gods in a good humor."

Voisin was full, as restaurants tend to be in wartime. Even people who are in no danger whatever feel that they have to get something out of life before it's too late. And they spend their money more freely in troubled times.

Kahn was depressed. "I'm feeling low," he said. "I've had a letter from Carmen. She thinks we should separate. She says we don't understand each other. She doesn't want me to write any more. Has she got someone else?"

The news had hit him hard. "I don't think so," I said. "She doesn't seem to see anybody but her landlady and the chickens in the back yard. I saw her a few times. She was happy to be doing nothing."

"What would you do? Should I go out there and bring her back? Would she come?"

"I don't think so."

"Neither do I. What should I do?"

"Wait. And stop writing. Maybe she'll come back of her own accord."

"Do you believe that?"

"No," I said. "Does it mean so much to you?"

He was silent for a moment. "It shouldn't. It never used to. It was sort of a whim. Not now. Do you know why?"

"Because she doesn't want to come back."

He smiled sadly. "It seems so simple. Except when it happens to us."

I thought of Natasha. Hadn't the same thing almost happened to me? And wouldn't it happen one of these days? I shook off the thought and wondered what to say to Kahn. The whole thing was completely out of character. It was absurd, incongruous, and for that very reason dangerous. In a poet, a man of imagination, it would have been absurd but understandable; in a coolheaded intellectual like Kahn it was merely absurd. He had been amused by Carmen's odd combination of tragic beauty and phlegmatic soul, and, because he was at loose ends, this amusement had become a kind of refuge for him. Now he was suddenly taking it seriously. That was a bad sign, a sign that he was going to pieces.

He raised his glass. "How little we find to say about women when we're happy! And how much when we're not!"

"That's true. Do you think you would have been happy with Carmen?"

"You think we weren't right for each other? That's true. But when people are right for each other, separation comes easier. It's like a pot cover. When it fits there's no difficulty in taking it off. When it doesn't, and you have to take a hammer to it, you're likely to break something."

"That's nonsense," I said. "All proverbial sayings can be twisted into their opposites."

"All situations, too. Forget about Carmen. I guess I'm just generally depressed. The war's coming to an end, Robert."

"Is that why you're depressed?"

"No. But then what? Do you know what you're going to do?"

"Who knows these things for sure? It's impossible to conceive of the war being over, and it's impossible to conceive of what we're going to do."

"Do you want to stay here?"

"I'd rather not talk about it today."

"You see? I'm always thinking about it. It's going to be a terrible letdown for us refugees. Up to now we've been sustained by the thought of the injustice that was done to us. And now all of a sudden the injustice is gone. We'll be able to go back. What for? Where? And who wants us? How *can* we go back?"

"A good many will stay here."

He waved that away. "I mean the vulnerable ones. Not the opportunists and careerists."

"I mean the whole lot," I said. "Including the opportunists and careerists."

Kahn smiled. "There speaks the lover of humanity. Of all humanity, except for the individuals. *Prosit,* Robert. I'm talking a lot of nonsense today. It's a good thing you're here. Radios are great talkers, but poor listeners. Can you see me selling radios for the rest of my life?"

"Maybe you'll take over the factory."

"Can you see me owning a factory?"

"Not really," I admitted.

"The Cheval Blanc is all gone," I said. "And we've forgotten to sacrifice the last drops to the gods. How about an enormous dish of ice cream? You always said it was your favorite weakness."

He shook his head. "That was an act, Robert. Mostly for my own benefit. The smiling cynic, the *bon vivant,* who takes life's little pleasures as they come. I'm through with all that. I'm just an old Jew."

"An old Jew of thirty."

"Jews are always old. We're born old. Each one of us carries two thousand years of persecution on his back—from the cradle to the grave."

"How about taking a bottle with us and continuing our conversation at my place?"

"That's another thing about the Jews. We're not drinkers. I'll just go home to my room over the shop, and tomorrow I'll laugh at myself. Good night, Robert."

He had me seriously worried. "I'll take you home," I said.

We stepped out into the bitter cold. "In some situations," I said, "there's no sense in trying to be heroic. Your cold room . . ."

"It's overheated," Kahn interrupted me.

"There are different kinds of coldness," I said. "Could anything be colder, for instance, than this damn neon light they have all over the place? It makes my teeth chatter twice as hard. Come on back to the hotel with me. Be reasonable."

"Tomorrow," said Kahn. "I have a date tonight."

"Don't be silly."

"I really have," he said. "With Lissy Koller. Now do you believe me?"

The twin, I thought. Why not? She was pretty and domestic, as hungry for love as a stray cat and a lot less stupid than Carmen. But suddenly in the glacial night it dawned on me why only Carmen would do for Kahn. Somehow her absolute futility helped him to bear the futility of his own uprooted existence.

The tail lights of the passing cars suggested scattered coals trying in vain to warm the darkness. We stopped outside the radio store, and I looked up. The light was on in Kahn's room. "Don't take on like a worried mother hen," said Kahn. "As you can see, I've left the light on. I won't be going into a dark room."

I thought of the twin who had been afraid of her room. Maybe she really was upstairs, combing her hair. "Does it get much colder in New York?" I asked.

"Much colder," said Kahn.

Natasha was covered with jewels: earrings set with enormous rubies, a diamond-and-ruby necklace, and a magnificent ring. Horst, the photographer, whispered in my ear: "That's a forty-two-carat ring. We're doing color photos of her hands. We wanted a big star ruby, but there was none to be had. It doesn't matter; we'll fake the star. That's what retouching is for. Everything is fake nowadays."

"Really?" I asked, looking at Natasha, who was sitting motionless on the platform in a white satin dress, her rubies aflame in the spotlights. It was hard for me to believe that this cold gleaming goddess had lain on my bed the night before, rending the air with her raucous screams: "Deeper! Deeper! Break me into pieces! Crush me! Deeper!"

"That's right," said Horst. "Women and politicians, for instance. False bosoms, rubber bottoms, made-up faces, false eyelashes, wigs, false teeth. Everything fake. When I come in with my off-focus lens and sophisticated light effects, the years melt away like sugar in coffee, and *voilà*."

"Where do the politicians come in?" I asked.

"Ah, the politicians. Most of them can hardly read and write. They have clever little Jews who write their speeches, agencies that supply them with jokes, ghost writers who turn out their books, actors who teach them personality, and sometimes even phonograph records that speak for them." Having got that off his chest, he bounded to his camera. "That's fine, Natasha. Hold it."

Natasha came down from the white light of the platform, and the goddess was transformed into the warm-blooded, bejeweled wife of an armaments magnate.

"One more pose and I'll be with you," she said to me. "I'm famished."

I knew these attacks of hers. They were brought on by hypoglycemia, a condition in which the blood-sugar level drops at an abnormal rate. While we were living on Fifty-seventh Street I had often been awakened by strange sounds. Leaping out of bed to do battle with burglars, I had found her naked by the icebox, magically illumined by the inside light, with a cold chop in one hand and a piece of cheese in the other.

I reached into my pocket and took out a waxed-paper parcel. "Steak tartare on rye," I said, "to tide you over."

"With onions?"

"With onions."

"You're an angel." She took off her necklace and began to eat. I had got into the habit of providing myself with these little packages when we were going to places where no food was available. If only in self-defense. Natasha could be pretty vitriolic when her blood-sugar level took a sudden drop. If there was nothing to eat, she lost control; it was a kind of momentary madness. She simply felt the pangs of hunger more acutely than other people.

I waited for Natasha to usher in the next season. Outside it was midwinter, but here it was May. Woolen suits in bright colors with the most seductive names: cobalt blue, Nile green, corn yellow, desert brown. May, I thought. They say the war will be over in May. What then? Kahn had asked. What then? I thought, and looked at Natasha, who had appeared in the background in a short two-piece suit, looking very slender and swaying a little, as though her legs were too long. Where would I be in May? Time seemed to be falling apart, like a bag of overripe tomatoes. We're spoiled for a normal life, Kahn had said; can you see me as a radio salesman, with a family, voting Democratic, putting money aside, and trying to become a leader in the community? We're spoiled for normal life. A lot of people have been hit by this explosion. Some have come off without grave injury, some have even profited by it, others have been crippled. The injured, and those are the ones who matter most, will never get their bearings again, and in the end they'll go to the wall. May 1945! Or June or July! Time, which had dragged on so painfully all these years, suddenly seemed to race. I watched Natasha, who was now on the platform, illumined from all sides. I saw her face in profile, bent slightly forward, and it passed through my mind that she must smell slightly of onions.

Suddenly the spotlights went out. Gray and diffuse, the regular lights seemed to fight their way through the fog. "That's all!" Horst called out. "Pack up and go home."

Amid the rustling of tissue paper and the clatter of boxes, Natasha emerged. She was wearing the borrowed fur coat and the ruby earrings. "I couldn't resist it," she said. "I've kept them for this evening. I'll send them back tomorrow. I often do that. They're so lovely."

"But what if you lose them?"

She looked at me as if I had said something obscene. "They're insured," she said loftily.

"Well," I said, "that determines our strategy for the evening. We'll go to the Pavillon."

"I won't have to eat much after that steak tartare."

"We'll get ourselves a meal fit for con men and counterfeiters," I said.

We went out. "Good God!" cried Natasha. "There's the Rolls! I'd completely forgotten."

I stood thunderstruck. "With Fraser inside?" I asked.

"Of course not. He left town today. He promised to send it because he thought it might be a late night. I'd forgotten."

"Send it away."

"Be reasonable, Robert. As long as it's here. We've often used it. It doesn't mean a thing."

"It was different then. Now I love you, and I'm a capitalist in a small way. I can afford a cab."

"But the Rolls is just the thing for con men and counterfeiters."

"It's very tempting, but let's not. It's a pleasant evening, crackling with frost. Tell the chauffeur we're going for a walk in the woods."

"If that's what you want," she said hesitantly, taking a step.

"Stop!" I said. "I've changed my mind. Forgive me, Natasha. Anything that gives you pleasure is more important than jealousy disguised as moral principles. Hop in."

She sat beside me like an exotic bird. "I haven't taken off my make-up," she said. "It would have taken too long and, besides, it's too hectic in the studio. They only give you time for a quick wipe with cold cream and you come out looking like a plucked chicken."

"You don't look like a plucked chicken," I said. "You look like a hungry bird of paradise, lost in the big city. Or like a virgin decked out for the sacrifice in Haiti or Timbuctoo. I like women to look different. I'm an old-fashioned admirer of woman as a miraculous creature from the jungle or the northern forests. I can't see her as a comrade and business partner and equal."

"You mean you're a barbarian?"

"A hopeless romantic."

"Am I barbaric enough for you? With false eyelashes, movie make-up, jewels that don't belong to me, a borrowed fur coat, and this new hairdo? Is that enough for my counterfeiter friend?"

"You haven't seen the last of my counterfeiting," I said. "Wait till I pay with counterfeit money."

"Don't we always?"

I took her hand. "Probably. But business practices should always be viewed with respect. In ancient times lying wasn't looked down on; it was regarded as a kind of wisdom. Think of the crafty Ulysses. How wonderful it is to be sitting here with you under all these lights, surrounded by waiters with venerable flat feet, and to see you digging into a sirloin steak. I worship you, Natasha, for all sorts of reasons. A very important one is that you're such a good eater in an age where diet is king on this great glutted island separated by two oceans from the world's hunger. The women here eat like rabbits while whole continents starve; but you have the courage to eat. Other women make you spend a pile of money, they pick at their food for a while, and it all goes back to the kitchen. But you . . ."

"What other women?"

"I'm generalizing. Look around. This fine restaurant is full of them. They eat salad and drink coffee. When they're through, they're so hungry that they kick up scenes with their husbands. That's the only passion they're capable of. In bed a fence post would put them to shame. But you . . ."

She laughed. "That'll do!"

"I had no intention of going into details. I was only intoning an ode to your magnificent appetite."

"I know, Robert. But I also know that you tend to strike up your odes and rhapsodies when there's something else on your mind. You may be a counterfeiter and double talker and double thinker, but you can't fool me. I don't ask you what's eating you and what you're trying to forget. But I know there's something." She stroked my hand tenderly. "We're living in crazy times. The only way we can get through is to make certain things bigger or smaller than they are. Is that it?"

"Maybe," I said cautiously. "But we don't have to do it ourselves. The lousy times do it for us."

She did not reply. We sat for a while in silence, and I wanted very much to be alone with her. "I talk a lot of nonsense," I said finally, "and I don't know anything about women. But I'm happy with you. Maybe I am hiding something, but that has nothing to do with my feeling for you. They're two separate things. All I really wanted to say is that I'm happy with you. Forgive me for taking so long about it, but you've got to remember that for years words were my stock in trade. I used to be a journalist."

"And you're not any more?"

"No. I can speak English fairly well, but I can't write it. Is it any wonder that my imagination sprouts like weeds and puts forth romantic blossoms? In normal times I wouldn't have been such an anachronistic false romantic."

"Do you really think so?"

"No, but there's something in it.

"There's no such thing as a false romantic, Robert."

"Oh yes there is. In politics. And in politics they're a disaster. There's one of them in a bunker under Berlin right now."

I took her home. I was glad to see that the Rolls was gone; she had sent the chauffeur away. "Are you surprised?" she asked.

"No," I said.

"Did you expect me to send it away?"

"No."

"What did you expect?"

"I expected you to come back to the hotel with me."

We were standing in her doorway. It was dark and cold. "It's too bad we haven't got the apartment any more."

"Yes," I said, looking into the unfamiliar face with the long eyelashes.

"Come up with me," she whispered. "But we'll have to make silent love."

"No," I said. "Come back to the hotel with me. Then we won't have to be silent."

"Why didn't you take me there straight from the Pavillon?"

"I don't know."

"Tell me *why*."

"Maybe because you looked so exotic—like a stranger. I don't know. Now I want you because you look so exotic."

"Is that the only reason?"

"No."

"Go find a taxi. I'll wait here."

I ran to the corner. It was very cold, and it was exciting to know that Natasha was waiting in the doorway. I felt the little muscles in my chest quivering. I found a cab and rode back in it. Natasha rushed out of the house. We didn't talk. We were both shivering. We tried in vain to warm each other's hands. We practically fell out of the cab. No one saw us. It was as though we had never been together before.

XXXI

Betty Stein died in January. The last German offensive dealt her the death blow. From day to day she had followed the advance of the Allied armies; her room was full of newspapers. When the Germans surprised the world by counterattacking, her courage failed her. The war would go on for years; the German people would never turn against the Nazis, as she had hoped. "They'll defend every town and village, every inch of ground," she said wearily. "They're all Nazis." Even when the German offensive collapsed, she did not rally. She grew weaker from day to day, and one morning Lissy found her dead.

She had insisted on being buried. Cremation reminded her of the German death camps. She had even refused to take German medicines. But to the end she had yearned to see Berlin—a Berlin that no longer existed. In spite of everything she had read in the papers, her image of it remained unchanged.

The day Betty was buried, the streets were deep in snow. The city was digging itself out. Hundreds of trucks were hauling snow to the Hudson and the East River. The sky was very blue and a cold, bright sun was shining.

The funeral chapel was overcrowded. Many of those whom Betty had helped had half forgotten her, but now they remembered. The usual organ pipes were in evidence, and as usual the music issued from a hidden phonograph. The records chosen for this day's ceremony were vestiges of a Germany that no longer existed. German folk songs were sung by Richard Tauber, a Jew, one of the finest singers of the century, who had died of lung cancer in England after the barbarians had driven him out of his country. *"Ach, wie ist's möglich dann,"* he sang, *"dass ich dich lassen kann / Hab dich von Herzen lieb, Nur dich allein."* It was almost unbearable; but that had been Betty's wish; she hadn't wanted to depart from this world in English. I heard a wheezing sob behind me and turned around. It was Tannenbaum. He looked gray and haggard and needed a shave. I guessed that he had just arrived from California. He owed his career to Betty's untiring efforts.

We gathered again in Betty's apartment—another of her wishes. She had left express orders for us to be gay. There were a few bottles of wine, and Lissy had brought cake from a Hungarian pastry shop.

It was not gay. We stood awkwardly about, all of us with the feeling that not only Betty, but many more were absent.

I was standing with Ravic and Tannenbaum. We were joined by a stocky, dark-haired man I had never seen before.

"What's happening with the apartment?" he asked.

"Betty left it to Lissy, Mr. Meyer," said Ravic. "The apartment and everything in it."

Lissy, who was serving wine, came up to us. Meyer turned to her. "You won't be keeping it, will you?" he asked. "It's too big for you. There are three of us, and we're desperately in need of a place."

"The rent's been paid till the end of the month," said Lissy, fighting back her tears.

Meyer took a sip of wine. "But you'll let us have it, won't you? We're friends of Betty's, after all. You wouldn't give it to strangers."

"Mr. Meyer," said Tannenbaum angrily, "do we have to discuss this right now?"

"Why not? Apartments are hard to find. We've been waiting a long time."

"Then wait a few days more."

"I can't," said Meyer. "I'm leaving town tomorrow and I won't be back until next week."

"Then wait until next week. Haven't you heard of piety?"

"Exactly," said Meyer. "Shouldn't piety toward Betty make you want friends of hers to get her apartment before some stranger snaps it up?"

Tannenbaum was boiling. Because of the other twin he regarded himself as Lissy's protector. "You expect to get it for nothing, don't you?"

"For nothing? Of course not. We could contribute something for the moving, or buy some of the furniture. How can you think of business details at a time like this?"

Tannenbaum's face had gone purple. "Lissy took care of Betty for months. For nothing. Betty couldn't pay her but she left her the apartment. We're not giving it away to any small-time chiseler."

"I must ask you to show respect for the dead."

"Mr. Meyer," said Ravic, "kindly shut up."

"What!"

"Shut up! You can make Miss Koller a written offer. But right now shut up!"

"A written offer? Are we Nazis? Isn't my word . . ."

He beat a retreat in midsentence.

"That scavenger," said Tannenbaum. "He never even came to see Betty when she was sick. And now he wants to get the apartment away from Lissy before she can find out what it's worth."

"Are you staying on here?" I asked.

"No, I've got to go back. A small part in a Western. Very interesting. Did you know that Carmen was married?"

"Since when?"

"A week ago. To a farmer in the San Fernando Valley. Wasn't she Kahn's girl?"

"I don't know. Are you sure she's married?"

"I was at the wedding. A witness, in fact. The husband's a big friendly guy who never says anything. They say he used to be a great baseball player. They've got a chicken farm, and they raise flowers and vegetables."

"Chickens," I said. "I see it all. How did she meet this man?"

"He's her landlady's brother."

I had been surprised not to see Kahn at the funeral. Now I understood. I decided to go and see him.

I found him with Holzer and Frank. Holzer was an actor, Frank had been a successful German writer before Hitler.

"How was it?" Kahn asked me. "I hate funerals in America, that's why I didn't go. Did the inevitable Rosenbaum make a speech?"

"They couldn't stop him. First in German, then in English with a Leipzig accent."

"That man is the refugees' nemesis," Kahn explained. "He used to be a lawyer. He can't practice here, so he delivers an oration whenever he gets a chance, especially at funerals. No refugee can be buried without his words of unction. If I were about to die, I'd try to do it on the high seas, to get away from him; but he'd probably stow away on the same ship or swoop down in a helicopter."

I watched him. He seemed to have himself under control.

"When they bury me in liberated Vienna," said Holzer darkly, "he can speak at the grave of an unemployed bald-headed juvenile lead."

"Bald heads can be covered with wigs," I said.

In 1932 Holzer had been a matinee idol—young, handsome, and talented. Since then he had put on fifteen pounds and lost his hair. He was sullen and embittered. In America he hadn't even been able to find work as an extra.

"Look at me," he said. "I could never face my audience."

"Your audience is also twelve years older," I said.

"But we haven't grown old together. They haven't seen me grow old. They remember me as I was in 1932."

"You make me laugh with your problems," said Frank. "Why can't you do character parts?"

"I'm not a character actor. I've always been the young lead."

"Then you can be a middle-aged lead," said Frank impatiently. "Caesar was as bald as a billiard ball. Or you can wear a shaggy wig and do King Lear."

"I'm not old enough. I've got to feel my part."

"I wish I had your troubles," said Frank. "In 1933, when they burned my books, I was sixty-four, at the height of my creative powers, as they say. Now I'm going on seventy-seven. I'm an old man; I can't work any more. I have eighty-seven dollars to my name."

Frank was so German that all attempts to publish him in translation had been a total failure. And he was also too German to learn English.

"Your books will be republished after the war," I said.

"In Germany? After twelve years of National Socialist education?"

"All the more reason," I said, but I didn't believe it.

Frank shook his head. "They've forgotten me," he said. "They don't need us any more. They need new writers. In 1933 I still had all sorts of plans. Now I have none. I'm an old man. It's awful to be old. It creeps up on you and you don't know it. But now I know. Do you know when it dawned on me? When I realized that the Nazis had lost the war and that maybe I could go back. Go back! What for? Where to? I'm finished."

No one answered. I looked out the window at the clear winter sky. The room trembled as trucks rumbled past. Frank and Holzer took their leave.

"I suppose you've heard about Carmen getting married," said Kahn.

"Tannenbaum told me. But it's so easy to get divorced in this country."

Kahn laughed. "Good old Robert! Any more words of comfort?"

"No. Except that you're better off than Frank or Holzer. You're not seventy-five and you're not a matinee idol."

"Did you hear what Frank said?"

"Yes. That he's finished. And has nowhere to go. That he's suddenly become an old man. We're not old men."

Kahn was a man of iron discipline. But for all his composure I could see that he was shattered. I laid it to Betty and Carmen and thought it would pass. "It's a good thing you didn't come to the funeral," I said. "It was horrible."

"She was lucky," Kahn said. "She died at the right time. If she'd gone back, she would have died of disappointment. As it is, she died with hope in her heart. I know she despaired at the end, but she still had a spark of hope."

I saw there was nothing I could do to help him. He was running around in circles like a constipated dog. He rejected the slightest attempt at consolation in advance. It was plain that he wanted to be alone, and, besides, I was tired. Only one thing is more tiring than running around in circles, and that is trying to keep up with someone else who is doing it.

"See you tomorrow," I said. "I've got to get back to work. But why were you hobnobbing with Frank and Holzer? You never used to be a masochist."

"They were at Betty's funeral. Didn't you see them?"

"No. There was such a crowd."

"They came straight here from the funeral parlor. They wanted me to cheer them up. I'm afraid I let them down."

I left. It was almost a relief to be back with Silvers in his somewhat baroque, yet wholesomely businesslike world.

"Isn't your friend on Fifty-seventh Street taking a winter vacation?" I asked Natasha. "Why wouldn't he go to Florida, for instance? Hasn't he got asthma or bronchitis or something? Isn't this cold weather bad for him?"

"It's the heat that disagrees with him. He always goes away in the summer."

"That doesn't help us right now. It's terrible to be a poor lover in America. Where does sex take place in this country?"

"In cars."

"But what if you have no car?" I couldn't help thinking of the spacious Rolls-Royce with the built-in bar. But maybe, I consoled myself, Fraser himself couldn't drive and the chauffeur was my guardian angel. "What do all these healthy young men do without brothels? In France they open at ten o'clock in the morning, psychiatrists are unknown, and you hardly ever hear of a nervous breakdown. Anyway, that's how it was before the war."

I was sitting in a wobbly armchair, upholstered with the same plush as the furniture in the lobby—and in all the other rooms from cellar to attic. The mysterious owner of the hotel must have hijacked a carload of plush thirty years before.

Natasha was lying on the bed. On the table in front of us were the remains of our dinner, supplied by the delicatessen, that magnificent institution, the salvation of all kitchenless Americans, where you can buy hot roast chickens, cakes, cold cuts, canned goods, luxurious toilet paper, dill pickles, caviar (black and red), bread, butter, and Band-Aids—in short, everything but condoms; for them you must go to the drugstore, where a white-clad clerk dispenses them with a hushed conspiratorial air.

I put a kettle of water on the electric hot plate. Then I lit a White Owl cigar to mask the smell of coffee that would inevitably seep out into the corridor. There was no real danger; though cooking was officially forbidden, nobody cared. But when Natasha was there, I was cautious; maybe the invisible owner would come creeping through the corridors. He had never done so, but that was what made me suspicious. Too many things that never happened had happened in my life.

As I was pouring the coffee, someone knocked at the door, softly but persistently. "Hide under my coat," I said. "Pull in your head and legs. I'll go see who it is."

I unlocked the door and opened it a crack. The Puerto Rican

woman was outside. She put one finger to her lips. "Police," she whispered.

"What!"

"Downstairs. Three cops. Be careful. Maybe search hotel. Be careful."

"What's going on?"

"You alone? No woman?"

"No," I said. "Is that why the police are here?"

"I don't know. About Melikov, I think. Not sure. Maybe search. Arrest woman if find."

"Why? On account of Melikov?"

"Don't know. Better hide."

In the bathroom, I thought. But if the police found Natasha in the bathroom, it would look even worse. She couldn't get away if the cops were downstairs. Damn it, I thought, what can we do?

Suddenly Natasha was standing beside me. She had dressed in two seconds flat. She was perfectly calm. "It's Melikov," she said. "They must have picked him up."

The Puerto Rican woman made hurried signs. "Quick. You come my room. Pedro come here. Understand?"

"Yes."

"See you later," said Natasha, and followed the woman. Pedro, the Mexican, emerged from the shadow of the corridor, hiking up his suspenders. "*Buenas tardes, señor.* Better this way."

I understood. If the police came, Pedro was my guest and Natasha the woman's. Much simpler than the melodramatic Anglo-Saxon solution of climbing through toilet windows and escaping over icy rooftops. A Latin solution. "Sit down, Pedro," I said. "Cigar?"

"Thank you. Better a cigarette. Many thanks, Señor Roberto. I have my own."

He was nervous. "Papers," he mumbled. "Tough spot. Maybe they won't come up."

"No papers? You can say you left them home."

"Not so hot. Are yours any good?"

"Pretty good. But who wants to tangle with the police?" I was nervous myself. "Care for some vodka?"

"Too strong. Better keep a clear head. But I'd like some coffee."

I poured the coffee, which Pedro drank quickly. "What's this business about Melikov?" I asked. "Do you know?"

Pedro shook his head violently. Then he closed one eye, cupped his hand, held it up to his nose and sniffed.

"Is it true?" I asked.

He shrugged his shoulders. I remembered the hints Natasha had thrown out. "Is there anything I can do?" I asked.

"Nothing," said Pedro. "Just keep quiet. Anything you do will make it worse for Melikov. Is there a little more coffee, Señor Roberto?"

I gave him the rest. Better put the hot plate away, I thought. You never know what the police can use against you. "A piece of cake with your coffee?" I asked.

"No, thank you. I'm too nervous."

I put the hot plate in my suitcase and looked around to see if Natasha had left any traces. Only cigarette butts with lipstick marks. I opened the window as quietly as I could and threw out the contents of the ash tray. Then I crept to the door, opened it, and listened.

I heard faint sounds from the lobby. Then steps on the stairs. The police. I knew that tread, I had heard it often enough in Germany, Belgium, and France. I closed the door quickly. "They're coming," I said.

Pedro dropped his cigarette. "They're going upstairs," I said.

Pedro picked up his cigarette. "To Melikov's room."

"Do you think they've got a search warrant?"

He shrugged his shoulders again. "A warrant? With poor people?"

"I see what you mean." I ought to have known. Why should New York be different from anywhere else in the world? My papers were good, but not so very good. Pedro was probably in the same situation. As to the Puerto Rican woman, I didn't know. The only thing I was sure of was that they would let Natasha go, but they could hold the rest of us till kingdom come. I cut off a big piece of the Sara Lee chocolate cake and stuffed it into my mouth. The food in police stations is notoriously bad.

I looked out the window. There was light in some of the windows across the court. "Where's your lady friend's room?" I asked Pedro. "Can we see it from here?"

He came to the window. His curly hair smelled of some sort of sweet oil. He looked up. "No. It's right on top of us. You can't see it from here."

We had quite a long wait. Now and then we opened the door and listened. Not a sound. The hotel guests seemed to know what was going on, and no one stirred from his room. Finally I heard the unmistakable heavy steps coming down. I closed the door. "I think they're leaving," I said. "I guess they were only interested in Melikov."

Pedro heaved a sigh of relief. "Why can't they leave people alone? What's the harm in a little snow if it makes a man happy? Over there they're killing millions with their bombs and here they get all hot and bothered about a little white powder."

His eyes were moist, and the whites were tinged with blue. He probably used cocaine himself, I thought. "Have you known Melikov long?" I asked.

"Not so long."

I shut up. What business was it of mine? I wondered if anything could be done to help Melikov. No, I decided—anyway, not by foreigners with dubious papers.

The door opened. It was Natasha. "They're gone," she said. "They've taken Melikov with them."

Pedro stood up. The Puerto Rican woman came in. "Okay, Pedro, we go."

"Many thanks," I said to her. "You've been very kind."

She smiled. "Poor people help each other."

"Not always."

Natasha kissed her cheek. "Thanks for the address, Raquel."

"What address?" I asked when we were alone.

"For stockings. She's got the longest I've ever seen. They're hard to find. Most stockings are too short. Raquel showed me hers. They're marvelous."

"Pedro was less entertaining."

"Naturally. He was scared. He takes cocaine. And now he's got a problem. He'll have to find another pusher."

"Was Melikov one?"

"The gangster who owns this hotel forced him. If he'd refused, he'd have been fired. He'd never have found another job. Too old."

"Is there anything we can do for him?"

"No. Only the gangster can help him. Maybe he'll get him out. He's got a very smart lawyer. He'll have to do something. Melikov might talk if he didn't."

"Who told you all this?"

"Raquel."

Natasha looked around. "Where's the cake?"

"Here. I ate the rest."

"Is that what danger does to you?"

"No. Just a precaution. And Pedro drank the coffee. Do you want some?"

"No, I'd better get out of here. The police might come back."

"I guess you're right. I'll take you home."

"No, stay here. Somebody might be watching the lobby. If I'm alone, I can say I was visiting Raquel. Isn't it exciting?"

"Too exciting for me. I hate excitement."

She laughed. "I love it."

I took her to the head of the stairs. Suddenly she had tears in her eyes. "Poor Vladimir," she muttered.

She went down quickly and very erect. I went back to my room and cleared the table. Clearing tables has always made me sad, probably because it reminds me of the impermanence of all things, even of a lousy chocolate cake. In a sudden access of rage I opened the window and threw out what was left of the cake. Let the cats have a party, now that mine was over. I went downstairs. There was no one in sight; people have a way of avoiding places where the police have been. I crept through the orphaned lobby. You never really appreciate a man until he's gone, I thought, a truth all the more crushing for being so banal. I thought of Natasha—it would be harder now to smuggle her into my room. A wave of self-pity swept over me. It had been a gray day. Weighed down with past partings, I had thought of the partings to come, feeling utterly wretched because I could think of no way out. I dreaded the night and my bed; I was afraid of being sucked in by my nightmares. The only hope, I thought, was to go for a walk and get good and tired. I went back to my room for my coat. Fifth Avenue was deathly still. In the light of the street lamps the shops glittered like glass coffins, as though rain had frozen on the panes. I heard my own footfalls and thought of the police and then of Melikov languishing in some cage. Suddenly I felt very tired and turned back. It occurred to me for no reason at all that now in February the almond trees in Sicily must already be in blossom. I walked faster and faster; someone had told me that brisk exercise relieves sadness, but I was too tired to notice whether it worked.

XXXII

The weeks melted away like the snow in the streets. For a while I heard nothing of Melikov. Then one morning he was back. "Is it all over?" I asked him.

He shook his head. "I'm out on bail. I'm coming up for trial."

"Have they got anything on you?"

"Let's not talk about it, Robert. And for your own good, don't ask questions. The less you know in this town, the better off you are."

"I understand, Vladimir. But you've lost weight. Why did they hold you so long?"

"No questions, I said. Believe me, it's better that way. And keep away from me."

"No," I said.

"I mean it. But now let's have a drink of vodka. It's been a long time."

"You're not looking well. You look thin and sad."

"I'm seventy. Had a birthday in jail. And I've got high blood pressure."

"There are cures for that."

"Robert," said Melikov under his breath, "there's no cure for trouble. I don't want to die in jail."

For a moment I listened to the drip drip drip of the melting snow outside. Then I said very softly: "Can't you do what I've always done in times of danger? This is a big country and nobody checks on your papers. Besides, each state has different laws."

"No, Robert. I don't want to be a hunted man. I'll just have to take my chances. Maybe the people who bailed me out can help me." He forced a smile. "Let's just drink our vodka and hope for a good heart attack while I'm still at large."

In March the Vriesländers announced their daughter's engagement—to an American. They were married in April. Vriesländer decided to give two receptions—one for Americans, the other for refugees. He was determined to become more American with each passing day, and he regarded his daughter's marriage to a genuine American as an important step in this direction. But at the same time he wanted to show us stateless waifs that, though he softpedaled his origins, he was not utterly unfaithful to them. The first reception, the real one, so to speak, was confined to his new connections and to a few selected refugees who were already naturalized or at least held academic positions. The other was for the deserving poor. I had no desire to go, but Natasha made me. She had developed a passion for the Vriesländer goulash and hoped I would bring home a jar of it.

As Vriesländer put it, this party was a kind of leave-taking, but at the same time it marked the beginning of a new era. "Our forty years in the wilderness are almost over," he said.

"Where is the Promised Land?" Kahn asked.

"Right here!" said Vriesländer in astonishment. "Where else would it be?"

"Then it's a victory celebration!"

"Jews don't celebrate victories, Mr. Kahn," said Vriesländer. "Jews celebrate escapes."

"Will the young couple be here?" I asked Mrs. Vriesländer.

"No. They've gone to Florida on their honeymoon."

"To Miami?"

"No, to Palm Beach. It's more exclusive."

I looked around. The same faces as usual, but the atmosphere had changed. Vriesländer gave a party for refugees every few months, chiefly to provide all these lost souls with a haven and gathering place. In this emigration, as in countless others before it, assimilation began with the second generation. The children went to American schools and slipped effortlessly into American ways. Not so the first generation, who found it as difficult to change their

286

habits as to learn English. They clung to each other and, thankful as they were for American hospitality, felt they were living in a comfortable prison without walls.

Tannenbaum was there. He was again playing the part of an S.S. man, but this time in the theater. "I'm here to stay," he announced. "New York is the only place where we're not treated as foreigners and intruders."

Vesel glared at him. "What if you can't find work? You've got a horrible accent, and when the war's over there won't be any more of those parts."

"Wrong again. They'll be rehashing the war for years."

"You know everything," said Vesel. "You must be God."

"I'm not God," said Tannenbaum. "But at least I've got a job."

"Gentlemen!" said Mrs. Vriesländer. "You mustn't fight. Now that our troubles are over."

"Are they?" asked Kahn.

"Not if you go back," said Tannenbaum. "What do you think the old country looks like now?"

"Home is home," said Vesel.

"And shit is shit."

"I've got to go back," said Frank. "What else can I do?"

That was the keynote of this dismal evening. Suddenly Kahn's prediction had come true. Because it would soon be possible to go back, those who wanted to stay were beginning to have their doubts, to fear that they would be losing something. America had not changed, but the prospect of staying there no longer seemed so attractive. And those who wanted to go back and still looked upon Germany as their home suddenly realized that, far from being a paradise, it was a devastated country, where life would be very difficult. Both those who had decided to go back and those who had decided to stay felt like deserters.

"Lissy wants to go back," said Kahn. "Lucy, the other twin, wants to stay. They've hardly ever been apart. They each accuse the other of selfishness. It's tragic."

I didn't know how he stood with Lissy. "Couldn't you talk to her?" I asked.

"No. It's in the air. Some go, some stay, and all will be disillusioned."

"What will you do?"

"Me?" he said, laughing. "I can't go either way. I'll just burst like a balloon. What about you?"

"I don't know. I've still got time to think about it."

"You've been doing that ever since you got here."

"Thinking is no help. It only complicates matters. One day you suddenly do something."

"Yes," he said. "Suddenly. That's it."

Vriesländer took me aside. "Don't forget what I told you about German stocks. After the armistice they'll be dirt cheap. And they'll go up and up. Even if you hate Germany politically, you can count on the German economy. The Germans are a schizophrenic people, proficient in industry, commerce, science, and mass murder."

"Yes," I said. "And sometimes you find all those gifts combined in the same individual."

"Exactly. Didn't I say they were schizophrenics? You be one, too: hate the Nazis and make a fortune."

"Wouldn't you call that opportunism?"

"Call it whatever you like. But why should we let the German corporations, which benefited by the Nazi regime and worked their slave laborers to death, pile up another fortune?"

"They will anyway," I said. "They'll be subsidized, and their directors will be honored and decorated. We saw what happened after the First World War. Are you going back, Mr. Vriesländer?"

"Certainly not. I can handle my business by phone. If you need money, I'll be glad to lend you a thousand dollars. That will be a lot of money over there."

"Thank you. I may take you up."

For a fraction of a second something seemed to have gone wrong with the light. It did not go out, but the people and objects around me were blanketed in mist. In that moment an anguished desire, which I had been able to live with until then because it seemed half-unattainable, became reality. I had no thought of investing the money Vriesländer offered me. What it meant to me was the possibility of going back to the country that was the substance of my nightmare, a lowering black cloud that threatened to engulf me. I stood dazed in the glare of the chandeliers. The room and everyone in it twisted and turned uncontrollably. Then in the midst of the confusion I heard Kahn's voice: "The cook is getting your goulash ready. You can pick it up in the kitchen, and then we can make our getaway. How about it?"

"What? Getaway? When?"

"Whenever you like. Preferably right now."

"Oh!" I blinked. At last I understood what he was saying. "I can't go yet," I said. "There are some things I want to attend to." I wanted to pull myself together and I thought I could do that most easily with people around me. And at that particular moment I had no desire to be alone with Kahn.

"All right," said Kahn, "but I'm leaving. I can't take any more of this atmosphere, this mixture of excitement, sentimentality, and uncertainty. All these people make me think of blind birds that keep dashing against the bars of their cage; then one day they discover that the bars are not made of steel but of cooked spaghetti. And they don't know whether to sing or weep. Some have started to sing. They'll soon find out that there's nothing to sing about, that they've only been deprived of their last possessions: romantic nostalgia and romantic hatred. It's not possible to hate what has been destroyed. Good night, Robert."

He was very pale. "Maybe I'll drop in on you later," I said.

"Don't. I'll just take two sleeping pills and go to bed." Then he saw the alarm in my face and added: "Don't worry. I won't do anything foolish."

"Good night, Kahn. I'll drop in tomorrow at lunch hour."

"Do that."

I had an impulse to run after him, but I was too befuddled by the dismal absurdity of this whole gathering and by what Kahn himself had said. I sat there, listening absently to Lachmann, who was telling me confidently of his recovery; for four weeks now he had been having an affair with a widow, and he felt that his performance, though not brilliant, could be qualified as normal.

I asked him if he was going back.

"Maybe in a few years. For a visit. There's no hurry."

I looked at him enviously. "What did you do before?" I asked. "Before Hitler."

"I was a student. My parents had money. I never learned how to do anything."

I couldn't ask him what had become of his parents, but I'd have been glad to know what was going on in his mind. Kahn had told me once that the Jews were too neurasthenic to be vengeful. Because they were neurasthenic, their hatred had no stamina; it soon gave way to resignation and, to preserve their self-respect, they turned their energies to *understanding* the enemy. Like all radical generalizations, this was only partly true. Still, there was something in it. Or maybe they were too cultivated, too sublimated to be vengeful. I wasn't. I was alone, I felt like a troglodyte, but there was a force within me that I could not ignore. All attempts to evade or repress it culminated in an unbearable rage of impatience. It was something in my blood; I hardly understood it myself, but I knew it would lead me to my destruction. I fought against it; I tried to get away from it, and sometimes I thought I was almost succeeding; but then came a memory, a dream, or, as now, an opportunity to set the wheels of destiny in motion, and that was the end of my illusions; then I knew that there was no escape for me.

"You must try to be more cheerful," Mrs. Vriesländer said to me. "After all, this is our last gathering as refugees."

"The last?"

"Our group is breaking up. The days of the Wandering Jew are over."

I looked at her in disbelief. Where had the simple, kindhearted woman heard that? All at once, for no good reason, my spirits revived. I forgot Kahn and my own thoughts. I looked at her plump, rosy-cheeked, mindless face and suddenly I became aware of the touching, innocent, almost magnificent absurdity of this mournful victory celebration. "You're right, Mrs. Vriesländer," I said. "We must try to get some pleasure out of each other before we all go off in different directions. We're all like soldiers when the war is over —comrades today, tomorrow friends or strangers. So in parting let's give a last grateful thought to what we have meant to each other."

"Exactly. That's just what I meant."

I became more and more euphoric. Despair may have entered in, but when doesn't it? It seemed to me that nothing bad could happen, not even to Kahn. Precisely because disaster had menaced me so blatantly, it no longer seemed possible.

XXXIII

I found Kahn at noon next day. He had shot himself. He was not lying on the bed. He had been sitting in a chair and had slumped to the floor. It was a very bright day. The curtains were not drawn. The light streamed into the room, and there lay Kahn on the floor. For a moment the sight seemed so unreal that I could not believe it. Then I heard the radio and, coming closer, saw his shattered head. Seen from the doorway, his face had looked intact.

I didn't know what to do. I had heard that in such cases you must phone the police and that nothing must be moved in the meantime. For a time I stared at the lifeless body, which seemed to have no more to do with Kahn than wax figures with life. Then suddenly I awoke to myself and to a terrible confusion of grief and remorse. I blamed myself for Kahn's death, and the thought was unbearable. He had been cruelly alone, he had needed me. The signs had been obvious, but in my eagerness to see Natasha I had overlooked them.

I turned off the radio and looked about for a letter, though it became clear to me almost at once that I would find none. He had died alone, as he had lived alone. I also knew why I had looked for a message. In the hope that it would dispel my sense of guilt. Now I saw his shattered head in all its reality, yet as though looking at it from a distance, through a thick pane of glass. In my confusion I was struck with surprise that he had shot himself; this was no fit death for a Jew. But even as the thought grazed my mind I remembered that this might well have been one of Kahn's sardonic remarks; it's not true, I said to myself, and was ashamed to have had such a thought.

I finally pulled myself together. I had to do something. I called Ravic.

"Kahn has shot himself," I said. "I don't know what to do. Can you come here?"

Ravic said nothing for a moment. "Are you sure he's dead?" he asked.

"Yes. His head is smashed to pieces."

A hysterical thought passed through my mind: maybe Ravic was thinking that in that case there was no hurry, that he had time to eat lunch.

"Don't do anything," he said. "Don't touch anything. I'll be right over."

I put down the phone, settled myself in a chair near the door, and waited. Then it struck me as cowardly to be sitting so far from Kahn, and I moved in by the table. Everywhere I found traces of Kahn's last moments: a displaced chair, a book that lay closed on the table. I opened it, hoping that it would throw some light on his state of mind; but it was neither an anthology of German poetry nor one of Franz Werfel's books, but some irrelevant American novel.

The silence was made more oppressive by the muffled sound of the traffic. Kahn was dead, and it was inconceivable, just as the death of a bird or rabbit is inconceivable, beyond our powers of thought.

Ravic came in quietly, but I started up as if I had heard an explosion. He went directly to Kahn and looked at him. He did not bend over and did not touch him. "We'll have to notify the police," he said. "Do you want to be here when they come?"

"Don't I have to be?"

"I can say I found him. The police will ask a lot of questions. Wouldn't you rather avoid them?"

"It doesn't matter now," I said.

"Are your papers in order?"

"It makes no difference now."

"Oh yes, it does," said Ravic. "And it won't do Kahn any good."

"I'll stay," I said. "It's all the same to me if the police think I murdered him."

Ravic looked at me. "You think so yourself, don't you?"

I stared at him. "What gives you that idea?"

"It's not hard to guess. Forget it, Ross. If we were to interpret every accident as fate, we'd be paralyzed for life." He looked at the rigid, no longer recognizable face. "I've always had a feeling that he didn't know what to do with himself when the war was over."

"Did you?"

"It's simple for a doctor. We patch people up again so they can be killed in the next war." He picked up the phone and called the police. He had to repeat the name and address several times. "Yes, he's dead," he said. "Yes. All right. When? Good." He hung up. "They'll come as soon as they can. Murders have priority. This isn't the only suicide in town."

We sat and waited. Time seemed to stand still. I discovered an electric clock on Kahn's radio. Kahn's radio, Kahn's clock, I thought, and sensed my mistake at once. Possession was bound up with life. These things no longer belonged to Kahn, because he no longer belonged to them.

"Are you staying in America?" I asked Ravic.

He nodded and gestured toward Kahn. "He had no illusions. They'll probably hate us the same as before. Do you still believe the fairy tale that the poor Germans were forced to do all those things against their will? Look at the newspapers. They know the war is lost, but they defend every single house. They defend their Nazis as a lioness defends her cubs; they're perfectly willing to die for them." He shook his head more sadly than angrily. "He knew what he was doing. It wasn't an act of desperation. He simply saw things more clearly." Ravic paused for a moment. "It makes me very sad," he said. "Kahn saved my life in 1940. I was in a French internment camp. The Germans were coming. The commandant refused to let us go. Kahn found out where I was. He turned up in the camp with two men, all in S.S. uniforms, and bellowed at the commandant, said he had orders to arrest me."

"Did it work?"

"Not right away. The commandant suddenly remembered his honor as a soldier. He said I wasn't there any more, that I'd been released. He would have been willing to hand over the whole lot of us, but a single individual touched his conscience and he tried to save me. Kahn turned the camp upside down until he found me. It was a comedy of errors. I was hiding. I thought it was really the Gestapo. Once we were out of the camp, Kahn gave me a drink of brandy and explained. I hadn't recognized him in his disguise. Hitler mustache and dyed hair. It was the best brandy I ever tasted." Ravic looked up. "I've never seen anyone who could be so lighthearted in difficult situations. The peaceful life over here depressed him. It got worse from day to day. He couldn't have been saved. Do you know why I'm telling you all this?"

"Yes."

"I have more reason than you to blame myself," said Ravic very slowly. "But I don't. We can't if we want to go on living."

Heavy steps were heard on the stairs. "The police," said Ravic. "That's a sound you never forget."

"Where will they take him?" I asked.

"To the morgue. They'll want to do an autopsy. Or maybe they won't, since the cause of death is not in doubt." The door burst open. Crude primitive life poured into the room. Stupid questions were asked, the sergeant took notes with the inevitable pencil stub (a full-length pencil has never been seen in the hands of a policeman), the body was lifted onto a stretcher and carried away. We were taken to the police station, but dismissed after we had given our addresses. Kahn remained behind.

"The undertaker greets us like old friends," said Lissy Koller bitterly.

She was less upset than I had expected. Strangely enough, Kahn seemed to make no lasting impression on women. Tannenbaum had wired Carmen. Later I heard that she had received the news without surprise or emotion and gone on feeding her chickens. Lissy, who had been deeply affected by the death of Betty Stein, looked fresh, pink, and serene. Maybe she had a lover, I thought, an amiable nonentity whom she understands. Neither she nor Carmen had understood Kahn, and he, for his part, had never taken an interest in women who did understand him.

It was a cloudy, wind-swept day. I had threatened to eject Rosenbaum bodily from the chapel if he tried to speak, and he had promised not to. At the last moment I had instructed the proprietor to remove the potted plants from the entrance of the establishment and not to play records of German folk songs. The man looked at me as mournfully as if I had wrenched his last crust of bread from between his gold teeth. There was a fee of five dollars for the music. I looked through his record collection and found Mozart's *Ave verum*. "Play this," I said. "And never mind about taking away the laurel trees."

The chapel was only half full. The mourners included a night watchman, a masseuse with only nine fingers, a masseur who had been a coal dealer in Rothenburg ob der Tauber, a waiter who had operated a corset shop in Munich, and a tearful old woman unknown to me. Kahn had saved them all from the Gestapo in France.

Suddenly I caught sight of Rosenbaum. He came creeping out from behind the coffin like a black frog. A habitué of funerals, he alone of all the mourners was dressed for the occasion—in a morning coat and striped trousers. He planted himself in front of the coffin and cast a sidelong glance in my direction; then he opened his mouth.

Ravic nudged me. He had seen me jump. I nodded. Rosenbaum had triumphed; he knew I wouldn't start a fight next to Kahn's coffin. I wanted to leave, but Ravic nudged me again. "Don't you think Kahn would have been amused?" he whispered.

"No. He even told me once that he'd rather drown than have Rosenbaum speak at his funeral."

"That's just it," said Ravic. "Kahn always recognized the inevitable, and made the most of it. This is inevitable."

I had no need to make a decision. Throughout the months of hesitation the decision had lain dormant within me, now rekindled by my nightmares, now lulled by the fascination of my new life. It rose to full consciousness the moment it became clear to me that I *could* go back. Then I knew I would go. I had to. It was no longer revenge that drove me. I was going in order to set things right with myself. Until I had done that, I would never find peace. Disgust at my cowardice, intolerable remorse, and the thought of suicide would follow me wherever I went. I had no precise plan, but I was fairly sure that whatever I did it would not have much to do with legal retribution, with courts and trials. I knew the courts and I knew the judges in the country to which I was returning. They had been docile servants of the government, and I could not conceive of their suddenly undergoing a change of heart. I had only myself to rely on.

When the armistice was proclaimed, I went to see Vriesländer. I found him radiant. "At last the rotten mess is over. Now we can start building."

"Building?"

"Of course. We Americans. We'll invest billions in Germany."

"Doesn't it seem odd to destroy something in order to build it up again? Or am I wrong?"

"Not wrong, but unrealistic. We've destroyed the system, now we'll rebuild the country. The possibilities are enormous. Think of the construction industry alone."

It was refreshing to speak to a man who dealt in hard facts. "Do you really believe the system has been destroyed?" I asked.

"Of course. After such a defeat."

"The defeat in 1918 was just as disastrous. But that didn't prevent Hindenburg, who had shared the responsibility, from being elected president seven years later."

"Hitler is dead," said Vriesländer with youthful enthusiasm. "The Allies will hang or imprison the rest. A new day is dawning, and we've got to be ready for it." He winked at me. "Isn't that what you've come to see me about?"

"Yes."

"I haven't forgotten my offer."

"It may be some time before I can repay you," I said, and no sooner had I spoken than a faint hope stirred within me. If Vriesländer backed out, I would have to wait till I had saved my passage money. That would give me a little more time in this country, which seemed like more and more of a paradise now that I was about to leave it.

"I keep my promises," said Vriesländer. "How do you want the money? In cash or a check?"

"In cash."

"I thought so. I haven't that much on hand, but you can pick it up tomorrow. And there's no hurry about paying it back. Are you going to invest it?"

"Yes," I said, after a moment's hesitation.

"Good. Let's say you'll pay me six-per-cent interest. You're sure to make a hundred per cent on your investment. That's fair enough, isn't it?"

"Yes," I said.

"Fair" was a pet word with Vriesländer, though he actually was fair in his dealings. Usually pet words are a habit and a subterfuge.

I stood up to go, torn between relief and despair. "Many thanks, Mr. Vriesländer."

With his right hand he patted me on the back, while with his left he pinched Lissy Koller, who was scurrying past, in the behind —quite an acrobatic feat. "Why, Mr. Vriesländer!" she exclaimed with a routine affectation of indignation.

"It's the spring," said Vriesländer. "It even creeps into these old bones."

For the moment I was devoured by envy. There he stood, a pillar of strength, surrounded by a family and a thriving business, in a world that was clear and simple. I remembered that Lissy had told me he was impotent and tried to believe it for a moment to down my envy.

"Going back soon?" he asked.

"As soon as I can get a ship."

"It won't be long. The war with Japan is almost over. Just a mopping-up operation. The traffic with Europe will be restored even before that. Are your papers in order now?"

"My residence permit is good for another three months."

"You oughtn't to have any trouble."

I knew it wasn't so simple. But Vriesländer was a man of grand strategy. Details didn't interest him. "Come and see me again before you leave," he said, as though we were already in the thick of peace and the ships were running daily.

"Definitely," I said. "And many thanks."

XXXIV

It wasn't as simple as Vriesländer had thought. It took me more than two months to cut through all the red tape and complete my arrangements. Nevertheless, I was easier in my mind than I had been for years. Everything that had tormented me was still present; but now it was bearable because my mind was made up, and I became more firmly convinced from day to day that no other course would have been possible. I had to go back, and I stopped thinking about what I would do when I got there. The rest would take care of itself. My dreams did not leave me. In fact, they were worse and more frequent than ever. I was in Brussels crawling down a shaft that became narrower and narrower, until I awoke with a scream. I saw the face of the man who had hidden me and been dragged away by the Gestapo. For years that face had been indistinct in my dreams, as though veiled from me through my fear of confronting it. Now I saw it clearly, the tired eyes, the creased forehead. I woke up in horror, but no longer as confused and close to suicide as before. The bitterness and lust for vengeance were still with me, but I no longer felt crushed and dejected. The horror was almost outweighed by a fierce impatience and by joy at finding myself alive and able to make use of my life. Those who had been tortured and murdered and burned could not be brought back to life. But there was something that could be done, and I was going to do it. The source of my determination was not revenge, though it sprang from the same primitive roots; it was the feeling that crime must not go unpunished, for if it did the foundations of morality would collapse and chaos would reign.

Those last months had a strange weightless quality. My whole picture of America changed. Shadowy unreality gave way to a serene, enchanted reality. It was as though the fog had lifted and colors had come into view—a late-afternoon idyll bathed in golden light, a gleaming mirage over a restless city. The scene was transfigured by my awareness of leave-taking, and sometimes it seemed to me that a life of perpetual leave-taking was the closest we could ever come to the dream of eternal life. In those months every evening was the last.

I had decided not to tell Natasha until the last moment that I was going back. I knew she suspected it, but I said nothing. I was willing to be taken, and to take myself, for a traitor and deserter rather than face the torment of a long-drawn-out parting, with its bitterness and reproaches, the brief reconciliations and renewed scenes.

Those were luminous weeks, as full of love as a well-tended beehive is full of honey. Spring turned to summer, and the first news of postwar Europe came through. It was as though a long-sealed tomb had opened. Previously I had avoided the news or let it glance off the top of my mind, for fear of being overwhelmed. Now I devoured the papers. Now the news had a bearing on my aim, my departure. I was blind and deaf to everything else.

"When are you leaving?" Natasha asked me suddenly.

For a moment I was silent. Then I said: "At the beginning of July. How did you find out?"

"Not from you. Why didn't you tell me?"

"I only found out myself yesterday."

"That's a lie."

"Yes," I said. "It's a lie. I didn't want to tell you."

"You could just as well have told me. Why not?"

"It's very hard for me," I mumbled after a pause.

She laughed. "Why? We've been together for a while. We haven't kidded each other. One of us has made use of the other. Now we're breaking up. What's so bad about that?"

"I didn't make use of you."

"But I made use of you. And you of me, too. Don't lie. There's no need."

"I know."

"It would be nice if you stopped lying for once. Now at the end at least."

"I'll try."

She gave me a quick glance. "Then you admit it?"

"How can I? And how can I deny it? You'll just have to believe what you like."

"Do you think that's easy?"

"No, it's not at all easy. I'm going away. That's true. I can't even explain why. I can only say that it's like having to go to war."

"Having to?" she asked.

This was torture, but I had to face it. "I can't answer that," I said finally. "But you're right. If there is any right and wrong in a case like this. I'm everything you've said. A liar, a cheat, an egotist. And then again I'm not. What does it matter? Only one thing matters . . ."

"Go on."

I found difficulty in speaking. "What matters is that I love you. But this is hardly the time to say so."

"No," she said, suddenly grown gentle. "No, Robert, it's hardly the time."

Her suffering was as painful to me as if I had cut into my own flesh.

"It's nothing," she said. "We meant less to each other than we thought. We both lied."

"Yes," I said helplessly.

"I've been with other men. While we were together. You weren't the only one."

"I know, Natasha."

"You knew?"

"No," I said quickly. "I didn't know. I'd never have believed it."

"You'd better believe it. It's the truth."

I knew her wounded pride had sought refuge in this dismal invention. Even at that moment I did not believe her. "I believe you," I said. "I'd never have expected it."

She thrust out her chin. I had never loved her more. I was in despair, but she was even more so. The one who is left behind always suffers more. "I love you, Natasha," I said. "I wish you could understand. Not for my sake. For yours."

"Not for your sake?"

I saw that I had blundered. "I'm helpless," I said. "Can't you see that?"

"We never really cared for each other. Chance threw us together for a while and now we're breaking up. We've never understood each other. How could we have?"

I was expecting her to bring up my German character; but I also knew she knew I was expecting it. What she did not know was that I would not have contradicted her. "It's just as well," she said. "I wanted to leave you, only I didn't know how to break it to you."

I knew what I was supposed to answer. I couldn't. But then I finally said: "You wanted to leave me?"

"Yes. I've been wanting to for a long time. We've been together much too long. Affairs like ours should be short and sweet."

"Yes," I said. "Thank you for waiting. I'd have been lost."

She turned around. "Why do you always have to lie?"

"I'm not lying."

"Words, words. You always have something to say."

"Not now."

"Not now?"

"No, Natasha. I'm miserable and helpless."

"More words!"

She stood up and reached for her dress. "Don't look at me," she said. "I don't want you to look at me any more."

She put on her shoes and stockings. I looked out the open window. Someone was practicing "La Paloma" on the violin. He kept making the same mistakes and repeating the first eight measures. I felt wretched and bewildered. It seemed to me that even if I hadn't been leaving it would have been all over between us. I heard Natasha behind me, slipping into her dress.

I turned around when I heard the door opening. "Don't come with me," she said. "Stay here. I want to go by myself. And don't ever get in touch with me. Ever. Don't get in touch with me."

I stood staring at her, her pale expressionless face, her eyes that were looking through me, her lips and her hands. She made no sign, she was gone, the door closed behind her.

I didn't run after her. I didn't know what to do. I just stood there gaping. Then I moved about the room, putting things away, the cups and glasses and left-over cold cuts. I moved automatically, not knowing what I had in my hands. I picked up an ash tray and saw two cigarette butts smeared with lipstick. I put it down again. The pain was brief and unbearable. I opened my mouth and took a deep breath. For a moment I couldn't move. Then I picked up the ash tray again, went to the window, and emptied it. Maybe I could catch up with Natasha if I took a cab, I thought. I was already at the door, but then I visualized what would happen if I did catch up with her, and abandoned the idea. For a while I stood still in the middle of the room. I didn't want to sit down. Finally I went downstairs. Melikov was there. "Didn't you take Natasha home?" he asked in surprise.

"No. She wanted to go by herself."

"Don't worry," he said. "You'll patch it up."

A senseless hope seized hold of me. "Do you think so?"

"Of course. Are you going to bed? Or shall we have some vodka?"

My hope hung on. I still had two weeks ahead of me before sailing. Suddenly I was flooded with joy. It seemed to me that if I had a drink with Melikov, Natasha would call up or come to see me next day. It wasn't possible that we should part like this. "Good," I said. "Let's have some vodka. What about your trial?"

"It's coming up in a week. I still have a week to live."

"What do you mean?"

"If they put me in jail for any time, it will be the end of me. I'm seventy and I've already had two heart attacks."

"I knew a man who got his health back in prison," I said. "No more liquor, light work out-of-doors, a regular life. A good night's sleep."

Melikov shook his head. "That's all poison to me. But we'll see. No use thinking about these things before we have to."

"That's right," I said. "If we could only stop."

We didn't drink much. We sat down as if we were settling in for the night; there seemed to be so much to say. But it turned out that there was very little. I knew I shouldn't have asked Melikov about his trial, but that wasn't it. We were both too deep in our own thoughts. Finally I stood up. "I'm restless, Vladimir. I think I'll roam around until I feel tired."

He yawned. "In that case I'll sleep, though I guess there'll be plenty of time for that."

"You really think they can convict you?"

"They can convict anybody."

"Without proof?"

"They can prove anything. Good night, Robert."

I walked until I was dead tired. I passed Natasha's house; I revolved around public telephones, but I didn't call. I still had two weeks ahead of me, I thought. The hardest was to get through the first night, because in such situations it seems very close to death. What did I want? A conventional parting, with kisses, at the foot of the gangplank and promises to write? A tender memory? But memories were a terrible burden; they could choke you like lianas in the jungle. Natasha had been right in making a clean break.

Why couldn't I? Why was I running around like a sentimental schoolboy, blubbering with love and desire and too cowardly to do anything about it? Instead of taking life as a matter of course and following where it led, I was circling around as in a room full of mirrors, looking for a way out and bumping into myself at every step. I was passing Van Cleef and Arpels. I didn't want to look, but I forced myself to stop. I saw the Empress Eugénie's tiara. I thought of how Natasha had worn it, borrowed jewels on a borrowed woman—just the thing for my counterfeiter's existence. At the time, I had enjoyed the irony with a spurious satisfaction. Now, as I looked at the glitter, I wondered if I was not making a big mistake, exchanging a vestige of fleeting happiness for a bundle of ridiculous moth-eaten prejudices and a quixotic battle with windmills. What should I do? I asked myself. I clung to the thought that I still had two weeks in New York. Somehow I had to get through that night. But shouldn't I call her then and there? What if she was waiting for my call? I stood staring at the jewels and whispered no, no, over and over again. In other bad moments I had found it helped me to talk to myself as I might have talked to a child. No, no, tomorrow, tomorrow, I whispered in a hypnotic, conjuring monotone until I felt calm enough to go on. Haltingly at first, then almost at a run, I went back to the hotel.

I did not see Natasha again. Perhaps we were both waiting for the other to make a sign. I often had an impulse to call her, but each time I told myself that it could lead to nothing. I could not jump over the shadow that pursued me, and I told myself over and over again that it was better to let what was dead be dead than to go on hurting myself, for what more could I have accomplished? Now and then it occurred to me that Natasha may have loved me more than she ever admitted; the thought took my breath away, but little by little my agitation blended with the general excitement of my departure. I looked for Natasha in the street but never saw her.

Melikov was sentenced to a year in prison. I spent the last few days alone. Silvers gave me a bonus of five hundred dollars. "Maybe I'll see you in Paris," he said. "I'm going over in the fall to buy a few pieces. Write me." I promised to write. It comforted me to know that he was going to Europe and for so humdrum a reason. It made the thought of Europe seem less forbidding.

I returned to an unfamiliar world. At the museum in Brussels no one could tell me what had happened since I had left. People remembered the man who had saved me, but no one knew what had become of him. For several years I searched for him and his murderers. I searched in vain for my father. In the bitterness of my return to Germany I often thought of Kahn; he had been right. It was a return to a strange country, a return to indifference, cowardice, and concealed hatred. No one remembered having belonged to the party. No one accepted responsibility for what he had done. I wasn't the only one with a false name. Hundreds had changed passports and gone scot-free—a new generation of murderers. The occupation authorities were well-intentioned, but there was little they could do; they depended for their information on Germans who either feared retaliation or whose code of honor forbade them to "soil their own nest." I never found the face from the crematorium; no one remembered the name or what he had done; many had no recollection that concentration camps had ever existed. I came up against silence, against walls of fear and indifference. The people were tired, I was told; they themselves had suffered too much through the war to worry their heads about others. The one thing they were never too tired to think about was making money. But wasn't that only natural? The Germans were not revolutionaries. They were a people who took orders. Orders were their substitute for conscience. How could a man be held responsible for what he had done under orders?

The story of my comings and goings in those years is blurred in my mind and has no place in these notes. Little by little the memory of Natasha gathered strength. I thought of her without regret and without remorse, but now for the first time I fully understood what she had meant to me. In the crucible of my futile searchings and bitter disappointments, the crude ore of memory became purest gold. The farther our time together receded into the past, the more shattering became my realization that Natasha had been the most important experience of my life. No sentimentality entered in, not even regret that I had found this out too late. If I had known it then, Natasha would probably have left me. I felt certain that if it had not been for my independence, she would not have stayed with me so long, and if I had not taken her too lightly, I would not have been so independent. Sometimes I reflected that if I had known what awaited me in Europe, I might have stayed on in America. But these were random thoughts; they brought neither tears nor despair, for I knew that if I had stayed, I would not have known what I now knew. But I also knew that there was no going back. One can never go back; nothing and no one is ever the same. All that remained was an occasional evening of sadness, the sadness that we all feel because everything passes and because man is the only animal who knows it.